# One Last Breath

# One Last Breath

## P S Cunliffe

First published in Great Britain in 2024 by

 **embla books**

Bonnier Books UK Limited
4th Floor, Victoria House, Bloomsbury Square, London, WC1B 4DA
Owned by Bonnier Books
Sveavägen 56, Stockholm, Sweden

A CIP catalogue record for this book is available from the British Library.

ISBN: 9781471416699

This book is typeset using Atomik ePublisher

Embla Books is an imprint of Bonnier Books UK
www.bonnierbooks.co.uk

To Mum and Dad

# 1

## Jessie – 12.07 a.m.

I reach up into the darkness and my index finger meets hard stone, a fingernail folding back with a neat click. It should make me scream, but my hands are almost numb from clinging to the rock – from holding on for dear life. There is only a soft throb, the promise of pain to come.

Try again. Stretch, reach, feel for the stone's edge.

Ticking insects scurry away from my touch. What might be a slug bursts under my palm with a wet pop. I ignore it all, have no choice. I can't let anything distract me from the climb.

I clear the narrow ledge as best I can, scrape away moss and dirt until it feels like there's enough room to hook my fingertips over the edge. I test it, let the stone take some of my weight. None have been loose, so far, but some have crumbled when I've tried to pull myself up, ancient pieces of rock fracturing and falling into the darkness below with a drumroll of splashes.

Up above, my destination: a violet disc of night sky, twice as big now as it was an hour ago – at least it feels like an hour. Hard to keep track. Time doesn't pass down here like it does on the surface. All I know is that progress is slow, and slow is bad.

I test my footing again, say a prayer as I pull myself up and search for a new place to dig in. For a terrible moment my shoe squeaks over wet stone and my arms begin to tremble – *No, no, no, no!* – then my toe lodges in some unseen gap. I twist my foot sideways, wedge it in tight and hoist myself up.

I stop to rest, remind myself not to look down, then do it anyway. I want to see how far I've come, but the bottom of the well is too dark to see anything of the filthy water below, and looking into that black

1

pool of nothingness only serves to unsteady me. I lift my head, take a few deep breaths, focus on the opening high above me.

Whoever did this to me doesn't know I can climb. Martin and I had a bunch of lessons at a climbing centre in Hackney a few years ago and got quite into it. The core principles have got me to where I am now: hips close to the wall, three points of contact at all times, don't rush. That last one is crucial. I can't afford to lose my grip because I'm rushing. Nobody will know the truth if I die down here, like Amy did.

I've dreamt about her final moments so many times, had nightmares so real I could feel the cold in my bones when I awoke, safe and sound, in my own bed. But this isn't a nightmare. It's happening right now. And if I don't get out of here soon, I'll be dead too.

So focus, Jessie. Keep going. Reach, clear, test. Pray, pull, breathe ...

The next four steps come in quick succession, as if the hand- and footholds are finding me, rather than the other way round.

When I started, the opening of the well was the size of my closed fist and it seemed to stay that way for a long time. Now, it's big enough to contain shifting clouds and pinhole stars. The air is fresher too. Not fetid, like it was at the bottom of the hole. Stinking and thick with mosquitoes.

I'm only ten feet from the top now.

Five ... four ... three ...

I reach up to dig out the next, and hopefully last, handhold I'll need, but when I run my fingers over the curve of the wall, something feels different. It's smoother, not so weathered and worn. A part of the well made from different materials, where the joins between stones are harder to find. An old repair that means I'm not going to find any cracks in the wall to hold onto. Please God, don't tell me I've got this far, only to find I can go no further.

Because if I can't go up ...

The muscles in my arms twitch and tremble, my thighs and calves sing out in pain, and the urge to relax my hold on the wall and surrender to gravity is so strong.

But I can't give in. Not now.

I close my eyes and picture Freya, my beautiful, perfect little girl. The thought of never seeing her again, of leaving her without a mum, is unbearable.

I can't let that happen.

I try again, search for a new handhold, and at the very limits of my reach, find what I'm looking for: a protruding edge I can just about hook my fingertips around. It isn't much, but it's enough to give me the leverage I need to move that bit higher, to clamber up the few remaining feet of the wall and eventually, with every last bit of strength left inside me, launch myself upwards and throw an arm over the lip of the well.

I climb through the violet disc and into the chill of the night, then fall across the well's broad rim and lie there panting, my belly pressed against the cold stone and my legs dangling over the void behind me.

My body vibrates with adrenalin, my muscles cramp, and my hands are on fire – fingers bloody, knuckles scraped, joints swollen – but relief crashes over me. I've actually done it! I can't decide whether to laugh or cry. Whoever did this to me, I've beaten them. Now, all I have to do is find my way through the woods, get back to town and raise the alarm. Get to a phone. Call Bill, he'll know what to do. He can protect us. Before long I'll be back at Dad's, safe and sound, with Freya in my arms. And I swear to God, I'll never let her go again . . .

A noise close by. I lift my head.

Someone's here. They must have heard my cries for help and come running. They'll probably already have raised the alarm. Any second now I'll hear sirens and see blue lights flickering through the trees. Police and ambulance, come to take me away from this awful place.

'Thank God,' I say, as the outline of a figure emerges from the shadows, reaches down with both hands and clamps them onto my shoulders to pull me to safety.

'Somebody did this to me,' I explain. 'They put me down there . . .'

Then I realise the person isn't pulling me to safety after all.

'No,' I plead. 'Don't, please—'

But it's too late. They're pushing.

I draw in a breath to scream on the way down, but hit the water before I make a sound.

# 2

*Five days earlier*

Seven miles of the journey left to go, with the town still crouched beyond the horizon, and it hits me: I don't know what the hell I'm doing.

Last night everything seemed so simple. Coming back not only felt like something I should do, but something I *must* do – despite Martin's objections. He warned me to stay away, insisted I at least wait until morning before making a decision, probably thinking I'd change my mind. But the feeling in my gut was too strong. So I plucked Freya from her bed, strapped her into her car seat still sleeping, and set off well before sunrise.

Now, last night's argument comes back to me in fragments; images of Martin, stalking around the living room, tidying – the way he does when he's really annoyed. I remember him raising a hand with a stuffed pink unicorn of Freya's in it and pointing it at me like a weapon as he spoke.

'This won't be like last time,' he said. 'People in that town really don't like you anymore.'

'Oh, do you think?' I replied, as if I'd forgotten the abuse that used to clog my social media on a daily basis, and probably still does – I just don't look now. My timeline used to be a near constant stream of accusations: I used my best friend's death to my advantage; I was only ever interested in money; I was, and still am, in league with the man convicted of her murder. Some even accused us of being lovers.

'I stopped caring what people think a long time ago,' I told Martin.

'Even me?' he said, squishing the toy unicorn to his chest.

'No, I didn't mean—'

'You told me you were finished,' he said. 'You *swore* to me you were done.'

'And I was,' I shouted. 'But things have changed. I've got to go, because—' I stopped, sighed. 'You know why.'

Martin knows better than anyone how the documentary I made still lives and breathes inside me, how no matter how many times I say it's over, it will never truly be finished. Not while Amy's killer is still out there.

He gave a resigned shake of the head, came over and pulled me into a hug. 'I know how much this means to you. I just don't want you getting hurt.'

'I won't,' I said into his shoulder. 'I'll be careful. But I have to go.' I pulled back, looked him in the eyes. 'We'll be back before you know it. It'll be a nice half-term break for Freya. She can finally spend some time with Dad, and you'll be super busy with work anyway.' I made it all sound so convenient.

'Fine,' Martin said, though it clearly wasn't.

At the time, I felt brave and self-assured, but now, as we approach the town, I'm starting to feel headachy and breathless. It's as if Westhaven is at the top of a high mountain and the closer we get, the thinner the air becomes. I'm starting to think maybe Martin was right, that I must have been temporarily insane to consider coming back to this place, to these people. And bringing our five-year-old daughter along for the ride? Madness.

I check the mirror. Miraculously, Freya has slept through most of the journey, strapped into her car seat. She looks even more angelic than usual this morning, the light streaming in through the car window turning her blonde hair gold and her soft skin white, except for the touch of winter eczema that reddens her cheeks.

Freya stirs, as if she knows she's being watched, lifts her head and peers around in a daze.

'It's OK, sweetie. I'm here.' I reach back between the seats and give her foot a squeeze. 'We're on our way to Grandpa's. We'll be there in a bit.'

I expect the news to be greeted with excitement – Freya adores her grandpa and often pesters to visit – but a shadow of concern darkens her face and she puts a hand to her chest.

'Need my breather,' she says.

'Which colour?' There's a brown asthma inhaler she has to take four times a day, twice in the morning and twice before bed, and a blue one that offers instant relief.

'Blue,' she says, the end of the word dissolving into an old-man wheeze.

I can't help thinking this is my fault. We're as close as can be, Freya and me. We spend almost every waking moment together – at least when she's not in school. No wonder the tightness in my chest, the panic inside me, has found its way to her.

'It should be in your bag,' I say. 'Can you find it?'

A feeling like falling in the pit of my stomach. I did put her inhalers in her rucksack, didn't I? I remember having them in my hand as I rushed around packing her things. Please tell me I didn't put them down somewhere before we left the house, that I didn't leave them on the kitchen table by mistake. We never go anywhere without her medication, but I wasn't thinking straight when we set off.

I hear Freya strain as she reaches for her rucksack, the straps of the car seat pulling tight. 'Can't . . . reach . . .' she says, her voice threaded with panic.

'It's OK,' I say, keeping my tone light. 'We're going to stop as soon as we can. I'll help you find it.'

Neither Martin nor I suffered from asthma when we were kids, but my best friend Amy did. At times like these, when Freya is in its grip, I can't help thinking of Amy's final moments – or at least how I imagine them: alone, terrified, and unable to find the breath to call for help – and I have to force myself to stay calm, because if I freak out, Freya will freak out, and then we'll be in real trouble.

I spy a petrol station on the other side of the road up ahead, change lanes and slow down to make the turn.

'We're stopping now, sweetheart,' I tell Freya, but we aren't, because the oncoming traffic is an unbroken stream, sunlight glancing off the bonnets of what feels like hundreds of early morning commuters heading in the direction we've just come from. There's nothing we can do but wait.

I turn to look at Freya over my shoulder. 'Remember what Mummy told you: stay calm and take slow breaths. In, hold for three, then out. In, hold for three, then out. Like this.' I make my breathing loud so she can hear.

Freya nods, but her shoulders are up near her ears, her body tightening around itself, trying to stop whatever air she has left inside her from escaping.

'Come on, darling. Do it with me.'

'I can't,' she cries, on the verge of tears, her breaths coming out in sharp, rasping gasps.

Fuck. I look ahead, search for that elusive gap.

*Come on, come on . . .*

'Hurry up, Mummy!' Freya calls out, desperate in the back seat.

Even the *tick-tick* of the indicator tells me we're running out of time. I picture a fist clenched around Freya's windpipe, squeezing tight.

Ahead, I see what looks like a possible gap and edge forward. The moment the first car passes, I jam my foot down on the accelerator and make the turn as fast as I can. I hear a dreadful screech of tyres and the honk of a horn and for a moment think I've made a spectacular mistake and this is all going to end terribly . . . but then we're through. I check over my shoulder, see the car that had to swerve to avoid us shrinking into the distance, unscathed.

I park up, spin round in my seat and snatch up Freya's rucksack. Where is it, where is it? There! Her blue inhaler. Thank God. I shake it, uncap it, then hold it out so Freya can wrap her lips around the nozzle.

'Head back, nice big breath in,' I tell her, like she hasn't done this a million times before. Freya inhales as I squeeze the end of the canister and hear the puff of medicine being released. 'Now, hold it. One, two, three . . .' I count to ten. 'And let it out.'

Freya exhales, long and slow, and a wisp of sunlit vapour emerges from between her lips, like she's breathing out a malevolent spirit.

Within a minute the wheezing has stopped.

'Better?' I ask. Freya nods, looks back at me and smiles. Then her eyes flick sideways, to the petrol station.

'I'm hungry,' she says. 'Can we get breakfast now?'

\* \* \*

Inside the petrol station, I pick up a copy of the *Westhaven Chronicle* and a coffee from the machine, plus a cereal bar, banana and juice for Freya. I carry the items over to the counter while Freya drifts over to a nearby stand of leaflets advertising local attractions: The Egg Theatre, the Children's Museum, Westhaven Market. I watch her cheerfully pluck a selection of leaflets out of the stand, finding it hard to believe my little girl was in such distress only moments ago, but that's the way it is with her asthma. It can flare up at terrifyingly short notice, then once she's had her medicine, be gone just as quickly.

We return to the car and I sit and drink my coffee, trying not to think about what comes next, while Freya eats her cereal bar and flicks through the leaflets she's collected.

'They've got dinosaur golf, Mummy,' she says. 'Can we go? Please?' She teases the word out between her teeth. *Pleeease?*

'We'll see,' I say, wondering what on earth dinosaur golf is. 'Maybe Grandpa will take you, if you're good.'

'I'm *always* good,' she moans.

'Oh, are you now?' I say, and she nods insistently.

She is good, mostly. Though Martin says I let her get away with murder, that I mollycoddle her. *You can't wrap her in cotton wool all her life*, he says, and he might be right about that. But I'm going to bloody well try.

With Martin on my mind, I take out my phone and video-call him, see my own face staring back at me from the little window in the corner of the screen. God, I look dreadful. My skin pale and washed out, green eyes bloodshot with tiredness. My shoulder-length hair, difficult to tame at the best of times, is a mousey mess of knotted curls. I push my hand through it, try to give it some shape, but it's hopeless.

There's a beep and Martin's handsome face fills the rest of the screen. He's still in bed, looking attractively dishevelled, his dark hair sticking up wildly and his muscular chest on show.

'Sorry, just woke up,' he says, his voice dopey and sleep filled. 'I take it you've arrived?'

'Not quite,' I tell him. 'We're stopped just outside of town. Freya needed her breather.' Martin looks worried and I turn the phone so that the camera points into the back of the car. 'She's fine now. Say hi to Daddy.'

Freya glances up from her leaflets and waves. 'Hi, Daddy.'

'Morning, sweetheart. You OK?'

'Yup. Mummy's taking me to dinosaur golf!'

'She is? Wow! I wish I could play dinosaur golf rather than go to boring old work. How about we swap places? I'll play dinosaur golf with Mummy, and you can go to work instead of me. Sound good?'

Freya laughs. 'No way, Daddy. *I'm* going to dinosaur golf, not you!'

I call out so he can hear, 'I said, *maybe* we'll go. If she's good.'

'I'm *always* good,' Freya says again, and I pull the phone back, stare at Martin for a moment, not knowing quite what to say, but not wanting the call to end.

I wish he were here. I might not feel so worried if he was. But he hates coming back to Westhaven, says it's the most depressing place on earth and that there's nothing here for him but bad memories. Plus, he has work. An important meeting with investors later in the week that he's spent forever preparing for under the watchful eye of his demanding boss, Laurence.

'You doing OK?' he asks.

I come back to myself. 'Yes.' Then, 'Do you think I'm mad?'

He gives a little laugh and holds a finger and thumb in front of the screen, a millimetre apart. 'Maybe a little,' he says. 'You know, you could just turn the car around and come home. I shouldn't have to work too late tonight. We can get a takeaway, a bottle of something nice, curl up on the sofa . . .' He waggles his eyebrows suggestively.

Sounds heavenly. But then I look down at the copy of the *Westhaven Chronicle*, folded on the passenger seat, the front-page headline cut in half, *Body Found in Search—*

I unfold the newspaper to reveal a picture of a teenage boy dressed in a purple school jumper, part of the uniform of Westhaven High School – I used to own one just like it.

I scan the first paragraph.

*A body has been discovered in the search for 15-year-old Evan Cullen from Westhaven, Avon and Somerset Police have confirmed. A police investigation was launched three days ago, with hundreds of people joining the search to help find Evan, who was last seen at around 6.30 p.m. on Wednesday. The body was found by a dog walker in Cooper's Wood, a local beauty spot, and the location of the tragic death of 15-year-old Amy Barnes, in 2007 . . .*

Martin's voice calls to me from far away. 'Hon, you still there? I think you've frozen . . .'

'Still here,' I tell him. 'But I've got to go. Speak later. Love you.'

'Hon—' He protests, but I press my finger against the screen to end the call.

I can't have him getting in my head with talk of takeaways and cosy nights in, curled up on the sofa. I'm too close to breaking as it is.

I take out my phone, send a quick message to Dad to let him know we're nearly there, then start the engine and move the car over to the exit, wait for a gap in the traffic so we can rejoin the road.

Last chance, I think. Turn left, and we can be home in three hours, maybe four. Turn right, and who knows what we'll be heading into . . .

A mile further on, the car crests a rise and the view of the town opens up. Shafts of morning light turn the tree-lined lanes that swoop down into the valley into ribbons of silver, while low-hanging clouds cast drifting shadows over cattle-filled farmland. In the distance, Westhaven sits, nestled in the wooded hills, the limestone buildings shimmering in the morning sun. And beyond the town, on the far side of the valley, Cooper's Wood is a dark shadow, smeared across an otherwise pristine hillside.

# 3

*Seven days earlier*

While my agent Laura enjoyed the city views from the fifteenth-floor meeting room at the London offices of BlinkView, the streaming service that, five years ago, made my documentary series one of the most watched TV shows in the world, I gazed at the framed posters hanging on the walls.

All of their biggest hits were there: the zombie show, already on its eighth season; the fantasy show, with all the dragons and nudity; the one about the terminally ill music teacher who becomes an assassin for hire; and my show, *Born Killer*.

I gave Laura a gentle nudge with my elbow. 'Do you think they switch them around every day, depending on who they're meeting with? You know, to make them feel special?'

Laura turned and eyed the posters, then cocked an eyebrow. 'Don't be daft. You *are* special,' she said. 'You're a prized asset. Besides, those things look heavy. They'd be too much of a pain to keep changing around all the time.'

'Hmm.' I nodded.

I didn't want to be there, but when BlinkView requested a meeting, Laura had insisted, saying it was essential to play nice, seeing as I am technically still under contract for another series of *Born Killer*. Plus, you never knew what they might want to throw money at next.

Laura smoothed down her skirt and gestured towards the door. 'Here they come.'

Through the office's glass wall, we could see Ellen Puglisi, BlinkView's Head of Factual Programming, heading in our direction, with two other staff members in tow: a young woman wearing a plaid skirt and a hoodie, carrying a laptop under one arm, and a well-built, middle-aged man, dressed in bootcut jeans, blazer and a formal shirt with no tie.

Ellen opened the door, came in and greeted me with a full-on hug and kisses on both cheeks, then did the same to Laura, before stepping back and gesturing to each of her colleagues in turn. 'This is Mark, Deputy Head of Programming, and Margot, Head of Analytics.'

Mark and Margot muttered their hellos, each coming in for their own awkward hugs.

They are big huggers at BlinkView, touchy-feely in a way that makes my skin crawl. It's as if they feel they have the right to put their arms around you whenever they like, just because they stream content into your living room.

While the BlinkView crew took their seats on the opposite side of the table, and I hung my coat over the back of my chair, Laura asked how business was. Ellen tugged at the neck of her shirt, blew out a jet of air and pretended to mop her brow, like she always does.

'Things are *so* crazy right now,' she said. 'Honestly, we're too exhausted to even think straight half the time, aren't we?' Mark and Margot nodded in agreement. 'And how about you?' Ellen said.

Laura nodded. 'Oh, same here,' she said, then she turned to me as I took my seat, passing the question over.

'Yes, lots going on,' I agreed, although the truth of it is, I haven't picked up a camera since the day I finished shooting season two of *Born Killer*. Instead, I've been focusing on making up for lost time with Freya, and right now I can't imagine any project taking priority over that.

'Well, we're *such* big fans of your work here at BlinkView,' said Ellen.

'Big fans,' said Margot.

'Hundred per cent,' said Mark, nodding his head.

Ellen leaned in over the table, close enough for me to get a hit of sour coffee-breath mixed with her perfume, and said, 'I myself binged both seasons of *Born Killer* all over again just last week, watched the whole thing in a single day.'

Unlikely, I thought, seeing as seasons one and two combined run to around sixteen hours, but technically not impossible.

Ellen went on, 'It's still one of our most watched shows.' She caught Margot's eye.

'Absolutely,' said Margot, turning her laptop towards me so I could see a graph on her screen, colourful lines rising and falling. 'As you can see, it's among our highest performing shows in terms of overall hours watched and completion rate.' She clicked her trackpad, and a new graph appeared. 'Obviously, the numbers took a bit of a hit for season two, but that's to be expected. And the key metrics were still *very* strong.'

'That's great,' said Laura, nudging me with her elbow. 'Isn't that great?'

'Great,' I said.

'And I don't mind telling you,' Ellen continued, 'bringing *Born Killer* to the platform did my reputation no harm whatsoever.' She grinned, flashing a row of tiny white teeth, and her team chuckled. 'With some things, you just know, right?' Ellen added. 'As soon as Connor appeared on screen, I could tell we had a hit on our hands, just like I could tell he was innocent.'

What rubbish, I thought. All Ellen could tell about Connor in those first few minutes was that he is handsome and charming, and possibly dangerous. And I'd bet she watched him talk about how much he missed his grandmother, and how his biggest wish was to get out of prison so he could see her again, and she felt for him – *fell* for him, even. Wondered what it would be like to have those deep blue eyes fixed on hers. His strong arms wrapped around her. Would she be scared? Would she be turned on?

'A lot of people tell me that,' I said. 'About Connor, I mean.'

*He has a kind face*, they'll say. Or, *He couldn't possibly have done it, you can tell just by looking in his eyes.* And I'll nod along, thinking all the while, *You don't know the first thing about him.*

Ellen licked her lips. 'How is he, by the way?'

'Doing well,' I said. 'Still adjusting to life on the outside, but he's getting there.'

This is what I say now when somebody asks after Connor, though I've no idea if it's still true – if he still needs to sleep with the TV on because the quiet unnerves him; if simple choices, like what to eat for breakfast, or what shampoo to buy at the supermarket, still overwhelm him to the point of panic.

'I suppose he's got a lot of catching up to do, after all that time . . .' Ellen trailed off, then cleared her throat and slapped the table with both hands. 'So, when are you going to put us out of our misery? We want another series, our subscribers want another series, and the algorithm tells us it would be a *huge* hit.'

'Absolutely,' said Margot.

'Hundred per cent,' said Mark.

I looked over to Laura who offered me a meek shrug. Of course, I realised. She wanted a new series of *Born Killer* as much as they did. A bigger payday for me would mean a bigger payday for her. No matter that I'd told her and them a dozen times already that it wasn't going to happen. Clearly, they either hadn't got the message, or had decided to ignore it.

'We have spoken about this, a few times,' I said. 'And I've already explained, it's just not possible.'

'But why ever not?' said Ellen.

'It's what our subscribers want,' said Mark, as if paying £9.99 a month gave their subscribers the right to dictate my career – my life, even.

*Born Killer* brought Amy's story to the attention of the wider world, and helped secure the release of an innocent man. But it did other things too. It put a community under the microscope and in the end, when it was all over, it left behind an open wound.

Connor, far from being welcomed back into the community, found that many of Westhaven's inhabitants still think of him as a child killer. John Dalton, the police officer who planted the evidence that secured Connor's conviction, lost his job, then his marriage, then his home. Worst of all, Amy's parents, Rob and Elaine Barnes, had their closure taken away, the murder of their daughter now *unsolved* all over again.

I thought about explaining this to Ellen and her colleagues, but didn't bother. Because I knew that for them, the people of my hometown are nothing more than characters in a TV show, no more real than a CGI zombie. Instead, I gave them the same line I gave the last time Ellen and I spoke.

'The story is over,' I said. 'It ended when Connor was released.'

Across the table, the three BlinkView staffers exchanged looks, as if they'd prepared for this moment, then Ellen nodded at Mark who laced his fingers together and cleared his throat.

'The thing is,' he said. 'I'm not sure our subscribers would agree. I mean, Connor's innocent, right? So, that means the real killer is still out there.'

'Right,' said Margot. 'So . . . ?' She spread her hands, as if Mark had just shared vital new information.

I said nothing while Ellen leaned back in her chair, tipped her head to one side. 'Come on, Jess. Tell us what it is you want.'

What I want most of all is to solve the murder of my best friend, but with every line of enquiry exhausted and no new leads, I'm beginning to come to terms with the fact that this is never going to happen. There will never be closure. Not for me, not for Connor, and certainly not for Amy's parents. And another series of *Born Killer* isn't going to do a thing to change that.

'You're in a great position here,' Ellen said. 'Whatever you need, you've got it. Bigger crew, better equipment . . .'

'The algorithm says it's a no-brainer,' said Margot.

'I think it's time to give the audience the ending they deserve,' said Mark.

What the fuck? I'd have been furious if I weren't so taken aback. The sheer nerve of it. The way they were talking, as if *Born Killer* was one of their scripted shows and the ending could be neatly wrapped up in the writers' room, was enough to make me laugh.

I looked over to Laura. 'I think we're done here,' I told her.

Ellen spread her hands. 'Jessie, don't be like that. You've got to admit we've done a lot for you, for your career. Let's talk. What will it take?'

'If this is about money, we've already spoken with the US office,' Mark added. 'They're very happy to up the budget.'

But it wasn't about money, and never had been. And the fact they thought it was only reinforced everything I'd already suspected about BlinkView. They didn't care about me, or Amy, or about the people of Westhaven. And they never had.

'For me to make another series of *Born Killer*, it would take a fucking miracle,' I told them. 'Do you understand? It's never going to happen. Not now, not ever.'

Ellen emitted a small grumble of displeasure then leaned back in her chair, while Mark and Margot stared at their hands, and the room crackled with tension before Laura cleared her throat beside me.

'Shall we agree to check in again in a few months?' she said, with false cheer.

Ellen smiled broadly. 'Excellent idea.'

'Hundred per cent,' said Mark.

It was as if a switch had been flicked and my outburst was forgotten, the meeting promptly dissolving in a shower of smiles and hugs. Soon, Laura and I were taking the lift down to the ground floor then walking through the cathedral-quiet lobby and out into the screaming construction and traffic noise of the city.

As we walked across the paved plaza in front of the building, Laura sighed. 'I do wish you hadn't lost your temper. We are under contract still, and you can't deny they did an incredible job of promoting and building *Born Killer*.'

'I know. Sorry,' I told her. 'I just wish they'd listen to me. I can't click my fingers and give them what they want. There isn't going to be any more *Born Killer*. Not now, not ever. Not unless—'

She waved a hand. 'I know. Not unless there's some sort of miracle.'

'Exactly. A new witness, new evidence. Something that turns everything on its head. But that's hardly likely after all this time.'

'You never know,' said Laura. 'Miracles do happen.'

'Not to me they don't,' I said, glumly.

'Nonsense.' Laura leaned out into the road and hailed a black cab. She asked the driver to take us to an expensive restaurant and, when we arrived, we ate and drank until we were stuffed and tipsy, and I felt much better about everything. Perhaps my outburst was exactly what had been needed, I thought. Perhaps now BlinkView would finally have got the message.

Of course, I didn't know then that it wouldn't be a miracle that brought me back to Westhaven, but a murder.

# 4

## Jessie – 12.56 a.m.

I come back to myself, sitting in the pitch black at the bottom of the well, my lower body submerged in a foot of stinking water. My chest hurts, my throat burns. It feels like I've swallowed glass. There's pressure, behind my ribs and behind my eyes. A terrible feeling of fullness that shouldn't be there. My heart races, beats in triple time.

*I'm dying, I'm dying.*

Then I pull in a ragged half-breath and vomit up a mouthful of bile.

It's fifteen years since Amy's body was found floating in this well. At least a part of me knows it isn't the same water down here now as it was then. Still, I can't stand the thought of having so much as a drop of it inside me. I retch and spit to get the horrid taste out of my mouth, then vomit again, and collapse against the curved stone wall.

Was it this dark down here before the climb? It must have been, but it seems darker now. The light from above doesn't reach the bottom of the well, and while not being able to see around me is bad enough, not be able to see how badly I'm injured is ten times worse. My entire body hurts in new and frightening ways. My chest, my shoulders, my neck. Most of all my right leg, where the pain throbs in steady waves from the back of my thigh. And my hands and fingers feel odd, bigger than they should. Still, I can't help peering at the opening high above me, a fine drizzle wetting my face as I look up. I was so bloody close. I wonder if I could climb out again, even with whoever did this to me still up there, waiting to push me back down. I could, I'm sure of it. Once I've got my breath and my hands have stopped hurting. And the second time would be easier than the first, seeing as I've already dug out all those footholds and handholds. Maybe I can get the jump on them, if I'm quick enough. Climb out before they realise I'm there and take off through the woods? Or I could grab hold of them and refuse to let go. Hold on for dear life . . .

What else can I do? I can't just sit here.

I'm over two miles from the edge of town and half a mile from the nearest building – though the Old Mill Tearooms won't be open again until the morning – so I know there's no use screaming for help. Nobody will hear me. The well is thirty yards off the trail, down an overgrown, hard-to-find path, and while it's possible the occasional hiker might wander in this direction, they don't tend to walk the woods in the dead of the night.

And that's the least of my problems.

When I try to remember the last few days, it's like trying to recall a dream. Images come to me, fuzzy and incomplete, as if viewed through frosted glass. It must be the shock: my brain has switched into emergency mode, putting all its effort into the here and now, surfacing only what it deems relevant to my survival. Which must be why, even though I haven't a clue how I ended up here, I know that the oppressive heat of the last few days is forecast to come to a thunderous end in the next few hours. A storm is coming.

Right now, the water in the well is neither deep, nor very cold. It barely covers my legs and is bordering on tepid, perhaps still holding some of the heat of the last few days. But that will quickly change when the rain comes. I need to get out of here, and soon. If I don't, there's a possibility I won't make it through the night.

My legs feel like they have gone to sleep. I need to stand, get the blood flowing, work out what to do next.

I shift position, brace a hand against the wall of the well to help myself up. But the moment I try to move, pain spikes through my right leg and steals all the breath from my body. I see stars, and slump back against the wall with tears in my eyes. I keep still for what feels like a long time, the darkness closing in around me. If I could only see what's wrong, I might not feel so afraid.

Once the pain isn't singing quite so loudly, I unclench my jaw, reach blindly down into the water and carefully run my hand down the back of my thigh until my fingers catch on something hard that shouldn't be there. The pain flares again. Explosive, dizzying.

Something is very wrong under the water.

What feels like a branch is growing out of my leg. No, worse than that, it's growing *through* my leg. I can feel the swollen places where it enters at the back and emerges through my inner thigh. It is gnarled and knotted. Sturdy. As thick as my finger.

I feel the blood drain from my face. I want to throw up again.

Oh God, this is bad. This is so, so bad.

I pull my hand away, don't want to touch the branch anymore. Don't want to think about what has happened, what it means.

*You're fucked. That's what it means.*

I got lucky, I realise. The first time I came to, down here, I was banged up, bruised and terrified, but by some miracle, not seriously hurt. Once the shock had subsided, I was able to pull myself together, get to my feet and make a plan to climb my way out of this mess.

But this time is different. This time there will be no climbing.

# 5

*Five days earlier*

The large, three-storey house I grew up in sits at the end of one of Westhaven's grand Georgian crescents, a monolith of dirty grey sandstone with ivy clambering over the lower reaches of the gable end. This morning the sash windows on the ground floor are shuttered, and the curtains in each of the rooms on the second and third floors are closed, the windowpanes holding only milky reflections of the overcast sky. The whole building gives the impression of sitting back, with its arms folded and its eyes closed to the world, as if it knows all my secrets and disapproves. Which is impossible, because it's just a house.

Then again, it's my dad's house.

I unfasten Freya from her car seat, and while she hops down onto the gravel drive and races to the front door shouting at the top of her lungs – 'Grandpa! We're here, we're here!' – I go round to the back of the car to get our things. As I lift out the bags, I hear the front door open, followed by a gasp of delight from Dad, and when I close the boot, I see he's scooped Freya up onto his hip and the two of them are gazing at each other with adoring grins on their faces. It's such an unrestrained display of affection I can't help but feel a flicker of jealousy.

Dad sets Freya down with a groan of effort. 'Oof! You've got so big.'

'Not *that* big,' says Freya. 'I'm only one hundred centimetres tall.'

As one of the smallest children in her class, Freya is keenly aware of her height. She has Martin or I check how much she's grown on the first of every month, the date-stamped pencil marks etched into her bedroom doorframe climbing ever-so-slowly upwards.

'I bet you'll be taller than me in no time,' Dad tells Freya, and he might be right about that.

In my memories, Dad is tall and strong, with big, callused hands, and fingertips permanently stained with varnish, as if a small part of him were turning into the furniture he spends his days building in his workshop. But today he looks small and fragile; hunched over and shrunken with age, his scalp visible through his thinning hair. He grips the doorframe with a blue-veined hand to steady himself as he drops to one knee and presses a palm against Freya's tummy.

'And I bet you must be very hungry after such a long journey,' he says. Freya nods. 'I'm *starving.*'

'You've just eaten, not fifteen minutes ago,' I call out.

Dad half-whispers into Freya's ear, 'If you go through to the kitchen, there *might* be some cakes on the counter. I'm sure your mum won't mind if you have one.'

Freya looks to me for permission, wide-eyed at the prospect. 'Go on,' I say. 'Just one, mind.' She races off into the house to find the kitchen as I reach the door, a suitcase in one hand and bags hanging from each shoulder.

'Cake at this hour?' I say.

Dad smiles as he gets to his feet, groaning with the effort. 'I'm her grandpa. I'm supposed to spoil her, it's in the job description.' Then he gives me a look that says, *Besides, what do you expect?* and a rush of guilt dries my mouth.

It's two years since I've been back, and in staying away from Westhaven, I've been keeping Dad away from his only grandchild, reducing their relationship to weekly Skype calls. The one London trip he did make, for Freya's fifth birthday last year, left him exhausted and overwhelmed, flustered by the tubes and the crowds, and seeing him that way made me snappy and irritable, as if it were his fault for struggling, rather than mine for choosing not to visit him instead.

The words of a half-apology I'll probably never deliver form in my mind, *Sorry, Dad. I just couldn't face it. This place, these people. That look you always give me . . .*

'We've just been so busy,' I say, instead. 'You know how it is. But we're here now, aren't we?'

'Indeed,' says Dad, warmly. 'I suppose you'd better come in then.'

Inside, I'm immediately hit with familiar sights and smells from my childhood. The high shelf in the hallway of coloured-glass bird ornaments Mum used to collect, the framed family photos on the walls, the collection of wellington boots under the stairs – a large yellow pair of Mum's slumped sadly in the corner, covered in cobwebs. I breathe in the house's distinctive odour, a signature combination of pipe smoke, old books, and the damp in the cellar, and it feels both like I've been away forever, and was here only yesterday.

'I'll make up the spare room for you,' says Dad. 'And I thought it would be nice if Freya had your old room.'

I shake my head as I set down the bags at the foot of the stairs. 'We'll both sleep in my room.' Dad raises an eyebrow and I add, 'Freya's asthma is playing up. She had an episode in the car.'

'Oh dear.' He looks worried. 'She's OK now though?'

'She's fine, but it gets worse at night. I want to keep an eye on her.'

Hopefully this morning was a one-off, but if Freya is having an asthma flare up, night-time is when it will be at its worst, when that malevolent spirit creeps up on her and has her waking up in a panic, clutching at her chest as her breathing crackles and whistles. I don't want her to be alone if that happens.

After cake, Dad gives Freya a tour of the house – except for Mum's old office, which he waltzes past without a word – and we carry the bags up to my childhood bedroom, still brimming with the remnants of my younger self. I look at the single bed, the old textbooks and folders of college work on the shelves, the smudges of Blu Tack on the walls from where posters of my favourite bands used to hang, and I feel young and old at the same time.

'This is where Mummy used to sleep when she was a little girl,' I tell Freya.

She sniffs, pulls a face. 'It smells funny.'

'No, it doesn't,' I say, but I open a window anyway to air out the room.

Once we're unpacked, Dad fishes out a stack of board games in battered boxes from the old dresser in the spare room, and we sit around the kitchen table, trying to find one we can all play that isn't missing essential pieces.

'You never did look after your things,' he complains.

Mousetrap is a no go, of course – was there ever a time when there weren't pieces missing from that one? The same goes for Buckaroo. In the end we crib a pair of dice from Ludo to play Snakes and Ladders, Freya doing a little victory dance around the kitchen when she wins and Dad pretending to be annoyed at losing. He seems younger already, as if being around Freya for half an hour has had a restorative effect on him, and perhaps it has.

After a lunch of sandwiches and more cake, we move through to the living room and lounge on the sofas and, once we're settled, I discreetly check my emails on my phone, and see the reply I was hoping for.

He'll meet with me, he says. But I'll need to be quick.

I ask Dad if he can watch Freya for a few hours. 'There's someone I'd like to catch up with in town, if it's OK with you.'

'Do I mind spending time with my only granddaughter?' Dad reaches over and tickles Freya's pink-socked feet, and Freya dissolves into giggles. 'I think we'll manage, won't we?'

'Her inhalers are . . . Dad, are you listening? It's important.'

Dad stops tickling Freya and looks up. 'Yes, dear?'

'Her inhalers are on the bedside table, up in my room. She shouldn't need them, but if she does, she knows how to take them by herself. She can have two puffs of the blue one and no more. If her breathing doesn't improve after a few minutes, call me and I'll come straight back, OK? Freya, be good for Grandpa.'

'I'm *always* good,' Freya says; apparently her new catchphrase.

I head for the front door, take my coat down off the hook, and am surprised to find that Dad has followed me out into the hall and is standing close by with a stern look of disapproval on his face. It's a look I remember well from when I was a teenager, when he caught me smoking out of the bathroom window when I was fourteen, or the morning he caught Martin sneaking downstairs after he'd stayed the night in my room without permission.

Dad leans in. 'Do you really think it's a good idea, going through all this again?' His voice is laced with concern.

'Dad, it's not like that—' I begin, but he isn't listening.

'Jessica, you turn up out of the blue after two years, and I'm supposed to believe you're here for a half-term holiday? Did you know, some more kids got lost in the woods the other week, trying to find that well? They'd flown in from God knows where. One of them even had on a T-shirt with Connor's face printed on it.'

Martin often reminds me that I can't be held responsible for the actions of each and every *Born Killer* fan, but who else is to blame for them coming to Westhaven? Most are harmless enough, content to visit some of the sights and landmarks from the show, take selfies in front of the town hall and perhaps stroll up to the Old Mill Tearooms. But others have different motives. They walk into Cooper's Wood convinced they'll find some missing clue or piece of evidence that might solve Amy's murder once and for all. They come to Westhaven to do what I could not: to find Amy's killer, and finish her story.

'I'm sorry,' I say, but Dad waves me away.

'Don't apologise to me, love. It's just that . . . If your mother was here . . .' He trails off with a shake of his head and I feel my throat tighten at the mention of Mum.

I'm certain he thinks that if she were still alive, I wouldn't have made *Born Killer*. That it is in some way a continuation of the disruptive behaviour I engaged in as a teenager when I first found out she was ill. An adolescent cry for attention, streamed into the homes of millions of people around the world.

Sometimes I think he might be right.

Dad raises a bony hand. 'All I'm saying is, and I'm sure your mum would have agreed with me, I think it might be best if you sit this one out.'

I don't blame him for not understanding, and for thinking I have a choice.

'You needn't worry,' I tell him. 'I'm not here to make another documentary. I haven't even got my equipment with me.'

He gives me one of his looks, with one eyebrow raised, and I hear his voice in the back of my mind, an echo from years passed, *Don't lie to me, young lady.*

I suppose he's used to the old me, who never went anywhere without her camera. But in the last twelve months, the only filming I've done has been on my phone; little videos of Freya, playing in the park, or opening her presents on Christmas morning.

'So, you being here has nothing to do with this young boy who's been murdered?' he says.

'I didn't say that,' I tell him, because there's no point in denying it.

He shakes his head. 'Thought as much. If all you wanted was someone to babysit while you go poking your nose in where it isn't wanted, I wish you'd have just come out and said so.' Then he turns away and walks back down the hall.

'Dad . . .' I call after him, but he's already closing the living room door behind him, and a moment later I hear the soft murmur of his voice through the walls, followed by laughter from Freya as he switches back into cheerful Grandpa mode.

I know I should stay and try to smooth things over, but I can't afford to be late.

I'm not here to make another documentary. I'm here because this is my chance to make things right; to help find Evan's killer, and to finish Amy's story.

I put my coat on and head for the door.

# 6

## Martin – 1.04 a.m.

Half an hour ago, Martin was struggling to keep his eyes open, drifting in and out of sleep, in front of the TV downstairs, still dressed in his work clothes. But now that he's tucked up in bed, sleep won't come. He couldn't be more awake if he tried, lying here in the dark, eyes open, listening to the whoop and holler of the wind outside and the distant crack and rumble of thunder. In comparison, the house seems deathly quiet. Not that Jessie or Freya would usually be making noise at this hour, they'd be sound asleep, just like he should be, but their absence is a presence in itself, a heavy silence that fills the house from top to bottom.

He misses his girls.

He rolls over, grabs his phone off the bedside table and checks for missed calls, even though he knows looking at the screen will make him even more awake than he already is, and that's the last thing he needs.

He has a big day at work tomorrow, a meeting with an important client he can't afford to mess up. He's spent the last few weeks preparing for it, fine-tuning his presentation, role-playing the meeting through with his boss, Laurence, so he can be ready for anything and everything the client might throw at him. He's as ready as he'll ever be. The only thing left to do is to make sure he gets a good night's sleep.

So much for that.

Every day Jessie has been away she's either called, or sent him a message, before bed. More often than not, she's video-called early in the evening so he can say goodnight to Freya. But tonight? Nothing. No call, no messages, either. The three times he's tried calling her have gone straight to voicemail, and his own messages have not only gone unanswered, they've also gone unread, the little grey tick marks beside each luminous block of text stubbornly refusing to change colour. He could have called Frank's landline, but he held off, thinking Jessie would call at any second and he'd end up feeling silly for worrying. If he calls now, he'll wake everyone up, so instead he lies here, with pictures of worst-case scenarios ambushing his thoughts: Jessie, unconscious and upside down, still strapped into an upturned car that has ploughed off the road; Freya, being wheeled through a corridor after having had an asthma attack, the gurney smashing through hospital doors as doctors fuss around her; Jessie *and* Freya, trapped in her dad's house while it fills with smoke, their fists hammering uselessly against a window that will not break as the fire blooms bright behind them . . .

What the hell. He shakes his head from side to side like a wet dog, as if that will dislodge the horrible images from his mind.

Just because he can't think of one right this second, that doesn't mean there isn't a perfectly good reason why Jessie hasn't called, or read his messages. It'll be something straightforward – certainly not a car crash, or an asthma attack, or a house fire, or anything else horrible, for that matter. She's probably just had a busy day and decided to get an early night. She'll most likely call first thing tomorrow to apologise and wish him good luck for his meeting. Right now, the best thing he can do is stop worrying, and start sleeping.

Martin puts his phone aside, turns over and closes his eyes, tries to calm his thoughts. He reaches back, searches the corners of his mind for a happy memory he can sink into, and after a while he finds one, from when he and Jessie were just teenagers, from back when they didn't have to worry about documentary films or client meetings.

He conjures up an image of the two of them, lying side by side on the single bed in Jessie's old room, dust motes swirling in the sunlight streaming through the window. Their heads are close together, lips almost, but not quite, touching. He looks into her eyes and is quickly lost in the greens and golds of her irises. A shiver races up his spine as her fingers walk a path down his bare arm—

A buzzing sound wrenches him from the brink of sleep.

He jerks upright. His phone is vibrating hard against the bedside table. He snatches it up. On the screen the caller ID says: Jessie's Dad. God knows why she's calling from her dad's landline, rather than her mobile, but at least Jessie's finally decided to check in. Martin swipes the screen to accept the call.

'What time do you call this?' he says, sharper than he intends. Now he knows that Jessie is safe, the worry that was keeping him awake has changed shape.

'Martin, I'm sorry,' a voice says. Not Jessie's, but her dad's. 'I hate to call so late, but . . .'

Martin sits up. 'Frank, what is it? What's happened?'

For Frank to be calling at this hour, something *must* have happened.

Those horrible images run through his mind again: the car on its roof, broken glass and blood everywhere; Freya in the hospital, struggling to breathe; the girls, thumping their fists against a window that will not break, with the glow of flames at their backs . . .

'It's Jessie,' Frank says. 'She hasn't come home.'

# BORN KILLER –
# SHOOTING SCRIPT

## S01 – E01: LOST & FOUND

**RECONSTRUCTION:** Dawn. A police car comes to a stop at the head of an overgrown trail. The car door opens. A pair of heavy boots hit the muddy ground.

**ON-SCREEN TEXT:** Westhaven, England. 2007

**DI BILL CALDER (Voice-over):** 'I'm not sure what made me go up there. Call it a hunch, I suppose. I'd just finished a night shift and the well just popped into my head. I knew I wouldn't sleep until I'd checked, so I drove over, walked down the trail until I reached the old well. It was still dark when I arrived, so I didn't see anything wrong at first, but when I got close I shone my torch and noticed that the metal grate that covered the well was gone.'

**RECONSTRUCTION:** Torchlight flickers through the trees as a uniformed police officer closes in on an old well, nestled in a small clearing. The opening is wide and dark, ominous looking. His feet squelch in the mud as he walks over, leans forward and shines his torch down into the well. Light slips over wet stone, briefly illuminating a section of twisted metal, before coming to rest on a kelp of hair floating on the surface of the water.

**DI CALDER:** 'At that time, everyone was still hopeful. Shops in town had her missing posters up in their windows, her mum and dad had just done another TV appeal. But . . . there she was.

I felt awful – for her, and for them. Still do. As bad as it sounds, I remember hoping she'd died in the fall, because I couldn't think of anything worse than the alternative; that she'd been stuck down there for four days. All that time calling for help and nobody coming? It didn't bear thinking about.'

**RECONSTRUCTION:** Calder takes out his radio, speaks into it, then shines his torch around the clearing. He sees something, narrows his eyes as he gets down on his haunches and studies the ground.

**DI CALDER:** 'I got on the radio and called it in. While I waited for backup, I looked around and that's when I saw the footprints. Two sets. One was mine, walking up to the well, but there were others, too, walking away. That's how we knew it wasn't an accident. Somebody knew she was down there, and kept that information to themselves.'

**MUSIC:** Sombre piano music begins to play.

# 7

## *Five days earlier*

At The Star Inn, I order an orange juice and a double whisky at the bar, then carry the drinks through to a wood-panelled side-room imbued with the odour of a thousand spilled drinks, and a carpet so threadbare the pattern only persists in the shadows.

Detective Inspector Bill Calder is sitting by the unlit fireplace, at a small round table with folded beermats stuffed under three of its cast iron feet. Bill is in his third decade in the force now, and on the cusp of retirement. He looks tired, and older than I remember, though that can happen with people who were in *Born Killer*, all that time spent looking at their faces in the edit suite having cemented a portrait of them in my head that's becoming less true to life with each passing day.

Bill drains the last of his Guinness, puts his glass down and wipes the foam from his moustache with the back of his hand.

'Perfect timing,' I say, holding up the whisky.

Bill lifts his hand in a wave and I step through the hazy light streaming in through the etched glass windows, and set the drinks down as he gets to his feet then gives me a brief hug. He smells of sweat and beer, and cheese and onion crisps, but I don't mind.

*Born Killer* is my documentary, but it wouldn't have happened without Bill. He was one of the first people I interviewed when I decided to investigate Amy's death. He told me all about finding Amy's body in the old well up in Cooper's Wood, and about the bad dreams that followed. Then he told me about the investigation, and how he never believed that Connor, Amy's boyfriend at the time of her murder, was guilty.

We spent countless hours together over the next two years, trying to piece together the story of what really happened that night. And I grew to enjoy the company of this quiet, clever man, who was willing to share his time and expertise with me, and whose eyes would sparkle whenever we thought we'd found a new lead.

'Good to see you.' Bill pats me on the back, whiskers grizzling my cheek, then returns to his seat, setting the table rocking with a nudge from his bulging stomach.

I take off my coat, pull up a stool. 'How are things?'

'Better now.' He sips his whisky and grimaces at the burn, then slides a beermat over to his side of the table with his finger and sets the glass down. 'Day off,' he says. 'But Lou's got her mum over.' The corner of his mouth twitches. 'I'd sit here all afternoon if it were up to me, but I promised I'd be back within the hour. So, shall we do ourselves a favour and save the small talk?' I nod and Bill lowers his voice, as if we might be overheard, though we're the only two people here. 'First things first, tell me you're not thinking of making another documentary, because if you are, I don't want any part of it.'

I tell him I'm not, that I don't even have my equipment with me.

'But come on, Bill,' I say. 'Two kids, same age, from the same school, murdered in the same location? I had to come, didn't I?'

He lifts a finger, slowly shakes his head. 'What happened to Evan Cullen is nothing like what happened to Amy. Someone did a real number on that kid, beat him black and blue.' He lifts a hand and taps the back of his skull. 'He died from a blow to the head, and his body was left where he fell, out in the open. He wasn't anywhere near the well—'

'But he was close, right?' I say. 'Half a mile away, maybe less?'

At least it looked that way, going from the map printed in the newspaper, next to a series of CCTV stills that traced Evan's last known movements. They captured him walking down Broad Street in his school uniform, his bag slung over one shoulder, buying a snack from a newsagent's, paying a brief visit to Westhaven Library, before seemingly vanishing. Thirty-six hours later, his body was found in Cooper's Wood.

'I thought maybe you could give me the inside story,' I say. 'What do you think? The two of us, working together again? It'll be like old times.'

I look for that glint in his eye but can't find it.

Bill shakes his head. 'This isn't like last time,' he says. 'This is a live investigation, and I don't want you getting in the way of that.' His expression softens, and he gives my arm a gentle squeeze. 'I get it, though. Really, I do.'

'Get what?' I say, pulling my arm away.

'Just that I know what it's like having unfinished business,' he says. 'Some cases, even when you're done with them, they're not done with you. But that doesn't mean you did a bad job, it just means you can't join all the dots, and there ain't a thing you can do about it.' He pauses for another sip of whisky, then pulls in a long breath, like a sigh in reverse. 'When we met, you told me you wanted to tell the world Amy's story, and that's exactly what you did. And you made a damn fine job of it.'

'Apart from the ending,' I say. 'I never got to tell that part.'

'No, but you did everything you could; followed every lead, left no stone unturned . . .'

'But this could be a *new* lead, Bill.' I lean forward in my seat. 'You're talking like I should just give up and go home.'

'You *did* go home,' Bill says, with a small laugh. 'We all did. Even Connor.'

There's no arguing with that. And a week ago, I was the one telling BlinkView it was over – *No more* Born Killer, *not now, not ever.*

But that was before another child was murdered.

'I just want to make sure,' I say. 'You understand that, don't you?'

Bill smooths his moustache down with finger and thumb, says nothing.

'Fine,' I say, with a sigh. 'What about the parents? Think they'll talk to me? Maybe you could put in a word?'

Bill laughs. 'You're not serious?' He looks at me as if I've gone mad, then leans back in his seat and crosses his arms. 'Evan Cullen's mum is John Dalton's sister,' he announces, then adds, as if I couldn't work it out for myself, 'The kid's his nephew.'

My God. I sit back, stunned into silence.

John Dalton is the ex-police officer who planted the evidence that helped convict Connor. *Born Killer* fans not only hate him, they celebrated every misfortune to come his way after he was exposed: his demotion, the loss of his job, the breakdown of his marriage. And I admit, I took some pleasure in his downfall too. But this? This is on a whole new level. A family member – a child, no less – taken away so cruelly? I wouldn't wish that on my worst enemy.

'I didn't know,' I say, as much to myself as to Bill.

'Heard they were close,' he says. 'The kid's dad wasn't around, so Dalton stepped up. He even lived with them for a while, after his divorce, before he moved back to his parents' old place.'

I nod, though am barely present.

How is it possible for such an important piece of information to have passed me by?

I think back to the articles I've seen in the papers and online, the pictures and video of Evan's mum looking harried and distraught. I don't recall any mention of Dalton. Perhaps there wasn't any, or perhaps I wasn't reading closely enough. One thing's for certain, the fans will be all over this.

Dalton has always insisted on his innocence. In every interview he's given, and there have been many, he's stuck to the same story: the discovery of Amy's bag in Connor's bedroom, two days after a thorough police search found nothing, is as much a mystery to him as it is to everybody else. Which is nonsense, of course. Body-cam footage, that the police insisted didn't exist during Connor's trial and then went on to claim had been mysteriously 'misfiled' when I uncovered it during the making of *Born Killer*, proved Amy's bag wasn't present during the original search, and that it had to have been planted while Connor was being held in custody.

Dalton put it there, I'm sure of that. What I've never been certain of is why. If the pressure to find the killer was too much, and he planted it to frame an innocent young man he had a grievance against, or if he did it because he truly believed in Connor's guilt and wanted to secure the conviction. If it's the latter, I can only imagine what might be going through his head now his nephew's body has turned up, less than half a mile from the place where Amy was killed.

I have a feeling the open wound *Born Killer* left behind in Westhaven might be about to get a lot worse.

'Shit.' I put my head in my hands. 'People are going to be looking for someone to blame.'

'Already are,' says Bill. 'There were protestors outside Connor's when I drove by this morning. You know the type.'

I do. When Connor was released, a handful of people made camp on the lawn in front of Westhaven Town Hall for three days, waving signs with slogans on them, chanting about their children not being safe with Connor back on their streets.

Bill continues, 'We've already spoken to him, of course. Just an informal chat at this stage.'

'And?'

'Says he was home all night, with his grandmother. Not exactly the most credible of alibis. We may need to bring him in for further questioning.'

'But why?' I say. 'There's no reason to suspect him any more than there is me or you.'

'Come on, Jess. Don't be naive,' says Bill. 'You know why.'

I do, but that doesn't make it right.

'You seriously think he'd take revenge on Dalton by killing his nephew?'

Bill holds up a hand. 'Right now, I don't think anything, but a kid's been killed, Jess. We have to look into every possibility. Besides, the sooner we exclude Connor from our enquiries, the better it'll be for him.'

That may be true, but it still doesn't seem right that Connor should automatically be considered a suspect because of something he didn't do, rather than something he did.

A warm hand lands on my arm. 'Look,' Bill says, sounding like he's already regretting what he's about to say. 'If you must know, right now the investigation is focused on Evan's online activity. We think he might have been lured to the woods by someone he was exchanging messages with on social media. An older man, maybe.'

'You think he was being groomed?'

A small nod. 'It's a possibility. We're still going through his accounts, trying to track down anyone he was in regular contact with online who might live in the local area, anyone with a record, anyone who seems suspicious. So, you see why we don't think there's any connection to Amy's case?'

It's a different M.O.

Amy wasn't beaten the way Evan was. She didn't die from a blow to the head, and while she might well have been lured to the woods the night she was killed, that didn't happen over social media. Amy didn't even have a Myspace profile. And as for WhatsApp, Instagram, Snapchat and TikTok? They weren't invented when she was killed.

Still . . . two kids, same age, from the same school, murdered in the same location – or near enough. Despite what Bill says, my gut is telling me there's something here.

'If anything comes up?' I say.

Bill nods. 'I'll let you know. But in return, I need you to keep a low profile. Don't go asking too many questions. If you're seen to be interfering with the investigation, we will step in. Understood?'

'Understood. I'll behave, I swear.' I put a hand over my heart, the way Freya does when she's making a solemn promise.

'Good,' says Bill. 'People have got enough to be dealing with right now. They're scared, worried for their children, worried for themselves. Something like this happens and it puts a community on edge, people don't behave rationally. What we need is for everyone to stay calm and let us do our job so we can catch the bastard who did this.'

'Got it,' I say, and I drain the last of my orange juice, get to my feet and start buttoning my coat.

'Not staying for another?' Bill looks at his watch. 'By my reckoning, I've still got thirty-five and a half minutes' drinking time left, and I intend to make the most of it.'

'Another time. I've left Freya with Dad,' I tell him. 'She'll be running him ragged.'

'Fair enough.' Bill glares at me over the rim of his empty glass. 'Remember what I said: low profile.'

Outside, I walk a little way down the road before calling Dad, both to check in on Freya, and to let him know I'll be a little while longer than expected.

'There's someone else I need to see,' I tell him.

I hear Freya's excited chatter in the background – *Grandpa! Come see, come see!*

'There in a minute, sweetheart,' Dad says to Freya, then to me, 'Someone else?'

It would be so much easier to lie, but if I'm going to be investigating what happened to Evan Cullen, I'm going need him to help look after Freya. I need him onside. So, I tell him the truth.

'Connor.'

Dad replies with an exasperated sigh and I follow it up with one of my own.

'I'm just trying to help,' I tell him.

'That's the problem, love,' he says. 'Some people are beyond help.' Then he hangs up, leaving me wondering if he's talking about Connor, or about me.

# 8

## Jessie – 1.10 a.m.

My thigh has its own heartbeat. It throbs and itches, and with every tiny movement the pain spikes and I picture the branch, scraping back and forth against muscle and bone, sharp edges dividing soft tissue, black dirt and filth, little insects and organisms and God-knows-what else, inside me – actually *inside* me – and oh God this is bad, this is so, so bad.

I can't tell if I'm bleeding, because I can't see a damn thing, but I must be, mustn't I? You don't get impaled through the leg by a branch and not bleed. If I could stand, get my leg out of the water, I might be able to work out how bad it really is, but the branch won't let me. When I try to lift my leg, there's a sharp downwards tug and a shocking bolt of pain as muscle and skin stretch to near breaking point.

I reach into the water, gently trace the shape of the branch with my fingertips, feel it thicken as it meets the floor of the well and disappears into the mud. That's why it won't move. It's not a branch. It's a root, growing out of the earth at the bottom of the well.

And now it's growing through me.

I pull back my hand as my stomach flutters and drops.

Don't panic, I tell myself. Maybe it's not as bad as it feels.

I make another attempt to free myself, moving as slowly as possible, but when I feel the sharp tug and the same shock of pain, I stop, worried that I'm going to make things worse, slice through an artery and bleed out at the bottom of the well.

Fuck. I'm going to die down here, aren't I? I'm going to die down here in the dark, just like Amy did.

Stop. Breathe. Keep it together.

Got to get a grip. Take slow breaths, just like I tell Freya when she's having an asthma attack.

*In, hold for three, then out. In, hold for three, then out . . .*

Think, Jessie. Think.

If I can't climb, the only way I'm going to get out of here is if somebody gets help, and right now there's only one person on earth who can do that, because they're the only one who knows I'm down here.

I look up, half expecting to see a figure peering down from the top of the well. Rain wets my cheeks – the storm isn't here quite yet, but it's coming – and I see shifting clouds up above, but nothing more. I picture whoever did this to me, crouched up there like some sort of gargoyle, listening to me suffer. Is that what they want? To hear me suffer?

'I know you're up there!' I shout. My voice spirals up and away, but the only reply is the drip-drip of water sweating from the walls.

I try again. 'You can't do this to me! You can't just . . . *leave* me down here. There's a storm coming. You can't leave me when there's a storm. I'll . . .' I don't want to say it. It feels like if I say the word, it'll make it more likely to happen. 'Do you hear me?'

A sound up above. The snap of a branch underfoot? That's good. They might not have responded to me so far, but if they're up there, they can hear me. And if they can hear me, it means I still have a chance. I've got to reason with them, convince them to do the right thing.

'People are going to be looking for me,' I shout. 'Lots of people. They'll rip this town apart trying to find me, and once they do, they're going to come for you, whoever you are. But if you get help, I'll tell them it was an accident. I'll tell them you saved me.' I stop to listen. Nothing. 'Hello? Are you still there?'

As I look, a dark figure leans over the edge of the well, a black silhouette against the deep blue of the night sky.

Oh, thank God.

'Please . . . You don't have to do this.'

No response.

'I'll leave, I promise. If you help me out, I'll pack my things and

I'll go and I'll never come back, I swear to God. Please, get help. Do *something*.'

I slap my hands down in frustration and my right leg explodes with pain. It fills me up, dizzies me, makes me grit my teeth so hard it feels like my jaw is going to crack. I wait for it to loosen its grip, just a little, enough so I can breathe again, and when I look up, I see the figure has extended an arm over the well. They're holding a large object. They swing it to-and-fro a few times then let go, and a black shape falls fast towards me. I cry out and press myself against the wall, lift my arms to shield my head as something hits the water with a great splash. I shut my eyes and brace for more impacts – a brick to the skull would finish me off for good – but none come. All is quiet. When I next dare to check, the person up above has gone.

Stupid of me. What the hell was I thinking, trying to reason with them?

Something bumps up against my arm and I shriek. My mind fills with images of rats, of giant spiders with thousands of babies clinging to their backs, of finger-thick millipedes wriggling their many legs, reaching out for me in the dark. There's no telling what might be living down here.

When the thing bumps into me again, I swat at it with my hand and my fingers graze something cold and thin that seems to coil away from my touch. I shudder, then catch myself – whatever it was, it felt familiar. I reach out into the dark, trail my fingers across the surface of the water until I find what I'm looking for. It's a thin strap. I snag it, pull it towards me, feel something drag through the water. I lift it up and press its familiar sopping weight to my chest.

It's a bag. *My* bag.

Of course. If they're going to get rid of me, they need to get rid of my things too. They can't afford to leave any evidence behind.

# 9

*Five days earlier*

I bring the car to a stop at the end of Connor's road, in a small council estate at the fringes of town. The Warren Estate is Westhaven's dirty secret, an area the tourists never see, and a far cry from the Georgian splendour to be found further down the valley. There are signs of deprivation here, of lives lived on the fringes, pay packet to pay packet. Graffiti, litter, St George's flags hanging from windows. A gang of kids loitering on bikes. In the gutters, dozens of little silver nitrous oxide canisters, like spent bullet casings.

I eye the protestors at a distance. There are around fifteen in all, grouped on the pavement opposite the row of small, beige brick terraced houses. Some are just standing around, vaping and looking bored, but others are jeering and waving banners made from taped-together pieces of cardboard with hand-painted slogans on them. A little further on, a grey transit van is parked half on the pavement, the logo of the local news programme emblazoned on the rear doors. A camera has been set up on a tripod, ready to go should anything worth filming happen, and a woman in a sharp suit is leaning against the side of the van studying an iPad.

Marching straight past the press and protestors isn't an option. If the reporter doesn't recognise me, there's a good chance at least some of the protestors will, and if I'm seen going into Connor's, it could prompt all sorts of rumours and speculation. I proved him innocent of one murder – at least as far as the wider world is concerned. Perhaps they'll think he's asked me to do it again?

I turn the car around, drive back the way I came a few blocks and park up, then put the hood of my coat up and walk back until I reach a narrow cut-through between houses. I wind my way through the alleyways behind the streets of the Warren Estate, and discover that this part of town is just as charming now as it was when I was a kid.

The high brick walls and concrete-slab fences at the foot of each garden are covered in graffiti – not the artistic kind I'm used to seeing back home in Dalston, but crude messages in black spray paint. Suchabody is a slag, somebody else sucks cocks, and so on. And the graffiti isn't the half of it. I count three abandoned mattresses, stained with God only knows what, slumped against the walls like hopeless drunks; two old fridges, one lying on its back, the other on its side, oozing brown liquid. Most disturbing of all, a blue holdall surrounded by a swarm of flies, with a dark patch of fur poking out between the teeth of its broken zipper. I cover my nose and hurry on until the chanting of the protestors grows loud, and I know I've reached the right place.

I stop to count the backs of the houses from one end of the street, to make sure I've got the right garden, then pull a filthy metal bin up to the high brick wall and, with some difficulty, clamber on top of it.

For as long as I can remember, the garden of number thirteen Milk Street has been full of junk. Useless off-cuts of timber, old car parts and broken bicycles. It was that way when I was a kid, and it was that way when I was last here, two years ago, when Connor was released. But what I find today when I peer over the wall, is a small, perfectly formed garden, with colourful plants and flowers of all kinds, and a trail of stepping stones embedded in a neat lawn that lead from the house's back door to a small tool shed.

Either I've got the wrong house, or somebody has been very busy. I count again. Definitely the right house.

With great effort, I hoist myself up on top of the wall, then swing my legs over to the other side and drop down onto the lawn, falling forwards and hitting the grass on all fours. I get to my feet, wipe the dirt off my hands, then walk over to the back door of the house. Putting a hand up to the glass to block out the reflections, I get a view of the kitchen leading into the hallway.

Perhaps I really have got the wrong house, I think, because what I see inside looks nothing like the kitchen I remember. Gone are the ancient appliances, stained yellow from years of nicotine. The sink, always piled high with dirty dishes, is empty, the taps gleaming. I'm pretty sure the rodent droppings I used to see on the kitchen work surfaces, like lost punctuation marks, will be gone too. Everything looks fresh and clean.

I rap my knuckles against the glass.

'*Connor*,' I whisper-shout, the way Freya does when she's pretending to tell you a secret, but there's no answer. I try again, not wanting to say his name too loudly, in case it attracts the attention of his neighbours. On my fourth attempt, the shape of a person leans into view in the hallway.

It's Connor, all six feet four of him, dressed in jeans and a checked shirt, sleeves rolled up to the elbows, showing off his muscular forearms. His dark hair has grown out, and by the looks of it, he's a few pounds lighter than he was when I last saw him, but it's definitely him.

I knock on the window again and hiss, 'Con, it's me!'

I get a glimpse of those piercing blue eyes of his, then he steps out of view for a moment before he reappears and rushes forward, closing the gap between us in four big steps. He unlocks the door and snatches it open in one swift movement, and before I know what's happening, he pulls a cricket bat from behind him and swings.

The bat whips through the air, inches above my head, and smashes into the doorframe. I half duck, half stagger backwards, snag an ankle on the edge of a flagstone and go sprawling across the lawn.

Connor looms over me. 'I've told you.' He snarls. 'Leave us alone!'

He pulls the cricket bat over his shoulder, getting ready for another swing, and by God, I'd forgotten how big he is, how powerful. The damage he could do . . .

'Con, it's me! It's me!' I say, trying to shield my head and pull back my hood at the same time. I close my eyes, brace for impact . . . But none comes. I feel the tension in the air slacken, look up and see Connor staring down at me.

'Jess?' He lowers the bat, reaches out a hand to help me up.

'Bloody hell, Con!' I say, as he hauls me to my feet. 'You nearly took my head off.'

'Sorry,' he says. 'I thought you were one of them.' He jerks his head towards the front of the house, towards the sound of the protestors. 'What the hell are you doing here?'

'Oh, you know,' I say, brushing the dirt off the back of my jeans. 'I was just passing.'

# 10

## Martin – 1.14 a.m.

'And you're sure she didn't say where she was going?' Martin clamps the phone between shoulder and cheek while he pulls up his jeans, then switches it to speaker and sets it down while he puts on a T-shirt. 'Frank?'

Frank sighs. 'She just said she had something she needed to do. She asked me to go up and read Freya her story and, once she was asleep, to listen out in case she woke up, and that was about it.'

'And she didn't say what time she'd be back?'

'Afraid not.'

'When was this? When did she go out?'

'Oh, I should think around seven, or seven thirty.' He pauses. 'Maybe somewhere closer to eight?'

Useless.

Martin has always got on well with his father-in-law – at least once they got over that initial awkward phase. In the early days, Frank would sometimes look at him and recoil like a salted slug, as if he was thinking, *This is the man my daughter wants to be with? Really?* But after a while – and after what happened to Amy – things settled down. Frank warmed to him, seemed pleased Jessie had someone who clearly worshipped the ground she walked on, who loved his daughter as much, if not more, than he did.

Things got a little rocky when Jessie's mum passed. Knocked sideways by grief, Frank became a different person. And Jessie struggled with that. She needed her old dad back, but he was nowhere to be found. Years passed, and the distance between them began to solidify, to become more permanent. Then Freya came along, and the sun came out, the birds began to sing, and Frank

45

became Frank again; doting on his granddaughter, wittering on about the furniture he hand-builds in his workshop, or his favourite jazz records.

So, Martin has always been fond of Frank, considered them connected through their shared love of Jessie and Freya. But tonight, Frank is testing his patience.

'And she didn't say anything else?'

'Not that I recall.'

'Did she seem stressed, or upset? Was she worried about anything?'

Jessie has been investigating a murder. It's not out of the question she's got herself wrapped up in something dangerous.

'Nope,' Frank says. 'She was in a hurry, but I thought she just wanted to finish whatever she had to do before the storm hit. I warned her it was going to get rough tonight, told her she'd be better waiting until the morning, but she wouldn't hear it. You know how stubborn she can be. She said she'd find somewhere to shelter if the weather got too bad, and I reckon that's what's happened. It's terrible here, Martin. The wind and rain are really picking up, and they say it's going to get a lot worse.'

Sounds feasible. Both Jessie's stubbornness and her need to take shelter. Westhaven isn't like London. Aside from the town centre, it's all winding country lanes. If a tree comes down, or a road is flooded, a route can be blocked for hours, or even days.

Plus, don't storms interfere with mobile phone reception? Might that be why Jessie hasn't got back to him?

Martin heads downstairs, turns on the lights in the hall and the living room. Things always feel better in the light.

'I'm sure she'll be back once the weather eases off,' says Frank.

He's probably right, thinks Martin. She's probably hunkered down in some countryside pub somewhere, enjoying an impromptu lock-in while she waits for the worst of the storm to pass.

Then Frank says, 'The only thing is . . .' and the muscles across Martin's back and shoulders pull tight.

'What is it?'

'I can't find Freya's inhalers. I looked in on her a little while ago – and you mustn't worry, she's sleeping like a baby – but I noticed they weren't on her bedside table. So, I checked her little rucksack, and they aren't in there either, and then I remembered . . .'

'Remembered what, Frank?'

'We went for a drive this afternoon, into town to get some ice cream, and Jess put the inhalers in the glovebox. She told me to bring them in when we got out of the car, but . . . I must have got distracted. They must still be in there and Jess has taken the car and . . . I've tried calling her, but there's no answer. It's like her phone's turned off. I'm sorry, Martin. I'm sure she'll be back at any second, but . . .' He trails off, leaving the crucial question unsaid.

What if she isn't?

If Jessie knew Freya was without her medication, she'd come home right away, no matter how bad the weather was. If the roads were blocked, she'd set off on foot, would walk through gale-force winds and wade through flood water up to her neck. But as far as she's concerned, Freya is fine, because Frank brought her inhalers back into the house after their drive.

Freya's asthma is always worse at night, and not only is she without her medicine, but without her mum.

That image comes back to Martin, of Freya on a gurney being rushed down a hospital corridor, doctors fussing around her. There are new details in it this time: an oxygen mask over her mouth, her eyes rolling back in her head. He can almost hear the terrible wheeze and rattle of her constricted breathing.

He pulls the phone away from his ear and checks the time. Twenty past one. Freya's spare inhalers are in the bathroom cabinet. If he sets off now, he can probably get them to her for five thirty, maybe even five, if he puts his foot down.

Shit. The realisation dawns that there's no way he can get to Westhaven and back in time for tomorrow's meeting. Even if he could, by some miracle of traffic and timing, he'll be in no shape to present to the company's biggest client after having not slept a wink. Laurence is going to lose his mind, he thinks. But what choice does he have? Frank's probably right; Jessie will be home any minute now . . .

But what if she isn't?

# BORN KILLER –
# SHOOTING SCRIPT

## S01 – E03: MANHUNT

**POLICE BODY-CAM FOOTAGE:** Helmeted police swing a battering ram against the front door of a small, beige brick terraced house. On their fifth attempt, the door crashes inwards and officers swarm inside.

**FLORA STARLING (Connor's grandmother):** 'It was six in the morning. I was still in bed, so of course I didn't answer. Next thing I knew they were in my room, shining a torch in my face and screaming at me. And there were three of them on Connor, they pinned him down on his bedroom floor. He was terrified. They turned the whole house upside down, and didn't find nothing, because there was nothing to find. They made a hell of a mess though.'

**RECONSTRUCTION:** The camera pans over the results of the police search: upended furniture; drawers pulled out of dressers, their contents emptied carelessly onto the floor; a framed family photograph with a dusty boot print on the shattered glass.

**FLORA STARLING:** 'When they were gone, I sat Con down and told him he had to be honest, that if he did it, or if he knew who did, he had to tell me, because this wasn't like those other times he'd been in trouble. This was serious. But he said to me, "Nan, I didn't do anything, I swear on my life." And that was good enough for me.'

**DS JOHN DALTON:** 'What you have to remember, is that Connor wasn't some wide-eyed innocent, despite what his grandmother would have you believe. He had a record of criminal activity going back to when he was just eight years old. He was a troublemaker, and he was a liar.'

**FLORA STARLING:** 'He never meant nobody no harm, he was just out having fun, doing what boys do at that age. But the police were always getting on at him, giving him grief. Harassing him on the street, accusing him of this and that. He was targeted, because of who he was. It was the same with his dad. They were always getting on at him.'

**DS JOHN DALTON:** 'Targeted? That's absolute nonsense. Jake Starling was a well-known local criminal, involved in drugs, theft, violence, threats of intimidation. And when he passed away, Connor seemed determined to take up the baton. He was engaged in criminal activity, on a frequent basis, from a very young age. It's as simple as that.'

**FLORA STARLING:** 'A few days later, Dalton turned up on his own, acting all concerned. He said he wanted to check on Connor, see how he was doing. I knew he was up to something. I told him Connor wasn't home, but he talked his way inside anyway, and went up to Connor's room.'

**DS JOHN DALTON:** 'A young girl had been murdered. Forgive me if I neglected to respect the privacy of the young man who was, at that time, our primary suspect.'

**FLORA STARLING:** 'He was only in there for two minutes. Next thing I know he's on his radio, saying he's found something, and I'm not allowed to go into my own grandson's bedroom. Two minutes, to find what an army of those bastards couldn't find in over an hour of searching. What does that tell you?'

# 11

*Five days earlier*

Connor makes tea, and we sit either side of his small kitchen table. I was right about the place having been cleaned up. Gone is the broken furniture, the scuffed linoleum, the rusty old cooker with only one working hob, and the pellets of mouse shit that gathered in the corners of the worktops. Now, there are new kitchen units, worktops, appliances – new for here, at least – and the whole place is so clean that it echoes. It's hard to believe it's the same room I spent hours in while making *Born Killer*, interviewing Connor's grandmother while she chain-smoked and answered questions between endless coughing fits.

'Place looks different,' I say.

Connor looks around, as if he isn't sitting in his own kitchen. 'Yeah, I made some changes. Nan's not so keen, but she doesn't come downstairs much now anyway.' He casts his eyes up towards the ceiling.

'How is she?' I ask.

He shakes his head. 'Good days and bad. She can't walk too well anymore. Her balance . . .' He puts one of his giant hands out and rocks it from side to side. 'You could go up and say hello, but she's just had her meds. She'll be dead to the world until dinner time.'

'Another day, then,' I say.

Connor gives a sad sort of smile, then brushes his dark fringe out of his eyes, a gesture I haven't seen from him since before he entered his first Young Offenders Institution and was given the close-cropped haircut he would keep for the next twelve years.

When we used to speak over the phone, when he was still inside, I'd try to lift his spirits by asking what he wanted to do when he got out. He'd talk of travelling the world, list the countries he'd like

50

to visit, the sights he'd like to see. When I told him he had fans in America, he got excited, said maybe he'd move to New York or LA, maybe meet someone and make a fresh start. The possibilities of freedom seemed endless. And yet, here he is, back in the same old two-up two-down council house he grew up in, because he refuses to spend any more time away from his beloved grandmother, and she is too old and infirm to move anywhere else.

'Sorry about them.' Connor jerks his head towards the front of the house, to the low murmur of the protestors.

'It's not your fault this town is full of idiots,' I say, and he laughs.

'It's good to see you,' he says. 'It's been a while.'

'Yeah.' I glance down at my tea. I suddenly can't look him in the eye.

When *Born Killer* finished, it didn't just leave behind an open wound here in Westhaven, it left one inside me. Because while I helped to secure Connor's release, I failed my best friend. No matter how hard I tried – and God, did I try – I couldn't finish Amy's story, and every day spent in Westhaven only served to remind me of that.

Not only did I discover that a considerable, and very vocal, part of the community believed I'd done the wrong thing in helping to secure Connor's release, but Amy's parents went from treating me like a member of the family, to refusing to speak to me. They did hold a press conference during which they told the assembled reporters that seeing Connor walk free was not only a miscarriage of justice, but a betrayal of their trust and an insult to their daughter's memory. I know they're wrong about that. I know Amy wouldn't have wanted to see Connor rot in a cell for something he hadn't done. But the hurt that *Born Killer* caused them was too much for me to bear. Staying away – putting distance between myself and everything related to *Born Killer*, including Connor – not only seemed like the easier option, but the right thing to do. For everybody.

I want to tell Connor this, so he knows he did nothing wrong, that I still care for him and have missed him, but I don't know where to start.

Instead, I clear my throat, stand up and carry my tea over to the back door and peer out into the garden, at the flowerbeds and the bird feeder, the stepping stones pressed into the lawn at regular intervals.

'You did this all by yourself?' I say.

Connor comes and joins me, and we stand shoulder to shoulder, admiring his handiwork.

'Funny thing,' he says. 'I always thought gardening was for boring old blokes, so I guess I must be one of those now. It helps keep my head straight. There's all sorts of little animals out there – not just insects, but hedgehogs, foxes. I even saw a badger once. When I'm in the garden it feels . . . good, y'know?'

Words never were his strong point.

'Yeah,' I say, and we stand and drink the rest of our tea, and in the pockets of silence between mouthfuls, the sound of the protestors finds its way to us.

*. . . fucking murderer . . .*

Connor gives a wry laugh, shakes his head. 'D'you know, I actually thought people would be pleased to see me when I got out, that they'd want to, I don't know, make up for what happened?' He catches himself, touches me on the arm. 'I don't mean to sound ungrateful, 'cos I'm not. I just thought if I kept my head down, kept myself to myself, people would leave me alone and let me get on with my life. Instead, they're standing outside my front door, calling me a murderer.'

'Come on, Con,' I say. 'Nobody cares what they think.'

He lets out a barking laugh. 'Remember last time? All those people coming out of the woodwork? Teachers, neighbours, the bloody vicar. Every bad thing I ever did since I was a little kid used against me. I didn't stand a chance.'

He didn't. Even as a fifteen-year-old, his reputation – and that of his father's – had preceded him. His card was marked long before he was arrested for Amy's murder. It was marked from birth. And the teachers he'd sworn at, the neighbours whose windows he'd broken, and the vicar who'd caught him stealing flowers from graves – they were for his grandmother, of course – were all too keen to speak out against him when the time came, to tell anyone who would listen that he was a bad kid, that they'd always thought something wasn't quite right with him. Never mind that there's a world of difference between petty vandalism and murder.

'Things are different now,' I tell him. 'Do you really think the police are going to make the same mistake twice?'

Connor doesn't look convinced. 'Why did it have to be him?' he says. 'I know that sounds horrible, because he was just a kid, and no kid deserves that. But it looks bad, doesn't it, Dalton's nephew being murdered? It looks bad for me.'

It does. Because if anybody is searching for a motive as to why Connor would want to hurt, or even kill, a member of John Dalton's family, they won't have to look very far.

Thirteen years of his life, up in smoke. There's your motive right there.

'Con?' He looks up, meets my eye. 'You know I have to ask . . .'

He does, but that doesn't stop his shoulders slumping with disappointment.

'I'm not accusing you of anything,' I say. 'But I have to know.' How bad things might get for him, and to a lesser extent, for me. 'You told Bill you were home all night?'

'Because I was,' Connor says. 'I spent the day working in the garden, had a shower, made dinner for me and Nan. She has to eat with her pills, so that would have been around eight. After that, we watched TV in her room. She likes all these old quiz shows on Challenge, you know, the really old ones, from when we were kids. *Bullseye*, *Wheel of Fortune*, that sort of thing. I fell asleep about midnight, at a guess, woke up about one, then went to bed. And that's it. That's where I was the night it happened.'

An alibi from his grandmother is hardly ideal, but it's better than nothing.

'OK,' I say. 'If they speak to you again, just keep telling them the truth. Everything's going to be fine, Con. You've got nothing to worry about.'

He shakes his head. 'I don't know about that.'

Connor sets his empty mug down on the counter, then leaves the kitchen and I hear him fussing around in another room, opening and closing a drawer. He returns a moment later with a blue ring binder under one arm, drops it onto the table and motions with his eyebrows for me to look inside. I take a seat, turn the folder the right way round and open it.

Inside, there are see-through plastic pockets, the sort I used to use for my college work. Each one has a typed letter inside it, along with the envelope it came in. I look at the first one, read the first few lines: *They should never have let u out u murdering bastard. U will rt in hell . . .*

Another: *It dont matter wht some stupid documentary says we all know that ur a murdering cnt . . .*

The next: *It's all lies u child killing bstrd . . .*

'I used to get hate mail every now and then, when I first got out,' Connor says. 'I'd just throw them straight in the bin, before Nan saw them. But these are new.'

'Oh, Con. I'm so sorry.'

'Why are you sorry?' he says. 'You didn't write them.'

'Of course not. But they're all so . . . horrible.'

I've received my fair share of abuse online, and a couple of nasty letters sent to my agent for my attention, but this is something else. Hate drips off the pages. They look like they were written in a fit of rage.

'It's Dalton, I'm sure of it,' says Connor. 'I've seen him a few times, parked up across the street. I recognise his car. Big Land Rover, it is. He just sits there, watching, hating. He blames me for everything; all the bad stuff that's happened to him, and now he's going to blame me for what's happened to his nephew. And I know he's not police anymore, but you know what they're like. They stick together, look after their own. If he does do something, they'll still protect him, they'll cover for him.'

I look down at the first letter again. *U will rt in hell . . .*

The language used is not dissimilar to the kind of abuse I used to get over social media.

'I'm not sure this is his style,' I say. 'Almost looks like it's been written by a kid. Plus, Dalton's not exactly shy about telling people how he feels about you, so why would he bother sending you anonymous hate mail?'

'Because he *hates* me, more than anything, that's why,' says Connor, through gritted teeth, as if I'm missing the point.

'Con, even if it is him, so what? They're just letters. Ignore them, and he'll go away.'

'I don't think so,' Connor says. 'I think he's planning something. Something bad.'

He turns to the cupboard under the kitchen sink, opens it and retrieves a plastic bag. After carrying it to the table, he sets it down and takes a small cardboard box from inside it.

'Someone left this on the doorstep the other day. I was going to throw it out, but I don't want those nutters outside going through my bins and finding it, thinking it was me that did it. I reckon I'll bury it in the garden.'

'Bury what, Con?' I ask, and he reaches down and opens the box.

# 12

## Jessie – 1.55 a.m.

I'm still stuck in the same sitting position, my legs submerged in the water, unable to stand, unable to move much at all. Although I know there's nothing useful inside the bag, nothing that's going to get me out of here, at any rate, I rest it on my lap, half in and half out of the water, reach inside and feel through the contents, identifying each of my belongings by touch.

Loose change, house keys, lipstick, mascara, a makeup compact. Tissues, tampons, purse. A spare pair of tights, a small bottle of sparkling water – I shake it from side to side, try to judge how much is left. Less than half. I'm tempted to use it to wash my mouth out to get rid of the lingering taste of well-water, but decide against it. I'd better save it for when I really need it.

I go through my things again, in case I've missed something, but there's nothing of use. I'm about to cast the bag aside when I remember the front pocket where I keep my phone. I check it now, if only to confirm what I already know; my phone isn't there, of course it isn't, because whoever put me down here doesn't want me to get out.

So why, when I dip my hand into the pocket, do my fingers close around cold metal and glass?

I don't understand. Why would they give me my phone? It doesn't make sense. Unless . . . they've disabled it, broken it, drained the battery. The police can track your location using your phone. When they start looking for me, it'll be the first thing they check. And if I have my bag and a lifeless phone with me when they find my body, me being down here might look more like a freak accident than the attempted murder it surely is.

I press the slim button on the side of the phone that turns it on. It won't work, of course it won't, because it's wet through, and if it does, there'll be no battery, and if there is, there'll be no signal . . . But after a moment, the phone emits three heavenly, electronic notes, and the screen bursts into life with a swooshing red and blue graphic. I hold my breath, expecting the phone to switch off at any moment – that can happen when your phone is super-low on battery. It can give one last gasp of life before realising it's out of juice – but the phone doesn't switch off. The swooshing graphic fades and is replaced by the home screen. Rows of icons hover over a picture of Freya I took on the morning of her fifth birthday, wearing her favourite unicorn jumper and with a great big, gap-toothed grin on her face. My heart blooms at the sight of her.

Unbelievable. The phone works.

There's battery – not just a little, the icon in the top right of the rain-spattered screen reads fifty-two per cent – and more importantly, there's a signal. I watch the little icon flicker, drop down to one bar, then back up to three, before settling in the middle. How this is possible, when I couldn't get a signal in the middle of town two days ago, I don't know. And I don't care. Through some lucky miracle of technology, some alignment of satellites, I have a *signal*.

Now, it really is over. Whoever did this to me is finished.

I'm getting out of here.

Then the phone beeps twice and a notification flashes up on the screen. A text message. It reads: If you want to see your family again, get ready to tell the truth.

# 13

*Five days earlier*

Back at Dad's, there are more board games at the kitchen table after dinner, followed by some TV for Freya, before I give her a bath and put her to bed. I make sure she takes her brown inhaler, then we video-call Martin and blow goodnight kisses over the Wi-Fi.

I search the bookshelves for something to read to her, and take down a dog-eared copy of *A Bear Called Paddington*, with barely enough spine left to hold its pages together. I know what I'll find on the inside front cover before I open it, but still get a lump in my throat when I see Mum's name, written in faded orange felt tip. My grandma bought this book for Mum and read it to her when she was little, then Mum read it to me when I was little, and now I'm about to do the same for Freya. How sweet, I think. How perfect. But when I show Freya the cover, she pulls a face.

'I don't want Paddington,' she says, pouting and folding her arms.

So much for that heart-warming image. 'Why not? What's wrong with Paddington?'

'It's *boring*.'

'It's not boring. You liked it the last time we read it.'

She gives me one of her sad looks, a frown line creasing her forehead.

'I'll tell you what,' I say. 'Tomorrow, we'll go to the library and borrow some new books. How does that sound?'

With no news from Bill, the library seems like as good a place as any to start my enquiries. And if I can combine that with an outing for Freya, everyone wins.

'The library at home?' Freya says, brightening.

I shake my head. 'No, the library in town. The same one Mummy and Daddy used to go to when they were little.'

'Oh,' she says, looking a little confused.

'You'll like it there, I promise,' I tell her. 'So, Paddington?'

'Paddington,' she concedes.

I read until her eyes grow heavy and her head starts to nod, then close the book and put it aside.

Normally I love putting Freya to bed. There's something restorative about that moment of peace at the end of the day, when the world outside collapses into nothing and it's just the two of us. But tonight, I can't quite shake the image of Connor, opening that little box in front of me in his kitchen.

There was a dead bird inside it – a starling, to be exact. Such a pitiful sight – its dark purple, green and blue feathers matted, its eyes grey and lifeless. Just thinking about it brings back the smell of decomposition and makes me want to gag all over again.

Connor explained that the bird had arrived with a typed note, rolled into a little tube and held in its beak. It was written in the same textspeak as the letters.

U ruined my life. Now I'm going to ruin urs.

Going by the message, I had to agree that Connor's suspicion that Dalton was behind the letters and the dead bird didn't sound so far-fetched. Who else could claim that Connor had ruined their life? Amy's parents, of course, but the thought of either Rob or Elaine handling a dead bird, stuffing it into a box, is ludicrous. They just aren't *that* kind of people. But Dalton? I can believe it.

I move over to the window and part the curtains, wipe the condensation from the glass so I can peer out into the street. Might he be out there now, parked up in his Land Rover, watching? While the threat was aimed at Connor, I'm the one who got him out. Might Dalton want to ruin my life too? What if he comes after me? Or after Freya?

I scan the street below, but there's nobody there. Of course, there isn't. I'm being paranoid, worrying over nothing. Dalton isn't going to do anything. He's grieving, for God's sake. He's just lost his nephew.

There's a gentle knock at the bedroom door, and it eases open. Dad pokes his head into the room. 'You've got a visitor downstairs,' he whispers.

My heart jumps into my throat. A visitor? Please God, not Dalton.

But Dad doesn't look like he's just welcomed an angry ex-police officer into his home. He has a glass of red wine in one hand and has that relaxed look he gets when he's taken the edge off. Which means the visitor is probably Bill, because apart from Connor, he's the only person who knows I'm here. Perhaps he's got news about the case already. I'll tell him about the threats Connor has received, I decide. And about the dead bird. If Dalton is behind it all, perhaps one of his former colleagues can have a word with him and warn him off.

'There in a minute,' I tell Dad, and he retreats downstairs while I turn back to Freya, who, despite the interruption, is now fast asleep.

I lean in close so I can hear her breathing, listening for signs that all is not as it should be; that the worry inside me has found its way to her. But tonight, her chest sounds wonderfully clear.

'Night night, darling,' I whisper, and I switch off the light.

When I reach the bottom of the stairs, I see right away that the visitor isn't Bill. It's a young girl, and the first thing I notice is her hair, which is jet black and cut short at the back and sides, but with a slanted fringe that curves down towards her right eye. A thought stirs, *Amy used to wear her hair just like that*, and I take in the rest of her: Dr Martens, faded black jeans worn through on one knee, black band T-shirt under a zip-up hoodie. She's dressed like Amy too. But so what? There's nothing unusual about a teenage girl wearing the same kind of clothes as Amy used to. Fashions come back around all the time. But still . . .

I used to dream about Amy all the time after she was gone. Nightmares, mostly, about her being stuck down that awful well, struggling to draw enough breath to call for help. But sometimes the dreams were more everyday, as if she were still alive and everything was normal. In those dreams, she'd be waiting for me in the hall at the foot of the stairs, having arrived to call for me on the way to school, and we'd set off together, arm in arm, sharing a pair of earphones and singing along to our favourite songs. The sense of loss I used to feel after waking from those dreams was so acute, so painful, that I almost preferred the nightmares.

Seeing this girl now, standing in the hallway, with Amy's hairstyle and Amy's clothes . . . I feel a flutter in my chest as some long-forgotten hope stirs.

'You're Jessica Hamill, right?' the girl says. Her voice is not at all like Amy's, at least not how I remember it. It's higher, sounds less grown up, and all of a sudden, the spell is broken. I notice other differences: that she's shorter than Amy was, her features sharper, eyes a different shape and colour. Were it not for the clothes and the hair, she'd hardly look like Amy at all.

I gather myself. 'That's me. Can I help you?'

The girl tugs the sleeves of her hoodie down over her fists and hunches her shoulders, as if she's trying to hide inside her own clothes.

'Need to talk to you . . . it's about Evan.' Her words come out as a murmur, directed towards the floor.

'Did you say Evan? Do you mean, Evan Cullen?'

She glances up, eyes wide and afraid. 'I knew him,' she says. 'We were . . . sort of friends.'

'I'm so, *so* sorry for your loss,' I tell her. I don't have to imagine what she might be going through. I know exactly what it's like to lose a friend at that age.

'Thanks.' She swallows, bites her lip. 'The thing is,' she says. 'I've got some information, about what happened to him.'

I'm not here to make another series of *Born Killer*, but in that moment, I wish I was. The girl, appearing out of the blue in this way, is exactly the sort of moment I might end an episode with, the story suddenly blown wide open.

'Have you spoken to anybody else about this?' I ask her. 'Have you told the police?'

She shakes her head. 'My dad says the police are all the same. He says they can't be trusted.' Why is that? I wonder. Might he have been treated unfairly by the local force at some point in the past, just like Connor? Or might there be another, more nefarious reason he doesn't want his daughter going to the authorities?

'So, you've come to me instead?' I say.

The girl nods. 'Because of what you do,' she says. 'You made *Born Killer*, didn't you? You help people.'

# 14

## Martin – 2.14 a.m.

The drive out of London is off to a bad start. It's a quarter past two in the morning and Martin is stuck in traffic. How that's even possible at this time of night, he doesn't know. Most of the bars, pubs and theatres will have closed their doors hours ago, and the rain is falling so hard and heavy the wipers can barely keep up. Any sane person would be at home in bed right now. Nevertheless, a long line of stationary cars and buses trail off into the distance in front of him, the world beyond the rain-slicked windscreen aglow with the pulsing reflections of dozens of brake lights.

He has Freya's spare inhalers in a paper bag on the passenger seat beside him – both the blue and the brown one – and he double-checked they were in full working order before leaving the house. As long as Freya doesn't wake up needing them in the next three or so hours, she should be fine. If she does, Frank has strict instructions to call Martin on his mobile and put Freya on the line so he can try to talk her down, a task that usually falls to Jessie – partly because she's around Freya more often and knows just what to say to soothe her, and partly because Martin is not very good at it. He struggles to be around Freya when she's having an attack. Of course, he'd never leave her to handle it by herself, but seeing the panicked look in her eyes, hearing the wheeze and crackle of her breathing . . . it's too much. To watch her struggle with the most basic of human functions, to know, that in another place or time, she might not have made it, is terrifying. Which is precisely why he's driving to Westhaven in the middle of the night, when he should be at home in bed. Because even though Jessie could be back at the house at any moment, he can't risk it.

The bus ahead lurches forward a few feet, then stops. Brake lights bloom in front of him, turning the interior of the car red, and Martin thumps the steering wheel with the palm of his hand. 'Come on, come on. Let's go, *let's go*,' he says.

As if in reply, his phone buzzes into life, Laurence's name on the caller ID.

'Oh, shit,' Martin says to himself.

Before leaving the house, he emailed over his presentation and all his notes to his boss, then sent him a text – given the time of night, he thought that more appropriate than a call. In the message, he apologised and let Laurence know that he won't be there in person to lead tomorrow's meeting due to an urgent family matter, though he can be dialled in if necessary. He's not expecting his boss to be happy about it – Laurence is a difficult person to work for at the best of times – but at least it means the meeting will go ahead.

He clicks the button on his steering wheel to accept the call, wondering if he shouldn't have waited until at least six to send the text. Now his boss has been woken up in the middle of the night he's going to be doubly annoyed.

'Hi,' he says. 'I take it you got my message?'

'Martin—' Laurence says his name in precisely the same warning tone Martin himself uses when he catches Freya about to do something naughty.

'I know, and I'm sorry,' Martin says. 'Couldn't have happened at a worse time, but it should be OK. Did you see my email? I've shared the latest version of the deck, and all of my notes with you. If you give it the once-over, you'll be up to speed in no time. Plus, you can dial me in and I can still run the Q&A at the end. Between the two of us, that should cover it.'

It's not a perfect solution, but it's as good as he could come up with at short notice.

'Martin, I'm in New York,' Laurence announces, in the flat tone he uses when he's really pissed off about something.

'You're what now?' Martin says.

'In New York,' Laurence repeats, and Martin's stomach drops.

Of course. How could he have forgotten? Laurence is at a

conference in the States. It's the entire reason Martin was tasked with running the meeting in the first place.

Martin winces. This isn't good. He supposes that all he can do is explain. No doubt Laurence will be annoyed, but once he finds out a kid's involved, he'll understand. People always do.

'I'm so sorry,' Martin says. 'I just . . . I've got a bit of a situation here. Freya's at her grandfather's, and there's been some kind of mix-up. She doesn't have her asthma inhalers and Jessie's gone AWOL, so I've got to take her spare medication to her in case something happens. If I could make it back in time, I would, but I won't even get there until five thirty, maybe later, and I won't have slept a wink. Let me speak to them first thing in the morning, reschedule the meeting and smooth everything over. I'm sure it'll be fine.'

'You're sure it'll be fine?' Laurence deadpans. 'Martin, we've been preparing for this for months. You know how important it is.'

'I do,' Martin says. 'But . . . it's my daughter.'

Not just his daughter. Frank is supposed to call the moment Jessie gets back, but so far he hasn't, which means she's still out there in the storm somewhere.

'So . . . let me make sure I've got this clear,' Laurence says. 'You're missing the most important client meeting of your career, because your daughter *might* have an asthma attack?'

Martin can see how that might sound to someone like Laurence, who prioritises work over everything else, who hasn't got kids, and who's never had to watch his daughter struggle to breathe in the dead of night. It could look like he's overreacting, making a big deal out of nothing.

'I know how it might seem,' Martin says. 'But believe me, you can't take any chances with this sort of thing. It can get very serious, very quickly.'

He hears Laurence exhale on the end of the line, long and slow. 'Martin,' he says. 'I need you at the meeting tomorrow. I'm telling you to be there, and if you're not, then . . .'. He trails off, doesn't finish. Doesn't have to.

He can't be serious. Is he really throwing threats around at two thirty in the morning, over a family emergency?

'I can't turn back, you understand that, don't you?' Martin says. 'It sounds like you're asking me to choose between my job and my daughter's life here, for God's sake.'

'Of course I'm not,' says Laurence. 'What I'm asking is that you come to me with solutions, not problems.'

'Sure, but—'

'I'm asking you to find a way to make this work.'

If only it were that easy. Maybe if Freya were back in London, they could find an all-night chemist, or take her to A&E, but there's no all-night chemist in Westhaven, and Frank hasn't owned a car for a few years now, so can't drive to the nearest major city to find one. A&E could still be an option, but that would mean calling an ambulance, in the middle of a storm. A bunch of strangers turning up in the middle of the night while Freya is without her mum is more likely to bring on an asthma attack than anything.

'It's just not that simple,' Martin tells Laurence.

'Then *make* it simple,' Laurence snaps. 'Find a way to make it work, or find another job. Just fucking fix it, Martin. That's what I pay you for, isn't it?'

Martin feels his heart quicken under his T-shirt, as he finds himself hurtling towards a choice he had no idea he'd be facing tonight. Just over an hour ago, he was still in bed, struggling to sleep with the pressure of tomorrow's meeting hanging over him. At least that's one thing he won't have to worry about any longer.

'You know what, Laurence? Why don't you fix it yourself,' he says, and he hangs up.

Adrenalin courses through him. *Did I just quit my job?* he thinks. He did, and he'd do it again.

He will not be pushed around, especially by people like Laurence, who've got it all back to front in their heads, who think the only thing that matters is the bottom line, who put their own family second, and believe their employees should all follow their fucked-up example.

He'll get another bloody job. Right now, the only thing that matters is finding Jessie and making sure Freya is OK. Everything and everybody else can wait.

# 15

*Five days earlier*

'Sorry about the mess,' I say, when I open the door to Mum's office, the cramped little room on the first floor of the house that I used as my base of operations while making *Born Killer*.

The last time I left Westhaven, I promised Dad I'd be back soon to collect all of my paperwork and equipment, but in the end couldn't face the idea of bringing it all back to London, into our family home. So here it sits, like some sort of cursed museum.

The desk is cluttered with equipment, including the big old desktop PC I used to use for putting together rough cuts of interviews, and the bookshelves are overflowing with film magazines, notepads, folders of interview transcripts and shooting scripts. The walls are covered almost entirely in paper: a map of Westhaven, a timeline of events, photographs, photocopies and newspaper clippings.

I step over a cardboard box marked 'Interviews: Jan 2015', move a stack of memory cards off a swivel chair that no longer swivels, then lean over the desk to switch the lamp on. A soft yellow light is cast around the room and I take a seat, side-saddle, so I can face the girl. I gesture for her to sit on the sofa, beneath the room's only window.

'So, you know my name, but I don't know yours,' I say.

She sits down, sinking into the soft leather. 'Um . . . it's Chloe.'

Chloe looks small and afraid. How old is she? I wonder. Fifteen, sixteen maybe? I'm going to have to tread carefully here.

'And you said you were friends with Evan?'

She brushes her dark fringe out of her eyes and gives me a shrug. 'I said we were *sort* of friends. I mean, we hung out sometimes. We were in the same class for some subjects. Mostly he was just . . .' Her voice contracts to a whisper, 'around'.

There's a sudden blast of music from elsewhere in the house and Chloe shoots a glance towards the door.

'It's OK,' I tell her, recognising the first few gentle piano chords of 'So What', the first track on *Kind of Blue*. I hope the music isn't so loud that it wakes Freya, and Dad must have the same thought because after a moment the volume dips. 'It's just my dad, listening to old records,' I tell Chloe. 'You're safe here. Plus, it means he won't be able to hear a word we say. Nobody will.'

She nods, then releases a trembling breath.

I give her a gentle nudge. 'You were saying?'

'Oh, just that . . . I don't think Evan had any proper friends, not really.' She looks down at her lap, drums the fingers of one hand against the palm of the other.

'OK. So, you went to the same school and were sort of friends, but you weren't close?' She nods. 'And you said you have some information about what happened to him?' Another nod. 'Do you want to tell me about it?'

She gives a little twist of the mouth, as if I've forgotten something important.

'Aren't you going to film me?' she asks, and I realise what this is.

She knows I made *Born Killer*, and must think I've come back to Westhaven to shoot another documentary.

'I'm not filming anything right now,' I tell her. 'I'm just here for myself. To see my dad, catch up with old friends.' I almost leave it there, but worry she'll think I don't want to hear what she has to say, so I add, 'Plus, Evan's murder has some similarities to the case I covered in *Born Killer*. I thought I should be here, just in case anything comes up.' In case Amy's murderer has waited fifteen years to kill again.

She lets out a small gasp of disappointment. 'Oh. It's just that, when I heard you were back, I thought you were, y'know . . .' She trails off, then a moment later pulls in a sharp breath, says, 'Just so you know, if you *did* want to film me, I'd be OK with that. I wouldn't mind. Honest.'

It can take days, even weeks of gentle coaxing to persuade some people to go in front of the camera, but Chloe *wants* to be filmed.

Why is that? I wonder. Because she's a *Born Killer* fan, and would get a kick out of being interviewed? Or because she wants whatever she has to say to go on the record?

'Even if I wanted to film you, I couldn't,' I explain. 'For one thing, I don't have my equipment with me. For another, I'd need your parents' consent. Do your mum or dad know you're here?'

'It's just my dad,' she says, matter-of-factly. 'And no, he doesn't know. Nobody does. It's just that . . . *Born Killer* is, like, my favourite show ever. I was totally obsessed when it came out.'

There's a sudden change in her, a spark in her eyes that I've seen before, in the fans who come up to me at events, or approach me in the street, to say how much they enjoyed the show, or to ask what Connor is like in real life.

Chloe goes on, 'My dad says I'm weird for liking stuff like that. I mean, I know not everyone enjoys watching documentaries about murders, but I think it's interesting, y'know?' She takes a breath, as if building herself up for a big announcement, then says, 'When I first saw *Born Killer*, it was like a lightbulb turned on in my head. Before then, I always wanted to be an actress, but now I want to make documentaries, like you. I'm planning to go to film school, once I've finished my A levels.'

A feeling of warmth spreads through me. Maybe *Born Killer* did some good after all.

'That's great,' I say. 'But you don't have to go to film school to make documentaries.'

'I don't?'

'Absolutely not. You've always got a camera with you, right?' I pat the hip pocket of my jeans. 'So, just find a story you want to tell and start filming. Or start filming and see what story finds you.'

Chloe digs her phone out of her pocket and turns it over in her hands, as if seeing it anew.

'Huh, I never thought of it like that,' she says, which strikes me as odd, because these days, thanks to YouTube and TikTok, kids are used to shooting video on their phones. Some become millionaires doing just that by the time they're Chloe's age. Though I suppose there's a world of difference between filming thirty-second clips of you and your friends, dancing to the latest Harry Styles track, and making a ten-hour true crime documentary.

'That's cool,' Chloe says, the trace of a smile on her lips. Then she shakes her fringe out of her eyes with a quick flick of the head, just the way Amy used to, and says, 'Can I ask you a question?'

What I really want to do is talk about Evan Cullen, but the first rule of interviewing is to build a rapport with your subject, to make them feel at ease. If sharing a few more words of wisdom with Chloe will do that, then so be it.

'Go ahead,' I say. 'Ask anything you like.'

'Could you tell Connor was innocent, right from the start?' she says. 'I mean, did you ever have any doubts?'

I shake my head. 'Never. I mean, don't get me wrong, Connor was no angel. He was always getting in trouble with his teachers, and sometimes with the police. Most of the time he deserved it, but sometimes he didn't. Sometimes he got blamed for things because of who he was, rather than what he'd done.'

'Right,' Chloe says. 'Like when he was accused of stealing that car, only he was with you and your friends when it happened, so he couldn't have done it.'

'Exactly,' I say, impressed that she's remembered this relatively minor detail from *Born Killer*. 'And here's something you might not know. That car was involved in a hit and run, so if we hadn't spoken up for Connor when we did, he might have ended up in prison even sooner.'

'Huh,' she says. 'Why did the police hate him so much?'

'Well, people weren't quite so understanding back then. When they looked at Connor, they didn't see a troubled kid who needed help and support, they saw a lost cause.'

'That's sad,' Chloe says.

'It is,' I agree. 'Maybe, if he'd had a different start in life, he'd wouldn't have got into so much trouble. And when it came to Amy, I know he cared for her very much. He'd never have hurt her. Someone else put her in that well, I'm certain of that.'

'Maybe the same person who killed Evan?' Chloe says, her eyes going wide.

'Probably not,' I say. 'But I'd like to rule that out.'

She looks more at ease now and I decide it's time to bring the conversation back to Evan.

'Now, do you want to tell me—' I begin, but she interrupts.

'Do you think I could help you?' she asks, and perhaps because the moment I first saw her, standing in the hallway, looking like the ghost of my dead best friend, is still lodged in my mind, something about her question catches me off guard. An absurd image comes to mind of Chloe, leaning forward and laying hands on me, like some sort of healer, as if she has the power to absolve me of all my sins.

'Help me?' I find myself saying.

'You know, like, follow you around and stuff? Run errands, see how you do things? I know you're not making a documentary right now, but I bet there's still stuff I could learn. And it's half-term, so I'm off school all week anyway.'

I come back to earth. Christ, what's wrong with me? She's not some magical healer. She's just a kid, looking for work experience – work experience I have absolutely no intention of giving her.

'I'm not sure that would be a good idea,' I tell her. 'I doubt your dad would be very happy about you getting involved in a murder investigation.'

She shrugs. 'He *might* be OK with it, if you talk to him. You could tell him it could help my film school application.'

At her age, I'd have given anything for some experience with a real film director. But despite that, and the pleading look in her eyes, the last thing I need right now is a teenager getting under my feet. It's going to be difficult enough trying to make enquiries with one child to take care of, never mind two. But I want to know what she knows.

I lean back and open one of the drawers in Mum's old desk, feel around for sticky notes and a pen, find both and hand them over.

'No promises,' I say. 'But give me your dad's contact details and I'll think about it.'

Chloe grins. 'Great! You won't regret it, I swear.'

I feel bad, giving her false hope like this, because I've no intention of calling her dad, but sometimes to get what you want out of an interviewee, you need to make them feel like they're getting something in return.

Chloe writes down an email address. 'I'll give you his number too,' she says. 'Probably best if you speak to him, y'know, given there's, like, an actual murderer running around.'

She cringes, aware that her words might come across as insensitive, and I smile to let her know it's OK. People react in all sorts of strange ways around death. When grief breaks us open, all sorts of emotions come spilling out.

Chloe hands over the sticky note and I take it from her.

'So, I've answered your questions,' I say. 'Now, how about you answer some of mine?'

# 16

## Jessie – 2.15 a.m.

I read the message again and panic chills my insides. If I want to see my family again, I must get ready to tell the truth, it says. What does that mean? That I'll be left to die alone down here unless I tell whoever did this what they want to hear? That they're going to hurt Freya, or Martin, or Dad? Please no. I'll do anything – *say* anything – to stop my family being harmed. But what is it they want from me?

Unless . . . The message must be from one of those crazy people who think Connor is guilty. And the truth they want to hear isn't the truth at all, but a story they've made up in their heads, sitting behind their keyboards, spouting myths and conspiracy theories on Reddit and social media: *Born Killer* is a pack of lies, Connor killed Amy, the retrial was a sham – the usual rubbish.

My God. I always thought some of them might have a few screws loose, but I never thought it would come to this, that they'd actually try to kill me, that they'd threaten my family. Now what? They want me to debate the facts with them over text message, while they're up there and I'm trapped down here, sitting in a foot of stinking water with half a tree through my leg?

It's nothing short of madness, and whatever they think is going to happen is irrelevant now, because for some reason – arrogance perhaps, or plain old stupidity – they've just given me a way out of here.

Holding the phone tightly in my trembling hand – because I'm terrified I'll drop it, and my one chance of getting out of here will be lost to sheer clumsiness – I bring up the keypad to dial 999, only to find that the phone won't register the press of my wet fingers. I try drying the screen on my T-shirt – which does no good whatsoever. Why is everything so bloody wet? I try again, manage to dial three nines in a row by repeatedly jabbing the screen, but when I press the call button nothing happens.

'Come on, you stupid thing!' I shout at the handset and, as if in response, the screen turns black. My heart freezes – *the battery indicator was wrong, the phone's out of juice after all.*

'No, no, no!' I cry, pressing the screen over and over. Suddenly the handset emits a loud beep, as if it were starting to ring but changed its mind. I stop pressing the screen and, to my astonishment, hear a faint voice: 'Hello?'

I put the phone to my ear. 'Hello? *Hello*?'

'Is somebody there?' It's a woman, calm and professional sounding. 'This is ambulance-emergency, we've been trying to call you back. Does somebody need assistance?'

Confusion clouds my thoughts. Did I call her, or did she call me? And what does she mean, 'call me back'? But confusion comes second to a wave of relief so strong it leaves me dumbstruck.

'Hello? Is there somebody there who needs help? Are you OK?'

'Yes!' I try to say, but my throat is raw from vomiting up well water, and what emerges is little more than a croak. I try again. 'I'm here, I'm here! I need help. I was just calling you.'

'We received a call from this number a short time ago. It sounded like someone was in distress. Can you tell me exactly what's happened?'

A call from this number? My brain is a black expanse as I scrabble to understand what she's saying . . . I must have dialled 999 before I was pushed into the well and the call must have cut off, or I was attacked before I had the chance to speak.

'I'm trapped! I'm in Dutton's Well. I'm trapped and I'm hurt—'

'Ma'am? Slow down. I can't make out what you're saying.'

I take a deep breath, so I can lay it out bit by bit, but my heart is beating too fast. I snatch lungfuls of air between words. 'I'm trapped in Dutton's Well . . . in Cooper's Wood . . . Someone put me down here . . . They tried . . . they tried to kill me. They've threatened my family.'

I can almost hear her sit up in her seat.

'OK, what's your name?'

'Jessica. Jessica Hamill.'

'And how old are you, Jessica?' I hear typing on a keyboard in the background.

'Thirty-one . . . I've got a little girl, she's five.' This last statement spills out of me, unbidden, and tears quickly follow.

'I'm arranging help for you right now,' the operator says.

'Oh, thank you, *thank you*. Please hurry.'

There's a brief moment of quiet, punctuated by flurries of keystrokes and mouse clicks, then the operator says, 'OK, Jessica. Please stay on the line so we can track your exact location. We'll have a rescue team out to you right away. We're going to do everything we can to get you out of there.'

# 17

*Five days earlier*

When the conversation turns to Evan, Chloe seems to retreat into herself. That spark in her eyes fizzles out, she puts her head down and stares at her hands, stutters and false-starts. At some points she talks so quietly I can barely hear her.

'I . . . erm . . . met Evan, like, a few years ago . . . next to each other for French and . . . and a few . . . and he was . . .'

'Can you speak up a little?'

'Um, yeah. So, there's, like, this stupid dance the school has . . . wasn't going to go.' Her volume dips again and I lift a hand.

'What is it?' she says. 'Am I doing something wrong?'

'No, it's not that. It's just . . .' This would all be so much easier if I were interviewing her, I think. Then I remember what she said, about going on camera, and an idea comes to me.

'Can I borrow your phone?' I say, and she looks at me as if I've just asked her to turn over her cashcard and PIN. 'I'll give it back, I promise. And can you unlock it for me?'

She holds the phone in front of her face to unlock it, then reluctantly hands it over and watches with cautious interest as I open the camera app and switch it to video mode. I turn to the desk, pull over a box of files and a stack of old film magazines to create a makeshift stand, then prop the iPhone up in such a way that the lens is clear and I have a partial view of the screen, if I lean back in my chair far enough. I centre Chloe in the frame.

'I thought you weren't allowed to film me?' she says.

'I'm not. Once we're done, I'm going to give you your phone back and the footage will be all yours. And you said you wanted to learn something, didn't you?'

'Yeah.'

'Lesson one. Most people aren't comfortable talking on camera, but that's not always the case. Sometimes it can help people to focus their attention. Do you ever make videos for YouTube or Instagram?'

'Sometimes.'

'Well, this will be just like that. You're going to look right into the lens, and imagine you're talking to your friends, or your followers. I expect you've got thousands.'

'A few.' She flicks her fringe again, the way Amy used to. 'Do I look OK?'

I check the screen. 'You look great,' I tell her, and she does. The lighting is far from ideal for filming, with the left side of her face completely in shadow, but the lamplight highlights her delicate features and adds a certain moodiness to proceedings that I think she'd approve of.

I press the button to start recording.

'OK, we're rolling. Now, head up, shoulders back, and look into the lens. Let's start over. First, I want you to introduce yourself, then tell me about how you first met Evan. I'll ask questions as we go.'

When Chloe next speaks it's clear she wasn't lying about being a *Born Killer* fan, or perhaps just a fan of documentaries in general. She's a little hesitant, and her words are still peppered with the 'likes' and 'sos' typical of people her age, but she soon hits her stride.

'So, my name is . . . um, Chloe Mitchell, and I went to the same school as Evan Cullen. We were, like, in some of the same classes. History and English, and we sat next to each other in French for a few terms. We weren't close, but we were . . . sort of friends.'

She looks over, unsure, and I give her a thumbs up.

She continues, 'I first met Evan around two years ago, when he switched to our school. Our form tutor introduced him to the whole class one morning and said we needed to make an extra special effort to be nice to him. She didn't say why, but word got around he'd moved schools because he was being bullied, and soon we all knew it was because of his uncle. We'd all seen *Born Killer* anyway. We knew what his uncle had done.'

Two years ago would make Chloe and her classmates just thirteen years old when Evan joined their school. I'm a little surprised by the idea of a class of thirteen-year-olds having watched *Born Killer*. Then again, when I was that age, I'd watch horror movies during sleepovers with Amy that were far more gruesome.

'Can you tell me what Evan was like at school?'

'He was . . . different. He didn't . . .' Chloe looks away from the camera while she searches for the word, then back. 'He didn't have his own group. He was a bit of a . . . nerd, I suppose, and he was teased, a lot. Kids made fun of him, said stuff behind his back. Some of the bigger boys pushed him around. He got beaten up a few times. I heard that one time, in his old school, some kid even broke his arm.'

'Some kid?'

She shrugs. 'He wouldn't tell anyone who'd done it. I guess he was too scared.'

Sounds about right. I think of Martin, who was bullied as a child because he was small for his age and had eczema, like Freya does. He hates talking about it, and has never told me the full extent of it, but he's shared enough over the years for me to know it was bad, that it soured his early school years. By the time I met him, he'd been through something of a growth spurt and his skin had all but cleared up, but the bullying had left its mark. To this day, when I think of what the little boy version of him went through, it breaks my heart.

'It must have been hard for you, seeing your friend treated that way,' I say.

'We weren't friends back then,' Chloe says. 'Like I said, he was just around. Then last year there was this stupid dance at school, and Evan came up to me at lunch break, all nervous, and asked if I'd go with him. I said no, because I have a boyfriend, but he didn't know that because my boyfriend doesn't go to our school. But I liked that he'd asked me, y'know? I thought it was sweet, and I felt sorry for him, because he was still being picked on by some of the boys. So, I started, like, making more of an effort with him, sitting next to him in class, talking to him at lunch break, that sort of thing. He was nice, and he could be funny. That's how we became sort of friends.'

'Sort of' friends. She keeps saying it, like she wants to preserve some distance between them, and I can imagine why. Status is everything at that age, and Evan was on the lower rungs of the school social hierarchy, or in her words, a nerd. As much as she seems to have enjoyed his company, she might have worried that some of his unpopularity might rub off on her.

'Thanks, Chloe,' I say. 'That's a great summary. Now, you told me you had some information to do with what happened to him?'

She nods, takes a few breaths to steady herself, then continues. 'Last week, it was the end of French and we were sitting next to each other, and everything was normal. We'd been joking around, talking like usual. But when he was packing up his things, this piece of paper fell out of the back of his textbook and landed on my desk, and I could see this look in his eyes, like he really wanted that piece of a paper back. So I looked at it and it was a letter, only not a proper letter, with an address at the top and yours sincerely at the bottom. It was full of swear words and threats, someone saying they were going to get someone, make them pay. I asked him what it was, but he snatched it off me and told me to . . .' She looks over. 'Can I swear?'

'If it's relevant to the story, then yes,' I find myself saying, like I'm her parent, rather than an adult she has only just met.

'He said, "Mind your own fucking business".'

She does a little impression of Evan when she says this, scowling and deepening her voice, then sits back in her chair, eyes wide with anticipation of what's next. She doesn't know I'm one step ahead of her, because I've already seen a letter full of swear words and threats today. A whole pile of them, in fact.

She goes on, 'I was worried because I thought someone had sent the letter to him. I told him he needed to talk to someone, tell a teacher, or his mum, and if he was too scared to, I could go with him.'

'That was nice of you.'

'I suppose.' She shrugs. 'But then he told me he hadn't been sent the letter, he was going to send it to someone. He was going to send it to Connor Starling. He said he hated Connor, that he'd ruined his uncle's life and that was why he was bullied all the time. I told him he was being stupid and that he'd get into trouble if he got caught. Besides, he only had to watch *Born Killer* to know that Connor is innocent. But he said *Born Killer* was full of lies, and that he was going to prove it. We had a big fight and he stormed off and . . . and . . .' Her face scrunches up and tears come. 'It's my fault,' she says, between sobs. 'What happened to him . . . it's my fault.'

Poor girl. She blames herself for her friend's murder. I want to put an arm around her, but I'm not sure if that's what she'd want. Instead, I move over and take a seat on the sofa next to her, our elbows touching.

'It's *not* your fault,' I tell her. 'Do you hear me? You mustn't think like that. If you had an argument and Evan stormed off and somebody hurt him, then that's not your fault. And it's not his either. The only person responsible is the person who did that to him.'

She pulls in a series of hitching breaths, like Freya does when she's really upset.

'Hey, come on,' I say, softly. 'It's OK to be upset, but you mustn't blame yourself. Now, I think what we should do is tell the police about this.' Chloe is shaking her head, but I go on. 'I understand that might sound scary, but I have a friend who's a police officer. He's really nice, and he can help us. He could speak to your dad, and then we could arrange a meeting, so you could tell them what happened.'

Chloe drags the sleeve of her hoodie under her nose, leaving a dark snot trail behind. 'We can't,' she says.

'Why not?'

'Because when I told Evan he was being stupid, that he'd never prove Connor was guilty of something he didn't do, he said I was wrong.'

I don't understand why this should stop us going to the police. Presumably, if Evan was looking for evidence that Connor killed Amy, the place he'd most likely think to find it, would be in Cooper's Wood.

'This could be important, Chloe,' I tell her. 'If this is why Evan was up in the woods that night, the police need to know.'

'But that's the problem,' she says. 'He didn't go to the woods.'

'He didn't?' I say, and my stomach clenches like a fist.

She shakes her head. 'He said he was going to go and see Connor,' she says. 'He said he was going to make him confess.'

# 18

## Martin – 2.41 a.m.

Martin resists putting his foot down, because while he wants to get there soon, he wants to get there in one piece, and with the storm still raging, driving conditions are treacherous and visibility is beyond poor. Besides, he's making good time. At this rate, he should reach Westhaven in a little over two and a half hours. Freya will have her inhalers and, once the storm has blown over, Jessie will arrive back at her dad's, safe and sound, although she's going to be surprised when she finds out he's driven all this way. Even more surprised when she finds out he's quit his job.

He hopes she's OK, wherever she is, and that she won't blame herself for tonight, that she'll accept that leaving Freya's inhalers in the car was Frank's fault, and not hers. It was an accident. There was nothing she could have done.

Jessie has a habit of taking responsibility for things that aren't her fault. You only need to look at the way she ran back to Westhaven to see it. The moment she heard about the murdered boy, it was like a switch flicked in her brain. Here was her chance to make everything right: solve the boy's murder, find Amy's killer, make Amy's parents like her again, and earn her hometown's approval. It says something about a person when they think they need to solve not one, but two murders, to be forgiven for trying to do the right thing.

It can be frustrating, seeing her take on everybody else's problems, but at the same time it's perhaps the thing Martin loves most about Jessie. How could it not be?

Whenever they're together and someone asks her how they first met, Jessie always takes the lead, but keeps the details light. She explains how they grew up in the same town, that they started dating when they were fourteen and have been together ever since, and leaves it at that. Not once, as far as Martin is aware, has she shared the fact that their first meeting involved her diving into a river to save him from drowning. It's as if she knows, without having to ask, that he finds the story embarrassing, that he thinks it makes him look . . . weak. She never brings it up, even though it would make her look good, and he loves her for that too, for putting him first, for knowing how he feels without having to ask.

When he thinks back to that Sunday morning, his memories are oddly truncated. He remembers next to nothing about the hours leading up to the incident and has only a vague sense of the conflict with the older boys that led to him being pushed into the river. What he does remember is the wicked bray of their laughter as he hit the water, which was as high as he'd ever seen it, and the panic that followed as he was knocked sideways by the current. Before he knew what was happening, he was being carried downstream, his body twisting and turning in the rushing water and his head repeatedly sinking beneath the surface. Every time he tried to take a breath, he'd get a mouthful of water instead, until his chest felt like it was going to explode, and he soon realised he was done for. He had only ever had one swimming lesson, couldn't bear the embarrassment of the walk from the changing room to the pool, all those people seeing the raw patches of eczema on the backs of his legs, the insides of his elbows and the base of his throat. And what little he had learned he could no longer remember as the current pulled him onwards and under. There was nothing he could do to help himself. In his final moments of consciousness, he thought of his mum and dad; how much he'd miss them – and how his imminent drowning was going to totally ruin his mum's birthday the following day – and then he caught a glimpse of someone in the water, swimming towards him.

After Jessie had rescued him, slinging an arm around his neck and dragging him to the water's edge, they sat on chairs outside the little coffee hut on the riverbank and the old lady who worked there brought them towels and polystyrene cups of hot chocolate while she went to phone their parents.

Martin mumbled a thank you to the pretty girl with wet hair sitting across from him, but only when she asked him what school he went to did he dare meet her eye, and then he recognised her as Jessica, one of the popular girls from school, who always hung around with another girl called Amy, which only added to how mortified he felt about the whole thing. She'd probably tell everyone at school what had happened, which would only lead to more trouble.

'Um . . . yours,' he mumbled into his chest. 'We're in the same year.'

'Oh,' Jessica said. 'I don't think I've seen you around.'

Martin shrugged. Of course she hadn't. To everyone but his friend Lex, and the handful of bullies who had made the first few years of senior school so miserable, he was practically invisible. He'd hoped the bullying would stop that year, given he'd gone through a growth spurt over the summer and had finally got his eczema under control, but it didn't seem to make any difference. His status as a victim and an easy mark still hung around him like the smell of Lynx deodorant in the boys' changing rooms.

'You should give me your number,' Jessica said. 'We should hang out sometime.'

He couldn't for the life of him understand why she was pretending she wanted to be friends with him, but he gave her his number anyway, because she had asked, and she had saved his life. It would have been rude not to.

When she called the next day to invite him to the cinema, he assumed it was some sort of cruel joke, that she wouldn't turn up and it would be yet another reason for his schoolmates to laugh at him. But to his amazement she arrived on time, with her friend Amy in tow.

Martin doesn't remember what film they saw, only that they kissed as the end credits rolled, and that her lips tasted of buttery popcorn and Sprite.

# BORN KILLER –
# SHOOTING SCRIPT

## S01 – E05: THE TRIAL

**ROBERT BARNES (Amy's father):** 'I wanted to kill him. Sorry, I know I shouldn't say things like that, but that's how it felt. I wanted to be shut in a room with him for five minutes . . . I know he was a big lad, bigger than I am, but if I'd have got my hands on him . . .'

**ARCHIVE NEWS FOOTAGE:** An explosion of camera flashes as a police van nudges its way through a booing crowd as it arrives at court. People hammer on the side of the van with their fists. There are shouts of 'Murderer!', 'Scumbag!'

**ELAINE BARNES (Amy's mother):** 'Rob was a typical dad. He always said nobody would ever be good enough for his little girl. But I told him we should give Connor a chance, try to get to him know a bit. Otherwise, we'd end up pushing her away. We knew he had a reputation, but Amy said he was trying to turn things around, so we agreed they could go out, so long as we met him first. So, we invited him over for dinner.'

**ROBERT BARNES:** (Looks down, shakes his head. Says nothing.)

**ELAINE BARNES:** 'We were quite impressed. He arrived on time, and he brought flowers. He was polite, well mannered, all "Yes please, Mrs Barnes. No thank you, Mrs Barnes." And I remember thinking that perhaps we'd been too hasty, that we'd misjudged him. I've always thought people deserve second chances, that they should be given the benefit of the doubt.'

**ROBERT BARNES:** 'He sat at my table, in my kitchen. Ate food off my plates, drank from my glasses. He laughed and joked and pretended he had nothing but good intentions. Then, six months later, he murdered my daughter.'

**DS JOHN DALTON:** 'In the end, the evidence was overwhelming. A neighbour saw Amy leaving her house on the night in question, carrying a small canvas shoulder bag. That bag was later found in Connor's room, hidden at the back of his wardrobe, with her asthma medication inside it. Clearly, they met up that night, and whatever happened between them led to her ending up in that well.'

# 19

*Four days earlier*

The next morning, I awake to the sight of Freya, standing by the side of the bed, holding a tray of tea and toast at a perilous angle – half the tea having slopped over the rim of the cup and the toast about to slide off the plate.

'Wake up, Mummy! I made you breakfast,' Freya shouts, delighted with herself.

I sit up and take the tray, before its contents end up on the floor, and set it down carefully on the bedside table.

'Thank you very much. Did you do all this by yourself?' Please tell me Dad hasn't had her handling a boiling kettle and putting her fingers near the toaster.

'Yes,' she says, 'but Grandpa helped.' I hear the creak of a floorboard out on the landing and a second later Dad pokes his head around the door. He must have carried the tray up the stairs, handing it over to Freya at the final moment so she could complete the delivery with the minimal risk of spillage.

'I only helped with the hard parts,' Dad says, glancing down at the tray, which is now swimming with a good amount of milky tea. 'I'm going to make a start on lunch, if you think you're about ready to join the land of the living?'

I snatch my phone up off the bedside table and check the time. Almost eleven. How did that happen?

'Oh no, I'm so sorry, Dad.'

'No trouble,' he says, sounding cheerful enough. Although, if Freya got up at her usual time he'll have been looking after her for nearly five hours already. He's probably in dire need of a break.

'I'll be down in ten,' I tell him, and he retreats downstairs. 'And you, young lady . . .' I grab Freya around the middle, pull her onto the bed and force a cuddle out of her. 'Why didn't you wake me up?'

She squirms and laughs. 'You were snoring, Mummy,' she says, then she does a passable impression of an oinking pig and breaks into a fit of giggles.

'I was not!' I tickle her sides, delighting in the sound of her laugher, then press an ear against her sternum. 'How's your chest today?'

'OK,' she says, though I can hear a small rattle at the end of each breath. Nothing too worrying, but her breathing isn't as clear as I'd like.

'Did you have your brown inhaler yet?' I ask. She doesn't reply, but her lips pinch into a thin white line and her eyes go wide, like she's struggling to keep in a secret.

'You'd better have it now then, hadn't you? Go on.'

I sit her up and pat her on the bottom and she grabs her inhaler off the bedside table and takes it. First dose, wait for ten seconds, then second dose.

'Good girl. Now, why don't you go downstairs and see if Grandpa needs any help with lunch. Tell him I'll be down in a bit.'

'Don't forget your breakfast, Mummy!' Freya calls out, as she leaves the room.

As soon as she's gone, I collapse back onto the bed. God, I'm tired. Fuzzy headed and heavy limbed, my eyes gritty and sore. I was awake half the night, turning Chloe's story over in my mind.

A few months ago, Freya had a bit of bother with a girl in her class – nothing serious, just a single incident involving a bit of hair pulling. But Martin acted like she'd been full on assaulted and confronted the other girl's mum at the school gates. Word of the resulting scene got back to me via the mums' WhatsApp group before he'd even arrived home from pickup.

'What were you thinking? You made her cry – the mum, I mean,' I said, but Martin stuck to his guns.

'Hopefully now she'll realise her daughter can't go around bullying other kids, making their lives a misery.'

'She wasn't *bullying* her. It was just a silly argument, that's all.'

'And who told you that?'

'Freya's teacher. She said it was over in two seconds, they were friends again by lunchtime.'

'And she knows everything, does she?' he snapped, then caught himself. 'Sorry. I don't mean to shout, it's just . . . I don't want Freya going through what I went through; getting picked on, teased by the other kids. I won't have it.'

His eyes grew dark, and I could see in them the residual hate for all the children who'd made his life a misery when he was a boy. He couldn't go back and protect his younger self, so he was making sure Freya was protected now, even if that meant making a little girl's mum cry at the school gates.

I've seen how bullying can affect people. How it can give rise to an anger, deep inside them. So I can understand Evan wanting to lash out at the person he considered ultimately responsible for the pain he had suffered; sending Connor hate mail, posting dead animals through his letterbox. But did Evan really think he could intimidate Connor into confessing to Amy's murder? Setting aside the fact that Connor is hardly likely to confess to something he didn't do, Evan was just a kid – a rather small, skinny one at that. He wouldn't have been able to force Connor to do anything he didn't want to. And if Evan really did set off to see Connor, how did he end up dead on the opposite side of town, in Cooper's Wood?

I'm not sure what to think, though one thing I do know: I don't want Chloe telling anybody else what she told me last night, not until I've done some digging. I need to keep a lid on the situation, make sure Chloe keeps her mouth shut. Fortunately, I think I know just how to do that.

After taking a bite or two of the cold toast and slurping down what's left of the tea, I have a quick shower and dress, then carry the tray downstairs to the kitchen – where Dad is acting as personal assistant for Freya, handing her different coloured crayons on demand.

'Yellow, please,' she says.

Dad tips his head to peer over his glasses, finds the right one and hands it over. 'And what colour are you going to make the man's hat?' he asks.

'Mmm, blue.'

'A fine choice. I once had a hat that exact colour.'

'I'm just going to make a call,' I announce. 'I won't be long, and then we can go out.' A visit to the library is on the cards, as promised to Freya last night.

'Don't mind us,' Dad says. Neither of them lift their heads.

I head back upstairs to Mum's office and close the door behind me, find the note with Chloe's dad's details scrawled on it, still stuck to the desk, and dial the number.

A sharp voice answers. 'Hello?'

'Mr Mitchell?'

'Yes, what do you want?' Two seconds into the call and I can already tell that Mr Mitchell and I aren't going to be the best of friends. Still, I put a smile into my voice.

'My name's Jessie Hamill, I'm calling because I met your daughter yesterday . . .'

'Chloe?' He says her name like a curse word. 'What about her? Are you from the school? I've told you, I can't make her go if she doesn't want to.'

Does he even know it's half-term? I wonder.

'I'm not from her school, and she hasn't done anything wrong, as far as I know. I'm actually a filmmaker—'

'Filmmaker? What sort of filmmaker?'

'Documentaries, mostly. You can find some of my work on BlinkView.'

'Really?' he says, sounding like he doesn't believe me, or if he does, that he isn't the least bit impressed.

'That's right, and . . . well, the thing is, I'm in the area and yesterday I met Chloe and she asked if she could help out; run some errands, that sort of thing. I wanted to ask you if that might be OK?' I keep the details light. No mention of the fact that I'm not actually filming anything at the moment, no mention of Evan Cullen, either.

'Like, work experience, you mean?' he says.

'Sort of. It'll be an opportunity for her to spend some time with me, ask any questions she wants to, learn how I do things. I'll cover expenses if any come up, of course, but there shouldn't be any.'

Come on, you miserable sod. What sort of parent wouldn't want their kid to get some work experience doing the thing they most want to do in life?

'Right,' he says, and I get the feeling he's about to tell me this isn't something he wants his daughter to be involved with, so I change tack.

'It's no problem, Mr Mitchell,' I say, breezily. 'I can tell you're busy. I've got other students who are really interested, so if this isn't right for Chloe, that's totally fine. It's just a shame, because it would have looked good on her college application—'

'Whoa, hold your horses,' he says. 'I didn't say she couldn't do it, did I? I was just thinking it over, that's all. I don't want some other kid taking a place that's rightfully hers.' He pretends that he's considering it. 'And you'll cover any expenses, right? It ain't gonna cost me anything?'

'It won't cost you a penny,' I tell him.

'Yeah, all right then,' he says. 'If it'll keep her out of trouble.'

'That's great, Mr Mitchell. Thank you,' I say, though if he had half a brain, he'd be the one thanking me. 'Is Chloe there by any chance? Could you put her on? I just realised she gave me your number, but not her own.'

'She's at her boyfriend's,' he says, giving the final word an emphasis that tells me Mr Mitchell has little time for Chloe's boyfriend, whoever he is. 'I've got your number in my phone. I'll pass it on, tell her to text you.'

'Thank you, Mr Mitchell—' He's already hung up.

What a charmer.

But I suppose it doesn't matter. I got what I wanted. Chloe has permission to become my assistant, and now I'll be able to keep an eye on her, and make sure she doesn't tell anyone else that the last thing Evan did, before he turned up dead, was tell his friend he was going to pay a visit to Connor Starling.

# 20

## Jessie – 2.43 a.m.

'We might get cut off,' the emergency operator says. 'If that happens, don't worry. I'll call you right back. The most important thing you can do right now is stay on the line. That'll help us monitor your condition, and zero in on your exact location. Can you do that for me?'

'Yes! Yes, I can do that.'

Dutton's Well is a local landmark, but my rescuers probably won't have heard of it. I expect they'll use the call to triangulate my exact location in the woods. Besides, I want to stay on the line, want to at least feel like I'm not alone down here.

The operator continues, her voice slow and measured, instantly reassuring. 'Now, I know this must be very frightening for you, but I want you to try to stay calm. My name's Fiona, by the way, and I'm going to be right here with you until help arrives. I'm not going anywhere, OK?'

I feel like a lost child delivered into the hands of a capable adult, one who knows exactly the right things to say and do. The fist of panic, clenched so tightly in my chest these last few hours, begins to loosen.

'Can you have someone check on my family, on my little girl and my dad?' I ask. 'And my husband too.'

'I can have that arranged for you. Right now I want to make sure you're OK. You said that you're hurt?'

'Yes. I tried to climb out – I *did* climb out, but they pushed me back down. I must have landed on something. A root, I think. It's stuck in my leg. I can't get up, I can't move.'

Beneath the water, pain flares deep in my thigh.

I hear more typing from Fiona. 'OK, Jessica. I'm just passing this information on to my colleagues at the ambulance service. Is that the extent of your physical injuries? Are you hurt anywhere else?'

Am I? It's hard to tell in the dark and in the grip of shock. I take a moment to check myself over, feel my way around my upper body with my free hand, hoping to God I don't find any more horrible surprises – open wounds, branches sticking out of places they shouldn't. I'm definitely bruised and bashed up, my body aches, and my hands still sting from the climb, but I don't think I have any other major injuries.

'I think it's just my leg,' I tell her, as if that isn't bad enough.

'OK, Jessica. Now ... I want you to listen to me very carefully. You said somebody put you down there. The person who did this to you, are they still there? Do they pose any immediate risk to your safety?'

I tip my head back, look up at the violet disc, blinking as the cool rain hits my cheeks. There's no sign of anyone up above, but that doesn't mean a thing. They could still be up there, lurking, listening.

I lower my voice. 'I think they're still up there. They threw my bag down, and my phone.'

'They threw down your phone?' She sounds confused, understandably.

'Yes, they sent me a message. They want me to talk to them, or make some sort of announcement. That's when they threatened me and my family.'

'You said that you have a little girl. Where is she right now?'

'She's with my dad.' I give her the address. 'And my husband will be at home, back in London. Can someone make sure he's OK too?'

Whoever did this to me is probably working alone, but I have to know that Freya, Martin and Dad are safe.

'OK, Jessica. I'm going to pass this information onto the police, and they'll be able to carry out welfare checks on your daughter and your husband so you know that they're OK. The most important thing right now is to make sure you're safe. You must let me know if you see anybody, or if they try to communicate with you again. Help is on the way.'

'How long until they get here?'

The well is only three miles from the edge of town, but it is deep in Cooper's Wood, down a series of dense woodland trails. It's not the easiest of walks in the daytime, when the weather is clear, but at night, during a storm? Who knows how long it'll take them to get to me?

I hear more keyboard tapping, more mouse clicking. 'I'll let you know when they're close,' Fiona says. 'I'm looking at a satellite view of the area your call is coming from and, from what I can see, that section of woodland is very overgrown, but they're professionals, they know what they're doing. As soon as I hear that the rescue team is nearby, I'm going to ask you to make some noise so they can locate you quickly. Do you think you can do that for me?'

'You want me to shout?'

'Scream, shout. Sing a song if you like, just as long as it's nice and loud.'

I tell her I'll scream my head off if it means I get out of here.

'That's good,' she says. 'I'll let you know when to start. For now, I need you to try to stay calm. You're doing really—' She stops herself. Was she about to say I was doing really *well*? 'You're doing really great. I'm going to put you on hold for just a minute while I check on a few things. I'll be right back.'

'Wait!' I don't want her to put me on hold, don't want to be alone down here again, but it's too late, she's gone.

How utterly surreal, to be on hold while I'm trapped at the bottom of a well. I suppose it doesn't matter now. With luck, when she comes back on the line, she'll tell me they are only fifteen minutes away and this whole thing will be over soon. I quieten my breathing, listen hard for sirens. Nothing yet. Just the constant dripping of water, the ticking of insects, and my own heartbeat thumping hard in my temples.

I think about turning the phone's torch on, but don't want to mess with the settings in case I accidentally drop the call, so I take the phone away from my ear and turn the screen outwards, flash the dim light around me. Until now, the picture I've had in my head of the well has been built solely from touch: from the feel of the wet stones, the tepid water sloshing around me, the feel of insects alighting on my upper arms to suck my blood, and the rotten dead-animal stink in the air. Now, by the light of the screen, I see the inside of the well properly for the first time.

It's wider than I thought, perhaps five feet across, though it narrows as it gets closer to the top. The stones that make up the well's walls are bigger and paler than I imagined, but just as encrusted with moss and lichen. At the bottom of the well, there's a foot or so of murky water with a thousand pieces of detritus floating on, or just beneath, the surface – sticks and dead leaves and pieces of litter. A crumpled old can, an ancient crisp packet, a beer bottle. My bag, still afloat, but listing to one side, like a sinking ship. There are no rats, or giant centipedes, thank God, but there are spiders, with large brown orbs for bodies and long black legs, and there are slugs, fat and swollen and grey. It is, I decide after taking in the view, no better having the light to see by than not. In fact, it might be worse. The more I see, the worse I feel. The more in pain, the more panicked, the more alone.

I put the phone back up to my ear. 'Fiona?' *Please be there.*

'Jessica, are you OK?' She's there, thank God.

'I'm OK,' I say, my voice high and trembling.

'You'll be relieved to hear that we expect help to be with you within the hour.'

Another hour is so much longer than I expected. It's practically an eternity. But I can get through it, I decide. As long as I know that Freya and Martin and Dad are safe, and as long as I have Fiona on the other end of the line, I can wait an hour.

'I know that might feel like a long time,' Fiona says, 'but they need to be properly equipped to get you out of there. Plus, the storm is getting worse. It's already hit some parts of the county. There are trees down, some of the roads are flooded. But I don't want you to worry; they're on their way and they'll be with you just as soon as they can, and I'm going to be right here with you the whole time. I'm not going anywhere until you do.'

# 21

*Four days earlier*

While Freya browses the children's section at the library, I take a seat on a low sofa nearby and do some browsing of my own, looking through Evan Cullen's various social media profiles on my phone.

His Twitter profile leads to his Instagram account – neither of which tells me very much – which then leads me to his YouTube channel, which is a little more revealing. It contains several home-made videos themed around the game Dungeons & Dragons. I make sure my phone's volume is turned down, then click on 'How to Create Your Own DnD Character' and, after a short advert, Evan appears, sitting in front of a cloth backdrop – presumably a sheet pinned to his bedroom wall – talking animatedly into the camera. It's the first time I've seen him up close and in motion, and there's something particularly moving about him looking down the lens at me. He seems so young and innocent. Awkward too, in the way teenage boys can be – as if they're still getting accustomed to their growing bodies – but with signs of the handsome man he would have become, had he lived. He reminds me of Martin at that age.

I'm tempted to nudge the volume up a notch so I can hear what Evan's saying, but I feel the ghosts of librarians past, hovering nearby with their fingers pressed to their lips, and decide against it.

Scrolling down, I see the video has a grand total of forty-five views. How many of those have been in the last few days? I wonder. From people like me, curious to find out more about the poor boy who was tragically murdered in the woods, or from the police for that matter, as they pick Evan's life apart in search of the person they think lured him to his death.

There are ten or so comments under the video, all but one a variation on the same theme: *RIP Evan xx*, *Gone too soon*, *Rest in Peace Bro*, etc. But the earliest comment, and the only one dating from before Evan's death, comes from someone called Fenchurch: *Awesome video. Keep up the good work.*

It's an odd choice of username. A reference to Fenchurch Street in London, perhaps? Or maybe someone's surname? I switch back to Evan's Instagram profile and scroll through the pictures. Pretty standard stuff for a nerdy fifteen-year-old: a couple of tentative, arty-looking selfies, a few *Game of Thrones* memes, and a bunch of photographs of painted miniature figurines – a wizard, a sultry-looking enchantress. Hardly any of the posts have any likes, though several have comments. I click on one, see that Fenchurch has been here too, replying to one of the memes with a string of laughing-crying emojis. Beneath another post, a picture of a little hand-painted goblin, he – or she – has written, *Brilliant work. You're very talented.*

I check Evan's Twitter profile, and sure enough, there are more likes and comments from Fenchurch there too, all rather positive and encouraging, as if Evan had his own little cheerleader. But when I click on the name, I see their profile has been locked down, the privacy settings on max.

Might Fenchurch be the person the police are trying to track down? The person who lured Evan up to the woods and killed him? Or perhaps they're just a friend of Evan's – despite what Chloe said, I'm sure he must have had some. I expect the messages that gave the police cause for concern were private, not posted for the whole world to see. Still, I file that particular combination of letters and numbers away in the back of my mind before slipping my phone back into the front pocket of my bag.

Checking in with Freya, I find that after thirty minutes of browsing, she's chosen four slim volumes from the shelves for me to read to her: two Horrid Henrys she already has at home, a Roald Dahl, and a book that promises to tell the true story of the wolf and the three little pigs. But when I ask her if she's done, she bursts into tears and throws herself to the floor, as if her whole world is coming to an end.

'I can't decide, Mummy,' she says, through her tears.

I crouch down beside her, stroke her back. 'There's no need to get upset,' I say. 'We'll be going home in a few days. Four books is plenty.'

'But you said I could borrow six!' she wails.

I try not to laugh. While I wasn't much of a reader when I was younger, the library was practically Martin's second home. I remember coming here with him one evening after school, expecting him to take ten minutes or so to select the books he wanted to borrow. An hour later, when I told him I was bored and wanted to leave, he didn't have a full-on meltdown like Freya, but he did sulk all the way home.

'You don't *have* to borrow six,' I tell Freya. 'We can just borrow these four.'

'But I *want* to borrow six and I can't choose!' she cries, bottom lip quivering.

'It's OK,' I say. 'Why don't I go and give these books to the lady, and I'll give you five minutes to see if there's anything else you want to borrow. But then we'll have to go.' Freya doesn't move, until I add, 'The café might close if we don't get there soon.' She peers over her forearm to check if I'm being serious. 'Five minutes,' I tell her. 'Then we'll get some cake. And later on, you can have an ice cream, if you're good.'

Newly determined, Freya gets to her feet and wipes her eyes on the sleeve of her pink unicorn jumper. Books will be chosen, cake will be eaten – maybe even ice cream.

'Stay where I can see you,' I tell her, then I head over to the counter, where a middle-aged woman with red cheeks, wearing a chunky knit cardigan, is sitting behind a computer.

I set the books down, fish my library card out of my purse and hand it over, and the librarian picks up each book in turn and scans their back covers. When she gets to the one about the three little pigs, she says, 'Your little girl is going to love this one. It's really fun.'

She seems friendly enough, and there's nobody nearby to overhear our conversation. It's the perfect opportunity.

'Terrible news, about the young lad,' I say.

She looks up. 'Isn't it just?' she says, and she tugs a tissue from a box behind the counter and holds it in her fist, ready should the need arise. 'Such a nice young man.'

'Oh, so you knew him? Would you mind if I asked you a few questions?' I say, and perhaps because she's already spoken to some journalists and thinks speaking to one more won't make much difference, or perhaps because a small part of her is enjoying the attention, she doesn't hesitate.

'When I saw his picture in the papers I couldn't believe my eyes,' she says. 'He was in here that very afternoon. He even said hello to me, and then, just a few hours later . . .' She shakes her head. 'It's just *awful*. His poor family. I can't imagine what they must be going through.'

She must see dozens of children every day, but she clearly remembers Evan, and he knew her well enough to say hello to.

'He came in here a lot, did he?'

'Oh, all the time,' she says. 'Everybody here knew his face. We all liked him. He was always polite and well mannered, not like some of the kids who come in. He never caused us any problems. Like I say, he was a nice boy.'

'And that afternoon, did he stay for long?'

She shakes her head. 'Ten minutes, maybe less.'

Ten minutes. Hardly enough time to browse the shelves. He must have known exactly what he was looking for. I wonder if whatever book, or books, Evan took out of the library that day might provide some sort of clue as to what was going through his head.

'You don't happen to remember what books he borrowed, do you?'

'Oh, he didn't borrow anything,' she tells me. 'Most kids his age don't use the library for that these days. They come in to use the computers, or because it's somewhere quiet they can do their homework.'

I glance over to the bank of computers, each in its own private booth, and wonder if Evan was using them to compose his letters to Connor. If he was, and if the librarian had ever stopped to look over his shoulder, perhaps she wouldn't think him such a nice boy after all.

'He must have really liked it here,' I say.

'I think so,' she replies. 'He was a . . . sensitive soul.' She glances this way and that, lowers her voice. 'I always got the feeling he was having a hard time at school, or at home. You get that impression sometimes. I'm just glad he had somewhere he could come. Somewhere he felt safe.'

I suppose the library isn't the typical stalking ground for the bullies who were making Evan's life a misery. And for the first time, I make the connection – maybe that's why Martin liked it here so much. It was somewhere he felt safe.

I glance over to Freya to make sure she hasn't wandered off, and see that she's sitting cross-legged on the cushioned floor, flipping through the pages of a picture book with a huge grin on her face. She's in her happy place.

Like father, like daughter.

'You know, I just had a thought,' the librarian says. 'If you want to know more about Evan, you should probably speak to Peter Rand. He runs the games club here, on Saturday mornings. Evan never missed a session.'

'Games club? Like, computer games?'

She shakes her head. 'Dungeons & Dragons. You know the sort of thing; when they pretend to be wizards and elves, and go on quests. They play for hours at a time.'

That makes sense, given the contents of Evan's social media.

'And Peter's one of the staff here?'

Another shake of the head. 'He's a volunteer, runs the whole thing. The children call him the dungeon master, or DM for short, but what he really is, is someone who gives up every Saturday morning so that children like Evan have somewhere to go. The kids really like him. He's more than just their dungeon master, he's a friend, someone they can look up to.'

My face must betray my thoughts, because just as I'm wondering if this Peter person is someone the police should be looking into, she says, 'He's cleared to work with children, in case you're wondering. All the proper checks have been done. Or we wouldn't have him here.'

'Of course,' I say, though all the DBS checks in the world won't tell you if someone is posting online under a false name.

The librarian goes on, 'He runs a little games café in town, just off the high street. I've never been there myself – it's not really my thing – but it looks nice enough.'

'And has he lived around here for long?' Might he have been in town fifteen years ago, when my best friend was murdered?

'Oh yes. The games club was up and running when I started here. That's nearly . . . let me think . . . Three years ago now, nearly four.'

I thank her and she hands over the books, and I start to make my way back to Freya, but before I get there, two things happen in quick succession.

First, I hear my phone ring, which sounds much too loud in the quiet of the library. I fumble it out of my bag, see Bill's name on the caller ID, then step between two bookshelves and answer in a whisper. 'Bill, I'm at the library. I can't really talk.'

I use my fingers to part the books on the shelf closest to me, make a gap so I can keep an eye on Freya, who is still sitting on the rug, engrossed in her picture book.

'That's fine,' Bill replies. 'I'll talk, you listen. Now, I'm sure you've heard about the vigil for Evan later on, and that you're planning on attending.'

I have, and I am.

Vigils are an opportunity for people to express their grief and pay their respects, but they're also a chance for the police, and for people like me, to observe while that happens. And while there's nothing nice about studying a grieving parent, asking whether they are crying too much, or not enough, it's a horrible truth that many children who are murdered die at the hands of abusive parents, or step-parents – from memory, around a third. So, I want to be there, to see Dalton, and his sister, to get the measure of their grief.

Bill continues, 'Well, I'm calling to ask you to stay away.'

'Stay away?'

'Tensions are running high. I don't want your presence making things worse than they already are. Now, it's a public place, so nobody's going to stop you from turning up if you choose to, but I'm asking you, as a friend, to keep your distance.'

Bill is a friend, but I can't let that get in the way of my chance of finding out what happened to Evan, and to Amy.

'I'll think about it,' I tell him.

The line goes quiet for a moment, then Bill sighs, 'You're still going to come, aren't you?'

'Depends,' I say. 'Any news for me on the investigation?'

He sighs again. 'I've told you already, Jess. I can't help you, not this time.'

'I'll see you at the vigil then,' I say, and I end the call.

The second thing that happens, at almost the exact moment I hang up, is that Chloe finally gets in touch. Her message says she's at her boyfriend's place. She shares the address, says she's ready to meet whenever I am.

A worm of worry twists in my belly.

What if she's told her boyfriend the same thing she told me? And what if he isn't a fan of *Born Killer*, or of Connor?

The other books, the cake and the ice cream – I decide it will all have to wait. It won't be fun disappointing Freya, but I have to see Chloe now. I've got to convince her to keep quiet about what she knows.

# 22

## Martin – 3.15 a.m.

As Martin passes the halfway mark of his journey, he feels a shift in his mood, as if he's just crossed an invisible line. Reaching the halfway point makes everything feel that bit more real, that bit more urgent.

He tries calling Jessie again but hangs up before leaving yet another voicemail, then takes a few deep breaths to calm himself.

'You're OK, you're OK,' he says, out loud in the car, perhaps to Jessie, perhaps to himself. He'll wait another ten minutes then try calling again.

In the meantime, he tries to think if there's anybody else in Westhaven who might be able to help track Jessie down, but he's long since lost contact with the few friends he had there when he was younger, and his parents moved away over a decade ago, after their very messy divorce. Jessie's friend Bill would be a start, if Martin had his number, but he doesn't. He supposes he could call the police, ask for Bill, and if he's not there, explain the situation to whoever is. But Jessie's not missing, she's not even hurt, as far as he knows. She's just out of mobile phone reception during a storm, like plenty of other people, probably. It'll seem like an overreaction, like he's making something out of nothing.

Jessie *will* be OK, he's sure of that, despite the imagined catastrophes that keep invading his thoughts. In weather as bad as this, all sorts of terrible things can happen. The wind can topple a giant tree that can crush a car like it's an empty Coke can, or blow an HGV across two lanes of traffic before tipping it onto its side, and if you're unlucky enough to be caught beneath it . . .

Stop, he tells himself. For God's sake, stop.

She's going to be fine. *Everyone* is going to be fine.

If only Jessie had stayed in London, like he'd wanted her to. But he knew, from the moment she said she was going, that he wouldn't be able to stop her, that the debt she feels she owes Amy trumps everything else. No matter how many times she told him *Born Killer* was finished, he should have known that sooner or later, something, or someone, would summon her back to Westhaven.

That winter after she saved him from drowning, when they became boyfriend and girlfriend, was one of the happiest times of his life. It was as if his entire world changed overnight. Not only did he feel different, but people treated him differently too, even when he wasn't with Jessie. It was as if he'd become better-looking, grown taller, become funnier and smarter, just by being around her. And as for the bullying? While he might still catch a mean comment from a boy during PE, or feel a wad of wet paper, shot from the barrel of a biro, whizz past his ear in the school corridor, things like that happened much less often than they used to, and when they did, it didn't bother him as much as it had. It was as if dating Jessie had made him bulletproof.

The only downside to that period, was Amy. While Jessie's best friend was nice enough, she was always . . . around. It was as if she and Jessie had some sort of magnetic connection. You could separate them, for a while, but they'd snap back together at the earliest opportunity. If they were at Jessie's house, Amy would invariably turn up. If they went to the cinema, or out for food, Amy would tag along. Even when they hung out at his house, Amy would invariably arrive, knock on the door and waltz right on in, as if Jessie being there was invite enough. Which was all fine . . . except for the fact that they had all these little in-jokes and words for things he didn't understand, like they'd developed their own secret language. Sometimes, all they had to do was look at each other and they'd burst out laughing, as if psychic messages were passing between them.

On the few occasions he'd suggested to Jessie it might be nice if they did something without Amy, she'd looked at him as if he'd gone mad.

'But it's Amy,' she'd say, with a confused look on her face. 'She's my best friend.' As if the idea they might spend time apart was not only ridiculous, but impossible. He might as well have asked her to go to the cinema without one of her limbs.

Before long, he realised that she liked Amy more than she liked him – more than she liked anyone, in fact – and if it came down to a choice between them, she'd pick Amy every time. He'd always be second best, and he could get upset about that, or he could get used to it.

Over time, he came to accept that if he wanted to be with Jessie, that meant Amy coming along for the ride. It meant them whispering in each other's ears, sharing little jokes that he didn't understand and speaking to each other using only their eyes, or a twist of their mouths. There was no point in trying to come between them. That was true then, when they were kids, and it's true now. Even if Amy has been dead for the last fifteen years.

# 23

*Four days earlier*

'I'm so sorry, sweetheart,' I tell Freya when I drop her back at the house. 'Mummy has something very important to do, but I promise we'll have cake and ice cream later on, OK?'

Freya nods, though her bottom lip is trembling.

Oh, my heart. I hate to upset her like this. Few things in life are as important to me as sitting in a café with my little girl, watching her eyes turn into saucers as she spoons ice cream into her mouth. But right now, time is of the essence.

'I'll see you a little later on, OK, sweetie?' I pull her into a hug as Dad appears in the hallway.

'Did somebody say something about cake and ice cream?' he says, as if he's just overheard the most delicious gossip. Freya's head whips around and she grins then sniffs back a tear as Dad comes and stands by her side, staring straight ahead as if he hasn't noticed her. 'Hmm. I was thinking about heading out for some ice cream myself, actually. If only there was somebody to go with me.'

'Me, Grandpa, me!' Freya shouts.

Dad lets out a yelp. 'Oh! Who was that?' And Freya cracks up.

'Thank you, Dad,' I say. He finds time to shoot me a wink as he backs down the hall, pretending to be astonished that his five-year-old granddaughter has turned invisible.

'Silly Grandpa!' Freya guffaws, clearly delighted.

Silly, brilliant Grandpa.

Twenty minutes later, I arrive at the address in Chloe's second message, a large, detached home in a well-heeled part of town; lots of flash cars in driveways, immaculate lawns, people walking around

104

in wellington boots and tweed. The kind of place where houses have names, rather than numbers.

Chloe's boyfriend's place – or his parents' place, to be more exact – is called Fairview, which I suppose is accurate enough, seeing how pretty it is. I duck under a garden arch festooned with flowers in bloom, walk down a perfect stone path to reach the front door and ring the bell. A moment later I hear the rumble of feet on stairs and a middle-aged woman answers. She's pretty and tanned, wearing a crop top under a tracksuit that offers a glimpse of her toned stomach muscles. A sheen of sweat shimmers at the base of her throat.

'Yes?' she says, with a breathless urgency that suggests she's in the middle of something.

'I'm here for Chloe?'

The woman, presumably Chloe's boyfriend's mum, eyes me cautiously. 'And you are?'

'My name's Jessie,' I tell her. 'Chloe's doing some work experience with me.'

'Ah!' She grins. 'She told me about you. How exciting!'

I wonder why Chloe has told her boyfriend's mum about me, but her dad didn't have a clue who I was when I called. Perhaps, with so little interest in her ambitions at home, she looks elsewhere for support and encouragement.

'She'll be in the studio.' She points into the house, down a long hallway. 'Straight through the kitchen, through the doors and out into the garden. You can't miss it.' She ushers me inside and closes the door, then gestures to the ceiling. 'Online yoga,' she explains, and with that, she jogs back up the stairs.

I move down the hall and into the kitchen, which is vast and has a rustic, farmhouse feel that probably cost a fortune. At the far end is an open set of French doors and I step through into the large garden and immediately see what the woman referred to as the studio: a single-storey garden office, set apart from the main house.

I see Chloe through the glass walls, lounging on a sofa, dressed in a grey hoodie and a band T-shirt, and I head over and knock on the glass. Chloe looks up and smiles, then gets to her feet, comes over and heaves open the heavy sliding doors.

'Hey!' she says, looking pleased to see me.

The studio is a man cave, I realise – or a teenage boy cave. There's a sofa and bean bags for lounging on, framed posters of action films on the walls, a shelf of rugby trophies, and a mini fridge stocked with energy drinks. There is also, I notice, a rather unpleasant tang of sweat in the air.

Chloe gestures to the corner of the room, where a man wearing a pair of giant headphones is sitting at a desk, playing computer games on a huge monitor.

'This is my boyfriend, Oscar,' she says.

He is not at all what I'd imagined. I'd pictured a male equivalent of Chloe, someone small for their age, perhaps a little nerdy – someone a bit like Evan, now I come to think of it. But Oscar appears to be twice Chloe's size and looks like he could be in his mid-twenties, with a mass of blonde hair, a patchy beard and long muscular legs, his grazed knees sticking out of the bottom of his cargo shorts.

The sound of frantic gunfire is leaking from his headphones.

'Hey, Osc?' Chloe says.

When Oscar doesn't respond, she reaches out and touches him on the shoulder, and he spins around in his chair and glares at her. 'Fuck's sake, Chlo! You messed up my game!'

Chloe drops her chin and hunches her shoulders, just like Freya does when she's getting a proper telling off, though we reserve those for when she's done something truly silly that risks causing her injury, or worse – like the time I caught her approaching an electrical outlet with Martin's keys in her hand.

'Sorry, babe,' Chloe says. 'It's just that . . .' Her eyes flick in my direction and Oscar turns to look at me. The hard expression on his face falls away and he looks suddenly younger, boyish, even. He pushes his headphones back, so they hang around his neck like a travel pillow, and looks me up and down, his eyes taking a quick cruise around my body, lingering on my hips and breasts.

'This is Jessie,' says Chloe. 'I told you about her, remember?'

Oscar sniffs. 'Yeah. Cool,' he says, then to me, 'Er, do you want a drink or something?' He gestures to the mini fridge full of energy drinks. 'Or I could get my mum to make you a tea, if you want?'

'No, thank you,' I say.

'Cool,' he says again, his head nodding. 'So, Chloe's doing work experience with you?'

'That's right,' I say. 'Just for a few days.'

'Awesome,' he says, still nodding, and because he doesn't seem to have much else to offer, I turn back to Chloe.

'Shall we make a move?' I say.

It's another two hours until the vigil, but I want to get Chloe on her own as soon as I can, so I can ask her to keep what she told me last night just between us.

Chloe points to a door over her shoulder. 'Let me use the loo,' she says, and she heads into the bathroom.

While I marvel at the fact that Oscar's boy cave has its own en suite, he takes a vape out of the pocket of his shorts, sucks on it and blows a pungent cloud of sickly-sweet vapour into the air.

'Sucks, what happened to Evan,' he says, which is rather downplaying it, in my view.

'Yes, it does,' I say. 'Did you know him at all?'

Oscar shakes his head. 'Nah, different schools,' he says. 'I go to St Mark's.'

St Mark's High is a private school, set in acres of lush woodland at the edge of town. The fees are no doubt extortionate, and from memory, they're big on sports there – rugby in particular – which explains the shelf full of trophies, and Oscar's grazed knees.

He goes on. 'I know Chlo used to hang around with him sometimes. I think she felt sorry for him, because he used to get picked on by some of the rougher kids. I told her, she should have brought him round here. He could have chilled with us, played games, watched movies, whatever, but I think he was a bit shy of meeting people, you know?'

'So I'm told,' I say.

Oscar leans back in his chair, spreading his legs. Thank God his shorts are of the long variety.

'So, you made *Born Killer*?' he says. 'That's super cool. I'm sort of a content creator myself, as it happens.' He lifts a hand to muss up his hair while he locks eyes with me, revealing a small cut above his right eye – another rugby injury, I expect.

Is he flirting with me? Is that what he thinks he's doing?

'Is that right?' I say.

'Yeah. I stream on Twitch, like, three times a week. I know it's not the same thing, but I'm building my audience. Everyone's got to start somewhere, right?'

'Absolutely,' I say, as Chloe emerges from the bathroom and I hurry her along.

She gives Oscar a long kiss goodbye, one with enough tongue to make me feel like I need a shower, and a moment later we're in the car.

Had I not met Martin, it's possible I might have ended up dating some inappropriate boys in my teens, the sort of guys that Dad wouldn't have approved of. It seemed normal for girls at school to date boys who were older, who could drive, who had facial hair and jobs, the imbalance of power and experience never once occurring to us. These days, young people are more attuned to that sort of thing, and Chloe seems to have her head screwed on, but I still feel a pang of unease at how Oscar spoke to her.

'Everything OK, between you two?' I ask her, as I start the engine. She looks back at me, blankly. 'The way he snapped at you, when you interrupted his game . . .'

'Oh, *that*.' She waves a hand. 'It's fine. He takes his gaming way too seriously, that's all. And he *has* told me, like, a million times, not to interrupt him when he's in the middle of a game. I mean, I don't like it when he interrupts me when I'm playing, either, so . . .' She trails off with a shrug, like she deserved it.

I want to tell her she doesn't have to put up with him speaking to her that way, but it isn't my place. And it isn't why I'm here.

'What you told me yesterday, about Evan . . .' I begin.

She turns to me. 'I haven't said anything to anyone, I swear,' she says, pressing a hand to her heart. 'Not even Oscar. I only told you.'

Relief flows through me.

'That's good,' I say. 'Because I wouldn't want people to get the wrong idea, or for Connor to get in trouble because of a rumour, or a misunderstanding. Before we tell anyone else, I'd like us to try to establish the facts. Does that sound OK?'

'Totally,' she says, as if it hadn't occurred to her there was another other option. 'That's why I came to you in the first place. So we can establish the facts.'

Music to my ears.

'So, what's next?' she asks, with an eager grin.

Given how quickly Chloe confirmed she was willing to keep her mouth shut, I feel guilty for rushing Freya home now. There was time for cake and ice cream after all. Still, I suppose it means I have time to follow up a different lead.

'Have you ever been to the games café, in town?' I ask her.

She does that fringe flick again that reminds me of Amy. 'No. Why?'

'Because there's someone there I need to speak to.'

She smiles. 'You're taking me along on an interview?'

Am I? Yesterday, the last thing I wanted was a teenager tagging along during my investigation. For one thing, it could be dangerous. For another, she could be a liability. Still, I find myself wanting to keep her close, not only because of what she told me about Evan, but because every time she flicks her hair out of her eyes the way Amy used to, I feel a small jolt of electricity that quickens my heart.

Taking her along for one meeting can't hurt, can it?

'It's not an interview, just a friendly chat,' I tell her.

'That's still cool,' she says. 'What do you want me to do?'

What do I want her to do, apart from stay quiet about Evan's supposed visit to Connor on the night he was killed?

'Observe,' I say. 'Don't just listen to how he responds to questions, but watch him closely. Look at his posture, his facial expressions, what he's doing with his hands, where his eyes are looking. And don't fill the silences. If he goes quiet, and things start to feel a bit awkward, that's fine. We don't mind silence, but he might. Got it?'

'Got it,' says Chloe, that sparkle back in her eyes.

# 24

Chloe consults a map on her phone as we walk briskly down the high street in search of the games café. It's late afternoon in Westhaven, and the town centre is in transition, the tourists who potter around the streets during the day thinning out and making way for the evening crowd. A handful of eager drinkers sit at tables outside Westhaven's oldest pub, The Grapes, making the most of the unusually humid weather, and the town's fanciest restaurant, named simply, Bistro, opens its doors as we walk by to welcome its first customers of the evening.

'Got it,' Chloe announces, coming to a stop. 'Down here.' She points down a narrow side street and we head in that direction and soon find the café, sandwiched between a pet shop and a vape shop, both with their shutters down. Stencilled in white above the front door is the name Food & Board, which seems to me as good a name for a games café as any.

Through the window, I make out a number of low tables with mismatched chairs, several sofas, an empty counter with fridges behind it and, on the opposite wall, shelves stacked to bursting with boxes of board games. The café is empty, except for one man, who's sweeping the floor and stacking chairs upside-down on top of the tables as he goes.

The sign on the door says closed, but I try the handle anyway and it opens.

'Ready?' I say to Chloe, and she grins back at me.

We step inside and the man sweeping the floor lifts his head and glances over. 'I'm afraid we're closing early today,' he says.

He is short and bald, though with a large and rather luxurious red beard, and his shoulders are a little hunched, perhaps from sitting down and playing games all day long. He's wearing trainers, corduroy trousers, a checked shirt and thick-rimmed glasses. The moment I see him, I can't help feeling like we've met before, but can't place him in my memories. Maybe I've seen him in town on a previous visit.

'Are you Peter?' I ask.

'That's me,' he says, cheerfully. 'But like I said, we're closing early today, for the vigil. Can I reserve you a table for tomorrow?'

'That's OK,' I tell him. 'We just wanted to ask you a few questions.'

'No problem.' Peter leans his broom against a nearby table, then proceeds to reel off information about the café in a breathless stream. 'We're open from ten in the morning, until ten in the evening on weekdays. Saturday, we don't open until two, and we're closed on Sundays. Admission is three pounds per person, though under twelves get in free, and we have around seventy games to choose from. We do advise reserving a table, especially if there's more than four of you, and please let us know of any dietary requirements in advance. The most important thing is to treat the games as you would your own. I think that's about everything . . . Oh, and children must be accompanied by an adult after 9 p.m. OK?'

He looks over at Chloe. He must think we're mother and daughter.

'Thanks,' I say, 'but we actually wanted to talk to you about Evan Cullen.'

He blinks back at me, says nothing for a moment, and I see him swallow hard. 'Are you a journalist?' he says. 'I mean, I've nothing against journalists, per se. I just don't want to . . . tread on any toes.'

I shake my head. 'I'm actually a filmmaker,' I tell him.

Peter tugs at his beard a few times, looking doubtful.

I push on. 'Do you mind? I promise we won't keep you long.' I set my bag down on a nearby sofa and take a seat, and Chloe follows my lead.

At this, Peter looks a little flustered, but eventually he comes over and sits down across from us.

He rubs a hand over his bald head. 'I suppose I can spare ten minutes,' he says, with a little shrug.

He didn't have to do that, I think. He could have told us to go away, and we would have, but instead, he came over and sat down. Either he's a pushover, or a part of him wants to talk.

'My name's Jessie Hamill, and this is my assistant, Chloe,' I say.

Peter points a finger at each of us in turn. 'I thought you two were . . .'

I shake my head. 'I do have a daughter though. She's five, and she loves playing board games. I might have to bring her here some time. I'm sure she'd enjoy it.'

He smiles broadly, flings his arms wide. 'A whole café, devoted to board games? How could she not?' There's a hint of children's TV presenter about him, a wide-eyed sort of enthusiasm and warmth that is at once endearing and a little too much. Freya would probably like him, I think. Maybe I will bring her here.

'Have I got this right?' I say. 'You run the games club, at the library?'

He nods. 'That's right. That's how all this,' he motions to his surroundings again, 'got started. Meetings at the library, every Saturday morning. I didn't know if people would come at first, but over time, word spread, and it became more and more popular. It got so popular, we had to expand, which is why I got this place. We've been open for about a year and a half now.'

'But you still run the sessions at the library?'

He nods. 'Some of the children prefer the quiet of the library to a busy café. Plus, it's sort of a tradition now. I started the club there when I first moved here, and—'

'When was that?' I interrupt. 'When did you move here?'

It's hard to tell how old he is. The missing hair and beard age him, and I've a suspicion he might actually be younger than me, which would mean he'd have only been a kid when Amy was killed. But I still have to ask.

He gives it some thought. 'Hmm. Four, maybe five years ago. Like I was saying, I started the club at the library, when I first moved here. I wanted to do something for the community, for the local kids. Especially for children who are a little different.'

'Different?'

As he explains, his voice softens, taking on an almost fatherly tone. 'The word some people use these days is neurodiverse, which covers a wide range of neurological variation: autism, ADHD, dyslexia, speech disorders, and so on. I wanted to create a club that was an inclusive space for all people, but with a particular focus on children who find some environments challenging. The games club is a safe place where they can feel at home and make friends – games are brilliant for that, helpful in all sorts of ways. They give structure to social interaction and help children to understand how their differences can work to their advantage, rather than hold them back. That's why the library sessions are still vital for the club's members.'

'Members like Evan?'

'Hmm.' He smooths down his beard with the palm of his hand then pinches the very tip of it between his fingertips, a gesture that looks at once thoughtful and self-soothing, like he's trying to hold a small part of himself in check. 'Evan was one of our first members,' he says.

'And was he . . . different?' I haven't read anything about Evan having any of the conditions Peter just mentioned in the papers, or online.

'He was . . . shy, painfully so,' Peter says, after a moment. 'He was almost frightened of the other children, especially the older boys. It took a long time for him to open up and trust others. But the more he played, the more comfortable he became. Once I got to know him, I found him to be a kind, clever young man. We became rather good friends.'

Friends? A thirty-something man, and a fifteen-year-old boy? Even if Peter was helping Evan, he must know how that could look to some people.

'Did you spend a lot of time together?'

'Oh yes,' he says. 'Some of the games we play can last for days, or weeks, even. It's only natural to talk while you play. I've grown close to many of our members over the last few years.'

Which makes perfect sense, though in the back of my mind an alarm starts to sound.

'And did Evan say if anything was troubling him recently?' I ask.

He shakes his head. 'Not that I recall. I do know he was bullied, sometimes quite severely. It got so bad at one point he had to move schools, though I'm not sure that helped. He talked to me about it sometimes, though I'm always careful not to overstep the mark. I'm not a trained counsellor, or anything, but I believe I can still be there for the children, like an older brother, or a trusted friend.'

Chloe jumps in. 'Did he ever mention *Born Killer*? It's a documentary—'

'I know what it is,' Peter says, his eyes flick back to me for a second. 'But no, it's not something Evan talked about. At least not recently.'

'So, you did talk about it, at some point?' says Chloe.

'We talked about all sorts of things,' he replies, and I search for an edge in his voice, a sign, no matter how small, that he is not being truthful, and can't find any.

I try something else.

'Evan went to the library the afternoon before he was killed. Do you think he might have been looking for you?'

Peter looks into space for a moment then blinks rapidly a few times before saying, 'I think that's highly unlikely. I rarely visit the library on weekdays and evenings because I'm busy running this place. If he'd wanted to speak with me, he could have found me here, or he could have sent me an email.'

'And did he? Did he come here? Did he email you, or call you, before he went missing?'

'Of course not,' Peter says. 'If he had, I'd have told the police.' He checks his watch, and I know he's looking to draw the conversation to a close, but I'm not quite done.

'Were you friends with Evan on social media? Did you follow him on Twitter or Instagram? Leave comments, or likes on his videos?' Perhaps under the username Fenchurch?

'Oh, no.' He shakes his head again, then laughs. 'I'm a total dunce when it comes to that sort of thing. I don't even have a website for this place yet. I keep meaning to pay someone to make one for me, but I never seem to get round to it. I suppose I'm just one of those people who prefers connecting with others in real life. Sitting down together, playing a game or two. There really is nothing quite like it.'

I nod, let the silence creep in, in case there's anything else he wants to tell me, but after a moment he leans forward, gives me another one of his children's TV presenter smiles, then gets to his feet. 'So, um . . . If there's nothing else, I'd really like to close up now,' he says.

'But I hope you'll come back again soon, and bring that little girl of yours with you. I'm sure she'd love it here.'

Back in the car, I ask Chloe if she remembers Evan ever mentioning Peter Rand, or the games club.

She pulls on her seatbelt, thinks about it for a moment, then says, 'Nope.'

'You're sure?'

She nods. 'I think I'd remember if he'd told me he was best friends with some thirty-year-old bald guy who ran a café.'

'Right,' I say, reminding myself that Evan and Chloe weren't close – they were only 'sort of' friends. It's entirely possible Evan never got round to telling her about his hobby, or that he chose to keep it to himself. He had a crush on her, after all. Asked her to the school dance. I wonder if he thought she wouldn't like him as much if she found out he spent his weekends playing Dungeons & Dragons? Though aren't kids of all ages more into that sort of thing these days? The sort of interests that made Martin stand out when he was a kid, and earned him the unwanted attention of his bullies, are now mainstream. Even Freya wears pyjamas with superheroes on them.

'And what about Peter?' I ask. 'Do you think he was telling the truth?'

'Sure,' she says. 'I mean, he seemed pretty nice to me. All that stuff he said, about starting the club to help kids who were different? That's a really kind thing to do.'

'It is,' I say. 'But just because someone does nice things, that doesn't necessarily make them a good person.'

She gives me an excited look. 'Do you think he could have something to do with what happened to Evan?'

'Probably not,' I tell her, which is the truth. 'But do you think you could do some digging for me? See what you can find out about him?'

'Totally,' she says, her eyes shining. 'What am I looking for?'

'Whatever you can find,' I tell her, because I don't know what Chloe should be looking for, but I do know that a small voice, deep in my subconscious, is trying to attract my attention. I can't hear what it's saying, not yet, but I'm certain it's trying to tell me something isn't quite right with Peter Rand.

Perhaps he really is just a kind-hearted local café owner who gives up his Saturday mornings so that shy, troubled kids like Evan have something to do. But I owe it to Evan, and to Amy, to make sure. Because if he isn't, he certainly wouldn't be the first person to use kindness as a way of showing the world he is a good man, when in fact, he is something else entirely.

# 25

## Jessie – 3.25 a.m.

The world has turned upside down. Now, when I look up, the disc of night sky is darker than the interior of the well, where the soft blue light from the phone's screen paints flecks of indigo over the wet stones. Up above, there's now a pitch-black hole, a bottomless chasm. A deep and dangerous well. There's a new sound too. A low, mournful honking, like a giant has his lips pressed against the opening of the well and is blowing, ever so gently. The wind is picking up, and the rain, until now no more than a persistent fine drizzle, is coming down in heavy drops, splashing down all around me. As if being stuck down here all alone wasn't terrifying enough. I might be at the bottom of a well, surrounded on all sides by thick stone walls, but I feel terribly exposed.

Please God, don't let the storm make it harder for them to rescue me. I so desperately want to go home. I ache to see my little girl. What if the storm wakes her up and she gets scared? I know Dad will be with her, but will he know what to say? Will he be able to soothe her? Freya's afraid of storms. Right now, so am I.

An image comes to mind of the water rising around me, the chill of it reaching my shoulders, my neck, my chin . . . I take a final last-gasp breath as it covers my mouth and nose, hold it until it feels like my lungs are going to burst, then the reflex to breathe takes over, opening my airways, and the water rushes in . . .

I once saved Martin from drowning when we were kids – it was how we first met – and I've never forgotten the look on his face as I swam over to help him. Not just one of utter terror, but also of pain. It hurt, swallowing all that water. Even now, he refuses to go in the sea when we go on holiday and always keeps to the shallow end when we take Freya swimming. I suppose some of the panic of that day has stayed with him. I think of that look in his eyes now, and can't help but wonder how painful it will be for me if I don't get out of here soon.

I push the thought away.

I'm not going to drown. Before long I'm going to see blue flashing lights up above and hear friendly voices, from people who know just how to help. An hour – less than that now. All I need to do is keep calm and focus on my rescue. Try not to let the fear take over my every thought. Don't worry about how they're going to get me out of here when they arrive, or about how they'll deal with the root in my thigh. Don't think about the rising water, or the darkness that has wrapped its arms around me like a living thing.

Like Fiona says, they're professionals. They know what they're doing.

I take the phone away from my ear and check the battery. Forty-four per cent remaining. Plenty. My heart is still beating too fast, adrenalin coursing through my body, but I'm a little calmer now. I can think straight.

'How's everything going down there, Jessica?' Fiona asks.

I usually hate it when people use my full name, but don't mind when Fiona does it. It reminds me of the way Mum used to tell me off when I was little. She'd cross her arms over her chest and tilt her head, give me one of those looks of hers that Dad used to say could turn a person to stone, then say my name with a slight rising inflection – not a question, but a warning – and I'd know I was in real trouble. But when Fiona does it, it has the opposite effect. It makes me feel safe, like she's the adult here, the one with all the answers.

'I'm OK,' I tell her. 'Have you heard anything yet, about Freya and Dad and Martin?'

'Should be soon,' she tells me. 'Welfare checks are in person, so can take a little time. Please bear with me. I'll let you know as soon as I hear back, OK?'

'OK.'

'How are you feeling?'

'Wet,' I say, which sounds like I'm being sarcastic, but I mean it. There's something extra unpleasant about sitting in the dark, surrounded by water. The sheer unavoidable, unremitting *wetness* of it. And is it my imagination, or has the temperature dropped a few degrees?

'Where's the water up to now?' asks Fiona.

'To my middle.' If I could stand, it wouldn't even reach my knees, but in this awkward sitting position, the waterline sits just below my breastbone.

'I'll let them know,' Fiona says. Tap, tap. Click, click.

I only wish I felt half as calm as she sounds.

'I want to speak to my husband,' I tell her. 'Just for a few minutes, to let him know what's happened, then you can call me back.'

I'll feel better once I hear Martin's voice, once I know he's OK. And I want him here, in Westhaven, to look after Freya, and to hold my hand at the hospital.

'I understand,' Fiona says. 'But right now, I'd prefer it if you stayed on the line. As long as we're connected, I can see exactly where you are on my screen, and I'd like to keep it that way.'

'But why? It's not like I'm going anywhere.'

'No, but the storm is affecting communications. If we break the connection, there's a small chance we might not be able to get it back, and the last thing we want is for you to spend a single second more down there than necessary. Plus, I have access to medical expertise here that could be required. So, like I say, I'd prefer it if you stayed on the line. As soon as my colleagues get you out of there, you'll be able to speak to your husband, but for now, just hang in there. You're doing great.'

It doesn't feel like I'm doing great, and I know I'd feel a hell of a lot better if I could speak to Martin. I'll text him, I think. Fiona doesn't even need to know.

I click on messages, start typing out a text to Martin, each letter taking an age to register as rain spatters the phone's screen. Even if it takes me an hour to type it out, and even if he can't do anything to help, I have to tell him what's happening.

**Call me**. **There's been a** . . . I manage, before stopping.

There's been a what, exactly? An accident? There's nothing accidental about me being down here. I delete what I've written, start again.

**Call me. I'm in trouble** – No, that's no good either. I don't want to panic him.

Perhaps it's stupid of me to send a text. Perhaps it's best if Martin hears about what's happened to me from the authorities, so he knows I'm going to be OK. I mull it over, thumb hovering over the screen.

'Is there anything else you can tell me?' Fiona says. 'Anything you can remember from before you woke up down there?'

I put the phone back to my ear. 'I don't really know,' I say. 'It's all . . . kind of a blur.'

The last few days are a jumble of memories, fragments that won't connect, like scenes from a film playing out of order. I see Dad and Freya and Bill, other faces I don't recognise and can't put names to. I see Westhaven Library and the town hall. Connor's living room . . .

'Take your time,' says Fiona. 'Anything you can remember might help the police catch the person who did this to you. Plus, it's good to keep talking. It'll help take your mind off things, and it helps me to know you're still wide awake and alert. The last thing we want is you losing consciousness.'

Slipping under the water and drowning. No, we don't want that.

'I know I came back here because of the boy who was murdered . . .' There's a blank space in my mind where his name should be.

'You mean Evan Cullen?' Of course, she'll have heard about Evan. His name has been all over the news.

'Right. I thought his murder might have something to do with an old case. My best friend was murdered. She . . . They found her body down here.'

There's a pause before Fiona says, 'In the well?

'Yes, a long time ago. I made a film about it. A documentary.'

'I think I might have heard of it,' says Fiona. 'I don't usually watch those sorts of programmes, especially if there's kids involved, but my husband loves that kind of thing. So, you came back to make a documentary about Evan's murder?'

'No,' I find myself saying. 'At least, I don't think I did.'

I didn't, did I? No, I remember meeting with BlinkView, leaving them in no doubt that I was done with *Born Killer*. And yet, I have a brief flash of me holding a camera in my hand – the old Sony that Mum and Dad gave me for Christmas one year. If I was filming, why on earth would I be using that old thing?

'I'm sorry, I . . . I can't remember,' I tell Fiona.

'Don't apologise, Jessica. It's the shock. Just take your time. You said you came back to Westhaven because of Evan Cullen's murder. Why don't you start there, and see what comes back to you?'

Evan Cullen. I try to picture him and get an image of a small, dark-haired boy dressed in a purple school jumper. Something else too. I remember leaving London, the argument I had with Martin. He didn't want me to come back to Westhaven, was worried about me. If only I'd listened to him.

'I thought if I could help solve Evan's murder, that people would forgive me,' I tell Fiona.

'Forgive you for what?' Fiona says.

There's a sudden, stuttering flash from up above and the inside of the well is lit up by a bright white light that imprints on my retinas, momentarily blinding me. A second later a crack of thunder echoes around the well, loud enough to set my ears ringing.

God no. The storm is here.

# 26

*Four days earlier*

A hundred or so people have loosely gathered in the fading light at Brookscroft Park, a fenced off square of lawn in the shadow of Westhaven's imposing town hall. Most stand in quiet reflection with their heads bowed, while others shuffle up to the old bandstand to lay flowers, or light candles – of which there are already a good number, burning brightly on the stage, their flames barely flickering in the still evening air.

Flowers, cards and handwritten notes cascade down the bandstand's steps, spill out onto the gravel path and pool around the splayed feet of an easel that holds a large picture of Evan in his school uniform. Music plays from a portable speaker behind an empty podium – tinkling piano under an over-earnest vocal – though the most notable sound is that of the crowd; low murmurs of consolation, and the occasional sob bursting out from behind a fist pressed to someone's lips.

I reach over, put a hand on Chloe's shoulder.

'You sure you're OK being here?' I ask her.

She nods. 'Look at all these people,' she says. 'I never knew he was so popular.'

I think back to Amy's vigil; this very park was packed with strangers, the whole town having turned up to say tearful goodbyes. People who'd never known she existed before they read her name in the papers were openly weeping, and kids from school who wouldn't give her the time of day when she was alive, were talking like they'd been her best friend now she was dead. It annoyed the hell out of me. Not for one second did I believe all those people who came – first to her vigil, later on to her funeral – were there for

Amy. For a time I suspected they were there simply because they wanted to be a part of something, like when the funfair would come to town and people would get caught up in the excitement of it all. But as I've got older, I've come to understand that their reasons were more complex. That when a child is murdered, a community experiences a special kind of grief.

I stand on tiptoe and scan the crowd. Some faces I recognise, but can't put names to – local shop workers I was once on nodding terms with perhaps, or old schoolmates who have aged out of recognition – while others are more familiar. There's Mr Harrington, the long-serving headmaster of Westhaven High, who is standing with a handful of pupils dressed in their school uniforms – some of them are in tears, though who's to say if they actually knew Evan or not. There's Joanne Hugard, the reporter from the *Westhaven Chronicle*, who was so helpful when I was making *Born Killer*. Next to her is George Tombs , one of Mum's old colleagues from the town council. And there, standing just thirty feet away from me, is Amy's mum, Elaine. She is as elegantly dressed as always, in a long, flowery print skirt and cropped blazer, and she's in conversation with another woman I don't recognise. At the sight of her, I feel a brief flash of warmth, of love, even – then reality crashes in and I remember how she feels about me, how she thinks I betrayed Amy's memory. I hope one day to prove her wrong about that, but today is not that day, and fortunately, the crowd is thick enough, and the light low enough that, as long as we keep our distance, she probably won't know I'm here.

I see no sign of Bill, though have no doubt he's around too, but there are police here and there: a pair of officers over near the entrance, either side of the gates; half a dozen more scattered throughout the crowd. Likely there'll be a good number in plain-clothes too, eyes peeled for anyone acting suspiciously.

We edge our way towards the bandstand, and when we get there a lady offers us each a candle from a box. We take one, and she carefully lights them for us, and we crouch down and add them to the pool of flickering tea lights on the gravel path.

Chloe looks on. 'It's beautiful,' she says, her eyes shining.

I remember how Amy's vigil hit me like a punch in the gut, made her death real in a way it hadn't been until then. I put an arm around Chloe's shoulders and give her a gentle squeeze.

I leave her with her thoughts for a moment, then we step aside and others take our place. More candles are lit, people join hands in prayer. The music is louder near the front. Robbie Williams sings about angels, and John Lennon sings about all the people living for today, while I stand on tiptoe and search the crowd for John Dalton.

So far, there's no sign of either him, or his sister. I only hope we haven't missed them.

'Do you think the killer's here?' Chloe asks, her voice a little too loud for my liking. 'That happens sometimes, doesn't it? They like to come to things like this, rub people's noses in it.'

A couple standing nearby shoot me a disapproving look, perhaps assuming that Chloe is my daughter, like Peter Rand did, and that I've failed to impress on her the solemnity of the occasion.

'I don't know,' I say. 'Maybe. And keep your voice down.'

She goes on, a little quieter this time, 'Do you think Amy's real killer might have been at her vigil?'

'No,' I tell her. 'I don't think so.'

Not that I didn't view the local news footage a hundred times, examining every face in the crowd, not sure exactly what I was looking for, but somehow convinced I'd know it when I saw it.

But there was nothing.

'Come on,' I say, and we edge our way over to the side of the bandstand, where the crowd is a little thinner. If Chloe wants to ask questions, I'd rather not risk being in earshot of any of Evan's extended family.

'Do you think it would be OK if I filmed some video?' Chloe asks, as she takes out her phone.

There are other press in the park. Photographers, with heavy cameras slung around their necks, even a couple of reporters doing pieces to camera.

'Sure, why not,' I say, and Chloe opens her camera app, hits record and starts shooting.

I reach over her shoulder and turn the phone ninety degrees. 'Shoot in landscape, like this. Remember, you're not filming a video for TikTok. You want to fit as much information in the frame as you can.'

'Oh, right.' She holds the phone steady, pans back and forth.

'Look for the little details that tell the story,' I tell her, and she presses two fingers against the phone's screen then widens them, making the camera zoom in on the bandstand and the flowers.

'Like this?'

'Exactly.'

She lingers on the candlelit portrait of Evan, then pinches the screen to zoom out, and as she does, the front of the crowd parts to let through a group of people, at the head of which is John Dalton.

He's given plenty of interviews since Connor's release, but it's a while since I've seen him in person. Normally clean cut, this evening he is unshaven, grey-faced and exhausted looking. He is supporting Evan's mother on his arm, a small, narrow-shouldered woman with her head bowed, her long brown hair covering her face. She takes unsteady steps forward while he whispers in her ear, and he walks her over to the podium then steps back, and the press swoop in like hungry gulls. Microphones are thrust under her nose, and she shields her eyes from a lightning storm of camera flashes.

'Thank you . . .' she says, and what little noise the crowd was making falls away. 'Thank you, everyone, for coming. I just want to say . . .' She chokes up, tries again. 'My son, Evan, meant the world to me and I miss him so, so much . . . I don't understand why someone would do this . . . I don't know why someone would want to hurt him . . .'

Tears set her shoulders shaking. She sways backwards, looks like she's going to go down and Dalton hurries up behind her, takes her arm and ushers her away from the podium and into a huddle of friends and family. A moment later he returns to stand before the press and speaks in a voice that is loud and clear, but thick with emotion.

'Evan was a sweet, kind boy, who never hurt a fly. Whoever did this to him is a monster, plain and simple, and they're going to pay. We want justice for Evan. That's what's important right now. So, if anybody knows anything about what happened to my nephew, please come forward and do the right thing.'

Chloe's elbow nudges against mine, perhaps accidentally, perhaps not.

Dalton surveys the crowd for a moment, then steps away from the podium, goes back to his sister and folds his arms around her, anger, pain and sadness radiating from the pair of them.

I wanted to get the measure of their grief, and now I have, there's no doubt in my mind it's as real as it gets.

It was a mistake coming here. I might not be shoving my camera in their faces, like the photographers who are crowding round them, trying to get the shot that will grace tomorrow's front pages. But maybe I'm just as bad. Maybe I've become one of *those* people, the sort who came to Amy's vigil, not for her, but for themselves.

I turn to Chloe. 'I think we should go now,' I tell her, but she doesn't respond. She's filming again, has zoomed in on Dalton and his sister.

I tug at her elbow. 'Chloe, come on. Time to go.'

'Just a minute,' she says, then a shout goes up.

'What's *she* doing here?' I lift my head, see that John Dalton is looking right at us.

There's a half-hearted attempt from his sister to stop him – *John, please*! – but he brushes her hand away and her head drops, as if even that small effort was too much for her, and Dalton starts making his way through the crowd towards us.

Fuck. I feel a rush of panic in my chest, and the heat of embarrassment in my cheeks.

'Are you filming?' Dalton shouts. He must have seen me helping Chloe. 'Who said you could film here? Who gave you permission?' Never mind the dozens of press he's walking right by.

I step in front of Chloe.

'Here to make money from another dead kid, is that it?' he says, as he draws near.

I glance over my shoulder in search of an escape route, but the crowd has bunched up behind me, closing me in.

Dalton comes to a stop, just three feet away. He's so hot with anger that I can feel it.

'Haven't you done enough damage?' he says. There is a murmur of agreement from the crowd.

'I'm just here to pay my respects, John,' I say. 'I know you're upset—'

'Upset?' He is all teeth and spittle, eyes wild.

We've got to get out of here. I turn to grab Chloe so we can go, but she isn't there. Where the hell has she gone? She was right behind me, just a moment ago . . .

'This woman . . .' Dalton is addressing the crowd now. 'This woman helps murderers get out of prison,' he says, and I see people nodding, hear more murmurs of agreement.

'John, please—' I say, trying to calm things down, but there's no talking to him. He takes another step forwards and I attempt to take a corresponding step back, but collide with someone. I have nowhere to go.

Dalton points a finger at my chest. 'If I find out *he* had anything to do with what happened to Evan . . .'

He doesn't say Connor's name. He doesn't have to, because everyone in the crowd knows exactly who he means, and the threat is as clear as day.

'He never should have been let out,' a voice says.

'He wants stringing up,' says someone else.

All those faces in the crowd I sort of know but can't put names to – the shopkeepers and old school friends – are turning against me.

Where the hell are the police? Shouldn't they be putting a stop to this?

And where the hell is Chloe?

I make a move, try to push forward, but a hand closes around my arm, starts dragging me back. Someone is pulling me into the crowd, and God only knows what will happen if I let them. I try to shake them off, but whoever's got hold of me clings on tight, pulls me with such force it feels like my arm might come out of its socket.

'Let *go* of me!' I shout, then a low voice speaks into my ear.

'Come with me.'

# 27

## Martin – 3.40 a.m.

Martin voice-dials Frank, asks if he's heard anything, even though he's pretty sure the answer is going to be no, because somebody would surely have called to let him know if Jessie had arrived back at the house – either Frank, or Jessie herself – and nobody has.

'Nothing yet,' Frank confirms, his voice a little crackly over the line. 'The storm's getting worse. I've tried calling her again, but can't get through. I got an engaged tone once, but the rest of the time it won't connect. I don't understand.'

Perhaps it's something to do with the storm damaging phone masts, thinks Martin. He isn't sure how these things work, but might that explain why he hasn't been able to get through, while Frank got an engaged tone? Perhaps Jessie has been able to call somebody because they're physically close by and connected to the same mast, whereas the signal is too weak for anyone at a distance to connect?

'If she was engaged, that's good,' he tells Frank. 'Means she's been able to get in touch with someone.' And it means she's still breathing – speaking of which. 'And Freya's still OK?'

'Still sleeping.' Frank sighs. 'Are you sure you need to drive all this way? I know you're concerned, but she seems fine, and I'm sure Jessie will make her way home as soon as it's safe to travel. She'll have taken shelter somewhere, you'll see. This isn't London, you know. People are more friendly around these parts. They help each other out in times of need.'

Frank seems to have forgotten that Jessie and the townsfolk of Westhaven haven't exactly been on the best of terms lately. Not since she helped release a convicted child killer back into the community. Martin thinks there are plenty of people who would have no issue turning Jessie away if she needed shelter during a storm. Some would probably take great pleasure from it.

'I should be there in an hour and a half,' Martin tells Frank. 'I'll call when I'm close, but let me know if anything changes. Anything at all.' And he hangs up.

It is, Martin thinks, the mistake people make about Westhaven. They see the beautiful old buildings and the quaint cobbled streets in the centre of town, and think the whole place is that way, and because it's nice to look at, the people who live there must be nice too. Never mind that there are parts of Westhaven, away from the tourist trails, that are just as deprived as anywhere in London, where drug use and crime rates are sky-high, and you'd be a fool to walk around on your own at night. Putting that aside, many of the people who live in the nicer parts of town are stuck up, narrow-minded and bigoted. Fearful of change, of anything that isn't white and middle-class. Just look at the way they've treated Jessie; turning their backs on one of their own, even though she was trying to do the right thing.

As far as Martin is concerned, every part of Westhaven, from the top of the valley to the very bottom, is rotten. He has been of this opinion ever since he was a boy, since the day a big kid wearing a faded denim jacket and trainers so worn it looked as if they were about to fall off his feet, approached him in the town centre, took a seat on the bench next to him, and asked him what was wrong with his face.

It would be another three years before Martin met Jessie. That morning, he was still the shy boy with the bad skin, who spent every school lunch break hiding from his bullies in the library and who hung back at the end of the school day, helping the teacher put chairs on tables so he didn't have to leave the school grounds at the same time as the other children. He knew better than to talk to bigger, rougher kids, like the one who'd just sat down beside him, so he said nothing, kept his head down, and prayed for the boy to go away. But the boy had other ideas.

'What are you, deaf?' he said. 'I said, what's up with your face?'

Martin felt himself flush hot with embarrassment. 'Eczema,' he managed to say in a small voice.

'Looks gross,' the boy said, and Martin felt the prick of tears at the back of his throat and said nothing. 'What you reading?' the boy asked, and Martin wordlessly angled the book's cover so the boy could see for himself.

'*The Hitchhiker's Guide to the* ... let me see.' The boy snatched the library book out of Martin's hand, flicked through the pages then, rather casually, tossed the book into the gutter where it landed with a splash.

Martin sprung to his feet. 'That's a library book!' The idea of a library book getting damaged appalled him. What if they took away his library card? What if they never let him borrow a book again?

'Is it?' the kid said, looking shocked. 'Sorry, I didn't know. I was only kidding around. Seriously.' Martin looked at him, tried to figure out if he really was sorry or not. He did look sort of regretful, like he perhaps understood that tossing someone's library book into the gutter was a step too far. 'Well, go on,' the boy added. 'You'd better go get it, before it gets totally ruined.'

Martin raced towards the kerb and saw, to his considerable relief, that despite the splash it had made, the book was only half in the water. It could still be saved. He bent down to pick it up, and that was when he felt a hard kick in his backside that sent him sprawling. He fell forwards, hit the concrete with his shoulder and landed on his side in the puddle.

It was a brutal and humiliating attack, made all the more shocking by the fact that the boy did not stop there. When Martin picked himself up, his clothes sopping wet with rainwater, the boy scooped up the copy of *The Hitchhiker's Guide to the Galaxy* and held it out to Martin.

'Sorry, mate, really,' he said, as if he'd been presented with an opportunity too good to resist, but felt bad for having taken it. Martin eyed him. He'd been tricked once and thought it very likely he was about to be tricked again. But he wanted his book back.

'Go on, mate, take it. I won't do anything, promise,' the boy said.

Martin reached out, but as he did the boy snatched the book away and opened it wide, so that the spine bent all the way back with a loud crack. Then, with some effort, he ripped the cover off the book and tore the pages in half. He laughed as he tossed what was left of the book over his shoulder, then he turned and strolled away.

It was far from the only occasion Martin was bullied. The destruction of his library book made that particular encounter more memorable than most, but what hurt more than anything else that day, what really stuck with him, was that as he ran around the street in tears, trying to collect the sopping wet pages of his library book, nobody came to help him. There were tourists passing by, people sitting on tables outside a café, two men leaning on the window ledge outside The Grapes smoking cigarettes – all of them must have seen what had happened, so why hadn't they done anything to stop it? He didn't understand. Weren't grown-ups supposed to protect kids? Wasn't it part of the deal, that you were safe from the bullies when you were around adults? What possible reason could there be for them not intervening? he wondered. Did they think he deserved it too?

# BORN KILLER –
# SHOOTING SCRIPT

## S01 – E07: INEXCUSABLE

The car stops at the start of the trail. Seatbelts are unfastened, doors slam, feet scuff the dirt. CLOSE UP: Elaine peers down the trail, into the woods, eyes big and afraid.

Two squirrels race a lightning-fast circle up an old oak tree. A bird alights on a branch, opens its beak and begins to sing. A butterfly parts its wings to reveal a flash of colour, red and yellow against the greenery.

**CUT TO:** Elaine, ducking under an archway of branches.

**ELAINE:** 'Down here? Are you sure?'

**JESSIE (Off camera):** 'Yeah, I'm pretty sure this is the way.'

The trees part and the clearing comes into view, and with it the old well. It is four feet across and three feet high. It looks ancient, like it has been there for centuries, although the rim is covered in faded graffiti. The surrounding area is scattered with litter – old Coke cans and beer bottles, pages ripped from pornographic magazines, countless cigarette butts.

A few feet from the well, Elaine comes to a sudden stop. She stands in quiet contemplation, swaying slightly, then takes a silk handkerchief from her pocket and holds it to her mouth. She takes a small step forward, then another.

**CUT TO**: Elaine, sitting on a cream-coloured sofa in the plush living room of the townhouse she has lived in for the last thirty-five years. She is flicking through a photo album on her lap, years passing by with each fingertip-turn of the page. For a moment the only sound is the creak of the album's spine and the soft crackle of static electricity.

**ELAINE:** 'When she was little, and her asthma was bad, she used to wake up in the middle of the night and call for me, and I'd always shout, "I'm here, darling," and I'd go and give her the medicine and stroke her forehead until she fell back to sleep. One night I ran in and gave her the medicine and she felt better, but as I went back to bed, I realised I'd picked up an old inhaler by mistake – it was empty, there was no medicine left, but it did the job. So that's what I did from then on when she woke up at night. I gave her the empty inhaler first, ready with the real thing if things didn't quickly improve, but they usually did. Rob said it was the placebo effect, that the reason she felt better was because she thought she'd had her medicine, even though she hadn't. But I think it was because I was there with her, and that once she knew she wasn't alone, she could breathe again.'

**CUT TO:** Back in the clearing, Elaine continues moving forward, taking small steps until she reaches the well. There, she drops down to one knee, puts her hands on the rim, then leans over and speaks into the darkness.

**ELAINE**: (Softly) 'I'm here, darling, I'm here.'

# 28

*Four days earlier*

Dad has already put Freya to bed by the time I get back to the house. We exchange whispers out on the landing. 'She was OK?' I ask.

He nods. 'Perfectly fine.'

'And you made sure she had her inhalers?'

'Of course.'

I check in on her anyway and find her sleeping peacefully. I plant the smallest of kisses on her forehead, so as not to wake her, then sneak out of the room and head downstairs to fret and worry about Chloe. I haven't heard from her since she disappeared at the vigil.

It was Bill who rescued me at the park, who grabbed me by the arm and dragged me through the crowd.

'You need to leave here, right now!' he barked, pulling me onwards, through the park gates. 'This is *exactly* why I told you to keep a low profile.'

He was right. I had no business being there, because I hadn't gone there for Evan – not in the way I should have.

'OK, I'm sorry. I'm going,' I told him. 'But I was with someone. I have to find her.' I took a few steps back in the direction we had come, but Bill grabbed hold of my arm.

'Stay away, do you hear me?' he warned. 'You leave that family alone.'

I had no intention of going anywhere near them. I just wanted to find Chloe.

I pulled away from him and walked back to the park gates, but when I got there I found a police officer blocking my way.

'I suggest you move along, ma'am,' he said.

'I'm trying to find someone,' I told him, trying to see around him, to spot Chloe in the crowd.

'Ma'am please. I've asked you nicely . . .' He spread his arms, blocking my way forward. Polite, firm. Non-negotiable. Bill must have told them not to let me back in.

I skirted the perimeter of the park, then walked the surrounding streets trying to reach Chloe in all the ways I could think of – calling, texting, leaving voicemails. After half an hour with no reply, it occurred to me that she could have made her was back to Dad's, so I did the same. But she wasn't at the house, either.

Now, I try her again. Calls, messages, voicemails. Still nothing. And with each unanswered call and unread text, the worry inside me grows. I can't help thinking back to that dreadful morning fifteen years ago, when Amy's mum turned up on the doorstep, grabbed me by the shoulders and shook me hard, *Where is she? Where is she?* Because isn't this how it starts? With unanswered calls and a string of voicemails?

That's not what this is, I tell myself. Chloe's fine. She'll turn up, you'll see. I resolve to wait until nine o' clock. If I haven't heard anything by then, I'll raise the alarm.

At two minutes to, I hear a knock on the door. I rush to open it with my heart in my throat, and there she is.

'Where the hell have you been?' I shout. 'I was worried sick. I've been calling, texting . . . I was about to call your dad.' I pull her in off the doorstep and hold her tight. Relief laps over me. She's not missing. Not dead in a ditch, or at the bottom of a well in Cooper's Wood. She's safe. She's here.

When I let her go, she gives me a 'no big deal' shrug. 'Yeah. Things were getting weird,' she says. 'So, I took off. I thought I'd go and do something useful, y'know? Sorry I wasn't checking my phone, I was doing research on Peter Rand, like you told me to.' She waves a slim folder of papers at me.

'You took off?' Relief at her being safe has given way to anger. 'You can't just . . . disappear like that. I can't work with you if you're going to vanish the moment I turn my back, I just can't.'

I take a breath, feel my heart begin to slow.

'I'm sorry,' Chloe says again. 'I didn't realise it might be triggering for you.'

The Gen Z turn of phrase grates, but she's right, that's exactly what it was. She goes on, 'When Mr Dalton came at you like that, and all those people started saying horrible things about Connor, I didn't know what to do. I just . . . freaked out, y'know? It was scary.'

She's right. It was.

What was I thinking, taking Chloe to the vigil? I wouldn't have dreamt of taking Freya. Anything could have happened. From now on, I'll do as Bill says, I decide. I'll keep a low profile. I won't take any chances, especially not while I'm with Chloe.

A small voice comes from behind me. 'Mummy?'

I turn to see Freya, standing barefoot at the top of the stairs, dressed in her *Bluey* pyjamas. 'Why are you shouting?' she asks.

'Sorry, sweetheart. Did we wake you?' I go to the top of the stairs, scoop her up and carry her down on my hip. 'It's OK, darling. I was just talking to my friend, Chloe. Do you want to say hello?'

'Hi!' Chloe says to Freya. 'I like your pyjamas. They're *really* cool.'

Freya smiles and buries her head in my shoulder.

'See? There's nothing to worry about,' I tell her. 'Now, let's get you back to bed.' To Chloe: 'Can you give me ten minutes?'

Upstairs, I tuck Freya in then read to her from one of her library books, the one about the three little pigs, though in this version the big bad wolf has been framed and reveals the true story of what happened from his prison cell. By the time I get to the part where the wolf visits the pig's house made out of bricks, she is fast asleep.

When I get back downstairs, Chloe is waiting for me in the living room with my phone in her hands. I must have left it behind when I went to answer the door.

'Looking for something?' I say, expecting her to panic at having been caught snooping, but she calmly lifts her head.

'Hope you don't mind,' she says. 'I saw it was unlocked and I just thought . . .'

She turns the phone towards me and shows me a new icon on my home screen for an app called Friend Tracker. When she presses it, the screen shows a map of the UK, then quickly zooms in, zeroing in on Westhaven. There's a little circle, with a picture of Chloe's face inside it, floating in the middle of the grey block that represents Dad's house.

'Now you don't have to worry about where I am,' she says.

Chloe's not a child – and she's certainly not *my* child. I don't have the right to track her every move.

'You didn't have to do this,' I say, taking a seat beside her.

'It's OK. I wanted to.' She smiles, and I smile back, grateful that she understands.

I can't have people disappearing on me. Not again.

Chloe reaches over to hand back my phone, and it's then I notice the purple bruise on her arm that has all the hallmarks of someone having grabbed her wrist too hard.

'What's this?' I say. 'Did this happen at the park? Did somebody hurt you?'

She drops the phone onto my lap then pulls away, pushes the sleeve of her hoodie down to hide the bruise.

It can't have happened at the park, I realise. Even if someone had grabbed her hard enough to leave a mark, it wouldn't look like this, not yet. So, if it didn't happen at the park, where did it happen?

'Did Oscar do this?'

She looks away, refuses to meet my eye, and the air grows heavy between us. There's a moment when I think she's about to speak, when her lips part and she draws breath, but then she shakes her head, plants her hands on her knees and gets to her feet.

'I think I'm going to go,' she says, heading for the door.

'Chloe, wait.' She stops, but doesn't look back. 'I won't try to stop you leaving,' I tell her. 'But you can talk to me, if you want to.'

A moment of silence, then she says, 'It wasn't Oscar, I swear.'

'OK. I believe you,' I say, though I'm not sure I do. Just because Oscar is well brought up and barely more than a child himself, that doesn't mean he couldn't be violent or abusive. Some young men have terribly misogynistic views about women, and how they should be treated. There are online influencers who've made a fortune peddling such 'alpha-male' bullshit.

Chloe hovers near the door for a moment longer, then turns to face me, comes back and takes a seat. Silence settles between us, and I give her space, room to talk on her own terms. And eventually, she does.

'It was an accident,' she says, her voice almost too soft to hear.

'OK...'

'Sometimes, when my dad's been drinking, he gets confused,' she says. 'The other night, he fell asleep in the bathroom, but I needed to go, so I tried waking him up, but I think he was having a bad dream, or a nightmare. Whatever it was, he freaked out and shouted at me, then he pushed me away and I hit my arm on the radiator.'

I only glimpsed the bruise for a second, but it didn't look like the sort of mark that would be left behind after her arm accidentally hit a radiator.

'Has this sort of thing happened before?' I ask her.

She gives me an urgent shake of the head. 'No! Never, I swear. I mean, the him being drunk part, yes. Every few months he'll like, get really drunk. Mostly he just goes to bed, but sometimes he doesn't make it that far and he falls asleep on the bathroom floor. Usually, I just hold it in if I have to go.' She gives me an embarrassed look. 'Once I had to pee in the garden.'

Poor kid. Having to go to the toilet in the garden because she doesn't want to risk waking up her drunken dad.

'It must be scary, being around him when he's like that,' I say.

Chloe gives a little twist of the mouth while she thinks of a reply – another little gesture of hers that reminds me of Amy. 'He isn't always like this,' she says. 'Just sometimes he gets all sad, and it's like he becomes this different person, you know?'

I do. That's exactly what happened to Dad when we lost Mum. The shock of the loss hit him so hard, it was as if his soul had been knocked out of his body. For a long time, he wasn't himself. I tried not to hold it against him, because I was distraught too. But sometimes I hated him for it, because I needed my dad, as much as I ever had, but he wasn't around.

'I know exactly what you mean,' I say.

She goes on. 'Every few months, I suppose it hits him all over again, and that's when he drinks. But he's getting better, he's trying to stop.'

Is that what he tells her when he wakes up in the morning with a terrible hangover having passed out drunk on the bathroom floor? Or when he shouts at her and pushes her hard enough to send her flying into a radiator?

'Promise me you won't say anything,' she says. 'He really is trying to get better, I swear.'

I don't know what to do. I'm going home in a few days, and I don't want to make any promises I can't keep.

'We have room here, if you want to stay tonight,' I tell her. 'I could call your dad, tell him I need you to work late on a project?'

'Thanks, but it's OK,' she says. 'He'll be back to normal in a few days. I'll just stay at Oscar's until then.'

I've barely known Chloe for twenty-four hours, but I feel oddly protective of her. I wish I could persuade her to stay here, rather than with her boyfriend, but if she feels safe at Oscar's, I suppose that's what counts.

'All right,' I say. 'But I want you to know that I'm here for you. You can tell me anything.'

'Thanks,' she whispers.

Before she goes, Chloe hands me the folder of papers she arrived with. 'Do you want to see what I found?' she asks, a quick flash of excitement in her eyes.

I do, but it's getting late. A lot has happened for one day, and last night's lack of sleep is catching up with me fast. I want to call Martin and say goodnight, then get some rest.

'Tomorrow,' I say.

'But . . .' she starts to object.

'Tomorrow,' I tell her, firmly.

'OK,' she says. 'As long as I can still help you.'

I tell her of course she can, then order her an Uber. Two minutes later we say our goodbyes in the hallway. As she moves past me to go, she stands on tiptoes and throws her arms around my neck.

'Thanks for worrying about me,' she says, then she's out the door, running down the steps and across the gravel driveway to the waiting car. I watch her go, glad she felt able to talk to me, but with a heavy feeling in my heart.

It is only half past nine, but I go upstairs and climb into bed behind Freya, wrap my arms around her and hold her tight.

# 29

## Jessie – 3.45 a.m.

Twenty terrible, and terribly long, minutes have passed. There have been no sirens, no flashing blue lights, no friendly voices calling down from on high to tell me that everything's going to be OK, that they'll have me out of there in no time.

I'm still pinned in place by the root in my thigh, with the phone held to my ear, waiting for word from Fiona that my rescuers are almost here.

The storm rages above me. Thunder rumbles and lightning flashes, and down here in the well, the water is rising. I can't see it, but I can feel the cold caress of it beneath my clothes as it climbs higher with every passing minute.

Rescue is coming, rescue is coming, I tell myself over and over, in an effort to stay sane, but I'm terrified. The dark, the storm, the pain in my thigh, the rising water and now the cold . . . I am having to work very hard not to let the panic overwhelm me entirely.

Rescue is coming.

With Fiona's encouragement, I've told her everything I can remember about the last few days; about arriving back in Westhaven; seeing Dad and meeting Bill at The Star. Some part of me knows she wants to keep me talking in order to keep me awake, alive . . . But I bury this thought, and the more I share with her, the more has come back to me. Little moments at first: playing Snakes and Ladders with Freya at the kitchen table, Bill wiping Guinness foam from his moustache. Then bigger things, like Connor nearly taking my head off with his cricket bat.

When we get to the part about the dead bird, there's a crack of thunder so loud it makes me jump, and the sudden movement causes the pain in my thigh to explode. It creases me in half, brings me to tears.

'I can't do this,' I sob. 'I can't . . .'

I take the phone away from my ear and tuck it into the top of my bra, the glass screen cold against my breast, then I let out a howl of fear and frustration.

Why is this happening to me? Whatever I have done, surely, I don't deserve this. Nobody deserves this.

I can hear Fiona's voice, coming from under my T-shirt – *Jessica, what's happened? Are you still there?*

Deep breaths. In, hold for three, then out. In, hold for three, then out . . .

I've got to try to keep it together, just for a little while longer.

I reach out blindly with cupped hands and catch a trickle of rainwater in my palms, splash some of it over my face and neck, then I tip my head back, open my mouth and let the cool droplets fall onto my tongue and slip down the back of my throat. It tastes good. Clean. I feel around in the dark until I find my bag, which, luckily for me, hasn't drifted out of reach. I dig inside it for the half-full bottle, drink what's left then hold it under a thin stream of pouring water until it feels heavy. I screw the top back on as tight as I can, put it back in the bag and loop the bag's strap around my forearm, so it doesn't float away.

There are layers of sound between the rumbles of thunder. Drips and drops and gurgles – water doing what water does, finding its way to the lowest point. It makes me want to pee, and I let go of my bladder without a care, enjoying the momentary warmth. It's not as if the water I'm sitting in could be any more disgusting. In comparison, the rainwater might as well be sparkling Perrier.

I feel a little less panicked now. Rescue is coming.

I take the phone out of my bra and check the time. Fiona said an hour. Shouldn't they be close by now? Shouldn't I at least be able to hear sirens? And shouldn't the police have been in touch with Dad and Martin?

'Fiona?'

'. . . right here, Jessica . . . you OK? What's happening?' Her voice fades in and out. I check the phone's signal. One bar, and even that is flickering on and off. Interference from the storm.

'Can you hear me?'

'. . . hear you just fine . . .' she says, breaking up again.

'I'm OK,' I tell her. 'But I can't hear you very well. You need to tell them to hurry up. The water is getting higher, and I'm getting cold.'

'They're moving as fast as they . . . almost with you.'

'Have you heard anything back about my daughter, and my husband?'

'. . . expect to hear back very soon. As soon as we . . . you know. You'll be able to speak to them yourself.' There's a moment of silence, then, '. . . ready to make some noise? You're . . . sing something for us?'

Sing something? I picture myself, belting out a showtune like I'm in some stupid musical – one about an idiot who gets stuck down a well, obviously – while my rescuers approach. The idea makes me laugh out loud.

'They'll think there's a dying animal down here,' I tell Fiona. She laughs too, and that makes me laugh some more, the sound echoing all around me.

Hell, maybe I will sing something.

What was that band Amy used to have all those posters of on her bedroom walls? Smileaways, they were called. Terrible name, terrible band. She used to have such good taste in music, but these guys, with their noughties post-punk haircuts and keychains hanging from their belt loops, were something else. They had one big hit. Lots of thumping guitars and heavy drums. 'If You Don't Mind', it was called. We used to sing it to each other all the time and copy their silly dance moves.

*If you don't mind . . . I can't dance, then I'll dance with you . . .* Something like that. So cheesy. But what I wouldn't give to sing it with Amy one last time.

That's what I'll sing, I decide. 'If You Don't Mind'.

'Jessica? Are you there?' Fiona's back on the line.

'I'm ready,' I tell her. 'I'm going to sing, but don't say I didn't warn you.' The line goes quiet, but for the gentle hiss of static. 'Fiona? Are you still there?'

There's a long pause, then I hear her say, '—essica? I'm afraid . . . got a problem.'

# 30

*Three days earlier*

When Chloe arrives at the house the next morning, we retreat to Mum's office so she can talk me through the folder of research she left behind last night. I resisted peeking at the contents over breakfast, decided to wait until she got here, to let her have her moment. After our talk yesterday, I feel like she deserves it.

I sit at the desk, while Chloe takes a seat on the sofa, resting the slim folder of papers on her lap.

The Chloe of today seems a long way from the wounded young woman I sat with last night. She looks lighter, as if a weight has been lifted. I hope it has, though I notice she's wearing a long-sleeved T-shirt under her usual grey zip-up hoodie, to make sure the bruise on her wrist doesn't show.

'Are you ready?' she says, a hungry look in her eyes.

She's clearly excited to show me what she's found out about the oh-so-kind owner of the Food & Board games café, with the children's TV presenter smile I don't quite trust.

'Ready,' I tell her.

'Cool,' she says, then she begins. 'First of all, he was telling the truth about him not having a website for the café. The only thing I could find about it online, were these . . .'

She opens the folder, peels off the first three printouts and hands them over, all articles about Food & Board from the *Westhaven Chronicle* website, the sort of gentle puff pieces you see in local newspapers, designed to celebrate businesses around town. *Westhaven's First Games Café Celebrates Grand Opening* trumpets one. I check the date and see it's from nineteen months ago. Another, more recent, article features a picture of Peter, stood out in front of the café, with that big smile of his fixed securely in place. The headline reads, *Games Café Charity Night Raises Money for Local Children.*

His story checks out, so far at least. I set the printouts aside. 'What else have you got?'

'So, there's no social media for the café, which is kind of weird,' Chloe says, 'but I suppose if he doesn't know how to do it, that makes sense. Plus, if business is good, maybe he doesn't think he needs to promote the café online.'

'Or maybe he just hasn't got round to it yet,' I add.

'Yeah, but what's weird is that I can't find any trace of *him* online, either. Like, nothing, apart from these few articles. There's no mention of him *anywhere*. I found other profiles for people called Peter Rand, but none of them were his. No Facebook, no Instagram, no Twitter. It's like he doesn't exist.'

I suppose that, for someone of Chloe's age, who has grown up with the internet, this could look not only odd, but suspicious.

'I don't think that's as weird as you think it is,' I tell her. 'Peter's around my age. The internet wasn't as much of a thing when we were kids, and social media barely existed. Some people just never got into it, or they think it's annoying, a waste of time. He said he prefers dealing with people face to face, didn't he?'

'I suppose,' Chloe says, undeterred. 'Anyway, seeing as I couldn't find anything about Peter, I did some more digging on Food & Board. And that was when I found *this*.'

She whips out the next piece of paper from the file, presents it to me like a prize.

It's a screenshot, with GOV.UK in bold letters at the top, and underneath, the company details for Food & Board: registered office address, incorporation date, company number and other official information. 'And then . . .' She hands over another page, much like the last one, except for a highlighted tab at the top that says, 'People', with space below to list significant figures in the running of the company. In this case there's just one name listed as company director: GRANTHAM, Alexander Peter.

'His business is in someone else's name,' Chloe announces. She grins, as if she's discovered a vital clue, but I know, from my early days of setting up my own production company to find a buyer for *Born Killer* that there could be all sorts of reasons for this.

I set the pages down. 'Businesses are complicated things,' I tell her. 'It's kind of like when I make a film; all sorts of people work behind the scenes, even if mine's the first name people see in the opening credits. Maybe this Alexander person put up the money for the café? Or maybe he handles all the complicated business stuff for Peter, and that's why he's listed as company director.'

'Maybe,' Chloe says, with a smirk, then she recaps, counting off her findings on her fingers. 'So, Peter Rand isn't online, neither is his business, and the director of Food & Board is someone called Alexander Peter Grantham.'

'Right,' I say. 'But there's nothing illegal, or particularly suspicious, about any of that.'

She peers back at me, her lips pinched tight and her eyes shining. Amy used to get the same look when she was especially thrilled about something, like there was a little sun burning brightly inside her, bursting to get out.

'What is it?' I ask. 'What else did you find?'

'I looked up Alexander Peter Grantham,' she explains. 'And I suppose it must be an unusual name, because I got a direct hit.'

She takes the final page from the folder and hands it over. It's another printout, this time of a school photograph. A hundred or more children in a school hall, arranged in rows according to height – shortest at the front, tallest at the back – all facing towards the camera. Every one of them is wearing a purple jumper.

'I found this on a Westhaven High Facebook group,' says Chloe. 'Old people seem to like posting stuff about their schooldays, for some weird reason. Anyway, someone had scanned it in, then tagged everybody in it. See anyone you recognise?'

The photo is blurry, the hundred or so faces little more than indistinct collections of pixels, but as I pass my eye over them, they rearrange themselves to become more than that – they become people from my past. Names, and half-names, drift up from my consciousness: Michael Cullen, Stephen Marsh, Jane Finlay, Rebecca . . . somebody. Mark, Lizzie, Claire. I recognise small details: the way a boy used to wear his hair or his tie, the girls who shortened their skirts by folding the waistbands, and the group of lads who lived for break time football, and had the mud-scuffed trousers to prove it.

This isn't just a photograph of pupils from my old school. It's a photo of my school year, which means . . .

I find Martin first, at the far right, on the bottom row. Unlike most of the children standing around him, he isn't smiling, which doesn't surprise me. He hated school. Next I find myself and Amy, standing shoulder-to-shoulder on the third row, grinning at the camera, and the ghost of a memory surfaces, perhaps of the very moment this photograph was taken, or maybe of another one just like it: the two of us, holding hands, trying our hardest to keep a fit of giggles at bay while a teacher shouts at us, *For goodness' sake, girls. Can you please stop fidgeting and look at the camera!*

The photo is an interesting find, but the younger versions of myself, Amy and Martin aren't the reason Chloe showed it to me. Alexander Peter Grantham must be here somewhere too, although I don't remember going to school with anybody called Alexander, or Alex. And what use is trying to spot someone in the crowd, if you don't know what they look like?

'I give up,' I say.

Amy leans over and points with her finger, and then I see him. A little boy on the second row, with red hair, wearing thick glasses and with a huge grin on his face.

Despite the years that have passed, it's unmistakably him: Peter Rand.

'Alexander,' Chloe says. 'At least according to the name tag on Facebook.'

'So, Peter Rand is – or was – Alexander Peter Grantham?'

She nods. 'He must have changed his name, which you have to admit, is kind of suspicious. And he told us he moved here five years ago, but he's been here all along. He lied.'

Rand said he set up the games club when he first moved to Westhaven, 'four, maybe five years ago'. At no point did he mention he'd lived here before then, or that he went to school here. I suppose he could have grown up in the area, moved away, then changed his name before moving back, and saw no reason to share that information with us when we spoke to him. Plus, people change their names for all sorts of reasons. Decide they prefer their middle name to their first, ditch their given surname and take their mother's maiden name after their parents' divorce. It happens.

But still . . .

If Chloe's right, if Peter *has* been here all this time, that would mean he'd have been around when Amy was killed. He'd have only been a boy at the time, but then so was Connor. And if Rand moved away and came back, when did that happen? And, more importantly, why?

This could be – and probably is – nothing. Or it could be the missing piece of information I've been looking for.

'So, what happens next?' Chloe says,

'Hmm. Not sure yet,' I tell her, thinking out loud. 'I should make some calls, maybe check in with some people. See if anybody remembers him. See if I can find out why he left town, if he did.'

I expect she wants me to take her with me, for us to tackle the next phase of the investigation together, but I think of my promise last night, to keep a low profile, to keep her safe.

'I'll let you know what I find,' I say, folding the picture of the school photo in half, then into quarters, and slipping it into the back pocket of my jeans.

She looks downhearted.

'We'll talk later, I promise,' I tell her. 'Are you going to be at Oscar's? I could come and find you.'

She shakes her head. 'Nah, he's busy with his mum today.'

I think about what Chloe told me last night, about her dad's binge drinking.

'Would you like to hang out here, until I get back?' I say. 'You can look through the archive, if you like.'

'Oh, no. I couldn't. This is . . .' She gestures to the shelves and files, as if she's standing in the British Museum, surrounded by priceless artefacts, rather than Mum's dingy old office.

'It's a mess, is what it is,' I say. 'I'll tell you what, if you get bored and want to make yourself useful, you can tidy up a bit. But if you just want to sit and read old film magazines, that's OK with me.'

'Really?' She moves over to the map of Westhaven pinned to the wall, eyes the printouts and photocopies, runs a hand along the timeline.

'So cool,' she says, in an awed whisper.

For lunch, Dad makes us all generous cheese and ham sandwiches, and we sit around the picnic table in the garden to eat, then Chloe plays with Freya on the lawn. They chase each other in circles, laughing as they go. At one point, Freya dives onto the grass and curls herself into a little ball. Chloe pounces on her and starts tickling her and they both end up rolling around in hysterics until there are tears in their eyes.

Dad looks on with something approaching approval. 'Your little helper seems nice,' he says.

Not only nice, but useful.

When lunch is over, Chloe and I head back to the office and I point out a few boxes she can rummage through. She opens one and is immediately thrilled by the contents: an old notebook with a hand-drawn map of Cooper's Wood inside it, a stack of audio tapes with Connor's name written on them, memory cards containing old interview footage.

'You must have done, like, hundreds of hours of interviews,' she says.

'Three hundred, at last count,' I tell her.

'Whoa!'

'I know, it's a lot,' I say. 'But I had to keep going, for Connor's sake. Had to keep asking questions until I got to the truth. At the end of the day, that's what's important. You keep going, keep digging, until you get to the facts.'

'So cool,' she says again.

That's the good thing about having Chloe around. Not only does she make me feel cool, she makes me feel like my work matters, like it means something.

Before leaving, I poke my head into the kitchen to let Dad know that Chloe's staying behind and to say goodbye to Freya. As I open the door to leave, I pause, wondering if it's OK to leave Chloe alone with the archive – which is odd, because I haven't wanted anything to do with it for the past two years, but I suddenly feel oddly protective of it. I decide that it is. Like Dad says, Chloe's a nice kid. I doubt she's the sort of person who would take something that doesn't belong to her. And even if she is, would it matter? Wouldn't that just mean I had one less cursed object to haul back to London?

# 31

I take the scenic route into town, walk the path down by the river, where the only sounds are my own footsteps, the lazy creaking of narrowboats, and the gentle splashing of ducks and swans on the water. The quiet offers my mind a chance to wander – and to worry.

I came here hoping to make things better, but I'm pretty sure last night's run-in with Dalton has made things a whole lot worse – especially for Connor. The way the crowd turned on me, the things they were saying . . . It's frightening to think of what could happen. I need to warn Connor, let him know to be on his guard. If I could climb over the back wall of his garden, what's to stop someone else doing the same thing? And while I know Connor is more than capable of defending himself, clobbering someone with a cricket bat certainly won't help his cause.

I take out my phone to call and let him know that I'm on the way, but before I get the chance, I spot a familiar figure heading towards me along the river path.

Amy's mum. She's loaded down with shopping bags and has her head down, looks lost in thought. I could turn back, perhaps avoid her entirely, but then she might see me walking away and that somehow feels like it would make me look even worse in her eyes. Short of jumping into the river, I can't see any way of avoiding her.

*So, the river it is, then, yes?* I think, but I take a few deep breaths to steel myself and am ready with a friendly smile when she looks up and recognises me. She comes to a stop, her shoulders slump and her face sets in stone. I suppose she's no happier seeing me than I am her.

Unlike some of the people in *Born Killer*, Elaine has hardly changed since the last time I saw her. Her hair is perhaps a little greyer, and there are a few more lines at the corners of her eyes, but she looks just as poised and elegant as ever. Despite the warm weather, she's dressed in a long woollen coat over a navy turtleneck, with a cashmere shawl draped over her shoulders.

P S Cunliffe

She gives a sigh as she comes forward, sets down her bags on a nearby bench.

'I heard you were back,' she says, wearily, as if seeing me has ruined her entire afternoon.

'Just visiting for a few days,' I tell her. 'With my little girl.'

'To see your dad,' she adds, and we both nod as something unsaid passes between us. She knows the truth, I'm sure – that while it's nice to see Dad, especially for Freya, the real reason I came back is Evan Cullen's murder.

'I've been meaning to get in touch,' she says.

'You have?' I'm surprised, because of the press conference she gave outside the courthouse after Connor's retrial. And because the last time we were in the same room, she could barely bring herself to look at me.

'Hmm,' Elaine says. 'We wanted to let you know, we're moving away.'

'Good for you,' I tell her, and I mean it. If I were them, I'd have moved out of Westhaven a long time ago, if only so I didn't have to see the shadow of Cooper's Wood on the horizon every time I left the house.

'We're going to join Rob's brother, over in Brighton,' Elaine adds. 'Spend whatever time we have left with family, by the sea. Amy used to love the seaside. You both did.'

We really did. Loved going to the beach, the funfair, the pier, the lights and noise of the arcades. Being dive-bombed by seagulls while we ate fish and chips, running into the sea, then running straight back out again, screaming at how cold it was.

It's no business of mine where Amy's mum and dad choose to live, but I'm glad it's going to be by the sea. It feels right.

A thought occurs to me. 'What about Amy's room?' I ask.

They didn't change a thing after she died, kept it just the way it was on the day she disappeared. And on the condition nothing was touched or moved, they agreed to let me film inside it for *Born Killer*. I included a lingering shot of it at the close of episode one, capturing on film the hundreds of little details that told the viewers what kind of a fifteen-year-old Amy had been: the pinboard containing photographs of friends and family, the posters of her favourite bands on the walls – The Libertines, The Strokes, Kings of Leon – her mini hi-fi system, perched on the window ledge, alongside a tower of CDs. Schoolbooks and magazines scattered everywhere. *Just Seventeen*, *Sugar*, *Heat*, *NME*. A pile of dirty laundry slumped in the corner of the room; black T-shirts, ripped jeans, hoodies. A box of costume jewellery on the bedside table. I can still remember the smell of the place – which was nothing like how Amy used to smell when she was alive. It was musty, like a winter coat taken out of a wardrobe for the first time all year.

The idea of them getting rid of Amy's things after all this time sparks an odd kind of panic inside me.

'We've put most of her belongings into storage,' Elaine says. 'But we've kept a few boxes back, things we'll be taking with us to the new house.'

'I see,' I say.

'Last month we had a little ceremony, in the back garden,' she adds. 'We burnt a few of her things in a fire. It was Rob's idea. He said it might help us to move on. I thought he must have gone mad when he suggested it, but we gave it a try, and it seemed to help. We've said goodbye to her so many times, but this time it felt different.'

Different because they are leaving the only home they every shared with their daughter, or different because this time, it worked?

I can't imagine burning anything of Amy's. I have so little of hers as it is. A CD she gave me for my fourteenth birthday, a tatty friendship bracelet, an old T-shirt I borrowed at a sleepover at hers and never gave back. Little pieces of her I keep in a box underneath my bed that I can barely stand to look at.

Elaine sighs and looks out over the water. 'We kept some things back for you,' she says. 'We thought it's what Amy would have wanted.'

I'm touched and, quite frankly, amazed. No matter what Elaine and Rob think of me, at least they still recognise that I loved their daughter, that we meant the world to each other.

'Thank you,' I say. 'Really. That's so kind of you.'

'It's not much,' she says. 'Just some photographs, a few bits and pieces of jewellery.'

'No, that sounds . . . wonderful,' I tell her. 'I can call round and pick it up later, if you'd like? I could bring Freya.'

Rob and Elaine have never met Freya. And, with Amy being an only child, don't have any grandchildren of their own. Given how big a part I expect Amy would have played in Freya's life had she lived, it feels right that they should meet.

But Elaine shakes her head. 'Best not,' she says. 'I'll drop it round at your dad's. Like I said, it's not much.' She tilts her head, fixes me with a cold stare. 'You could have a ceremony of your own, if you like. Or, just throw it in the bin. It's up to you.'

Just as I was starting to think we were taking tentative steps to rebuilding bridges. How stupid of me.

Elaine takes a final look out over the water, perhaps to calm herself, then picks up her bags.

'I'd best be going,' she says.

'Elaine—' I begin, but I don't know what to say that might help, that might make things better between us, and she simply nods and leaves without a further word. I watch her go, wishing I could sit down with her and talk the way we used to. Reminisce about old times, about the silly things Amy used to do that made us laugh, the things that remind us how much we miss her. But those days are long gone, and I know there's only one way I'll ever fix things between us.

# 32

## Martin – 3.58 a.m.

It's been nearly twenty minutes since Martin checked in with Frank, but he knows that if Freya had woken up needing her inhaler – the one still in the glovebox of Jessie's car – Frank would have called, and seeing as he hasn't, Freya must still be sleeping, which means she's fine, for now at least. And while Frank's silence also means Jessie isn't back at the house yet, given how bad the storm is, her staying put is probably the smartest and safest thing she can do.

Right now, Martin has no real reason to believe that either his wife or his daughter are in any immediate danger. So why doesn't it feel that way? Why is the fight or flight response in him so strong that his palms are sweating and his heart is thumping in his chest?

He thinks about Jessie and Amy, how close they were. They were connected at a deep, almost psychic level. Multiple times, he saw Jessie try to call Amy, only to find the phone was engaged because Amy was calling her. They'd often wear the same outfit, down to their choice of earrings, without having consulted each other beforehand. And Jessie once told him that, when Amy went missing, she knew something terrible had happened to her – could *feel* it in her bones.

Is that what he's feeling now? he wonders. Can he feel Jessie's distress in *his* bones?

It stands to reason that if such a connection can exist between two people, if they can feel each other's pain, even when they're apart, he would have that with the woman he has shared so much of his life with. On the other hand, maybe the panic in his chest is simply due to the fact that he's heading back to Westhaven, a place so full of bad memories – from the bullying that made his schooldays so miserable, to Amy's murder, to his parents' divorce – that when they bought their house, he made sure they had enough room for Frank to come and live with them. Jessie said that was just about the kindest thing she'd ever heard, but the truth was he only did it so he wouldn't ever have to visit that awful town again.

Sometimes Jessie likes to remind him that growing up in Westhaven wasn't all bad, even for him, and she's right. There was a short period, of around six months, when everything was fine. Better than fine, in fact. The bullying had all but stopped, and he had a girlfriend, who he loved very much. He was truly happy, for the first time in his life. And then, one rainy afternoon, everything changed.

The summer holidays had been a total washout. It had rained pretty much every day, and he, Jessie and Amy were forced to spend most of their time indoors. Sometimes they went to each other's houses but, more often than not, they'd end up at Doolallys, a trendy coffee shop at the bottom of town. They'd huddle by the rain-slicked window, drinking marshmallow-loaded hot chocolate, reading books and magazines, playing board games, or idly watching the tourists, who filed past the café in their transparent ponchos, clutching sopping wet street maps.

Martin didn't mind the rain, because he couldn't remember a time when he felt more at ease, more himself, than when he was sitting in that quiet little café with his girlfriend. It was the perfect place to be. At least it was until Amy's boyfriend turned up.

She'd told them she'd met him at school, that he was in the year above but had failed one of his exams so was retaking some classes, and the teacher had sat them together, saying she hoped Amy would be a good influence on him.

Martin liked the idea of there being another boy around, and the idea of Amy having someone else to hang out with. Maybe now he'd finally get some time alone with Jessie.

But when Amy's boyfriend arrived at the café – Amy rushing over and standing on her tiptoes to greet him with a kiss – Martin's heart sank. He recognised him immediately as the boy who'd assaulted him three years earlier, who had thrown his library book in the gutter, kicked him as he bent down to pick it up, then ripped the book in half. He knew the boy's name, had overheard it on the school sports field once and that night had written *Fuck You Connor Starling* on a piece of paper, folded it into quarters and hidden it under his mattress, a little talisman of hate he'd hoped might bring bad luck to his bully.

What on earth was Amy doing with *him*? She was petite and looked young for her age, whereas he was built like a barn and looked like he was in his twenties. He wore a leather jacket and had stubble on his cheeks, for God's sake. She was clever, top of her class for some subjects, whereas he was undoubtedly a total thicko, seeing as he'd been held back a year. And worst of all, Amy was nice, whereas he was a thug.

He would have to say something, he decided. She deserved to know what her new boyfriend was really like, what he was capable of. Of course, he wasn't going to do that in front of Connor, but at the earliest opportunity, he'd take Amy aside and tell her what her new boyfriend had done to him. She'd probably dump him on the spot, he thought – and wouldn't that be fun to see.

For now, he just had to sit tight and pretend that everything was normal, a task made that much the easier by the fact that although he recognised Connor, Connor didn't seem to recognise him. It made perfect sense. Victims dream about their bullies' faces at night, while bullies don't care enough about the people they hurt to remember them.

Connor took a seat at their table, though he pulled a face when Amy suggested he get a hot chocolate for himself.

'What, we're just going to sit here all day, in this boring café?' he said. 'Why don't we go and *do* something?' The girls giggled. 'Let's go to Bristol. Let's go ice skating!'

The girls loved the idea. Of course they did.

Martin demurred. 'Um . . . I think I'll give it a miss,' he said to Jessie. 'But you go, if you want.'

He didn't much like the idea of Connor laughing at him while he embarrassed himself on the ice, but Jessie insisted she'd show him how to skate, and Amy gently teased him until he agreed to come. Perhaps while they were on the ice he'd get a moment alone with Amy; then he could tell her the truth about Connor.

Before heading out, the girls went to use the bathroom together, whispering in each other's ears as they walked away, and Connor and Martin were left alone at the table. Connor sniffed, then took a packet of tobacco out of his inside pocket and started rolling himself a cigarette. Ugh, he was a smoker too. No surprise there.

When Connor was done, he popped his cigarette behind his ear, then looked up at Martin with a smirk, and said, 'Read any good books lately?'

Martin felt a rush of panic and a sudden need to use the toilet.

'You remember?' he said, and for a split second he wondered if Connor was going to apologise. After all, it had been three years since the incident. Martin had changed plenty during that time. Perhaps Connor had too?

But Connor didn't apologise. He leaned back in his chair and said, 'Oh yeah, I remember. You had that weird rash on your face, didn't you?' Then he checked over his shoulder, presumably to make sure the girls weren't on their way back from the bathroom, and added, 'You'd better not say anything to Amy, or it won't be your book I rip in half next time. OK, mate?' He leaned over and slapped Martin hard on the upper arm, the way bullies do when they're pretending to be your friend.

A moment later, Jessie and Amy returned from the bathroom in a cloud of perfume. Amy immediately sat on Connor's lap, and they kissed, noisily. Jessie tried to kiss Martin too, but he wasn't into it – couldn't be further out of it, in fact.

'What's up with you?' she asked him.

'Nothing,' he said. 'I just don't feel well.' Which was true. He'd had a stomach-ache from the moment Connor arrived.

'Aww, poor baby.' She kissed him on the tip of his nose, the way he liked, which usually made him feel better, but didn't work that day.

'Guys, Martin's not feeling good,' she told the others, while she stroked his arm. 'Maybe we can go ice skating tomorrow instead?'

'Aww, what?' moaned Amy.

'Hmm. You do look a bit peaky there, mate,' said Connor, acting all concerned.

'Cool,' said Jessie. 'We'll go tomorrow then. Our first double date!' She looked over at Amy and a psychic message passed between the two of them. They laughed, and Martin felt his world shift, because he knew that his perfect place, his perfect time, was ruined.

# 33

*Three days earlier*

I park up in the same nearby street as on my last visit, then weave a path through the filthy back alleys, past the fly-tipped mattresses, abandoned fridges, and the holdall with the broken zipper. I know which garden wall to climb over, but if I didn't, the soundtrack of the protestors on the other side of the house would have told me.

The bin is where I left it, up against the wall, so I clamber up and over, knock on Connor's back door, and stand well back. This time, he doesn't try to take my head off with his cricket bat, but quickly opens up and ushers me inside.

'Thought I'd come and see how you're getting on,' I tell him. 'Maybe say hi to your nan, if she's awake.'

We move through to the living room, which has been redecorated like the rest of the house, but looks dark and gloomy with the curtains drawn. On the coffee table, an ashtray is overflowing with cigarette butts, alongside a pyramid of empty beer cans. The air is thick with the smell of smoke and alcohol, like a pub from the nineties.

Connor is unshaven, his hair unwashed, his normally bright blue eyes dull and tired.

'Are you doing OK?' I ask him. 'Do you need anything?'

'More beer wouldn't go amiss,' he says, glumly.

'I was thinking food,' I say. Assuming he hasn't jumped over the back wall himself to go on a secret shopping mission, they might be getting low on supplies.

'We've got enough in, for now,' he says. 'Nan likes to keep the freezer well stocked.'

'OK. Let me know if you start running low. Don't starve because of those idiots outside.'

157

He nods his thanks, then says, 'How about you?'

'Me?' I say. 'I'm fine.' A little shaken following my run-in with Elaine, perhaps, but this morning's revelation about Peter Rand – or Alexander Grantham – has fired up the engine of curiosity inside me. It feels good to have a fresh mystery to solve.

'I meant after last night,' says Connor. 'That trouble with Dalton, in the park?'

It was crowded and dark at the vigil, but if Connor was there, even if he was keeping to the shadows, he's lucky not to have been spotted. Lucky to have got out of there in one piece.

'You were there?' I say.

'Course not,' he laughs. 'I overheard the neighbours talking about it while I was out in the garden earlier. Sounds like he really had a go at you.'

'He did,' I tell him. 'He's angry, looking for someone to blame, understandably.'

'I suppose,' Connor says. 'Thanks for having my back though.'

'Always,' I say, and he smiles at that. Which reminds me . . .

'Do you remember a kid called Alexander Grantham, at school? Red hair, short, big smile?' I take the printout of the school photograph from my back pocket, show it to him and point to Alexander on the second row. He squints at the picture, turns his head this way and that.

'Hmm, maybe,' he says, then he nods. 'Actually, yeah. I mean, I think I remember him. I wouldn't say I knew him exactly . . .' He gives me a sheepish look.

Of course, the little tubby boy with the red hair and glasses isn't the sort of kid Connor would have hung around with at school, but he is the sort Connor might have teased, maybe even bullied.

I tut, and shake my head at him.

'I know,' he says, holding up his hands. 'I'm sorry. I was a little shit, I get it.' He looks down as a darkness passes behind his eyes. 'Yeah, I think I remember giving him some hassle, calling him a few names,' he says. 'I was just . . . you know.'

I know.

He was a troubled young man, who terrorised his neighbours, his teachers and his schoolmates. He caused chaos, never missing an opportunity to disrupt a class, to sling abuse at an authority figure, or to kick out at the world. It doesn't take a genius to work out that much of the anger inside him probably came from his losing both of his parents when he was just a boy. Only the hardest of hearts could fail to have some sympathy for him. But the fact remains, he caused damage, to property and people. If he could have his time again, do things differently, I'm sure that he would. Wouldn't we all?

'What happened to him, anyway?' he asks now. 'Did he move away?'

'Not sure yet,' I tell him. 'That's what I want to find out.' I reach out to take the printout back from him, but he keeps hold of it, scanning the kids' faces.

'Hey! There's you and Amy, on the third row.' He holds the picture closer to his face to get a better view. 'Look at you two,' he says, wistfully. He loses himself for a moment, thinking about the past perhaps, before handing the picture back. 'Where d'you get this from, anyway?' he asks, his face open, curious.

'A friend found it, on Facebook.'

'Oh,' he says. 'They put stuff like this up there, do they?'

'Some people do,' I tell him. He looks surprised, impressed, even, like Dad did when I first showed him how to stream music. *You just type in who you want to listen to, and it just . . . plays? How marvellous.*

'You don't go online much?' I say.

'Me?' Connor shakes his head. 'Nah, we don't have internet. Nan wouldn't have much use for it, so I figure we're better off saving the money. I don't know much about computers, anyway. I'm still getting used to paying for things without having to type in my PIN. Why do you ask?'

'They reckon Evan met the person who killed him online,' I tell him. 'Someone was sending him messages. They lured him up to the woods, on the night he was killed. So don't go joining Facebook any time soon, OK? Don't give them any excuses. The police, I mean. Or those bastards outside.'

'I won't,' Connor says. 'In case you're forgetting, I've been through this before.'

* * *

Upstairs, Connor knocks on his grandmother's bedroom door. 'Nan? Someone to see you.' He pushes the door open, then stands aside and motions for me to go on in.

The room is lit only by the glow of a small TV set, perched on top of a chest of drawers, and it takes a moment for my eyes to adjust. Once they do, I make out Flora Starling, lying in bed, propped up into a half-sitting position by a stack of pillows, smoking a cigarette.

'Can I come in?' I say, my voice all but drowned out by a burst of applause from some old quiz show. Flora turns to look at me through a haze of blue cigarette smoke, the reflection of the TV filling the lenses of her glasses.

'It's me, Jessie,' I say, and something clicks and she comes to life.

'Jessie! Oh, it's *you*,' she says, her voice a tar-soaked rumble from deep in her throat. 'Come in, come in!' She reaches over and stubs the cigarette out in a saucer on the bedside table, waves the smoke away with her hand, as if it'll make any difference. The room smells even more like an ashtray than the living room downstairs.

I go to her, kiss her on the cheek and take a seat in an old armchair by the side of the bed, sinking down into a cushion that has long since lost all shape and purpose. Presumably, it's the same chair Connor fell asleep in on the night Evan Cullen was killed.

Flora takes my hand in hers and squeezes it tight.

When I first started making *Born Killer*, Flora was reluctant to go on camera. Not that she didn't want to get justice for Connor – nothing was more important to her than that – but she was wary of what people might think of her,

'Look at me, then look at her,' she said, speaking of Elaine. 'Who do you think people are going to believe?'

I told her it wasn't about who believed what. All that mattered was getting to the truth, because that would be how we could best help Connor. Though secretly, I thought she might be right.

Elaine was highly educated, well spoken and always immaculately turned out, with an elegance that came across well on camera. I knew after our first interview that viewers would respond positively to her, would want justice for her, and for Amy. Whereas Flora was anything but elegant. Her house was a mess, she didn't seem to care how she looked, she chain-smoked constantly and could barely get through a sentence without cursing.

I worried people would judge her harshly, that they'd think of her and Connor as *those* kinds of people – the sort you would dread having as neighbours – and in turn would be more likely to think Connor guilty.

In the end I needn't have worried. No doubt, people sympathised with Elaine; they cried along with her, felt her pain and loss through the screen. But audiences really connected to Flora. They loved her no-bullshit attitude. Most of all they liked her fierceness.

But there's nothing fierce about Flora today, sat smoking in bed, watching repeats of forty-year-old TV shows. Now, she looks thin and frail. I picture her in my mind, climbing into bed the very day Connor walked through the door a free man, and staying there, having finally got what she wanted after all those years.

'Where have you been?' she says. 'We haven't seen you in ages.'

'I live in London now, Flo,' I tell her. 'I'm just visiting for a few days, while my daughter is on half-term, and thought I'd call in to say hi.'

'Oh yes,' she says. 'Silly of me. Staying at your dad's, are you?'

'That's right.'

'And are you still with that fella . . . Martin, was it?'

'Yes, we're still together. We've got a little girl now, remember?'

I take my phone out of my pocket with my free hand, open the gallery and thumb through the pictures. Nearly all of them are of Freya, but I find one of my favourites of her, from last Christmas morning, where she's still dressed in her pyjamas and has a look of delight on her face as she is presented with her first bike. The picture never fails to make me smile.

I show Flora. 'She's five now.'

'Aww,' she says. 'Isn't she pretty? She looks just like you.' She smiles and I put the phone away.

'It's good you're here.' Flora rubs a thumb over my knuckles. 'Con's been lost without you. I keep telling him he needs to get out more, make new friends. It's no good, him being cooped up inside all day.'

Does she know what it's like for him out there, I wonder – even before these last few days? How people look at him, speak about him? That they cross the street when they see him coming? I'm not sure she does. The idea of him making new friends seems ludicrous.

'I'll try to visit more often,' I tell her, though I think she knows I don't mean it. Her eyes drift back to the TV, where two contestants dressed almost entirely in shades of brown are trying to win a prize by answering a series of questions and throwing darts at a board.

We fall quiet, and I suppose that's OK, that just being here, holding her hand, is enough.

The host goes to a break and there's a moment of silence during which we hear a shout go up from outside: *Murdering bastard!* One of the protestors, making themselves heard.

Flora looks over to the window. 'Did you hear that?' she says. 'There's been people outside, shouting things. They've been at it for days.' She looks back at me, as far from the fierce Flora I remember interviewing as I can imagine. She looks scared.

'Don't worry about them,' I tell her, giving her hand a squeeze. 'They'll be gone soon.'

Maybe not today, or tomorrow, but as soon as the police find out who killed Evan, the protestors will move on.

'It's to do with that lad who was killed, isn't it?' she says. 'Do they think our Connor did it? Are the police going to come and take him away?'

What a question.

'Of course not,' I tell her. 'They might want to speak to him again, but if they do, it'll just be routine. Once he explains he was here with you the night that boy went missing, that'll be the end of it.'

Flora looks puzzled. 'He was here, was he?'

My stomach flips. 'That's right. You watched TV together, remember?'

'Oh,' she says, sounding unsure, then a moment later she looks relieved. 'Well, that's OK then.'

Fuck. She doesn't remember.

Connor only having an alibi from his grandmother is bad enough, but at least it's something. Now it looks as if he doesn't even have that.

Another possibility surfaces: the reason she doesn't remember him being here, is because he wasn't . . .

I push the thought away. Connor wouldn't lie to me, of all people. He spent the evening sitting here, in this old armchair, watching terrible quiz shows from the eighties with his grandmother, and she doesn't remember because she fell asleep. Or she's forgotten, because her memory isn't what it used to be.

Connor says he was here, so that's where he was.

'Nineteen sixty-four!' Flora shouts at the TV, in answer to a question I didn't hear. A moment later the host confirms that she's correct and awards one of the teams ten points.

I feel a chill clamber up and down my spine.

She's old and unwell, and judging from the number of pill bottles on her bedside table, she's on plenty of medication, but she's not stupid. Far from it.

'I'd better be going,' I tell her. 'It was lovely to see you.'

'Oh, are you off, love?' she sighs. 'You will look after him, won't you? He's all I've got.'

'Of course I will,' I tell her.

'Good,' she says, her eyes narrowing. 'And make sure those bastards don't fit him up again.' Then she squeezes my hand so tightly that it hurts.

Perhaps she hasn't lost all of her fierceness after all.

# 34

When I arrive back at the house, I find Freya sitting at the table in the kitchen colouring, while Dad is standing by the stove, stirring the simmering contents of a pan and consulting a tatty old notebook with all the concentration of a scientist mixing volatile chemicals.

'Something smells good,' I say, as I go over and give Freya a hug – much needed after my run-in with Elaine, and my conversation with Flora.

'Look, Mummy.' Freya shows me a drawing she's in the process of making, in which stick-figure versions of herself, Dad, me and another smaller figure with dark hair are floating above the lawn in front of a house.

'Bolognese,' Dad calls over his shoulder. 'Your mother's recipe.'

That explains the wonderful smell, and why he's looking at the notebook so intently.

Mum wrote down all sorts of recipes for him before she died, worried he would attempt to subsist solely on red wine and cheese sandwiches after she was gone, which he mostly does.

'Is that Daddy?' I ask Freya, pointing at the dark-haired stick figure.

'It's Chloe,' she says, with a puzzled look, as if the likeness is obvious.

'Of course it is. Silly me,' I say. 'And are you playing in the garden?'

She nods, then takes the picture back, selects a green crayon and starts colouring in the grass.

'Would your friend like to join us?' Dad says, turning to look at me, and it takes me a moment to realise that he's talking about Chloe too.

'She's still here?'

Dad tastes the sauce, licks his lips, then gently lobs the spoon in the direction of the sink where it lands with a rattle. 'Assume so,' he says. 'I haven't heard her leave.'

I thought she'd have gone home hours ago. Perhaps the opportunity to rifle through the archive, or flick through old film magazines, proved too hard to resist, which is fine by me. In fact, I'm glad she's still here. On the walk back from Connor's, I had an idea of how I could thank her for her hard work.

I head out of the kitchen and up the stairs. When I open the door to the office, I find Chloe, sitting in the swivel chair that no longer swivels, though she isn't reading magazines, or looking through old papers. She has her coat on, looks about ready to leave.

The office looks tidier than it has in years. All the papers, tapes, folders and equipment have been neatly stowed away, or arranged in piles. I can't remember the room ever being this organised, not even when Mum was using it as her study.

'Oh, wow. Thank you, Chloe,' I say. 'You really didn't have to do this. But I won't lie, I'm very glad that you did.'

She shrugs, says nothing.

'Would you like to stay for dinner?' I ask. 'Dad's making pasta. He's not much of a cook, but it's my mum's recipe. It should be good, as long as he can read the instructions.'

Dad once offered me Mum's notebook of recipes to take home with me, said I'd have more use for it than he would, but when I looked through it, I saw the way her handwriting gradually deteriorated as I turned each page, and found the thought of keeping it too painful. I slipped it back onto his bookshelf without a word.

'No, thank you,' Chloe says. She stands. 'I should probably get going, now that you're back.'

'Oh, OK. Of course,' I say. I'm a little disappointed, but she's been here all day. She's probably tired, perhaps even a little bored.

I hold up a finger. 'Before you go, I've got something for you.'

I scan the newly organised shelves until I find what I'm looking for, take down an old canvas camera bag and set it on the desk, open it and reach inside. I pull out a silver Sony Camcorder, enjoying the brief flash of memories that accompany the feel of the plastic in my hand: glimpses of Mum and Dad at Christmas; Martin, Amy and Connor, larking around and pulling faces.

I offer it to Chloe, a tingle of pleasure in my stomach at the thought of how happy it will make her.

'I thought maybe you'd like to have this. It was one of my first cameras. It's pretty old, but I bet you can still get tapes for it on eBay. Some of the footage I shot on this ended up in *Born Killer*. I can show you how it works, if you'd like, and you can get some practice filming?'

Chloe looks down at the camera. I see a brief flicker of interest in her eyes before she looks away. 'No thank you,' she says, her voice flat and disinterested. 'You can keep it.'

I don't understand. I thought she'd be delighted, because while the camera is old, and getting hold of tapes for it probably will be a pain, it should still work just fine. Plus, what I'm holding in my hands is a genuine piece of *Born Killer* history. What fan wouldn't want to own that?

I put the camera down. 'What is it?' I say. 'Is this because I left you here on your own this afternoon? I'm sorry, I know today was a little boring, but sometimes working in film is like that. It's dull. Waiting around, doing paperwork, tidying up. But you didn't have to stay. I honestly wouldn't have minded if you'd gone home.'

Chloe shakes her head. 'It's not that,' she says.

'Well, what is it then?'

She glares at me from under her fringe, and I can't quite place the look in her eyes. For a moment I'd swear that she hates me.

'I know you lied,' she says. 'I know that you betrayed Amy.'

Where on earth has this come from?

'What are you talking about?' I say, as Chloe reaches inside her coat and pulls out her phone.

Her fingers dance across the screen for a second, then she turns it towards me and shows me a picture of Connor. She presses it with the tip of her finger, and a video starts to play.

# 35

## Jessie – 4.05 a.m.

'What do you mean, *problem*?'

'. . . taking longer than we thought. The roads are impassable . . . tried to get an Air Ambulance, but the conditions right now are . . . it's too dangerous. They're trying to find a different way to reach you. You're going to need to sit tight for a while longer, Jessica.'

No, no, no! This can't be happening.

She said an hour, and an hour has been and gone, and I have been so good. I have done everything she asked. I've been calm-*ish*, I haven't panicked, I have stayed on the line, and I have sat here while the water rises around me and done *nothing*, because she *told* me help was coming.

'Jessica . . . still there?'

'Where else am I going to be?' I cry. 'You *told* me to get ready to sing!'

'I know, and I'm sorry . . . afraid the situation on the ground has changed. The storm is making things a lot harder for . . . but don't worry . . . just going to take a little while longer than we thought.'

A little while. OK. That doesn't sound so bad. Another five minutes, maybe ten. I can live with that.

'How much longer?'

'. . . sure right now. It could be . . . maybe more.' The signal drops out at the worst possible moment. Of course it fucking does.

'I can't hear you!'

'. . . tell me it's going to be another hour. Maybe more.'

Another hour? She can't be serious.

Emptiness blooms in my chest, then the panic rushes in. I can't breathe. There's suddenly no air in the well. I throw my head back, let the rain pour down onto my face, try to stop myself from losing it entirely.

If it weren't for the rain, maybe I could spend another hour down here without going mad. *Maybe*. But the situation hasn't only changed on the ground, it's changed underground as well.

I'm still half-sitting on the bottom of the well with my legs bent at the knee, part submerged beneath the filthy water. Before the storm hit and the rain really started coming down, the water was tepid and came up to my breastbone. Now, not only has the temperature dropped considerably, but it's lapping at the neck of my T-shirt. How much has it risen in the last hour? Impossible to tell in the dark, without having some sort of marker to go by, but by the feel of it against my skin it must have risen by five, perhaps six, inches. The same again and it will be up to my chin. Again, and it'll cover my mouth and nose, and that's if the cold doesn't kill me first.

At this rate, I'll be dead in an hour.

'I'm going to freeze to death down here, or drown, do you hear me? The water's rising. You have to *do* something.'

'OK, Jessica. Please try . . . remain calm.'

Fiona is still using that oh-so measured tone that I have, so far, found reassuring. But now it infuriates me. It's like she's a satnav, politely asking me to turn the car around as I barrel towards the edge of a cliff. Why is she so bloody calm? Why isn't she panicking, like I am?

'I'm going to die down here! Do you understand? I don't *have* an hour.'

'Jessica, they're working on . . . promise . . . doing everything they can . . . just having some difficulties.'

Everything they can? Jesus. The only thing they need to do is get me out of here. What could be so difficult about that? I'm trapped at the bottom of a well on the outskirts of town. I'm not miles below ground in a mine or cave system in some far-flung country. It shouldn't be this bloody hard.

'You said you're stuck,' says Fiona. 'But is there . . . you can try . . . Very important you keep . . . above the water.'

No shit. 'I told you, I can't *move*. There's a root through my leg.'

'. . . break it . . . uproot it, maybe?'

The thought of it, of the pain that trying to pull the root out of the mud at the bottom of the well would undoubtedly cause, has me shaking my head, but I suppose I haven't tried, not since the last time I attempted to stand and the pain had me in tears. But Fiona's right, if I can break the root, or pull it up, I'll be able to get to my feet. I'll be able to survive long enough for my rescuers to get here.

'I'll try,' I tell her.

'Well done, Jessica. I'm right there . . . you.'

*You're not right here with me though, are you?* I think. You're sitting on a comfy chair, at a desk in a warm office somewhere. You couldn't be further away from here.

The water is now too high to risk putting the phone in my bra. I feel around for a safe place to stow it and find one of the footholds I dug out earlier on, a gaping hole where the stone fractured under my weight. The resulting gap feels deep enough, and has a slight slope backwards. If I'm careful, I should be able to keep the phone there until I'm done. I put the phone on speaker, set it down in its new home, then cradle my hands beneath it, in case it falls, but it stays put.

With the phone safely stowed, I lean forward and reach down under the water, touch the root at the place where it enters my leg, then run my hand all the way down until I reach the thickest part at the bottom of the well. It doesn't feel like I could break it. I'm not strong enough. But maybe I can uproot it.

I wrap my fist tight around the base of the root, then draw in a breath, hold it, then count to three in my head and pull as hard as I can.

The muscles in my arms and side stretch tight, and the movement results in an explosion of pain, deep in my thigh, that has me seeing stars. I let out a scream but keep pulling until it feels like I'm going to pass out.

The root doesn't move.

I stop, breathless and broken, nauseous with the effort. 'I can't . . . it won't . . .'

'That's OK, Jessica. Just take . . . moment. Get your breath back.'

Bit by bit, the pain eases. I sit there, in the dark and the wet, desperate and distraught, the rain pouring, the water rising.

It wasn't supposed to be this way. I was going to make things right. Find Amy's killer, Evan's too. Help Connor. Bring closure to Amy's parents. That's what was supposed to happen. But instead, I'm going to die down here, just like Amy did. Well, not exactly like Amy, because she didn't drown, despite how it looked when Bill found her. She was dead long before the rain came.

'Hold on, Jessica . . . contact with our ambulance response team,' Fiona says, then the line goes quiet.

This is pointless. I might as well hang up. At least then I could use however much time I have left to call Martin and Dad and say my goodbyes. Perhaps even speak to Freya. I wouldn't want to frighten her, but if I could just hear her voice, one last time . . .

'Jessica?' Fiona's back on the line. 'I've spoken with . . . you're going to have to pull the root out.'

Wasn't she listening?

'I just told you, I *can't*,' I yell. 'I tried, and I can't.'

'I don't mean pull it out of the ground,' she says. '. . . mean . . . out of your leg.'

Is she mad? Everyone knows if you're impaled by something, you don't try to take it out yourself. You wait for the professionals, so they can remove the object, stem the bleeding, repair damage to torn blood vessels and muscles, and make sure you haven't severed an artery. That way you don't bleed to death.

'You're not serious,' I say.

'Under the circumstances, I'm afraid . . . only option. I have medically trained colleagues with me . . . exactly what to do. But before we . . . is there anything in the well you can use as a tourniquet?'

The thought of all that pain is too much. 'I can't,' I say. 'I just can't—'

'One step . . . time, Jessica,' Fiona says. 'Don't think about what comes next, just focus on my voice. You need to make a tourniquet, that's all we want . . . right now. Is there anything you can use? Can you tear a strip off your clothes, maybe?'

'I don't know . .' Then it comes to me. 'My bag. There's a strap on my bag.'

'OK, that's good,' Fiona says. 'Find it, Jessica. Get it ready.'

# 36

*Three days earlier*

It's a video of a video. By which I mean the slightly shaky footage on Chloe's phone is the result of her filming a video file playing on the computer monitor on my desk, just two feet away from us.

'What is this?' I say. 'If you wanted to see some of the old footage, you could have just asked me. I wouldn't have minded.'

'Just watch,' Chloe says, a new coldness to her voice.

In the video, Connor is sitting on the old brown sofa in the living room of the house on Milk Street, a patch of black mould darkening the peeling wallpaper behind him. His hair is buzz-cut short, which means this must have been shot for *Born Killer* season two, in the days after his release.

The room is dimly lit by a single lamp on a nearby sideboard, plus the blue light from the TV. *Match of the Day* is playing in the background, highlights of the weekend's football.

Connor takes a swig from a can of beer, sets it down then starts rolling a cigarette. He looks blurry eyed, perhaps a little drunk. I hear the sound of a wine bottle being uncorked off camera, followed by the glug of a glass being filled, which means I'm drinking too.

My voice: *Tell me how it feels, Con.* Not quite slurred, but loose in my mouth. I'm not drunk yet, but I'm getting there. Is that why I don't know what this footage is? Did I dismiss it as unusable the moment I watched it back?

On screen, Connor looks over to where I'm sitting, and shrugs. *I don't know,* he says, half grinning. *Good, I suppose. But weird.*

*Weird how?*

*Everything's just . . . different.*

171

'I don't know what you're trying to show me here,' I say to Chloe. She glares back at me. 'I said, just watch,' she snaps, and I have this horrible feeling in the pit of my stomach, a growing dread at what Connor or I might have said in the privacy of his living room, our tongues loosened after a few drinks.

I look back at the phone.

*I keep thinking they've made a mistake*, Connor says. *That they're going to turn up at the door and tell me I've got to go back.*

*Relax*, I tell him. *That isn't going to happen, Con. You're out now, for good.*

*Yeah.*

*Everything's going to be all right.*

*Yeah*, he says again. He lights his roll-up, takes a long drag and exhales, and the living room fills with smoke. *People don't seem very happy about it though*, he says.

*You mean those idiots in front of the town hall?* I reply. *Don't worry about them. They'll soon get bored, find something else to get their knickers in a twist about.*

This must have started out as an interview, but now it's just two old friends, talking and drinking. And while the camera might still be rolling, either we've forgotten all about it, or no longer care.

This isn't good.

I want to reach over, press the screen to stop the video playing, but the connection between my brain and body doesn't seem to be working as it should. I'm rooted to the spot, frozen in apprehension of what we might say next.

*It'll just take some time to get used to things*, the tipsy version of me in the past tells Connor.

He nods, then plucks a stray strand of tobacco from his lip, wipes on it on his jeans. *I know*, he says, then he turns back to the TV, watches the football and swigs his beer while I no doubt drink my wine, and I briefly entertain the hope that whatever Chloe has seen, whatever made her take out her phone so she could have a copy of this footage for herself, might not be that bad.

She said I betrayed Amy, but that could mean any number of things. Perhaps this is just a misunderstanding? She's heard one of us say something about Amy that sounds mean, or unkind, but wasn't meant that way. Might that seem like a betrayal?

On the screen, Connor leans back, sighs heavily, then says, *You ever think about what we did?*

Shit. I will him to stop talking, because there are long-kept secrets between us we promised never to speak of, and until now I thought we'd both kept that promise.

But it's my voice that comes next.

*We were just kids, Con. We didn't know what we were doing. If we could go back and change things, we would. But we can't.*

Christ, this sounds bad.

*I know*, Connor says, then he lowers his head, rubs his hand back and forth over the short hairs at the nape of his neck. *I still feel guilty though. About the accident. It's our fault. It all started with us . . .*

I've seen enough.

'Turn it off,' I tell Chloe, but she stays exactly where she is, holding the phone out in front of her.

*If we hadn't done what we did, she'd still be alive—*

'That's *enough*.' I reach for the phone and Chloe steps back, out of reach, then presses the screen to pause the video. The picture freezes: Connor, looking over to one side, guilt etched into his face.

Fuck. Of all the hundreds of hours of footage Chloe could have watched, why did she have to watch this one? This is either an astonishing stroke of bad luck, or the result of her going through every memory card she could find. And now she has her very own copy on her phone.

I turn to her. 'It's not what it looks like. Really, it isn't. We weren't talking about what happened to Amy, not in that way.'

Chloe looks back at me, hurt in her eyes. 'All that stuff you said this morning, about getting to the truth . . .'

'I can explain.'

She shakes her head slowly. 'What did he mean by "accident"? What did you do?'

'Nothing,' I say, too quickly, the result of a burgeoning panic that is clouding my thoughts and making me sound far more desperate than

I'd like. I backtrack. 'OK, it wasn't nothing, but you must understand, we didn't hurt Amy, not in that way. Connor loved her, and she was my best friend, more like a sister.'

A sound from downstairs. The clunk of a door opening, followed by Dad's footsteps in the hall. I hear him walk to the foot of the stairs, then he calls up to us. 'Food's ready!' He waits for a response, and I look to Chloe, worried she'll make a run for it, but when she doesn't move, I risk the few steps to the door and call out into the hall.

'We'll be down in a bit.' There's a little tremble in my voice, but I sound almost normal and after a moment, Dad retreats, closing the door to the kitchen behind him.

I turn back to Chloe. 'Just come downstairs and eat with us, and later on we can have a long talk and I'll explain everything, I promise.'

Chloe takes a step away from me. 'I don't think I want to be around you right now,' she says. She puts her phone into her pocket and heads for the door.

I can't let her go like this. Can't let her leave with that footage.

As she moves past me, I reach out and grab her by the wrist. She winces, pulls in a sharp breath through gritted teeth, and all too late I realise I've grabbed her in the exact spot where her bruise is.

'I'm sorry,' I say, as I release my hold on her. 'I didn't mean to . . .'

'I thought you were different,' she says. 'I thought I could trust you.'

'You *can*,' I plead. 'You can!'

She looks heartbroken.

'Promise you'll come back tomorrow,' I say. 'Give me a chance to explain.'

Chloe looks back at me with an expression of disgust on her face, then leaves the room and I hear her footsteps thump down the stairs, followed by the sound of the front door opening and slamming shut.

She's gone.

What am I going to do?

I've worked so hard to keep our secret safe, but now, because of one stupid mistake, we risk the truth being exposed. And if the lies Connor and I have told come out, it will be bad for both of us. That footage could ruin everything.

# BORN KILLER –
# SHOOTING SCRIPT

## S02 – E01: LOOK AGAIN

**ELAINE BARNES:** 'They said it would be better for us if we didn't know all the details, but we wanted to know everything. We wanted as much information as possible, no matter how painful it would be to hear. It felt like the more we knew, the closer we'd feel to her, the more connected. Not knowing is the worst part. It's horrible. It's torture.'

**ROB BARNES:** 'You'd have thought, after it was proven in court what he did, that he might have done the decent thing, but we tried just about everything to get him to talk. Elaine wrote to him, plenty of times. He always replied, and he always said the same thing, that he couldn't tell us what he didn't know, and that he wanted the truth just as much as we did. Which just goes to show you what kind of a sicko we're dealing with here.'

**ELAINE BARNES:** 'There were so many theories about what really happened that night, but we wanted facts. On the tenth anniversary of her death, we decided that we should find someone to tell her story, in case there were witnesses who hadn't come forward, or in case somebody could convince Connor to talk. There were a few journalists who'd shown an interest over the years, but it had never felt right to us. We needed somebody who would handle Amy's memory with care. Somebody we could trust.'

**JESSIE (Voice-over):** 'I'd worked hard to move on from what happened, to build a life, a career, a family. But when Amy's parents reached out and told me they were looking for somebody to tell her story, I knew I had to do it. Partly because she was my best friend, but also because it wasn't just her story. It was the story of my hometown and of my childhood. It was Connor's story, and it was my story too.'

# 37

## Jessie – 4.17 a.m.

The strap of my bag is still looped around my left arm. I take hold of it and pull it towards me, lift the bag out of the water. It's heavy, waterlogged. I turn it upside down to empty it, the contents splashing into the water, then fumble with the metal clasps that secure the straps at each end, but can't seem to figure out how they work by feel alone. It probably doesn't help that my fingers are stiff with cold, and everything is wet through.

I turn the bag this way and that, try squeezing the clasps, twisting them. There must be a simple trick to it, but whatever it is, I can't work it out in the dark. Eventually, I clamp my teeth around the strap and pull as hard as I can until I hear the stitches tear, and with a final tug, one end comes loose. I do the same on the other side and let the bag slide back into the water, then wrap the strap around my left wrist, so I have it to hand when I need it.

'OK, I've got the strap,' I tell Fiona.

'That's great, Jessica. Good work,' she says, the phone's speaker just loud enough for me to hear her over the hiss of rain and the rumble of thunder. The signal is still shaky too. There are moments when her voice drops away to nothing.

'OK, Jessica. So, what . . . want you to do, is to take hold of the root. Don't think about . . . comes next. Just . . . hold of it.'

I do as she says and reach down into the water with my right hand. Electric shocks of pain spread through my leg, the muscles tightening in anticipation of what's to come as I take hold of the root close to where it punctures the skin under my thigh. I have a beauty mark there, I think. At least I did. Perhaps it's gone now, obliterated by the foreign body that has torn its way through me.

'Now, I know the temptation is to try to do it quickly, so you can get it over with,' says Fiona. 'But that could . . . your femoral artery . . .'

I freeze. 'What? What did you just say?'

'If you'd already . . . wouldn't be talking to me now. But we want to minimise the chance of causing any further damage. So we want you to go slowly. Slide the root out . . . smooth . . . one movement. And when it's done, we want you to . . . strap around the top of your thigh, as tight as you can. You can do this . . . deep breath and hold it. When you pull, push the breath out at the same time.'

I tighten my grip around the root and the pain flares.

'I don't think I can,' I tell Fiona.

'Jessica, listen to me. That little girl of yours is waiting for you. She needs you, and I know you'd do anything for her.'

I would, of course I would. I picture Freya at her most adorable, on one of those lazy weekend mornings when she climbs into bed between us, and she's all warm and snuggly, and I'm reminded of how lucky we are to have her, how blessed to have brought this perfect little life into the world . . .

'Now, take a deep breath . . . and pull.'

The pain is instant. It is a scream in my throat, an explosion of colour in my head, a white-hot fire in my thigh. There's a feeling of enormous pressure inside my leg that builds and builds – but the root doesn't move. In the short time it has been inside me, it has grown, wrapped its branches tightly around my bones. It's a part of me now, stuck inside me, like I am stuck inside this well, and it will keep growing until the distant day comes when they find my body down here, and when they cut me open.

The root moves, begins to rub against muscle and sinew as it slides, inch by agonising inch, out through one side of my leg, re-entering my inner thigh as it passes through me. The pain builds, and I want to stop, more than anything I want to stop, because it's too much, but if I do, I know I won't start again. So I keep going, keep pulling, and the root keeps coming, long after it should be out.

And then, all of sudden, I feel the last of it slip out of my body, and it pulls free.

'It's out,' I yell.

I feel faint. I'm going to throw up.

'That's good,' Fiona says. 'You're doing so well, Jessica. Now, the tourniquet. High up . . . as tight as you can.'

No time to get my breath. I unwrap the strap from my wrist and loop it behind my thigh. A fresh wave of pain crashes over me and I cry out.

'. . . thing OK?'

I cinch the strap tight, tie a knot and pull hard. My leg feels like it's on fire, like it's being dipped in acid. I push out a scream and grit my teeth and the world turns fuzzy at the edges. I press my back against the wall of the well, feel the cold stone against my skin and the rain on my face. I think of Freya and I breathe through the pain.

'I'm OK,' I tell Fiona, through gritted teeth. 'I'm OK. I've done it.'

'Brilliant. Well done, Jessica. Now . . . minute, catch your breath.'

But I don't want to take a minute. I want to stand up, get out of the water.

I brace my hands against the well wall behind me, transfer as much of my weight as I can onto my left leg, then push myself upright, water streaming off my body, until I'm up.

I rest my head against the stone and now I take a moment to try to steady my breathing, to make sure I don't pass out from the pain and slip under the water and drown.

*In, hold for three, then out. In, hold for three, then out. Nice and calm, nice and slow . . .*

I'm OK. Dizzy and nauseous, but on my feet.

I look for the phone and for a terrible moment I can't find it. I must have knocked it off its little shelf when I was trying to stand up and it's fallen into the water. But then I see a haze of light between stones, the faint glow of the screen. As I pick up the handset, I hear Fiona's voice in the darkness. 'Jessica, talk to me. What's happening?'

I put the phone to my ear. 'I'm here. I'm up,' I say, with my heart thumping so hard in my chest that it hurts.

'Amazing,' says Fiona. 'You've been so brave, Jessica. You've bought us time now, time to talk. We're going to get through this, me and you. We'll get through this together.'

# 38

*Two days earlier*

A near sleepless night, Freya curled up beside me, the warm curve of her back pressed against my tummy and my arm stretched around her middle. I draw small comfort from the gentle rise and fall of her breathing, while I worry about what might happen if Chloe decides to share the footage she has on her phone with the rest of the world.

It doesn't matter that she doesn't know what Connor and I did. She knows that we lied, and that's enough. If she puts the video out there, the consequences will be catastrophic, for me, and for Connor. The integrity of the entire *Born Killer* project will come under question. People will jump to the wrong conclusions. They'll think that, because we kept one secret, we must have kept others.

I lie awake into the early hours, running through all the ways my life might be about to turn upside down. At best, my reputation will be in ruins. Nobody will want to work with me, and although there have been lots of times over the last twelve months when I've wondered if I'll ever feel the urge to pick up a camera again, the idea that the choice might be taken out of my hands hurts more than I could have imagined. But I suppose I can live with that, with the end of my career. If that's all that happens to me, I'll consider myself lucky, because there's a risk that the video coming out could cost me a hell of a lot more than that.

When morning comes, I get Freya ready in a daze, then shower and dress in a fog of panic, repeatedly going over to the window, hoping to see Chloe walking up the driveway. But by mid-morning, there's still no sign and she hasn't replied to any of my messages. I'm starting to think that this is it. It's over.

I sit on the sofa, take out my phone and brave a scroll through social media, check the usual *Born Killer* hashtags. There are plenty of messages: fans singing the show's praises after their third rewatch, haters declaring it little more than a pack of lies. Connor is obviously innocent to some, obviously guilty to others. John Dalton is either the ultimate villain of the story, or the ultimate hero. Theories, memes, gifs, behind-the-scenes pictures. But no mention of any new footage. Which means Chloe hasn't posted it, at least not yet.

I put my phone down, lean back and press the palms of my hands to my eyes. I'm exhausted. If Chloe is going to post the footage, a part of me wishes she'd just get on with it.

I suppose, if I'm being honest with myself, it might be good to have everything out in the open. I feel mad for thinking it, because the consequences could be dire, but there's something freeing about the thought of having to face up to it all. I can't remember what it was like to have no secrets, they are heavy things to carry around.

Perhaps it's time to face up to what I did and take whatever punishment is coming my way. At least then I'd come out clean on the other side.

'What's wrong, Mummy?' a little voice says. 'Are you sad?'

I look up and see Freya, a concerned expression on her face.

Bless her for noticing. I pull her onto my lap, give her a big hug and rub my nose against hers. She squirms and giggles and the sound of her laughter calms something inside me.

'Nothing's wrong, darling,' I tell her. What else can I say? I can hardly tell her that our lives might be about to be ruined because of something Mummy did ten years before she was even born.

'If you're sad, you should do something that makes you happy,' she tells me, as if it's that simple. Oh, to be five years old again. On the other hand, perhaps she's right. If the truth is going to come out, I should be making the most of today. I should be treasuring every last second of normality we have left.

'Do you know what would make me happy?' I say. She shakes her head. 'A game of Dinosaur Golf!'

Freya gasps and her eyes go large. 'Really? We can go? When, *when*?'

'Right now! Go and get your shoes on, and ask Grandpa if he wants to come with us. Hurry, hurry!'

Fifteen minutes later the three of us are in the car, Freya in the back, strapped into her car seat, Dad sitting beside me, adjusting the headrest.

'Does anybody need the toilet?' I look over to Dad. 'That's meant for Freya, rather than you.'

'I gathered,' he says.

Freya assures me she doesn't, but when she's as excited as she is right now, there's no telling if she's being honest or not. I turn to her over my shoulder. 'You're sure? Because we won't be able to stop until we get there.' She nods as Dad nudges me with his elbow.

'I thought you weren't working today,' he says.

'I'm not,' I tell him.

'Well, I think you forgot to tell your little friend,' he says.

I turn back to see a familiar figure, wearing a grey zip-up hoodie, walking up the drive towards us.

Chloe. She's come back. Oh, thank God.

'Give me a minute,' I say. I get out of the car to go to her and we come to a stop a few feet away from each other. She eyes me warily.

'I'm so sorry about yesterday,' I say, keeping my voice low.

Chloe shrugs, looks down at her shabby trainers.

'I didn't mean to – you know . . . I shouldn't have . . .' I shouldn't have grabbed her like that.

'S'OK,' she grunts, rubbing her left wrist with her right hand.

I want nothing more than to give her a big hug, but the events of last night have built a wall between us. Still, I have to know how bad things might get, and whether or not it's too late.

'Have you shown it to anyone?' I ask.

She knows exactly what I mean. She looks away, her face set in stone, and for a moment I fear the worst, but after a few deep breaths she shakes her head, and the wave of relief nearly knocks me off my feet.

'Thank you,' I say. 'And thank you for coming back, for giving me a chance to explain.'

If I'm going to tell Chloe the truth, and I feel like I'm going to have to if I'm going to persuade her to delete that footage, then we need room to talk, in private, ideally as soon as possible. I can hardly let Freya down now that she's all excited, but I don't want to risk sending Chloe away, either. I want her close, where I can keep an eye on her.

'We're taking Freya to Dinosaur Golf,' I tell her. 'You could come with us, if you like?'

Chloe considers it for a moment, then shrugs. 'I guess.'

A few minutes later we set off, driving out of town, following the directions on the little map on the back of the leaflet Freya picked up at the petrol station days earlier.

Dad grumbles in the passenger seat, fiddles with the car stereo, while in the back Freya and Chloe play rock, paper, scissors, like they're the best of friends. And I eye Chloe in the mirror, a little time bomb, dressed like my dead best friend, who could explode at any moment.

# 39

## Martin – 4.25 a.m.

Despite the violence of the storm outside, the low thrum of the tyres on the wet road, along with the persistent drumming of rain on the car's roof, acts as white noise to Martin. It lulls him into a state of reminiscence – which is at least better than a state of a panic – and fills his head with memories of those first few months after Connor entered their lives.

He sees the party where Amy got so drunk she threw up all over her new dress and had to be carried home. He sees Jessie – a different side of her emerging following the news of her mum's cancer – taking her first drag of a joint and becoming so pale and out of it that he'd wanted to call an ambulance – and would have, if the others hadn't stopped him. He sees the fight that broke out near the bandstand in the park after a boy made a lewd comment to Amy. Connor hit him so hard that blood gushed from his nose and turned his grey T-shirt a deep shade of crimson. And he sees Connor, turning up at Jessie's birthday party and presenting her with a bottle of vodka stolen from the supermarket, the white security cap still in place. Moment upon moment of teenage recklessness, their lives transformed by the presence of this new person. They were the sort of firsts many kids experience – the first time they get drunk, do drugs, see a fight . . . Martin wasn't such a prude that he didn't recognise such behaviours as normal for some kids, in some towns. But it hadn't been normal for them, until Connor arrived.

To the girls, Connor was a tour guide, taking them to new places, introducing them to new people and new things – here, drink this, smoke this, swallow this. And there could be no denying that sometimes they had a good time, that it felt like a door had been opened to a more grown-up world they were being given early access to. But often things went too far. Someone needed their hair holding back while they threw up in the toilet, someone had to call their parents for a lift home because they had missed the last bus. Somebody got hurt.

And then there was the kiss, and what happened afterwards.

A pair of red lights materialise out of the darkness up ahead. Martin comes back to himself in time to hit the brakes and there's a moment of vertigo-inducing weightlessness as his internal organs lurch forward in his ribcage, and for a split second he thinks this is it, this is how I die . . .

Instinct takes over. He turns the wheel and narrowly avoids colliding with the back end of the SUV that has, for some insane reason, abruptly stopped in front of him. There's a screech of tyres as he swerves into the outside lane, and he somehow manages to wrestle control of the car before it smashes into the central reservation. He straightens up, eases off on the accelerator, heart pounding, adrenalin pumping.

'You're OK, you're OK,' he tells himself. He inflates his cheeks, blows out a long puff of air to slow his breathing.

Fuck, that was close. If he hadn't reacted as quickly as he did, that could have been nasty. It's dangerous out here. The rain is a constant, thunderous shower that hits from all sides, limiting the view in front and behind. Nobody should be driving in these conditions.

He's unharmed, but he's shaken, and newly annoyed. Not at Jessie – not even at Frank – but at the world, for having conspired to make tonight such a shit show. And perhaps at Connor too, who is still on his mind, and who, he is in no doubt, was at least part of the reason Jessie returned to Westhaven.

He dials Jessie's number, not expecting her to answer, but keen to hear her voice.

'Hi, this is Jessie. I can't take your call right now, but if you'd like to leave me a message, I'll get back you.'

'Hey, it's me,' he says, after the beeps. 'So, guess who's on their way to their favourite place in the whole world? That's right, I'm driving to your dad's. It looks like he left Freya's inhalers in the car

185

and you're . . . wherever you are. But don't worry, I've got her spares right next to me on the passenger seat. I'll be there in a few hours and hopefully we'll be eating breakfast together fairly soon. Hope you're OK. Call me as soon as you can and . . . I suppose I'll see you when you get back. Love you, honey.'

He hangs up, not sure if hearing the voicemail and leaving the message has made him feel better or worse, just knowing that it felt like something he had to do. He feels a little calmer now at least.

It would be ridiculous for him to still be annoyed at Jessie because of the kiss she shared with Connor when they were teenagers. She'd just found out her mum had cancer; she was lost, desperate for human affection, and Connor had just happened to be there. It would be childish and petty of him to still be pissed off at her because of a mistake she made all those years ago. After all, she went on to marry and have a beautiful little girl with him, not Connor.

What does piss him off though, is how Connor has managed to remain a part of their lives for so long. There were a few years, when they first moved away from Westhaven and Connor was still in prison, when he thought they'd escaped his influence entirely, that they had moved beyond the reach of his gravitational pull. Connor belonged to the past, like their schooldays, or the bands they used to like when they were teenagers that had long since broken up. He was nothing but a bad memory, his name occasionally brought up in conversation, but mostly consigned to history.

Then Amy's parents reached out to Jessie, and she began working on *Born Killer*. Soon, Connor's voice would drift down the hall from her office as she edited his interviews. She would talk to him on the phone for hours, trying to keep his hopes up. His name would reverberate through the house.

Martin could have coped with all of that – could have accepted that Jessie's drive to make things right meant that Connor would be a presence in their lives – if Connor had deserved it. But Connor Starling was not, and never will be, a good person. He was trouble then, and he is trouble now, and as Martin closes in on his destination, he can't help thinking that if Jessie is in some sort of trouble tonight, there's a good chance Connor has something do with it.

# 40

*Two days earlier*

Half an hour later, we arrive at Dinosaur Golf, which turns out to be just like normal crazy golf, only instead of hitting the ball through the spinning blades of a windmill, or into the yawning mouth of a demented-looking clown, you knock it along the arched spine of a brontosaurus, or into the open jaws of a roaring T-Rex.

There's a café with a dinosaur-themed menu, a gift shop stocked with erasers, keyrings, posters and cuddly toys – the sorts of trinkets that little girls like Freya go crazy for – and, throughout the grounds, large fibreglass models of dinosaurs. When we come across our first one, I tell Freya to go and stand next to it so I can take her photo, but she shakes her head.

'Don't want to,' she says, fear overwhelming her curiosity.

'Do you want me to go with you?' I ask her, and she nods. I hand my phone to Dad and take her by the hand and a moment later he snaps a picture of us standing next to a rather docile-looking triceratops as big as a car. When he hands back my phone, I send the picture to Martin with the caption: **Guess where we are?** That should brighten his day.

We work our way around the course, armed with a ball and a putter each. Chloe clearly enjoys helping Freya learn how to hit the ball just hard enough to make it to go where she wants it to, and Freya quickly gets the hang of things. Even Dad joins in, begrudgingly at first, but his competitive edge soon takes over and he's unable to hide his delight when he gets his first hole-in-one. Seeing everyone having a nice time is not only soothing, it makes this morning's worries start to feel overblown. If Chloe was determined to turn my life upside down, she wouldn't be here now, wouldn't be helping Freya and joking around with Dad. She came back because at least a part of her believes in me, trusts me. Perhaps it's time to repay that trust.

When the game comes to an end, Dad takes Freya to the gift shop to pick up a souvenir of our trip, and Chloe and I take a seat at a picnic bench on the lawn in front of the Jurassic Café and pretend to browse the menu.

There's nobody sitting close enough to overhear us and I know Freya will take an age choosing something from the shop, so we have time to talk.

'There are some things you need to know,' I tell Chloe. She looks up and nods, ready to listen. But am I really ready to talk? Secrets might be heavy things to carry around, but they can be hard to let go of too. If this goes wrong, I could lose everything. My life will come undone, unravel like a badly knitted sweater.

I take a few deep breaths to mentally prepare myself, then begin.

'A couple of months before Amy died, Mum and Dad sat me down and told me that Mum had been diagnosed with breast cancer. They said the next few months were going to be really hard for her, for all of us, but the doctors had told them that, with the right treatment, she should make a full recovery.'

She didn't, in the end, but that's another story, a long and painful one. The tough months turned into tough years, our lives branching off into an alternate reality of endless hospital trips, of remission and relapse, of hopes raised and hopes dashed, until, eight years later, the cancer finally took her.

I go on. 'They warned me that Mum would probably get a lot sicker before she got better, and that her hair might fall out because of the treatment. She always had lovely, long hair – not like mine.' I reach up and scrunch my unruly curls with my fist.

'I think you have nice hair,' says Chloe.

'Thanks,' I say. 'Anyway, I tried to be strong, to keep it together in front of Mum and Dad, because I thought they had enough to deal with without me freaking out, but once I was on my own, that's exactly what happened. I fell to pieces. I ran out of the house, and I suppose I could have gone to see Martin, but it was Amy I really wanted. Only when I got to her place, her mum said that she was at

Connor's, so I went to find her, but by the time I arrived she'd already left. When Connor told me I'd just missed her, I burst out crying on his doorstep. He invited me in, said he'd call Amy and get her to come back. But in the end, that didn't happen.

'Connor gave me a glass of his nan's whisky. It tasted horrible, but it helped calm me down, and I told him what was happening. He was very sweet. He told me he was there for me. They all were. He'd lost his mum when he was just a kid, you see. Maybe that was why I trusted him, why I felt like I could talk to him. He gave me a big hug and let me cry on his shoulder for what felt like hours, and then . . .' I feel my cheeks flush with shame at the memory of what happened next. 'And then I kissed him.'

Chloe's lips part in surprise, then her brow furrows. 'You were upset, and you'd been drinking,' she says. 'He took advantage of you.'

I shake my head. 'It wasn't like that. I hadn't drunk *that* much. No.' I pause, try to find a way to explain. 'Have you ever been so hurt and sad that you just wanted to feel . . . something else? Anything else? Does that make sense? Connor was there, and he was handsome and strong, and he was being kind to me. He didn't force himself on me.'

If anything, it was the other way around. I remember looking up at him, getting lost in the blue of his eyes, and wanting him to kiss me. But he didn't. So, I leaned in, and . . . It was a good kiss. Warm, wet, hungry. Memorable, in the way only the very best kisses in life are.

'After a minute, reality came crashing in and we came to our senses. We stopped, and I know we both regretted it immediately. Everything got awkward between us, and I left, ran all the way home. I couldn't believe what had just happened. I'd kissed my best friend's boyfriend . . . Such a stupid thing to have done, such a stupid mistake.'

'It was an accident,' Chloe says. 'Like Connor said, on the tape.'

I pause for a moment. Can you kiss somebody by accident?

'Right, yes,' I say. 'An accident. Just like Connor said. So, you see, we didn't hurt Amy, at least not physically. But he cheated on her, and I betrayed her. We both felt awful. Neither of us wanted to lose her, so we agreed to pretend it had never happened, to keep it a secret. But secrets have a way of coming out.'

'Amy found out?'

I nod. 'The thing is, me and Amy were like sisters. We told each other *everything*. So, even though Connor and I tried to behave normally around her, I think she could tell something had changed. She could tell I had this secret inside me.'

I look over to the gift shop, see Dad and Freya through the glass, standing in front of a rack of cuddly toys. Freya has her head tipped to one side as she struggles to make her selection.

We still have time.

'Around then, something else happened that put a strain on our friendship. You don't need to know the details, but we had a bit of a falling out, and I think that's what pushed her over the edge. She came to the house while I was out, said she wanted to pick up a CD she'd left at mine, and she went through my things and found my diary. At least I think that's what happened. Maybe she just stumbled across it, and curiosity got the better of her. I hadn't written down everything that had happened between me and Connor, but I'd written enough for her to know that *something* had happened.'

'What did she do?'

'Nothing, at least not right away. She waited a few days, until we were all together, then she confronted us, and all hell broke loose. Martin was furious with me, of course. He said we were over, and he made me give him back the ring he'd given me for Valentine's Day. I loved that ring; it was the first thing he ever bought me. It had a little garnet stone in it, and he'd had it inscribed with our initials. Later on, he said he'd lost it, but I think maybe he threw it away, out of anger. He was very upset, and don't get me wrong, it was horrible to see him so hurt. But it was Amy I was really terrified of losing. I tried telling her I was sorry, that it was just a stupid mistake, but she wouldn't listen. She was angry with Connor, but she was *really* angry with me. She stormed off home, and that was the last time I saw her.'

Chloe gasps. 'That was the night she went missing?'

'Right. In the morning, Amy's mum came to the house, and I thought she was there because Amy had told her what I'd done and now she was going to tell my parents and I was going to be in all sorts of trouble.'

'But that wasn't the reason.'

'If only. Instead, she told us that Amy was missing.'

That unforgettable image of a distraught Elaine, standing on our front doorstep, comes back to me now. The look of desperation on her face, and the hope in her voice as she asked me where Amy was, because if anybody would know, I would. We were like sisters, after all.

I go on. 'Within hours it was chaos. The police came, started asking questions, and I was so upset. I felt responsible. I'd kissed her boyfriend and now she was missing. I tried telling the police it was my fault, that we'd had a fight and she'd stormed off, but they weren't interested. It turned out that Amy had gone home after the fight – her mum and dad had seen and spoken to her. Then, for some reason, she'd left the house again. Nobody knows why.'

'You must have been so scared.'

'We all were. We were desperate to find her. Martin and Connor and I joined the search. We handed out posters all over town. I remember thinking I didn't care if she never spoke to me again, just as long as she was OK. But she wasn't.'

A memory surfaces, of Mum holding me for what felt like hours after we got the news. I cried into her shoulder and all I could think was that it was my fault Amy was dead.

'Then we found out someone else had been at the well, that someone had pushed her in . . . When they arrested Connor, I thought the police would talk to him, then let him go, because I knew, in my heart, that it couldn't have been him, because he loved her, and there couldn't be any evidence for something he hadn't done. And then . . . somehow, there was. Amy's bag, with her inhaler inside, was found hidden at the back of his wardrobe. I didn't understand how that could have happened. I was so confused. It felt like a bad dream, and after that, it seemed even more important that people not know about me and Connor, because they might think it was something more than it was. More than just a stupid mistake.' A motive, even.

'What about Martin?' says Chloe. 'He knew, didn't he? Weren't you worried he'd say something?'

I shake my head. 'At first, but then we talked, and he said he'd forgiven me. He accepted it was a mistake, a moment of madness, and nothing more. What with Amy's murder and Connor's trial, we had bigger things to worry about. I was . . . lost without Amy, and my mum was still poorly, and Martin was brilliant. He saved me, kept me sane. He was there for me then, and he's been there for me every step of the way, even when I told him I was coming back to Westhaven to tell Amy's story, and to find her real killer.'

Chloe smiles. 'You must really love him,' she says.

'I do,' I tell her. 'And I loved Amy, despite the fact that I hurt her.'

'That's why you've tried so hard to find out who really killed her, isn't it?' she says. I nod, and she blows out her cheeks and exhales, long and slow. 'Wow,' she says. 'All that, from a kiss.'

'I know,' I say. 'I still feel terrible about it, and I know Connor does too.'

'But you didn't know what was going to happen,' she says. 'It was a mistake. An accident.'

'Right, but if it hadn't happened, Amy wouldn't have found out and she wouldn't have stormed off that night. She wouldn't have been up in the woods on her own. She'd have been with us. She'd have been safe.'

Chloe lets out a heavy sigh, seems lost for words.

'Nobody else knows about this,' I tell her. 'Apart from me, Connor, Martin, and now you. I know I told you filmmaking was all about getting to the truth, and here I am, with this big secret, but if people see that footage, they'll think the worst. They'll jump to conclusions and think that because we lied about this, we lied about other things. It'll be bad for me, but it could really mess things up for Connor, especially right now. You understand that, don't you?'

Chloe looks down at the table, runs a thumbnail back and forth along the woodgrain.

'Don't do that,' I tell her. 'You'll give yourself a splinter.' I reach out and still her hand and she looks up at me.

'I won't tell anyone,' she says. 'It was a mistake. It's like you said about Evan. The only person responsible for his death, is the person who killed him. It's the same with Amy, isn't it. You didn't push her in the well.'

She takes her phone out of her pocket, makes sure I can see the screen as she brings up her photos app. She selects the video file, then clicks the trashcan icon on the bottom right of the screen. Her phone asks her if she's sure, and she immediately clicks yes, then she goes to her deleted items folder and wipes the file from there too.

Thank God . . .

I lean over and offer her a hug, which she accepts. 'Thank you,' I say into her ear, and I hold her for a while longer, feeling grateful for this young girl who has come out of nowhere and now knows my oldest secret. I'm not sure I feel any better for having shared it, but maybe I will, in time.

Five minutes later, Freya comes barrelling out of the gift shop with Dad in tow. 'Look what I've got!' she shouts, waving a large, blue cuddly dinosaur at us.

'Wow!' I say. 'I hope you've said thank you.'

'Thank you, Grandpa!' she hollers and Dad smiles.

Chloe acts suitably impressed as Freya shows off her new friend, and they discuss whether the dinosaur is a girl or a boy and what name it should be given. I look across the table at Chloe, and she grins back at me. Thank God. The little time bomb in a hoodie has been defused.

I clap my hands. 'Right, who's for a Brontoburger?'

Chloe nods and Freya cheers and jumps up and down. Dad looks somewhat less enthused at the idea. I wave the menu at him. 'It's either that, or Plesiosaur nuggets.'

He rolls his eyes. 'I suppose it'll have to be the burger then,' he says, as if he's disappointed at ruining his strict diet of sandwiches and red wine.

I get up and head over to the café, my phone ringing as I push open the door. I take it out, see Flora Starling's name on the caller ID, and stop in front of the counter.

Why on earth is Connor's grandmother calling me?

'Jessie? Jessie . . . that you?' she says, when I answer.

'Flora? Is everything OK?'

'They've taken . . .' I can't hear her. The signal is too weak inside the café.

'Hang on,' I tell her. 'You're breaking up.' I head back outside, stand out in front of the café. On the lawn ahead of me, Chloe is walking Freya's cuddly blue dinosaur across the table and making it talk. Freya is laughing like a drain.

'Flora, are you still there? What's happened?'

'They've taken him, Jessie,' she says. 'They've taken Connor. You've got to do something.'

Oh God. It's finally happened. The protestors have tipped over the edge, broken into Connor's and dragged him out into the street to beat him up, or worse. I know Connor wouldn't go down without a fight, that he'd do everything he could to stop the mob from taking him, but if there were enough of them, even he wouldn't stand a chance.

'Flo, you have to call the police,' I say. 'Call them, right away.'

'What do you mean?' she says. 'It's the police who have taken him, Jessie. He's been arrested.'

# 41

## Jessie – 4.33 a.m.

I thought I'd feel better, now that most of my body is out of the water, but I'm still stuck down here in the pitch black, propped up against the wall, so I can keep my weight off my right leg as much as possible. I'm still exhausted, nauseous, scared and wet – so utterly, unbelievably wet – and I'm feeling the cold now in a way I wasn't before. And there's something new to worry about.

My right leg feels strange. It doesn't hurt the way it did. I'm no longer hit by shocking bolts of pain whenever I try to move, but an initial warming sensation has given way to pins and needles and a spreading numbness. Is that supposed to happen? Is the tourniquet doing what it's supposed to? I have no idea. I suppose I could use my phone's torch to find out, but I'm scared of what I might see – scared of using up the phone's battery too. I have to believe it's going to be OK, that Fiona's advice was correct and that I've stemmed the bleeding. Otherwise, I'm done for.

Her voice comes to me now over the phone's speaker.

'Jessica? Say something. Let me know you're OK, Jessica? Talk to me.'

I wish she'd stop saying my name so much.

'Of course I'm here.'

'There you are,' she says, sounding relieved. 'I thought we'd lost you.'

I say nothing.

'Jessica? I know it's hard, that you're tired and you're hurt, but you're doing so well, being so brave. I need you to keep talking, though. I don't like it when you go quiet on me.'

I've already told her everything I can remember: about Chloe, the young girl who dresses like Amy, who came to see me, worried she

195

was responsible for her friend's murder; about meeting Peter Rand at his games café; about the vigil, and our run-in with John Dalton who tried to turn the whole town against us. But what's it all for? And I'm starting to feel tired, so tired . . .

'We need you to stay alert,' Fiona says. 'And talking to me is the best way you can do that. Besides, the next thing you tell us might help the police catch the person who did this to you. You want them to get caught, don't you?'

'What I want is to know that my little girl and my husband are safe, and for you to get me out of here,' I say, as a shiver shakes through me.

Fiona has told me that everything is taking longer than it usually would because of the storm. She's quite sure we'll hear back any moment on the welfare checks on Freya, Martin and Dad, and I should try not to worry, which is easier said than done. I suppose it makes sense, that the emergency services would be overrun tonight. I've stopped asking how far away they are, because each time I do, it seems like a new problem has come to light. Roads are blocked by flooding and fallen trees; specialist equipment has been requested and is being rushed to the scene; telecommunications have been damaged, and so on – and with each delay, the possibility I'll die down here, while still on the phone with Fiona, becomes that bit more real.

'Of course you want to know your family is safe, and of course you want to get out of there,' Fiona says. 'That's what I want too. And there's a whole team of people doing everything they can to make that happen.'

They don't seem to be having much luck though, do they?

Is that why she keeps pushing me to talk? I wonder. Because she knows that, while my rescuers are doing everything they can to get to me, it won't be enough, and whatever information I have inside my head will soon be lost forever?

I picture a press conference, a uniformed officer sombrely reading from a pre-written statement: *Unfortunately, by the time our officers arrived on the scene, it was too late to save Ms Hamill, but we can confirm that we have some very promising leads . . .*

I don't want that. I don't want to die talking on the phone with a stranger.

'I'm going to call my husband,' I tell Fiona. 'You can call me back in . . .' How much time will I need to tell Martin I'm trapped in a well, that the water is rising, and that the people who are supposed to be rescuing me might not make it in time? How long to say goodbye?

'Jessica, we've talked about this,' says Fiona. 'I'd strongly . . . you not to end our call. It'll be much safer for you if you stay on the line. Not only are we tracking your signal, but I have access to specialist medical support here. Should anything go wrong—'

'I want to speak to my husband,' I tell her. 'And you can't stop me.'

'I don't want to stop you from doing anything,' she says. 'But if you end our call, there's no guarantee we'll be able to re-establish—'
I take the phone away from my ear and hang up.

According to the little icon at the top right of the screen, there's now eighteen per cent battery remaining. I don't know how long that will last, but I'd rather it run out while I'm talking to my husband than to some emergency call handler I've never met before who just happened to be working the night shift.

I bring up my recent calls, scroll down and press Martin's number. There's no sound from the phone's speaker for a moment, just ominous dead air, then it rings twice, and the call connects.

Out of a hiss of static, I hear Martin's voice: '—llo? Jess? Are you OK? What's going on?'

My God, how wonderful it is to hear his voice, and how heart-breaking. I immediately start to cry, big full-bodied sobs that make it hard to catch my breath. But I can't afford to waste time.

'I'm here, love,' I tell him, through my tears. 'Are you OK? And Freya?'

More dead air, then Martin says, 'Jess? I can't hear you. Are you there?'

The phone beeps three times and the call drops.

Please, no. Not this. Not now!

I call him back right away and get an engaged tone. He must be trying to call me at the same time I'm trying to call him. How ridiculous. I hang up, stare at the phone's screen and force myself to wait for a moment, in case his call comes through, but after twenty seconds, it still hasn't – he's probably doing exactly the same thing I am – so I try again. This time he picks up right away.

'Hon . . . you there?' he says. 'The signal's terrible . . . you hear me?'

'I can hear you!' I tell him. 'Can you hear me?'

'Yes!' he says. 'Only just, but yes.'

Thank God.

'What's happened?' Martin says. 'Where . . . you?'

He sounds relieved to hear from me, but not panicked. I feel instantly better knowing he's OK. And if Freya were hurt, it would have been the first thing out of his mouth, which means they're both OK, thank goodness. It looks like I'm the only one in danger here.

I don't want to scare him, but I have to tell him the truth, don't I? If things were the other way around and he was the one calling me while he was stuck down here, I'd want to know precisely what was happening. So, no playing it down, I decide. No telling him there's nothing to worry about and everything's going to be fine when there's a chance it won't be.

'Something bad's happened, love,' I say, taking hitching breaths as I fight back tears. 'There's been an accident and . . . I might not see you . .' No. I don't want to say it. 'I'm at the bottom of Dutton's Well. I've hurt my leg and there's a storm. Martin . . . It's really bad. The water's getting higher, and I don't know how long . . . People are coming. They keep saying they're going to get here soon and that they're going to get me out of here, but I don't know if that's going to happen. Someone did this to me and—'

'Jess?' Martin tries to cut in, but this might be the last time we talk. I have to finish.

'Martin, listen to me. I need you to know, in case they don't get here in time, that I love you, and I love Freya, more than anything. I need you to go to her, make sure she's safe. I'm *so* sorry I came back here, I should have listened to you—'

'Jess, you still there? You're breaking up.'

Breaking up? Did he hear any of what I just said? From the frustration in his voice, I'm guessing he didn't. 'I'm here,' I tell him. 'Martin?'

'Jess?' he shouts, then to himself, 'Oh, come on! I can't hear a bloody thing.'

'I'm *here!*' I holler. 'I'm here, I'm here!' He calls my name a few more times, lets fly a curse, then hangs up.

I call back again. This time, he doesn't answer, and there's no engaged tone. Instead, a robotic voice, not entirely unlike Fiona's, says, 'Sorry, it has not been possible to connect your call.'

I hang up, try again. 'Sorry, it has not been possible—'

Again. 'Sorry it has not—'

'Sorry—'

This is unbelievable. It's like a bad dream come to life. Squinting through tears, I press the button to send Martin a text, delete the half-finished message I typed out earlier and start again. I take my time, wiping the rain off the phone's screen between key presses, my trembling hands moving carefully, deliberately, until I have the message written: In Dutton's Well. I'm stuck. Hurt. Help is on way. I stop, not sure what else to say.

How awful it will be for him, to get this message. He'll go mad with worry. He'll probably jump straight in the car and drive through the storm to get here, though it will be far too late by the time he arrives. Still, I want him to know. At least then he'll be here for Freya.

Call me pls. I love you, I finish, then hit send. There's a whooshing sound and I stare at the phone's screen, hoping for a quick reply, or for Martin to call back, but after a few seconds, two little words appear under the message: *Not delivered.*

No!

I press the message and an option asks if I want to try again. I click yes and a little wheel spins for a few seconds, then the same notification appears. I copy the message and paste it into WhatsApp, hit send and hold my breath . . .

*Not delivered.*

I let out a scream of frustration. All I want to do is to talk to my husband and tell him how much I love him and our little girl, so that if I die down here, they'll know what they meant to me. But I can't even have that.

Then my phone bursts into noisy life. My heart leaps. Martin got my message and he's called me back, of course he has! But when

I look at the screen it says, Unknown Number. It could still be him though, couldn't it, calling from a different phone in the hope of a stronger signal?

I press to answer. 'Martin?'

'Oh, thank goodness,' Fiona says. 'You had us worried there for a moment.'

Disappointment fills me up. I feel like sitting down at the bottom of the well and letting the water have me.

'Did you manage to get through to your husband?' she asks.

'No,' I tell her, holding back a sob. 'No, I didn't.'

'Oh, I am sorry,' she says.

She doesn't sound sorry. She sounds like her usual robotic, unfeeling self. It would be nice if, just for once, she could show a little emotion.

'I have to keep trying,' I tell her. 'I can't just give up.'

'Jessica—'

'Or I could try my dad?' I say, more to myself than to Fiona, who is fading in my thoughts. 'Maybe the signal will be better if I'm calling a landline . . . I could even speak to Freya. I won't tell her what's happening, but if I could get Dad to put her on the phone, just for a minute, I could say goodnight to her. I could hear her voice . . .'

'Jessica, no.' Fiona's voice on the other end of the call is firm, shocking me into focus. 'I know it's hard for you down there, and I know you're desperate to speak to your family, but we are so close now. If something should happen to you in these final moments and I'm not in contact with you . . .'

'Nothing is going to happen,' I cry.

'We don't know that. Now, as soon as you're safe, you'll be put in contact with your husband, and your daughter, but I must insist you stay on the line until we get there.'

I suppose she has a point. If they're that close and Fiona needs to check something, to help them to help me, then it's best if we keep in contact. Otherwise, it could cause problems, delay things even further – if that's possible.

I take a breath. 'Fine. Just tell me they're almost here.'

'They are,' she says. 'Not long now. And we've been talking here, and we were thinking, in the meantime, perhaps we can try a different approach?'

'A different approach to what?'

'You said whoever put you down there wanted you to get ready to tell the truth. If we can work out what it is they want to hear, perhaps that will help you remember, and that could help the police work out who did this to you.'

'I don't know,' I say. 'Can't this wait until I'm out?'

'Of course,' she says. 'But in cases like this, every second counts, Jessica. We can't afford to waste any time. Now, think. What is the truth they want to hear?'

# 42

*Two days earlier*

How surreal, to hear of Connor's arrest while I'm stood on the lawn in front of a dinosaur-themed café, with the sounds of children playing nearby and Freya's laughter in the air. Just when I thought that everything was going to be OK.

'You said you'd look after him,' Flora moans down the phone. 'You promised it would be OK.'

I did, perhaps unwisely. But I didn't for one second think Connor would end up being arrested again. Surely the police must realise how bad this is going to look for them? An innocent man, arrested for another murder he didn't commit?

'It *will* be OK,' I tell Flora. 'There must have been some sort of mistake, but I'm going to make some calls, find out what's going on.' Speak to Bill. He'll know what's happening. 'I'm going to fix this,' I tell Flora, though God only knows how.

I hang up and dial Bill, and while the phone rings, I gaze out across the lawn at the picnic table where I was sitting just moments earlier. How quickly things can fall apart. Freya and Dad are still sitting there, although Chloe's nowhere to be seen. She must have gone to the bathroom, which is good, because when Dad catches my eye and mouths the words, *You OK?* at me, I shake my head and point at the phone. He nods, knows immediately to keep Freya distracted and entertained.

I get through to Bill's voicemail, hang up without leaving a message and call back twice more until he answers.

'Jessie. What is it?' he says, curtly, with the low murmur of office chatter in the background.

'You know what, Bill.'

'Suppose I do,' he says, with a sigh. 'Yes, we've brought him in for questioning.'

'On what grounds?'

'Come on, Jess,' he says. 'You know I can't tell you that.'

'Please, Bill,' I say. 'Help me out here. You know what this means to me.'

Don't make me beg, I think. Because if I have to, I will.

Bill lets out an exasperated groan. 'Hold on a minute,' he says, and I hear footsteps, followed by a series of doors opening and closing before he comes back on the line. 'Still there?' he says, his voice echoey. I picture him, stood in a stairwell, somewhere a little more private, where he can talk.

'Yes, I'm still here.'

'OK,' he says, quietly. 'Now, this is strictly between me and you. Understand?'

'No talking to the press, no posting anything online. Got it,' I say. 'And thanks, Bill. I appreciate it.'

'Oh, I'm not doing you any favours,' he says. 'I'm only telling you this because I think you need to hear it.'

My heart stops beating for a second. What does he think I need to hear?

'We had a call,' he says. 'It was anonymous, but it was a detailed enough description. Someone claiming to have seen Connor, near the woods, on the night of the murder.'

'That's it?' I say. 'Surely you haven't arrested him because of an anonymous call? There are enough people who hate Connor around here for you to have received dozens of those.'

'We know that,' Bill says, 'but we had to check it out regardless.'

'He was with his nan, all night long.'

'That's what he says, but you know as well as I do, him being home with his grandmother is about as flimsy an alibi as he could get. Everyone knows she'd do anything – *say* anything – to keep him out of trouble. But putting that aside, I spoke with Flora myself, and while she backs up his story . . .' He sucks in air through his teeth. 'She's just not credible, Jess.'

'She's old, not well. She forgets things.'

'She doesn't remember him being there,' Bill says. 'She's trying very hard to pretend that she does, but she doesn't.'

I think back to yesterday, that vacant look in Flora's eyes when I mentioned that Connor was watching TV with her on the night of the murder. It was enough to make even me doubt Connor's story for a moment, to consider that he might have been lying to me.

Still . . .

'An anonymous call, and an old lady you think is lying but who barely knows what time of day it is? That's not evidence, Bill, and it's not a good enough reason to arrest him.'

'Not on its own,' Bill says, then I hear him swallow hard, and I know whatever he's about to tell me, I'm not going to like it.

'Remember I told you someone lured Evan up to the woods that night?' he says.

'Yes, but that can't have been Connor,' I tell him. 'He doesn't own a smartphone and he barely knows how to use a computer. His house doesn't even have internet. It must have been somebody else.' And I have at least a suspicion of who that could be. 'Perhaps I should have told you this before, but I spoke to a friend of Evan's, an older man. His name's Peter Rand and he runs a games club at the library that Evan was a member of. Peter told me they were close—'

'Jessie—'

'Please, Bill. Just listen for a moment. When I spoke to Rand, he told me he only moved to Westhaven four years ago, but he was here before that, when he was a kid. He was in my year at school, only he went under a different name back then: Alexander Grantham. He might have even been around when Amy was killed. He's hiding something, I'm sure of it. You need to speak to him and find out what.'

'We already have,' Bill says, frustration coming through in his voice. 'We spoke with Mr Rand several days ago. He was very helpful, as it happens.'

'Of course he was, because he wanted to throw you of the scent. He lied to me, Bill. Why would he do that?'

'Maybe he doesn't like journalists poking their nose into his business,' Bill says. 'Whatever the reason, he's not a person of interest.

And as for Connor . . .' he sighs. 'I'm sorry, Jess. He clearly hasn't been entirely truthful with you.'

'He hasn't?'

'After we spoke with Flora, we executed a rudimentary search of the house on Milk Street, and we recovered a laptop from Connor's bedroom. And while you're right in saying he doesn't have internet, his neighbours do. We think he's been using their connection.'

No, that can't be right.

Bill goes on. 'From what we can see, he was a member of numerous *Born Killer* message boards and forums. He posted under a number of different accounts, using false names, mostly to argue with people who say he's guilty of Amy's murder, and that your documentary's a load of old rubbish. He also followed Evan on social media, commented on some of his posts, but that's not all.'

Oh, please no. Don't tell me . . .

'There are messages on the laptop, sent on the night Evan was killed. It looks like Connor lured him up to the woods. He told him he'd found something he needed to see, evidence that could prove his uncle was telling the truth all along.'

Which means evidence that Connor is guilty.

I can't imagine a better way of grabbing Evan's attention, of getting him to agree to meet a stranger in an isolated location, than a chance to prove that his bullies were wrong the whole time.

'Looks like Connor's not quite the Luddite he'd have you believe,' says Bill.

Just yesterday, Connor told me he didn't go online. He said he was no good with computers, that he was still getting used to contactless payments. And I believed him, because it fit so perfectly with my view of him as someone who is still at least a little broken after his time in prison, who gets overwhelmed at having a choice of what to eat for breakfast or when doing the weekly shop, never mind navigating the relative complexities of using social media.

Oh, Connor. What have you done?

On the way back to Dad's, we drop Chloe off at her boyfriend's and I get out of the car and walk her to the front door so that we have a moment to talk. I want to make sure she's OK after our discussion earlier on, and that we have a clear understanding, because while I thought her silence essential this morning, it is even more crucial now that Connor has been arrested.

'What I told you earlier on . . ?' I begin, but I don't have to say any more.

'It's cool,' she tells me. 'You don't have to worry. I don't want to cause trouble, especially not for you or Connor. I know how rumours can get out of hand. I won't say anything to anyone, I promise.'

She gets it, thank goodness.

'Thank you,' I say. 'And thank you for today, for being so good with Freya and showing her how to play golf and . . . for everything else.' For giving me a second chance.

'No worries. I had fun,' she says, then she chews her lip. 'I overheard you on the phone, back at the café. I wasn't trying to listen in, I promise. You just looked so worried and . . . Connor's in big trouble, isn't he?'

I nod. 'I think so, yes.'

'What are you going to do?'

Good question. 'Everything I can to help him, I suppose. I'm sure it's some sort of mistake, that's all.'

'Yeah,' she says. 'It's got to be, right? I mean, they can't frame him twice, can they?'

I only wish I believed her. But the truth is, Connor being framed for Evan's murder isn't all I'm worried about. Ever since Bill told me about Connor's hidden computer, a worm of doubt has been wriggling in my belly.

I keep coming back to that moment when I first climbed over the rear wall of Connor's garden, and he swung for me with his cricket bat. Of course, he didn't know it was me at the time. He thought I was one of the protestors, trying to break in. But I remember the look in his eyes, like he wanted to take that second swing, and I remember thinking how big and strong he was, the damage he was capable of . . . and suddenly the idea he might have bashed Evan's head in doesn't seem so far-fetched.

I hate myself for thinking that way, but can't help it.

Yesterday, I told Chloe that I've never doubted Connor, that I've always been certain of his innocence, but that's not entirely true. There were times, during the making of *Born Killer*, when I considered the possibility that I might be wrong. Tired after a long day's shoot, or exhausted in the stifling heat of the edit suite at some godforsaken hour of the morning, the task ahead of me seemingly insurmountable, the question would pop into my head, unbidden: what if I'm wrong about him? What if he really did kill Amy?

It was an intrusive thought, too dark and too horrible *not* to contemplate. Just imagine spending years of your life trying to prove that the man convicted of killing your best friend is innocent, only to discover that he's actually guilty. The idea was so preposterous, so outrageous, that it was almost funny. What a cruel trick that would be for the world to play, I used to think. Only now, it would be ten times crueller. Because imagine finding out he actually did it, *after* you've succeeded in securing his release. Imagine finding out that everything you have believed, everything you have fought for, is a lie? How could you possibly live with yourself?

# BORN KILLER –
# SHOOTING SCRIPT

## S02 – E03: BREAKTHROUGH

**FLORA STARLING**: 'I like to think she was trying to help Connor from beyond the grave, because that box must have been sitting in that cupboard for, oh, I don't know, a decade, maybe more? Then the very day he loses his appeal, I decide to open it. The photo was right near the top, and I knew right away it was him. He was this skinny thing back then and his hair looked different – there was a lot more of it for a start – but I could tell it was him, and it all began to make sense.'

**CUT TO:** A colour photograph of a young couple in their early twenties, sitting within a triangle of sunlight in a park, their legs entangled. His hair is parted into curtains, and he has an arm flung around her shoulders. She's wearing a strappy vest top and combat trousers. While she smiles and looks at the camera, his head is turned towards hers. He gazes at her adoringly.

**ON-SCREEN TEXT**: Holly Starling & John Dalton, 1989

**DS JOHN DALTON:** 'Holly Starling? Sure, I knew her. I grew up in the area. I knew lots of people.'

**LESLEY POWELL (Connor's maternal grandmother):** 'They were together for about a year, maybe longer. She was nineteen and he was a little older – this was about the time he joined the police. They were quite the happy couple for a while, but then things went wrong, as they often do. I think he wanted to settle down, get married and have children, but she wasn't ready for that. She was a free spirit. It was a bad break up and he took it hard, wouldn't accept that she didn't want to be with him. I remember he used to come to the house, late at night, park up outside and just sit there, watching. Soon after she met Jake Starling. He was . . . different. The total opposite to John – I can't say I thought much of him, but he seemed to make her happy. I think there was some sort of rivalry there, between Jake and John. I think they even came to blows at one point. Jake was a big lad, though. He could take care of himself.'

**FLORA STARLING:** 'Holly chose Jake over him. I think that's why Dalton was always causing trouble, first for Jake, then later on, when Holly and Jake weren't around no more, for Connor. And when he saw a chance to really mess Connor's life up, he took it. It was his way of getting even.'

**DS JOHN DALTON:** 'Romantically involved? No, I wouldn't say that. I knew her, and we were . . . sort of friends, you might say. Maybe we went out on a few dates? To be honest, I don't remember. It was a long time ago.'

# 43

*One day earlier*

In a glass-walled meeting room, down a short corridor at the very back of Westhaven Library, Peter Rand is sitting at the head of a long table with five other members of the games club, all children – the youngest perhaps no more than nine or ten, and the oldest in their mid-teens. They are gathered around a large board with plastic figurines arranged on it, each player armed with pencil, paper and a handful of what looks like playing cards. I've no idea what game they're playing, but it looks like they're having fun; sounds like it too. As we approach the door, a small boy in glasses gets to his feet and jumps up and down with excitement while the other children cheer.

It doesn't feel right, interrupting their game, and I don't want to go barging in, encroaching on their safe space. But I have to speak to Rand.

I knock on the glass and heads turn, all eyes looking in our direction. The boy promptly sits down and shrinks into himself while Rand looks up from his notebook, registers our presence, then gestures to the children, moving his hands in a calming motion.

He comes over, opens the door and pokes his head out into the corridor. 'Can I help you?' he says, his kids' TV presenter smile nowhere to be seen.

'Sorry to interrupt,' I tell him. 'But we need to speak with you.'

'Can't it wait?' He gestures behind him. 'You can see we're in the middle of a game. I should be done in half an hour, or if you want to come by the café later, we can talk then.'

I don't want to wait, don't want to give Rand the opportunity to avoid us, but I scan the kids' faces, and decide that, despite my concerns about Rand, I don't want to cause a scene.

'That's OK,' I say. 'We'll wait until you're done.'

While Rand disappears back into the room, Chloe and I take a seat on a pair of low chairs, out of sight of the children, but with a clear view of the room's door. Not that I think Rand is about to make run for it, but it would be a clear indicator that he's been up to no good if he did.

Chloe leans over and says, 'He looked kind of annoyed, but . . .' She shakes her head. 'I dunno. I'm not sure he's the type. He's too nice.'

'The type?'

'You know . . .' She leans in closer and whispers, 'A murderer.'

'I suppose,' I say. 'But not all murderers look like creeps, you know. And maybe that way of thinking is why some don't get caught. It's like I said, just because someone seems nice and does nice things, that doesn't necessarily make them a good person.'

'Right,' she says.

In the end, forty-five minutes pass before the glass door wings open and the members of the games club begrudgingly file out of the room.

'I know, I know,' Rand tells them, 'but we'll pick up right where we left off next week. And Ryan?' The little kid in glasses turns back. 'Great job today!' Rand gives Ryan a half hug, a hand briefly slipping around the little boy's shoulders.

'Thanks, Mr Rand!' Ryan chirps, then he walks off down the corridor, grinning to himself.

Seems like the librarian was right. The kids really do like him.

Rand waits until the last of the children are out of sight, then turns to us and his smile falls away. 'Come in,' he says, and we follow him into the room where he snaps a few pictures of the game board on his phone, then begins tidying, sweeping the little figurines into a box and folding the gameboard into quarters.

'Thank you for giving us some space,' he says. 'Some of the children can be a little nervous around strangers.' He moves around the table, collecting notebooks and pencils. 'And they're especially fragile at the moment, seeing as one of their friends is no longer with us. Now . . .' He puts both hands in his pockets and perches on the edge of the table, the way a teacher about to lecture his pupils might. 'What can I do for you?'

'We have a few more questions, if you don't mind,' I say.

He sighs. 'All right. Make it quick. Like I said, I've no problem with journalists, or filmmakers, per se, but I already told you everything there is to know about my friendship with Evan the last time we spoke.'

'Whatever you say . . . Alex,' says Chloe.

His head whips in her direction and he fixes her with a flinty look, but I watch his Adam's apple rise and fall as he dry-swallows. I can see his thoughts behind his eyes: *Where did you hear that name?*

'Why didn't you tell us that you grew up here?' I ask.

Rand pulls a confused face. 'I don't know what you're talking about.' He lets out a small laugh, as if it's a ridiculous question, and I take the picture of the school photo from my back pocket, unfold it and hand it to him.

'Second row, third from the left. That's you, isn't it?'

He looks at the photo, then back to me. 'What is this?'

I don't say a word, and neither does Chloe – we don't mind silence – and eventually Rand throws up his hands.

'Fine. *Fine*,' he says. 'If you must know, yes, I lived in Westhaven when I was a kid. I moved away when I was twelve, and moved back at the tail end of . . .' His eyes flick up and to the left. 'I think it was 2018, not that it's any of your business.'

He says this like it's an unimportant detail. But if that's the case, why does he suddenly look so nervous? And why is he taking deep breaths through his nose, as if trying to keep his emotions in check?

'And can I ask why you moved away?'

'Because I was having a difficult time, that's why,' he says.

'A difficult time?'

He's blinking rapidly, engaged in some internal struggle that is bringing a sheen of sweat to his top lip. Finally, he slumps his shoulders and takes a seat at the head of the table. He clasps his hands together, bounces them softly against his lips, like he's trying to pray but has forgotten how, then looks over to me.

'I remember you from school, and your friend Amy,' he says. 'You and her were always together. You were inseparable. I tried talking to you, several times, actually, but you looked at me like I was from another planet.'

I shake my head. I've no memory of this, and it would have been nearly twenty years ago, but I feel a pang of guilt. Kids can be so cruel sometimes, even unintentionally.

'I don't expect you to remember me,' Rand says. 'Nobody does.' He picks up the printout again, takes a closer look. 'You know some people say their schooldays are the best of their lives? Well, for me they were the worst.'

'You don't look like you were having a bad time. In the picture, I mean,' says Chloe.

'No, I suppose I don't,' Rand says, with a forlorn chuckle. 'I was very good at hiding it. Until I wasn't. Until, at eleven years old, shortly after this photo was taken, I tried taking my own life.'

'Jesus,' I say, softly, and I hear Chloe gasp behind me.

Rand goes on, 'Fortunately, my parents found me in time, got me to hospital, got me the help I needed. In the end, they decided it would be best if we moved away and made a fresh start, in a new school, in a new town. And that's exactly what we did. We moved to Bristol, and I got better. Everything got better.'

'But you came back?' I say.

'Hmm.' He nods. 'My grandmother died and left me a house. I thought I'd stay here for a few months, do it up, then sell it on, but it turns out I'm not nearly as good at DIY as I thought I was. A few months turned into six months, then a year. I decided if I was going to stick around, I might as well do something useful, so I started the games club, to help kids who were like me. Outsiders.'

'But you didn't come back as Alexander?' says Chloe.

Rand shakes his head. 'I said goodbye to Alex a long time ago. You see, people didn't like him very much. They thought he was a strange little boy, someone who you should not, under any circumstances, be friends with. And if enough people tell you something enough times, you start to believe them. So, it got to the point where I didn't like Alex very much, either. I hated him, in fact. So I left him behind when I left Westhaven. I had to, to move on with my life, to make a fresh start.'

The idea of any child being made to hate themselves so much that they want to take their own life is appalling. And it's made all the worse by the fact that while Alex was going through hell, Amy and I were giggling away to each other on the row behind him, that we didn't help, that to us, he didn't even exist. Back then, Amy and I were so wrapped up in each other, nobody else mattered. It was as if the world, and everything in it, was divided into two. On one side, there was me and Amy, and on the other, there was everything, and everybody else.

'I don't blame you for ignoring me back then,' Rand says. 'You were just a kid, too young to understand the impact of your actions.' He stops, tips his head. 'But I'd hoped you might be a little more self-aware now, that you might understand the impact your documentary had on Evan, how it ruined his life.'

'That's not fair!' says Chloe, and I wave a hand to signal that I've got this.

'If Evan's life was made difficult because of a documentary I made that told the truth about his uncle, then I'm sorry about that, I truly am,' I tell Rand, keeping my tone calm and measured. 'But Evan didn't take his own life. Someone killed him.'

'And you think that someone was me, don't you?' Rand says. 'That's why you're here, isn't it, because the idea of a grown man being friends with a young boy doesn't sit right? It triggers an alarm, makes you think I must be a weirdo, or a pervert? Am I right?'

I don't reply.

'I was running a game at the café on the night that Evan . . .' He trails off, doesn't want to say it. 'The CCTV is already with the police, but if you give me your email address, I'll send you a copy. Then you can leave me alone.'

'Oh,' I say. Bill told me they'd already spoken to Rand, said he'd been helpful, but I thought he was just fobbing me off.

'I became friends with Evan because I knew what he was going through,' Rand says. 'I knew how hard it was for him, what the teasing and name calling was doing to him, what it could lead to. Did you know that a boy broke Evan's arm a few years ago, and Evan was so scared, he wouldn't even tell his teachers who'd done it? He pointed the boy out to me once—' Rand's comes to a stop, his voice choked with tears.

Chloe mentioned this attack on the night we first spoke. Perhaps it was a playground fight that got out of hand, but given what Evan was going through, it strikes me that perhaps it was more serious than that. A deliberate act of harm.

'Did Evan tell you the boy's name?' I ask, and Rand shakes his head.

'I don't think so,' he says, scratching at his beard. 'Maybe he mentioned it once, in passing; it was a long time ago.'

'He probably didn't want to say,' Chloe jumps in. 'He told me that even if he did want to tell, he didn't think his teachers would believe him.'

'Exactly,' says Rand. 'That's what happens. Victims are disbelieved, the crimes against them minimised. They're told that it's just boys being boys, that it was just a game that got out of hand and before long they begin to feel isolated and helpless. That's what happened to me, and I could see it happening to Evan. He was desperate to be listened to, to be believed. So forgive me for being there for a young boy who needed somebody to talk to. And if you think there's something wrong with that, then that's your problem, not mine.'

He wipes his eyes on his sleeve of his jumper, and I don't blame him one bit for feeling emotional. He tried to save Evan, to give him the help he himself had so badly needed as a boy, but Evan still ended up dead.

'I'm sorry,' I say. 'I know this must be really difficult for you.'

He sniffs, nods. 'You have no idea,' he says.

I suppose I don't.

'We won't bother you again,' I tell him. 'But if you think of anything else that might be useful, please get in touch. And I know it probably doesn't mean much now, but I'm sorry, for ignoring you back then, when we were kids. And for interrupting your game.'

'Yeah, sorry about the game,' Chloe adds.

I take a card out of my bag, put it down on the table and push it towards him with a finger. 'If you think of anything else . . .'

Rand picks it up, scans the name on the front. 'Huh,' he says. 'Do you know, I did have one friend back then.' He looks up at me. 'You married him, as it happens.'

Martin? I'm taken aback, but I suppose it makes sense. They were both victims of bullying. No doubt they sought each other out, clung to each other. Safety in numbers, perhaps. Plus, Martin has always been kind. Unlike me and Amy, if Alex had tried to talk, he wouldn't have looked at him like he was from another planet.

Rand goes on, 'But even he turned against me at the end, joined in the with the rest of them, teased me, called me names. I don't blame him. He was just trying to find a way to survive, like the rest of us.'

This, I find very hard to believe. Martin, a bully? His own schooldays still haunt him, so I can't imagine for a second he'd have ever wanted to inflict a similar torment on someone else. Rand must be mistaken. I wonder if the trauma of being victimised made him ultra-sensitive, unable to distinguish between mean-spirited name calling and good-natured banter between friends – not that Martin has ever been in the habit of poking fun at people. Because the way he talks about Westhaven High, you'd be forgiven for thinking it was a brutal, dangerous place, more like the prison yard than a normal school. It wasn't that bad, even for him, was it? I think. Then I recognise in myself the very behaviour he has just outlined: minimising, disbelieving. Maybe he's right about Martin, that he turned against his friend to save his own skin. God knows, we all do regrettable things when we're young.

Rand is slumped down in his chair with his head in his hands. He looks drained, and I feel bad for having dredged up old, no doubt painful, memories. Worse, because I believe him. I believe every word.

Chloe and I leave him to it, and walk back through the library and to the car in silence. As we put on our seatbelts, she gives me a look, sending me a message without moving her lips, the way Amy used to: *This is bad, isn't it?*

I nod. It is. Because if Peter Rand is out of the frame, the only person left in it is Connor.

# 44

## Jessie – 5.15 a.m.

The water is up to my sternum now. I can feel it. Or rather, I can feel the hundreds of bits of detritus floating on its surface, brushing up against my skin. An unsettling feeling of being lightly touched all over by dead leaves and twigs and cigarette butts and old crisp packets . . . And as the water has risen, the smell has got worse. It was bad enough earlier on, a rotten stink that made me want to throw up. Now it coats the back of my throat like a paste and makes me gag. I imagine, if I make it out of here, it'll still be with me years from now. Every drink I swallow and every mouthful of food will be accompanied by the bitter aftertaste of stagnant well water. But the feeling of the dirty water against my skin and the horrible stink is nothing compared to the cold which has got so much worse. I feel like it's inside me, radiating from me. I can't go on like this for much longer.

Fiona's voice comes to me out of the darkness, from somewhere just above and behind my left shoulder. I've stowed the phone away again, put it on speaker and wedged it into one of the footholds I dug out earlier on, so I don't drop it out of sheer tiredness.

'They'll be with you soon,' she says. 'Right now, you have to keep talking.'

She's like a broken record. Or a broken computer, churning out the same instructions, over and over again.

*Talk to me, talk to me. Tell me the truth they want to hear . . .*

At one point I contemplate taking the phone from its hiding place and dropping it into the water, so I don't have to listen to her going on and on about the truth, about what the person who put me down here wants to know.

'I've told you already,' I say. 'I don't know. *I don't know!*'

'Jessica, please remain calm,' she says, her automatic response whenever I raise my voice.

'I'll be calm once you get me out of here,' I shout back, as a shiver races through me.

'I'll give you a moment,' she says, like I'm a naughty child who needs a time-out.

I shouldn't be arguing with her. I know it's not her fault there's a storm and my rescue has been delayed, time and time again. I'm sure she's doing her best, and it can't be easy for her, being on the phone with me for hours, trying to coordinate my rescue. But time is running out, and all the talking in the world won't change that.

If help doesn't arrive soon, I'll join a list of names I know off by heart, of people who fell into wells and could not be saved. Amy's death gave me a morbid fascination with these stories, of these terribly unlucky people – most often children – who fell into man-made holes in the ground, and the great efforts that went into rescuing them. Their names come to me now, which is ridiculous, because I can barely remember what happened to me twenty-four hours ago, but I can remember Kathy Fiscus, who was three years old when she fell down the shaft of an abandoned well in 1949, and was dead by the time the authorities reached her. I can remember Alfredo Rampi, who was six years old when he fell thirty metres into a well and became stuck, until the heavy machinery being used to dig a parallel tunnel to save him shook the earth and caused him to slip thirty more. It took a month for them to recover his body. And I remember they used explosives to try to reach Roselló García in 2019, but he too was dead by the time they got to him.

Not all of the stories have a tragic ending. Jessica McClure was eighteen months old when she fell into a well in her aunt's backyard in Texas. She could be heard singing the theme from *Winnie the Pooh* as her rescuers dug a cross tunnel to save her. She was brought out alive after fifty-six hours. So, there is hope – there is always hope.

I just don't have much right now.

'I don't want to die,' I tell Fiona, suddenly swamped by tears.

'Hey,' she says. 'You mustn't talk like that. I know you're scared, but I'm still here, Jessica. I'm still . . . you. I'm not giving up on you, so you mustn't give up on yourself. Do you hear me?'

I sniff back tears.

Fiona might be annoying and frustrating at times, but right now, she's all I've got.

'And I've just . . . good news,' she announces. '. . . back from the welfare checks on your daughter and husband. They're both absolutely fine.'

'They are?' Oh, thank God.

'Officers are with them as we speak; with Martin, at your home in London, and at your dad's house too. They've been updated on the situation and . . . obviously very concerned about you, but they're safe and well.'

A fist, held tight around my heart, suddenly releases its grip. To know, for certain, that they're OK, makes me feel a hundred times better and I break down with the sheer bloody relief of it all.

'You're not going to die, Jessica,' Fiona tells me as I sob into the handset. 'Help is closer than you think, I guarantee it. You're going to be back with your family in no time.'

Is she allowed to say that, to tell me I'm not going to die? Probably not. But I'm grateful to her for giving me hope when I need it most.

'Do you promise?' I whisper into the darkness.

'I promise,' she says.

Whatever would I do without her?

# 45

*One day earlier*

The rest of the day passes in a state of high anxiety as we wait for news about Connor and try our hardest to pretend that everything is normal, for Freya's sake. Chloe is a godsend, joining in with all of Freya's games and getting down on the rug to help her colour in pictures, and in the afternoon, the three of us play hide and seek, taking turns in each role. Freya loves hide and seek; we play it all the time at home. Today the game is a welcome distraction as we race up and down the house's three storeys, looking for the most inventive place to hide.

After I'm caught for third time, I retire to the living room for a rest and leave the girls to it while I put in a quick call to Flora. I ask how's she doing, and she asks me when Connor's coming home.

'I don't know yet,' I tell her. 'Soon, I hope. I'll let you know the moment I hear anything.' Connor was arrested more than twenty-four hours ago. Another twenty-four, and they'll have to either release him, or charge him.

'I told them he was with me,' Flora says. 'I said we watched TV all night. I don't know what more they need to hear. They're trying to fit him up, just like last time.'

Of course, she doesn't yet know about the laptop the police found in Connor's room, and I'm not going to be the one to tell her.

'It's going to be OK, you'll see,' I say.

'I hope you're right,' she says.

So do, I Flora. So do I.

I hang up and a moment later Chloe stalks into the living room, singing softly, 'Freya, where are you?' But instead of finding Freya, she finds me, curled up on the sofa with my phone clutched tightly in my hand. 'Sorry,' she says. 'I didn't mean to—'

'It's fine,' I say. 'You're not interrupting anything.' I pat the space on the sofa next to me and she comes over and takes a seat.

'Have you found her yet?' I ask, and she nods.

'She's upstairs, hiding in the laundry basket. I'm just sort of going through the motions.'

I lay my hand on top of hers. 'Thank you,' I say. 'You're so good with her.'

She shrugs. 'It's OK. I like playing with her. It's fun.' She pulls in a sharp breath and holds it for a moment, then clamps her lips tightly shut, as if she was just about to ask me something, but changed her mind at the last moment.

'What is it?' I ask.

She waves me away. 'Oh, it's nothing. Really.'

'No, go on,' I tell her. 'It's OK. You can talk to me.'

'I was just wondering . . .' She licks her lips. 'If you found out that Connor did do it, that he killed Amy and Evan—'

'But he didn't,' I say. 'I *know* he didn't.'

He can't have, because he's Connor, and because I've spent years of my life telling everyone that he is, if not a good person, then at least not a killer, and I have to believe I'm right about that, because if I'm not, it won't just be my career that comes crashing down, it'll be my entire world.

Chloe persists. 'But if you found out that he did, could you ever, like, forgive him?'

Nobody has ever asked me that question before, and I've never let those brief moments of self-doubt live long enough to ask myself. But I don't have to think about it for long.

'Somebody killed Evan, beat him so badly that he died,' I say. 'And he might have been wrong about his uncle, but nobody could blame him for trying to defend him. And what happened to Amy was . . .' I take a breath. 'It was unspeakably cruel. Her asthma inhaler was right there, in her bag, at the top of the well. Whoever pushed her in could have easily dropped it down to her, could have given her a chance of survival. But they chose not to. So, no. If he did it, if he killed one, or both, of them, I couldn't forgive him. We've known each other for half our lives, but some things are just . . . unforgiveable, aren't they?'

'Yeah,' Chloe says, softly. 'If somebody hurt someone I loved, I don't think I could forgive them either.' From the serious look in her eyes, I don't doubt she means it.

We sit quietly for a moment, neither of us able to find a way back from the dark turn our conversation has taken, until a voice drifts down the stairs.

'Chlo-eee, come fiiind me . . .'

Looking somewhat relieved, Chloe gets to her feet. 'I'd better go,' she says. I nod, and she leaves the room and races upstairs, and a moment later I hear her giggling as Freya's hiding place is discovered.

An hour later, Chloe leaves and I hurry Freya upstairs to change her out of her clothes, which are dusty from having hidden in some of the house's less housekept corners. I strip her down to her underwear, then help her change into a clean top and a pair of shorts, then send her on her way with strict instructions that hide and seek is off the agenda for the rest of the day.

'Aww,' she moans.

'Never mind "aww",' I tell her. 'Now, go and get your shoes on, and ask Grandpa if he wants to join us for ice cream.'

She whoops with delight. Freya never passes up an opportunity for ice cream.

When I go to get changed myself, I find that I've run out of clean T-shirts. We've stayed in Westhaven longer than I expected. I gather our dirty clothes into a pile to take downstairs and put into the wash, then search through my old dresser, in the hope of finding an old top or T-shirt I can wear.

To my surprise, in the bottom drawer, I glimpse a familiar swatch of red fabric and pull out an old Bruce Springsteen Tour T-shirt I thought I'd lost years ago. I must have left it behind after a previous visit to Dad's and he tidied it away. I hold it to my nose, give it a sniff. It smells musty, and could probably do with a wash, but I put it on anyway, relieved to find that, while it's a little snug, it still fits, more or less. It feels good to be wearing it. Martin bought it for me when he took me to see Springsteen for my twenty-first birthday. Having it on brings back happy memories, and makes me feel closer to him. Martin that is, not Bruce.

It's funny how the smallest of things can make us feel better.

I wonder what Martin is up to right now. He's probably stressing about his big meeting tomorrow, putting the final touches to his presentation. Doing whatever it takes to make his boss happy. I take out my phone and drop him a message: **Hope everything is going OK and you're not working too hard. We miss you xxx**. Then I grab Freya's inhalers off the bedside table, and head downstairs.

Ten minutes later, we park up in the middle of town. While I get Freya out of the car seat, Dad goes and pays for parking, and comes back three minutes later grumbling to himself, 'Two pound, for an hour? Daylight robbery.'

The three of us stroll down the high street, to what used to be a trendy little café called Doolallys that I occasionally used to visit with Martin and Amy. Now it's an ice cream parlour, selling what appears to be a hundred different flavours and toppings. Dad and I stick with vanilla, but Freya goes nuts and has three scoops – chocolate, caramel and strawberry, with sprinkles and raspberry sauce.

Outside, Freya and Dad eat their ice creams and hold hands, walking a short way behind me as we meander through the streets, and the sound of them chattering away about this and that is almost enough to lift my spirits. Things are going to be OK, I tell myself. Connor is going to be released without charge. The police are going to find out who really killed Evan. Everything is going to be just fine.

And then I see Dalton and his sister, sitting at a wooden table outside The Grapes. Please God don't let them have seen me, I think, but it's too late. As I draw level, Dalton lifts his eyes, as if he can sense my presence, and looks directly at me. I come to a stop, stand there, frozen, with ice cream dripping down over my fingers. He looks so full of hate, and now his sister notices him staring and turns to peer over her shoulder too. She looks broken, in ruins. And here I am, walking down the street eating ice cream like everything's fine. What must they think of me? That I am heartless? That I don't care that they are in pain, that they are grieving for the little boy so cruelly taken from them? But I do care, I really do. As mad as it sounds, I even consider going over and saying something, because surely, anything would be better than just standing here. But then Dad bumps into the back of me.

'Oh dear!' he cries. 'I've got ice cream on you.' He makes a fuss of digging a tissue out of his pocket and wiping at the arm of my T-shirt.

'It's OK, Dad,' I tell him.

'Nonsense,' he says. 'Just hold still a minute.'

Dalton is still staring at me, and he's not the only one. There are others looking in our direction now. Some sitting outside The Grapes, like Dalton and his sister, but others merely passing by, loaded down with shopping. It's as if everyone knows what's happened, as if Connor's arrest has confirmed what they've believed all along, about him, and about me. He is a child killer, and I am the woman who got him released from prison so he could go on to kill again.

Even Freya notices. 'Why are those people looking at us?' she asks.

'They're not, darling,' says Dad, rather sweetly, and our eyes meet, and I know he's lying, and I love him dearly for it. He blots away the last of the ice cream on my sleeve, then balls up the tissue and throws it in a nearby bin.

'Come on, you two,' he says, cheerfully. 'Let's go.'

We head back to the car, though I dump my ice cream in a bin on the way, having lost my appetite.

I drive us back to the house in near silence, pleased that Dad is here to keep Freya entertained, but otherwise in a dark and desperate mood. I feel helpless, waiting for news that I'm frightened to hear.

As much as I try to deny it, to myself and to others – to Chloe and Flora – the monstrous possibility that I've built my entire career on a terrible lie has got its teeth into me. It's a prospect so huge and terrible, that I'm having to fight the urge to drive right past Dad's and keep going all the way back to London. I want to be far away from Westhaven. I don't want everyone here to be right, and me to be wrong. I don't want to face up to what might happen if Connor doesn't come home soon.

Martin was right. I shouldn't have come back here. I wanted to help, but what help have I been? To Evan and his family, to Connor and his grandmother? None whatsoever.

I was a fool to think I could finish Amy's story.

I feel nauseous and, even though we're nearly back at Dad's, I wind down the window for some fresh air. A moment later, when I pull into the driveway, I tell him to grab Freya's inhalers from the glovebox while I release her from the car seat, then I get out and lean against the door, breathless and panicked.

Freya knocks on the window. 'Let me out, Mummy!'

'Just a minute, sweetheart.' I open the door, start unfastening the straps, and am almost finished when she points over my shoulder. 'Who's that man?'

I spin around, convinced that Dalton has made his way back to the house, that seeing me, sauntering through town eating ice cream, has tipped him over the edge.

But it isn't Dalton sat waiting on Dad's doorstep. It's Connor.

# 46

Dad hurries Freya through the door, and tells her to go upstairs and wash her hands. 'Don't touch a thing until you're done,' he calls after her. 'I don't want your sticky fingers all over the furniture.'

'Yes, Grandpa,' replies Freya.

Once she's out of earshot, he comes back, looks at Connor before saying to me, 'You're OK with this? Because if you're not, I'll ask him to leave.' He fixes Connor with a steely glare, which is the sweetest of things, because Dad's a full two feet shorter than Connor, and probably seventy pounds lighter. The idea of him forcing Connor do anything he doesn't want to do is frankly ridiculous, but bless him for wanting to protect me.

'Thanks, Dad,' I tell him. 'But it's OK. Go on in, I'll let you know if I need you.'

With a parting glance, one not dissimilar to the look he used to give Martin when we first started dating – *You hurt my daughter, and it'll be the end of you* – Dad leaves us to it.

'He still doesn't like me much, does he?' Connor says, once we're alone.

'Nope,' I tell him. 'Come on.'

I lead him around the side of the house and into the garden, where there's less chance of us being spotted by the neighbours, and we stand on the lawn, a short distance from the house.

'What happened, Con? Why are you here? *How* are you here?'

Even if the police didn't have enough evidence to charge him, which they clearly didn't, I'd have thought they'd have kept him in custody for the maximum time permitted. But somehow, a day after his arrest, he's standing here in front of me, unwashed and dishevelled, but otherwise OK.

'Released without charge,' Connor announces, a little smugly, then he catches my eye. 'What, did you think the next time you saw me would be in court?'

'Of course I didn't,' I say, but something in my voice gives me away, lets him know that it had at least crossed my mind.

He looks offended, let down. 'Jesus, Jess.'

'What do you expect, Con? You lied to me,' I say. 'You told me you didn't go online, that you didn't use the internet. You said you barely knew how to work a computer, and now I find out that you followed Evan on social media, that you sent him messages—'

'That's not true,' he cries, then catches himself. 'I mean, not all of it.'

'Not all of it?'

Connor sighs and shakes his head, as if he's sick of talking about it, and usually I'd be right there with him, because an innocent man shouldn't have to keep explaining himself. But if he wants my help, he's going to have to come clean.

'Come on, Con,' I say. 'Help me out here. What am I supposed to think?'

He takes a seat on the steps that lead down to the lawn and hangs his head, and after a moment I go to him.

'Move over,' I tell him, and he shuffles along to make room, and I take a seat beside him.

'Last year, I started going to the library,' he tells me. 'I thought it would be a good idea to learn how to use the computers, so I could maybe get a proper job one day, and . . . I suppose I got curious. I went on some of the *Born Killer* forums and message boards.' He looks over and his eyes go wide. 'You should have seen it, Jess, the things they were saying about me, and about you. Horrible things. I mean, I can understand it with me, after what I was accused of, but you? I couldn't just let people say that stuff. It isn't right.'

'Oh, Con,' I say. 'You just have to ignore them.'

Though I know how hard that can be, given the amount of time I used to spend trawling the message boards myself, stoking my own outrage and wallowing in the negativity of it all.

'I know that now,' Connor says. 'But at the time . . . It just seemed wrong. So I started posting, under a fake name, setting some of them straight. Anyway, there was this one user who kept saying all this stuff about you being a liar and me being a murderer. Called himself Racor Dragonstorm, whatever that means. He posted all the time, and I'd post a reply, and we'd go back and forth. He used to make me so mad sometimes, but I suppose I sort of got used to us writing to each other . . .'

The name gives it away. 'It was Evan, wasn't it?'

He nods. 'I didn't know that at first, but when I searched, I found that name in other places too, on message boards about Dungeons & Dragons, nerd stuff. Then I found his social media and his YouTube videos, and I couldn't believe he was just this little kid. He'd say all these horrible things about me and you over here, and then he'd go and post a silly video that nobody would watch, or a picture of a little painted model, over there. And nobody ever commented or liked anything he did. He didn't seem to have any friends, online or otherwise. And I suppose we had that in common. I started feeling sorry for him, you know? So, I liked a few of his pictures, commented on his videos, always under a fake name, just so he knew he wasn't alone.'

'So, you're Fenchurch?'

He nods. 'It's a character from *The Hitchhiker's Guide to the Galaxy*.' I give him a look of surprise and he adds, 'I read a lot while I was inside. Anyway, I thought he might trust me more if he thought I was a bit of nerd, like he was.'

I'm not sure Evan would have made the connection, but it's good thinking.

Connor continues. 'Most of the time I'd go to the library when I wanted to post, but one day last month I was in there and I saw him. He was right there, using the computers, just like me. I usually went in when it was quiet, when there were no kids around. Maybe it was the holidays or something. Anyway, I don't think he noticed me.'

Oh, he noticed you all right, I think. That's why he visited the library when he was looking for you, on the night he was killed.

'I thought I'd better be more careful after that,' Connor goes on. 'I got myself a phone and that's what I used from then on in. And I'm sorry I lied to you, I just . . . I knew it would look bad.'

I sigh. 'You were right about that.'

'When I found out he'd been killed, I got worried. I deleted all my accounts and thought that would be that, but now they tell me you can't really delete things online, that it's always still there, if you look hard enough.'

'And the laptop? The messages that lured him up to the woods?'

He shakes his head, holds up his hands. 'That wasn't me, Jess. I've never even seen it before, I swear on Nan's life.'

'You're telling me someone planted a laptop in your bedroom?'

'Right.'

'They snuck into your house, past all the protestors and press, and planted it in your bedroom, and you knew nothing about it, even though you haven't left the house in, what, five days now?'

'Exactly,' he says. 'I know how it sounds, but it's the truth. And that's what I told the police. I followed Evan on social media, but there ain't no laws against that. Someone must have planted that laptop before all this got started, before the protestors appeared. Maybe even before the lad's body was found.'

He's starting to sound like one of the *Born Killer* conspiracy nuts. 'Con . . .'

'Do you really think I'd be standing here now if it was mine? Don't you think the police have been all over it? They couldn't even find my fingerprints on it.'

'I suppose,' I say.

'You have to believe me, Jess.'

But I don't *have* to, do I? I've given him the benefit of the doubt for so long, have fought for him, put my career, and my reputation, on the line. And this isn't just a question of whether I believe him or not, it's about whether I trust him to be here, to be around me and to be around Freya. Would anybody blame me for walking away? For not taking that risk?

'Jess. Come on . . .' He fixes those big blue eyes of his on me, so full of sadness and regret at how things have turned out.

I want to believe him, truly I do. Until now, the drive to protect him, to save him from those who brand him a born killer, and even from himself, has eclipsed any doubts I might have secretly held about his innocence. Amy loved him, and I loved her, and if I can't find out who killed her, the least I can do is look after her boyfriend.

But there has to be a limit, doesn't there? A threshold where the possibility, however slight, that I've been sheltering a monster in the guise of a friend becomes a risk too big to take; a moment where I must put myself and my family first.

'I just . . . I don't know anymore, Con,' I admit.

His mouth falls open, his face clouded with disbelief. 'You too?' he whispers, then he pushes himself to his feet.

'Con, wait,' I call after him. 'Don't go. I didn't mean . . .'

But he isn't listening. He walks away, disappearing around the corner without a further word and without looking back. I think about going after him, but then I hear the sweet sound of Freya's laughter from somewhere inside the house, and instead I head indoors.

# 47

## Martin – 5.22 a.m.

When Martin passes the petrol station at the top of the valley, relief washes over him. He's reached the edge of town, which means, with only seven or eight miles of the journey left to go, he'll be at Frank's in less than twenty minutes. Freya will have her inhalers, and Jessie will head back to the house as soon as it's safe for her to travel.

He wishes he'd been able to hear more of what she was saying when she called, but the signal was beyond awful. He only managed to catch a few words, something about the storm and hoping someone would arrive soon, presumably him. She must have spoken with Frank, so already knew about the inhaler situation, which made perfect sense. If she had signal, the first thing she'd do would be to check in on Freya.

After the call dropped, he'd tried phoning her back several times, but the call refused to connect. Nevertheless, hearing her voice, even in those brief, broken fragments, soothed him. Now, that niggling worry about her being caught up in some in dreadful accident, the car swept away by floodwaters, or crushed by a windblown HGV, has retreated entirely. Wherever Jessie is, all she has to do is sit tight and wait for the storm to pass. She even said she was well – at least that's what he thinks she said.

Everything is going to be fine.

He's tired, and his body is aching from having been sat in the same position for so long but he's feeling good. He made the right choice, he thinks. Even if Freya has slept through, better a long drive, through treacherous conditions, than her waking up in a panic and having a full-blown asthma attack. And then, as if on cue, his phone rings. 'Jessie's Dad' on the caller ID. He presses the button to answer.

'. . . awake . . . for you,' Frank says, his voice a broken whisper over the car's speakers.

'Say again, Frank. You're breaking up,' Martin shouts, as if that might somehow improve the signal between them.

'I said, . . . ya's awake. She's . . .'

'You still there?' It's no good, he's gone again. But Martin pieces together Frank's message from the fragments of syllables he's heard so far. Freya's awake, and she's asking for him. Which isn't good, but at least he's almost there. He has just crested a rise at the top of the valley that would usually offer him an elevated view of the town, but right now is washed out by the rain. Between the rapid push and pull of the wiper-blades, he can make out a haze of lights in the distance, but nothing more.

'Frank?' Martin tries again, but the signal has dropped off entirely.

He pulls in a few deep breaths. On a normal day, it would take him another twenty minutes to get to Frank's. This morning he can probably do it in half that time. Even if Freya's asthma is bad, she can hold on for another ten minutes, can't she?

*Hang in there, baby-girl*, he thinks. *I'm coming.*

Then Freya's voice fills the car. 'Daddy?'

It is loud and oddly clear. An explosion of warmth spreads through Martin's chest.

'Hey, sweetheart. Are you OK?'

'. . . ant Mummy.'

Of course she wants her mummy. 'I know sweetheart, but Mummy's not there right now. I'm going be with you really soon though, OK?'

A pause, and then the words come that he has been dreading.

'. . . need my breather.'

Is it just his imagination, or can he hear her wheezing on the other end of the line? Perhaps it's just interference, the thin hiss and crackle of a bad signal. Still, panic unfurls inside him.

'Listen to me, sweetie,' he says. 'Do you remember how to breathe slowly, like you do for Mummy? Breathe in, hold it in for three seconds, then breathe out. Nice and calm, nice and slow. Do it with me.'

'I can't . . .'

'Yes, you can. Come on, sweetheart. In, hold for three, then out . . .'

He makes his breathing loud so Freya can follow his example, but what good is that if she can't hear him?

'Daddy . . . ?'

There's that high- pitched hiss again. Please God, let it just be interference on the line.

'Freya?' Nothing. '*Freya?*'

There's a series of beeps, and the call drops.

Fuck. Martin puts his foot down.

# 48

*One day earlier*

It's just past seven, and Freya's bedtime, but tonight she's too excited to sleep. She jumps up and down on the bed in her nightie. The air is thick and clammy, heavy with heat, electric with anticipation of the storm the weather forecast promised would come this afternoon but is yet to arrive. Perhaps that's why she's so restless.

She fires questions at me, breathless between bounces.

'Who's that . . . man you . . . were talking to . . . downstairs?'

'An old friend of Mummy's,' I tell her, neatly draping her top and leggings over the back of a chair, so she can wear them again tomorrow.

'Has he . . . gone now?'

'Yes, he's gone.' Walked away, no doubt feeling that his only friend in the world has turned her back on him. The hurt in his voice comes back to me now – *You too?* – and my stomach churns. How is it fair that I should feel so awful after everything I've done for him?

I'll call round and see him tomorrow, I decide. Make things right.

'What's his name?' Freya asks.

'His name's Connor.' I turn to her. 'Get down, please. You're going to make yourself wheezy. Have you had your brown inhaler?' She nods. 'Right, well it's time to go to sleep then, isn't it?'

'But I'm not . . . sleepy,' she groans.

She might not be, but I am, and I'm not in the mood for a long, drawn-out battle of wills with Freya tonight. Worrying about Connor all day has worn me out, left me emotionally drained. I want to call Martin, say goodnight and wish him luck for his big meeting tomorrow, then take a bath perhaps, decompress.

'Come down, right this second, and get under the covers. Otherwise, there'll be no story.'

Freya bounces up and down a few more times, but I give her my best serious-mummy look, the one that tells her that my patience is wearing thin, and she stops jumping, scrambles up the bed and slips under the covers.

'That's better. Good girl.'

I perch on the edge of the mattress and take a book from the pile on the bedside table, the one about the wolf and the three little pigs. The librarian was right, she does like it.

'Is the man that was downstairs the same as the man on the picture in your office?' Freya asks, out of the blue, and I'm not sure what she means for a second, then I realise she's talking about the framed *Born Killer* poster I used to have hanging above my desk. I'm impressed she remembers it well enough to recognise Connor.

'That's right,' I say. 'Clever girl.'

'Is he a scary man?' she asks. 'He looked scary in the picture.'

Perhaps she means he looked scary because Connor's portrait was composed of two half-faces – the young, and the old him, combined into a single, disjointed portrait. Or maybe she's referring to the part of the poster that showed the older Connor, with his prison tattoos and that troubled look in his eyes.

'No, he's not scary,' I tell her, although right now, I'm not a hundred per cent sure about that.

Freya seems satisfied though. 'OK, good,' she says.

I open the book on my knee. 'Are you ready? Nice and comfy?'

She nods, and I'm about to start reading when my phone vibrates in my pocket.

'That'll be Daddy, messaging to see if you're ready to say goodnight,' I tell her, but when I look, the message isn't from Martin, it's from an unknown number. I press to open it and read it through once, then again, my insides clenching with fear.

God no.

'Mummy? Story time,' Freya moans.

'I know sweetheart, just . . . give Mummy a minute.' I set the book aside, get to my feet. 'I'll be back in just a second.'

I call Chloe as I leave the room, hear the phone ring as I race down the stairs.

Come on, come on, pick up, pick up . . .

She does. 'Hey, what's up?' she says, sounding pleased to hear from me.

'Where are you, right now?'

'At Oscar's,' she says. 'We're going to stay up and watch the storm. Why?'

Shit.

'Can you talk, in private?'

'Sure,' she says. 'It's just me and Oscar. There's no one else here.'

'I didn't mean that. I meant . . .'

I hear a voice in the background. *What does she want?*

I've got to be careful. I can't afford to slip up here.

'It's just that . . .' Think, Jessie. Think. 'We're going home tomorrow,' I announce. 'We'll probably leave first thing, to beat the traffic, and I don't want to go without saying a proper goodbye. I know it's getting late, but do you think you could meet me somewhere?'

'You're going home?' She sounds surprised, and a little disappointed.

'Yes. Um, I think it's for the best. So . . . can I see you?'

'Sure,' she says. 'Come over if you like.'

No, that won't work. 'Could we meet at yours instead? Freya's asthma isn't so good and I don't want to be away from her for long. Your place is closer, isn't it?'

'Um yeah, I mean, not by loads, but sure. I can be there in, like, twenty minutes?'

'Twenty minutes. Perfect. I'll see you there,' I say, trying to sound casual, like I'm not panicking inside, like I'm not doing my utmost to get her away from her boyfriend as quickly as possible, because Peter Rand has just messaged me to tell me that he has remembered the name of the boy who broke Evan's arm.

# 49

Jessie – 5.30 a.m.

Either the rain has got worse, or water is finding its way into the well by other means, seeping through the ground, through little cracks between the stones, or through the hand- and footholds I dug out earlier. Because the water around me is rising faster now. When it covers my breasts, I feel a new chill deep inside me, as if an ice-cold hand has closed around my heart.

'Please, tell them to hurry. It's getting worse,' I tell Fiona, as I fumble the phone from one from hand to another, my arms aching from having to hold it above the waterline.

It's getting worse, and I'm getting worse too. Exhaustion, confusion, drowsiness . . . Are these signs of hypothermia?

'They're really close now,' she tells me. 'We just have to make sure that you stay conscious. Keep talking, Jessica.'

I do my best, to trust her, to believe her when she says help is nearly here, and I do my best to remember, to talk her through what happened as fragments of memory come back to me.

'He lied . . .' I say, through chattering teeth. 'Oscar . . . he said he didn't know Evan, that they'd never met and that they went to different schools . . .' I trail off, suddenly too tired to continue.

God, I'm exhausted. My leg hurts, everything aches. The cold is in my bones and the water is rising and I have so little time left. Is there any point in going on?

'Jessica . . .'

'I know,' I say, because she's going to ask me to keep talking. 'Just . . . give me a minute.' Time to catch my breath.

It's funny. It feels like I've been down here forever, as if it's been days, not hours, since I've seen daylight.

I used to try to convince myself it was a good thing Amy died from an asthma attack, rather than from her injuries. Don't get me wrong, it would have been horrible for her, of course it would. I've seen the panic in Freya's eyes when she's having an attack, when she can't get enough air inside her lungs no matter how hard she tries. For that to be happening to Amy, while she was down here, all alone in the dark . . . She must have been terrified. But I always thought that at least it would have been relatively quick, and the pathologist who carried out the post-mortem confirmed that the progression from respiratory arrest to cardiac arrest was very swift, the whole thing over in a matter of minutes. I thought that far better than her being alive down here for days, waiting to be found while she bled out into the murky water. Only now, I'm not so sure. Because time is different down here. It goes slow when it should go fast, and fast when it should go slow. Did it feel like minutes to Amy? Or did her suffering go on and on, for hours, or days, even?

Fiona's voice: 'Jessica?'

I come back to myself, take a deep breath, try to focus. 'When Rand messaged me . . . I realised that Oscar was right about the schools in a way; he and Evan . . . they did go to different schools. But they didn't used to. They did know each other, because he was the boy who'd broken Evan's arm. He lied to me about it. Why would he do that? Why would he lie to me, unless he had something to hide? And then there were the grazes on his knees, the bruise on Chloe's wrist . . . It all started to add up.'

# 50

*One day earlier*

'You're going out now?' Dad says, alarmed. 'You know there's a storm on the way, a bad one. Is everything OK?' He's in the kitchen, washing up, jazz playing on the radio.

'It's fine,' I tell him. 'There's just something I have to do.'

There's no time to explain. I need to see that Chloe is safe with my own eyes, and that she is far away from Oscar. Once I've done that, I'll call Bill and tell him everything. If Oscar is the bully Rand claims him to be, and if he is lying about never having met Evan, that's reason enough to consider the possibility he might have been the one who lured Evan up to the woods on the night he was killed. I think back to my first meeting with Oscar, the grazes on his knees and the cut above his right eye. How stupid of me not to make the connection sooner.

'If you can go up and read Freya her story, and once she's asleep keep an ear out, just in case she wakes up. I won't be back late.'

'Can't it wait until the morning? You don't want to end up getting stranded.'

I shake my head. 'If it gets bad, I'll take shelter somewhere. Sorry, I've got to go.'

It's too warm for a coat, so I leave without one and fifteen minutes later I'm jogging up the path to Chloe's front door. I knock, and after a moment the door opens, though it isn't Chloe who answers, it's a man in his late thirties. He's well turned out, clean shaven and wearing suit trousers with a light blue shirt, open at the collar and cuffs. He stands at the doorway in his socked feet, looking for all the world like he's just got home and kicked off his shoes after a hard day's work at the office. He looks tired, a touch bedraggled, but if this is Chloe's dad, he certainly doesn't look like he's just come off a three-day drinking session.

'Hi,' I say. 'I'm looking for Chloe.'

*Please be here*, I think. *Please be safe.*

'Sorry,' the man says. 'She's probably at her boyfriend's place. I'm her dad though, is there something I can help you with? Is everything all right? She's OK, isn't she?'

Concern is etched into his face, and I'm struck by how different he seems, and sounds, to the man I spoke to over the phone. I'd expected a rather shambolic figure, someone who carries with him the soft features and the bad complexion of a heavy drinker. But he looks together in a way that doesn't fit with the picture Chloe painted of him. Not that this means anything, I remind myself. Just because he looks all smart and well-presented, that doesn't mean he doesn't have a problem. People are good at hiding the less attractive parts of their personalities, especially addicts.

'I'm Jessie,' I explain. 'She's been doing the work experience with me, and she was supposed to meet me here.'

His brow furrows. 'Work experience?'

'We spoke about it over the phone?' I say, but he shakes his head, looking genuinely puzzled. 'Look, it's fine,' I tell him. 'But when we talked, I asked if you minded Chloe doing some work experience, and you said you didn't, just as long as it didn't cost you anything. She's been helping me for the last few days. I spoke with her twenty minutes ago, and she said she'd meet me here.'

'There must be some sort of mistake,' he says. 'I'd remember if we'd spoken.'

Perhaps if he was three sheets to the wind he wouldn't.

'I think I know what's happened here,' he says. 'I think Chloe might have been having you on, playing some sort of joke. That girl's a law unto herself these days. I do try, but . . . I just can't get through to her half the time. Teenagers, right?'

'Right,' I say. And now I'm the one who's confused.

The more he speaks, the more at odds he is with my expectations, and the more I believe that he really doesn't remember our conversation. But if I didn't speak to him, then who did I speak to?

He goes on. 'You know, she used to be a real daddy's girl. We were so close. But then . . . I don't know what happened. It's like she hit puberty and became an entirely different person. I hardly see her these days. She comes and goes when she pleases, shows up when she wants to borrow a tenner, but that's about it.'

In all of our interactions, Chloe's been kind and considerate. She doesn't strike me as badly behaved, but kids are different with strangers than they are with their parents.

'Teenage girls can be a challenge,' I say.

'You're telling me.' He gives an exhausted-sounding laugh. 'I keep telling myself it's just a phase she's going through. That one day, I'll get my little girl back, but . . . I don't know. Maybe once she's moved out, and gone to drama school? Maybe a bit of distance will do us good.'

*Film school*, I think. It's film school she wants to go to, not drama school. An easy mistake to make. But it just goes to prove the distance between them.

I don't want to doubt Chloe's story about her dad being a drinker, about him being violent towards her. But I've got to admit, having met the man, I'm starting to wonder. Not that I think she'd deliberately set out to deceive me, but might she lie for another reason? To protect someone, perhaps?

'Do you want to come in and wait?' Chloe's dad says. He seems at a loss, doesn't know what to do. He's not the only one.

'No, thank you,' I tell him. 'I'll catch up with her another time.'

'No problem,' he says. 'I'll tell her you came by. Take care, now.' His eyes flick heavenward. 'And you might want to get home pretty sharpish. There's a storm coming.'

He closes the door and I head back to the car, get in and sit there, unsure of my next move, unsure of what's true and what isn't. I could be wrong, of course: about him, about Chloe, and about Oscar too. I suppose the only way I'll find out for sure is by speaking to her, but how can I do that if she doesn't turn up when she says she will and doesn't answer her phone?

And then I remember. I know exactly how to find her.

I open the Friend Tracker app, wondering if she put it on my phone in case of a scenario like this one. Chloe might love her boyfriend, but does she also, on some level, fear him? Did she put the app on my phone not because she didn't want me to worry if she went missing, but because she wanted someone to know how to find her if she did?

The app takes a moment to open, a little wheel turning circles in the middle of the screen, then her name pops up, I click on it and a new screen appears with a pin at its centre with a little picture of Chloe's face on it. But the map doesn't finish loading. There are no roads, streets or buildings shown. Chloe's icon floats in a field of grey. It's found her, but it can't find seem to find anything else. What use is that?

I jab the screen with my finger, move the map around until a small L-shaped building slides into view at the bottom of the screen. The label next to it reads: The Old Mill Tearooms.

Oh no. Please don't tell me . . .

I pinch-zoom out, and the building shrinks and I realise that the app is working perfectly well. It's not that it can't find any nearby buildings and roads, it's because there aren't any.

Chloe is in Cooper's Wood.

# 51

## Martin – 5.45 a.m.

Martin tries calling Frank back, voice-dialling him, over and over as the car drops down into the valley on its final descent into Westhaven, but each time he calls, a robotic voice answers, telling him they are sorry, but his call cannot be connected at this time, and with each failed attempt to get through, the feeling of dread in the pit of his stomach grows.

What if he's too late? What if, by the time he gets there, Freya has already taken her last breath?

It could happen. Asthma is so common, a lot of people think it's no big deal, but people die from it all the time. Martin knows this, has done the research. Thousands of people every year suffer fatal asthma attacks, their airways narrowing until they can't breathe enough oxygen in, or enough carbon dioxide out. If it gets bad, their skin can become cyanotic, taking on a bluish tinge. If it gets *really* bad, and treatment isn't administered in time, vital organs begin to fail.

How stupid of him, he thinks. Instead of driving halfway across the country with Freya's spare inhalers on the passenger seat, he should have stayed in London and put all his efforts into calling people – doctors, chemists, hospitals – anybody who could get a supply of asthma medication to someone who needs it. But he didn't do that, because in the panic of the moment, it felt too risky putting her safety in somebody else's hands.

Martin is not a praying man. But right now, as he speeds through Westhaven's empty, rain-soaked streets as fast as he dares, he mutters under his breath – *Please God, let her be all right. Please God, let her be all right.* He only hopes Frank has the good sense to call an ambulance if Freya's attack gets any worse.

The final mile to Frank's house seems to take forever, as if new streets have sprung up out of nowhere since he was last here, but eventually, he turns into Frank's driveway and parks up, the car skewed across the gravel. He grabs the medication off the passenger seat. The second he steps out into the open he is drenched from head to toe by the rain, but he barely notices as he runs the few steps to the front door, not wanting to lose a single second, and hammers on it with his fist.

*Come on, come on . . .*

A moment, then he hears the sound of the door being unlocked from the inside. It opens and Frank steps back so Martin can come in out of the rain.

'Everything's OK,' Frank tells him, as he closes the door. 'She's fine. Don't worry.'

Fine? She didn't sound fine over the phone. She sounded like she could barely breathe, but Frank doesn't look in the slightest bit worried. He looks almost relaxed, as if Freya having an asthma attack isn't something to be overly concerned about.

'Where is she?' Martin is breathless with panic, can feel his heart thumping hard behind his ribcage. He's been sat in car for the last four hours, but it feels like he's just run a marathon.

'She's up in Jessie's old room,' says Frank. 'But, Martin, before you go up there, there's something you should know . . .'

Frank steps in front of Martin, partly blocking his path to the stairs.

Something he should know? What is this? One minute he's saying Freya's fine, the next he's acting like Martin needs to brace himself before seeing his own daughter.

'I just . . . I don't want you to be upset,' Frank says.

Martin pushes Frank aside, takes the stairs two at a time and rushes down the hallway to Jessie's old bedroom.

As he pushes open the door, he can't help picturing what he'll find on the other side; his little girl in distress, struggling to pull in the breath she so desperately needs. Or worse, his little girl no longer struggling, her lips tinged blue, her chest horrifyingly still, having already taken her last breath.

He doesn't find either of these things, but what he does find is terrible in its own way, because Connor Starling is sitting on the edge of his daughter's bed.

# 52

*One day earlier*

I park up in the small and otherwise empty car park outside the Old Mill Tearooms, the quaint little café closed for the evening, the gingham curtains drawn and the menu boards and signs advertising ice cream packed away. I'd hoped there might still be some people milling around; tourists, having just finished a day's hiking, or locals out walking their dogs, someone who might have seen Chloe or Oscar perhaps, but it looks like the oncoming storm has sent everyone home early.

I grab my bag off the back seat, get out of the car and head for the broad trail that leads into the woods.

Rain spots the earth, fat drops that make a sound as they land in the dirt. The trail will turn to mud when the storm hits, but right now dry leaves crunch underfoot and clouds of dust kick up with each step. Sweat dampens my T-shirt under my arms and at the base of my spine, but I pick up the pace and, as I walk, I check the Friend Tracker app on my phone. The little pin with Chloe's face on it is still floating in a field of grey. She's out here somewhere, and I have to find her, before it's too late, before Oscar does to her what he did to Evan.

I should dial 999, of course I should, but some stubborn part of me resists. I come to a stop in the middle of the trail, stare at my phone, appalled at myself. How selfish of me, to cling to the hope that I can be the one to fix things, to make up for my past failings by being a hero. I need to make the call, and I'm about to do just that when I hear a sound up ahead. I look up in time to see a flash of colour racing through the trees in the distance.

It could be a startled deer, but instinct tells me otherwise.

I put my phone away and start to run. If Oscar has hurt Chloe, I need to find her fast.

Heart pounding, I race down the trail and before long find myself in a familiar part of the woods. Please don't tell me he's taken her there, anywhere but there. I scan the ground to my right, in search of the place where a thread of the trail curves off and disappears down a small embankment.

For a moment, I worry the woods are too overgrown, that the path has been obscured and that I'll never find it. But then something stops me in my tracks, a view that tugs at my memory, that tells me I'm in the right place.

There it is. The path to the well.

I clamber down and push my way through the branches, my arms held up in front of my face to protect my eyes. Sharp twigs tug at my clothes and scratch warnings into my skin. A root snags my foot and I stumble, almost go down. I reach out, grab a branch to steady myself and get a palmful of thorns. I snatch back my hand and watch as a spot of blood beads along my lifeline.

It's almost as if Cooper's Wood is trying to stop me from going any further, from reaching the well. Does it know what happened here? I wonder. Does it know the well is a cursed place? It sounds like silly superstition, but is it so mad to think that places might have memories too?

I press on, thirty or so yards down the muddy path, until I reach a low tunnel through the trees, branches that have interweaved in an intricate arch that looks almost man-made. I duck my head, squeeze through the gap, and emerge into the clearing. And there it is, nestled among the overgrown trees. A low, ominous stone structure, emerging from the earth. The place where my best friend took her last breath.

The sight of it doesn't just make my stomach churn and flip. It dries my mouth. It makes my heart beat twice as fast as it should. I want to turn around and run in the opposite direction. But I can't do that. Not if Chloe's here, not if she needs me.

There is litter scattered around – empty beer cans, scraps of tin-foil, faded pages from dirty magazines – but no sign that anybody has been here recently.

I call Chloe's name, the sound of my voice oddly muted in the clearing, and listen hard for an answer, but hear nothing. Not even the birds are singing here.

Did the app get it wrong? Has it brought me here for no reason?

I take my phone out of my bag and check again. A message on the screen tells me I've lost internet signal, but Chloe's pin is still hovering in the same place it was when I last looked. She should be standing right in front of me.

Maybe she's left already, or maybe she was never here, but I can't leave without making sure.

I move forward, taking slow steps towards the well, my heart thumping in my temples.

When I reach it, I pull in a deep breath and hold it. I don't want to do this, I don't want to look down there, but know that I have to.

I lean over and peer into the darkness, down into the depths, and see . . . nothing. There are no desperate faces peering back at me, no beaten, broken bodies. There's nothing down there, thank God.

I breathe out, am overcome with relief, made dizzy by it. I take a seat on the well's broad stone rim, so I don't fall down, and try to calm myself. Take deep breaths.

*In, hold for three, then out . . .*

What am I doing here? Why didn't I call the police as soon as I thought Chloe might be in danger and let them handle it, like a normal person would? Is it perhaps because some part of me wanted her to be here? Did a part of me want to find her at the bottom of the well, so I could save her, because I never got the chance to do that for Amy?

Jesus, what's wrong with me?

It is such a sad and awful place . . . So why can't I let it go? Why can't I move on?

Chloe isn't trapped down Dutton's Well, but perhaps I am. Perhaps I've been trapped down there ever since Amy died, unable to find out who killed her, unable to let go. Unable to forgive myself.

I've worked so hard to make things right. But the truth is, you can't ever go back. You can't undo what's done, no matter how hard you try. It's time I accepted that. And it's time to say goodbye.

A rushing sound behind me, the quick snap of branches underfoot.

Someone's coming, racing through the trees at speed. I start to stand, to turn my head in the direction of the sound so I can see who it is, but before I have the chance, I feel a hard shove in the middle of my back that knocks me forwards. My balance goes. I slam both hands down on the stone rim of the well to stop myself from falling, but my centre of gravity has already moved beyond me.

My palms slip over wet stone, my feet leave the earth, and down I go, head first into the dark.

# 53

## Jessie – 5.53 a.m.

I remember why I came here now. I was trying to find Chloe. I had the app on my phone and I followed her signal, and it led me right here, to Cooper's Wood, to the well.

What if Oscar's hurt her, or worse? Killed her. Left her body in the woods, like he did Evan's?

'You have to tell the police. They have to find her,' I tell Fiona.

'Jessica, please try not to worry,' she says, in that oh-so-measured way of hers. 'I'll let them know and they can . . . officers to Chloe's address . . . she's OK.'

I know keeping calm is what Fiona does, but shouldn't she be at least a little bit more concerned that a young girl's life might be at risk here? And from the possible killer of Evan Cullen?

'You must tell them to hurry,' I say. 'Oscar's dangerous. I think he might have been the one to put me down here. If he thought I was getting close to the truth, he might have done something to Chloe, then decided he needed to get rid of me too.'

It makes perfect sense. He lured me here, just like he did Evan. Only instead of pretending to be somebody else on the internet, he used Chloe's phone.

'Jessica, slow down. You're . . . tired, confused . . .'

'I am *not* confused. Why aren't you listening to me?'

'Jessica . . .' The signal drops, Fiona's voice reduced to a series of broken syllables, '. . . hard . . . you . . . Evan . . .'

'Fiona?'

'. . . the cold . . . you mustn't . . . Focus on remembering . . . truth . . . to you, wants to hear.'

I can't hear a bloody thing.

I check the phone's screen, see the single bar of signal flickering on and off in the top right corner. Not this again. I know it's a miracle that I have any sort of signal down here at all, but seeing as I do, why does it have to fail on me when I need it most?

I hold the phone up as high as I can and wave it back and forth, as if I can pluck some extra signal from the air.

I call out. 'Fiona? Can you hear me?'

'. . . essica? . . . can hear you, is . . . OK?'

A little better. I pull the phone down, and as I do, it beeps twice. I check the screen, see a notification slide in from the top, and my heart leaps.

'Jessica, are you there?'

'I've got a voicemail, from Martin,' I tell her, thrilled to receive some contact from the outside world.

He must be going out of his mind, sitting there with the police, waiting for news of my rescue. He's probably been trying to call me for ages.

'. . . good for you,' Fiona says. 'I'm sure you can't wait to hear . . . but it would be better to wait until we've got you out of there, then you'll be able to speak to him properly.'

'I want to listen to it now.' I *have* to listen to it now. I need to hear his voice.

'Jessica, we've talked about this . . . must stay on the call. We can't afford to lose . . .'

'It's OK,' I tell her. 'I can put you on hold . . .' At least I think I can.

I bring up the phone's keypad, and sure enough there's a button that says Add Call. If I click on that, I can call my voicemail and keep Fiona on the line. That should work, shouldn't it? I know it's a risk, but it's one I'm prepared to take to hear my husband's voice for what could be the final time.

'Jessica, don't—'

'I'll be back,' I tell her. I hit the Add Call button to put her on hold, then press 1 to dial my voicemail and a voice tells me I have a new message from four twenty-six this morning.

Do I want to play it now? Damn right, I do.

I press 1 again and Martin's voice, breathless and a little stressed sounding, comes over the speaker, and what he tell me leaves me reeling. He's driving to Westhaven because Dad didn't bring Freya's medication in from the car when I asked him to – no doubt he was distracted by the sight of Connor on his doorstep – but I mustn't worry because he has her spare inhalers with him. He should be with her soon. He signs off: 'Hope you're OK. Call me as soon as you can and . . . I suppose I'll see you when you get back. Love you, honey.'

Relief at hearing his voice is cancelled out by the news that Freya is without her medication. I remember now; she told me she'd taken her inhaler when I was putting her to bed, but she can't have. I should have checked, should have made sure they were by her bedside table like I usually do . . .

And then it hits me.

I check the time on the phone's screen. Martin left the voicemail an hour and a half ago, by which time he was already on the way to Westhaven. But Fiona told me the police carried out welfare checks on Freya and him, that they visited both Dad's place, and our home in London. But Martin isn't at home. He can't be sitting with a police officer, nervously waiting for news of my rescue, because he's on the road, and has been for hours. I suppose the police could have called him while he was driving, told him what's happened over the phone – but that's not what Fiona said. She was quite clear. She told me everything was fine, that Martin and Freya and Dad were all OK, which isn't true either seeing as Freya is without her medication.

She's lying to me. Why would she do that?

The voicemail hangs up, and as I try to make sense of what I've just heard, I hear Fiona's voice, clear and unbroken. 'Jessica? Are you still there? Is everything OK?'

'Yes. I'm still here,' I say, in a daze.

'That's good,' she says. 'I hope hearing your husband's voice has helped you to feel a little better. Remember, the police are with him right now. They'll make sure he's OK.'

Another lie. What is going on here?

As she steers the conversation back to me, back to the unspoken truth that has resulted in someone putting me down here, I begin to wonder: what else has she lied about? Because the fact is, after hours of waiting for rescue, I'm still stuck down here, and even if the storm is raging up above, and the roads are flooded and blocked, they would have found a way to get to me by now, wouldn't they?

# BORN KILLER –
# SHOOTING SCRIPT

## S02 – E05: RELEASE

**DI BILL CALDER:** 'What would I say to those who still think Connor's guilty? I'd say look at the evidence, look at the way this young man was treated because of who he was, then ask yourself, if mistakes were made, shouldn't we hold our hands up and try to make things right? We shouldn't be too ashamed to say, "We got this wrong, let's go back to the start and look at this again," because that's the only way we'll ever get to the truth of what happened.'

**JESSIE (Off camera)**: 'And do you think the truth will come to light, that we'll eventually find Amy's real killer?'

**DI CALDER:** (Sighs) 'Plenty of cases colder and more complex than this one have been solved, so yes, I'm hopeful that, one day, somebody will find the person who killed Amy.'

**JESSIE:** 'And in your view, what will it take to make that happen?'

**DI CALDER:** 'Like I said, go back to the beginning, start with the night she died. Keep digging, keep asking questions, keep searching for that individual who knew the landscape, and who knew Amy well enough to get her to go to the woods with them. One thing we know for sure: somebody out there knows who did this. Somebody has a secret they've been keeping for a very long time, and my bet is that, sooner or later, that secret's going to come out.'

**MUSIC:** Suspenseful music begins to play.

# 54

## Martin – 5.55 a.m.

Martin has seen Connor plenty of times over the last decade and a half – in *Born Killer* footage, newspapers, magazine features and online articles. He even remembers the stomach-churning shock of exiting Old Street station one morning and being confronted by a ten-foot-high portrait of Connor, courtesy of a BlinkView billboard promoting season two of *Born Killer*. But Martin hasn't actually *seen* Connor, face to face, since they were both teenagers. Since the day before the police came and took him away for Amy's murder.

He was big back then, built like a fully grown man, rather than a fifteen-year-old boy, and he's still tall and broad shouldered, the thick muscles in his neck bunching up as he turns his head. But Martin is a long way away from the weedy kid with bad skin he was when they first met. He might not be as big as Connor, but he's put in plenty of hours at the gym and the climbing centre over the last decade. He is fit and he is strong, and he would do anything – *anything* – to protect his little girl.

'What are you doing?' Martin says. 'Get away from her, right now.'

'Daddy!' Freya leans forward and reaches for him, arms outstretched. Her face looks blotchy, and her eyes are red, but she looks better than he expected, given how she sounded over the phone. In fact, she looks . . . happy. Not relieved that Daddy is here to save her from the bad man sitting next to her, but relaxed and cheerful, as if she's been having a good time.

Connor puts up his hands and slowly gets to his feet. 'We were just talking—' he starts to explain, but Martin doesn't want to hear it. The only thing he wants right now is for Connor to get the hell away from his daughter.

As Connor retreats, Martin moves forward and takes his place on the bed. He opens a paper bag with Freya's inhalers inside it. 'It's OK,' he tells her. 'Daddy's here now.' He keeps one eye on Connor as he takes out the blue inhaler, uncaps it and gives it a quick shake before offering it her. 'Here you go. Head back, nice big breath in.'

Freya pushes his hand away. 'I don't want it,' she says, shaking her head.

He was worried this might happen, that she's grown so used to Jessie being the one to soothe her when her asthma is bad, that she no longer trusts him to help her.

He tries again. 'Come on, sweetie. You can do it.'

Frank, having taken time to climb the stairs behind him, enters the room. 'See?' he says. 'It's OK, she's fine. Connor's . . .' He pauses to catch his breath, a hand on his chest. 'He's here to help.'

Martin is too angry at his father-in-law to say anything. What the hell is Frank talking about? What possible help could Connor be when Freya is having an asthma attack? And what on earth was Frank thinking, leaving a grown man – not just a stranger, but Connor Starling, of all people – alone with his granddaughter? Anything could have happened . . .

The possibility Connor might have done something unspeakable to Freya hits him like a punch to the gut. He pulls Freya closer. 'Are you OK, sweetheart? Are you hurt? Did he hurt you?' He lifts up her pyjama top to check for bruises, then pushes up her sleeves.

'Stop it, Daddy!' Freya squirms away from him. 'Mummy's friend helped me!'

Martin pulls back. 'He did?'

She nods. 'He talked to me, like Mummy does when I need my breather.'

'I used to do it all the time with Amy, when she had an attack,' says Connor, who's now standing next to Frank, over by the door. 'I thought it was worth a try, that if I could just keep her calm until you got here . . .'

'He's a miracle worker.' Frank grins and slaps Connor on the back.

Martin takes a breath. He doesn't know how to process what's happening here. A moment ago, he was in the grip of a panic-fuelled nightmare, half convinced he was going to arrive at the house and find that his daughter had taken her last breath. But now he's being told there's nothing to worry about.

'You're sure you don't need your breather?' he asks Freya.

'Daddy, I told you already,' she says. 'I don't need it. Mummy says I shouldn't take it if I don't need it.'

'Mummy's right,' he says, beginning to cool. 'Good girl.'

Relief is a rising tide inside him, strong enough for him to feel the scratch of tears at the back of his throat. He lets out a shaky breath and gives Freya a big hug, holds her small body close while his heart slows and his head clears.

She's fine. She's OK, thank God.

'Daddy, you're squeezing me too tight,' says Freya. Martin relaxes the hug, then looks up and sees that Frank and Connor have left the room.

'I'm just going to talk to Grandpa for a minute, OK?'

At home, Freya would usually be waking up around this time, running into their bedroom and climbing up onto the bed between them for morning cuddles. But the asthma attack must have taken it out of her. She nods and yawns, lies back and snuggles down under the duvet.

Out on the landing, Martin does his best to keep his voice down.

'What were you thinking, Frank?' he whisper-shouts. He points at Connor. 'What is *he* even doing here?'

'Ah, perhaps I should have said something,' Frank says, sheepishly. 'But I didn't want to worry you, and I wasn't sure how to explain over the phone. Connor happened to call round – I only answered the door because I thought it might be Jessie. When I told him we were having a bit of a crisis, he offered to help.'

'Happened to call round? In this weather?'

Connor's discomfort is evident as he lowers his gaze and mumbles, 'Jess and I had a bit of a . . . disagreement, earlier on. I got the hump, stormed off. Then I got worried she might disappear back to London without us making things right, so . . . here I am.' He raises his head. 'Anyway. I brought round some candles and a torch. Thought they might come in handy.'

'Jesus, Frank.' Martin puts his head in his hands. 'You should never leave her alone with a stranger. Never.' Not just a stranger, but a man who's spent fifteen years of his life in prison and who has witnessed, or been a part of, all sorts of terrible things. Even if you set that aside, there are people out there who hate Connor, who want to do him harm. Just him being in the same house as Freya puts her at risk.

'You should be thanking him,' Frank says, more sternly now. 'If it weren't for him, I don't know what might have happened. For a minute there, she was . . . I thought we were in real trouble.' Frank looks glassy eyed for a second, then clears his throat. 'Anyway. Things turned out OK in the end, didn't they?'

They did. There's no denying that.

Martin offers Connor a begrudging nod of gratitude. If he's the reason Freya's OK, then he deserves at least that. And perhaps Martin was a little too hasty in berating Frank, who was likely in a panic himself when Freya started to struggle. Still, tomorrow he'll have a word with Jessie. Frank has to understand that he can't ever do anything like that again.

'Did Jess say what time she'd be back?' he asks.

Frank pulls a face that says, *Your guess is as good as mine.*

'You haven't spoken to her? I thought she called you, earlier on?'

'I told you,' Frank says. 'I'd let you know if she turned up, but we've heard nothing.'

As if on cue, the wind lets out a howl and a gust of wind rattles the windows in their frames.

Damn it. Jessie's still out there.

When they managed to exchange a few words over the phone, he'd thought she said that she was well, but now he isn't so sure. It seems an odd way to let him know that she's safe. Wouldn't she have just said, *I'm fine*, or, *I'm OK?* Maybe he misheard her, and she isn't well? That feeling of dread, deep in his bones, that he thought was probably down to him returning to Westhaven, is still there, and now it's stronger than ever.

Something's wrong, he's sure of it.

'We have to find her,' he says. He takes a few steps down the stairs, ready to go out into the storm and look for her, but Frank catches him by the elbow.

'Now hold on a minute,' he says. 'Before you do anything, why don't you rest up a little. And maybe make sure Freya's OK before you go charging back out there. It's no good her having both of her parents out in this. Plus, it'll be light soon. It'll be easier to track her down in the light.'

He's right. Martin's been awake for more than twenty-four hours. He's dog tired and aching from the drive. Plus, Jessie would want him to stay with Freya.

'Yeah, OK,' he says. 'But once it's light . . .'

'Of course.' Franks nods.

'But *he* has to go,' Martin adds, nodding in Connor's direction.

Connor sniffs, but raises no objections. 'Fine by me,' he says. 'I was planning on leaving once it eases up a little. I need to get back to Nan anyway.'

Martin nods, and the two men stare at each other across the landing, the air briefly charged with mutual dislike, until Frank claps his hands.

'Who wants coffee?' he says. 'I'll dig out the old pot.'

'Yes please, Mr Hamill,' says Connor.

While Frank and Connor head downstairs, Martin goes back into Jessie's old room and finds Freya curled up on her side with her thumb pressed to her lips, snoring lightly. He hovers over her, holding his breath and staying very still, and is relieved to hear that her breathing sounds crystal clear, without even the slightest hint of a wheeze or crackle. Whatever Connor said to her, it worked. She's going to be just fine. He only hopes the same is true of her mum.

# 55

## Jessie – 5.57 a.m.

Panic rears up inside my chest and Fiona's voice fades into the background, folding itself into the hiss of the rain.

Fiona *must* be an emergency call handler. Why would she have been on the phone with me for the last God knows how many hours if she isn't? She's been with me every step of the way, ever since I called—

Wait. Did I call her, or did *she* call me?

I'd just got my hands on the phone and was trying to dial 999 but couldn't get the bloody thing to work, then the phone made a noise like it was about to ring and . . . there she was. She said they'd had a call from this number, that it sounded like someone was in distress. I couldn't, and still can't, remember calling the emergency services, but I was so muddled and confused, and there was no reason for me not to believe her.

I take the phone away from my ear and with trembling fingers press the screen to show my recent calls. At the top of the list is the incoming call from Fiona I'm on right now, below that the several attempts I made to contact Martin, followed by Fiona's original call, three and a half hours ago – so she *did* call me. The outgoing call before that was to Bill. There's no record of me dialling 999. Fiona was lying about that too.

It doesn't make sense. We've been on the phone for hours. She's been calm and professional throughout, if a little robotic. She even talked me through pulling the root out of my thigh and applying the tourniquet. But now I think about it, what she has done most of all is try to get me to talk, to remember the truth the person who put me down here wants me to tell.

I think of the text message: **If you want to see your family again, get ready to tell the truth** . . . then tune back into Fiona's voice as she's attempting to make me do just that.

'. . . worth considering the possibility that what's happened . . . might not be anything to do with Evan. It might have something to do with your past, which is why it's so important that you keep trying . . .'

Fiona and the person who put me down here want the same thing.

I interrupt. 'Who are you?'

She stops. 'Jessica, are you feeling OK?' Is that a hint of surprise I hear in her voice?

'I want to know who you really are, and why you've been lying to me. You said the police were with Martin, but they can't be.'

'Jessica . . . you know exactly who I am,' she says, but my mind is already racing, considering possible suspects, people who would want to hear me suffer. Is she something to do with Dalton? His sister, maybe? She probably hates me just as much as he does, blames me for what happened to Evan. Or Elaine? She still thinks I betrayed Amy. Could she have decided that I must face the same fate as her daughter? No. Fiona doesn't sound anything like Elaine. So perhaps Fiona's nothing more than a crazed *Born Killer* fan, one of those obsessives who gets their kicks abusing me on social media.

Fiona lets out a small noise of concern. 'Listen to me, Jessica. You're cold, and I've no doubt you're exhausted. It's understandable you might be feeling confused right now, that you're misremembering things. That can be one of the side effect of hypothermia.'

I'm not misremembering. She told me the police were with Martin, more than once. She told me that Freya was fine, when she isn't.

'I'm not confused,' I tell her.

'I think it might be best if I consult with one of our medical experts here, then we can let you know what the best course of action might be.'

A voice inside my head is screaming at me to hang up, because if she's not who she says she is, I can't afford to waste another second on the phone with her. But I hesitate, a part of me still clinging to the reassurance that calming voice has provided me with.

'Nobody's coming for me, are they?'

'Of course, they are,' Fiona says. 'They're very close. In fact, I'd be surprised if you don't hear people calling your name any moment now.'

She's lying, and she's been lying to me from the start. Which can only mean one thing. She's the one who put me down here. She's the one who sent me the message, then did everything she could to keep me on the line to prevent me from calling for help.

'I understand you're under a lot of pressure,' she says now, 'but I'm not the enemy here, Jessica. I'm the one trying to help you.'

'Just stop,' I shout. 'Stop saying my name. And stop pretending!'

Fiona lets out a long sigh, then the line goes quiet and in the silence I can almost swear I hear her smile.

'Fine,' she says, eventually. 'You've got me. You win.'

# 56

## Martin – 6.00 a.m.

Martin lies down beside Freya and lets her snuggle into him. He's missed his little girl. Having her lying next to him doesn't quite make everything OK, because the sound of the rain beating against the windows is a constant reminder that Jessie is still out there, but it helps. It warms his insides. Reaches inside him, puts a hand to his heart and steadies its beating.

He thinks about last night, when he conjured up a memory of him and Jessie, lying face to face in this very bed over fifteen years ago, to help him drift off to sleep. How bizarre to be here, just five hours later, lying next to their daughter. Who would have thought, all those years ago, they'd be back here one day with their very own little girl? It seems impossible that time could have moved on so fast, that so much, and yet so little, could have changed. Births, marriages. Deaths . . .

Frank has switched out some of the furniture in Jessie's old room and filled some of the shelves with his own belongings – a shelf Jessie used to have her CD player on now bows under the weight of multiple stacks of Ken Folletts and Bernard Cornwells – but so much of Jessie's younger self is still here: old books and schoolwork, soft toys, VHS tapes; the desk they used to sit at while he helped her with her maths homework; the pinboard she covered with dozens of photographs, handwritten notes, cards and concert tickets; the cobwebbed orange lampshade with stickers of Disney characters around the rim. Even the bedsheets and pillowcases smell the way they used to, with the lingering scent of Jessie's shampoo, plus whatever washing powder Jessie's mum used to use – and that Frank probably still does.

Being back here conjures up all sorts of memories, moments of discovery from the early days of their relationship, firsts that felt thrilling and momentous at the time, but would go on to become routine. The first time they saw each other naked, the first time they had sex, the first time they said I love you.

He closes his eyes, tries to let the memories carry him away, but they only serve to remind him that Jessie isn't here with them, where she should be.

He kisses Freya on the forehead, then gets up, leaves her to rest and goes downstairs. He finds Frank and Connor in the kitchen, sitting at opposite sides of the table, drinking coffee, a single candle fluttering between them.

'There's fresh coffee on the stove. Help yourself,' says Frank.

Martin is wired enough as it is, but he pours a small cup from the silver coffee pot, then goes over to the table and takes the seat furthest away from Connor. *Why is he still here?* he thinks. He wishes Connor would leave, but supposes Frank doesn't want to kick him out while the storm is still raging.

Frank pats him on the arm. 'She'll be OK, you'll see,' he says.

'I know,' Martin replies, even though he doesn't, and that's the whole problem.

Frank leans back in his chair, a wistful look in his eyes. 'She went missing once, when we were on holiday,' he says. 'She couldn't have been more than five or six years old. You know how people say they only turned their back for a second – well I don't even remember doing that. One minute she was making sandcastles right in front of us, and the next she was . . . gone. Vanished, from right under our noses. We went out of our minds trying to find her. We thought someone had snatched her, or that maybe she'd been swept out to sea. We were about to call the police when I spotted her, wandering back up the beach, wearing a little sailor's hat, of all things. Turned out she'd found a pound coin buried in the sand, which was just enough for her to buy the hat she'd seen in the shop on the way to the beach. We could have throttled her.' He laughs at the memory. 'But in the end, it was all fine. She was fine and well then, and she will be now, you'll see.'

Martin says nothing. He'd rather not be listening to stories about people going missing at the moment.

Frank gets to his feet. 'Top up?'

'I could do another,' says Connor, lifting his cup. Frank takes it from him and goes to the stove while Martin stares into the flickering candleflame. Anything to avoid making eye contact with Connor.

A sudden, shrill ringing comes from outside the room – the landline.

Time stands still for a moment. Connor looks to Martin, who looks over to Frank, holding the coffee pot and grinning. 'What did I tell you?' he says. 'That'll be her now. Well, go on . . . answer it.'

Martin jumps to his feet, races down the hall to the small table at the bottom of the stairs, home to the Hamill residence's landline since he was a boy. He snatches up the handset, breathless with excitement. 'Jessie, what's happening? Are you OK?'

A stern woman's voice responds. 'Is she there?'

It's not her. Disappointment blooms in Martin's chest.

'Jessie. Is she there?' the woman repeats. Whoever she is, she sounds not just angry, but on the verge of tears, struggling to hold herself together.

'Um . . . no, she's not. She's—' Martin starts to explain, but the woman interrupts.

'Well, you tell her from me, I have questions – *serious* questions – and she'd better have some damn good answers, because if this video is what it looks like, I'll . . . I'll . . .' She trails off, her voice shaking with emotion.

'Now, just hold on a minute,' says Martin. 'Who is this?' But even as he asks, a door to the past swings open at the back of his mind and he knows precisely who he's speaking with: Elaine Barnes, Amy's mother. What on earth is she doing calling the house at this time in the morning, ranting and raving?

'Mrs Barnes? This is Martin, Jessie's husband. I don't know anything about a video—'

'You *know*,' Elaine all but screams. 'The one posted online. I've seen it, everyone's seen it. You tell her from me, I want answers. If she lied for him . . . I'll make sure she pays. You *tell* her.'

'Mrs Barnes, please . . .' But he's speaking to the dial tone. She's hung up on him.

Martin stares at the handset for a moment, then places it back in the cradle and returns to the kitchen in a daze.

Frank gives him a puzzled look. 'What was that all about?'

'No idea,' Martin says, shaking his head at the absurdity of being shouted at by the prim and proper Mrs Barnes, who was always so warm and kind to him when he was a kid. 'That was Amy's mum. Something about a video?'

'What video?' Franks asks.

Martin shrugs, but he takes out his phone and opens Twitter. He can't imagine Elaine would be up browsing the internet at this time in the morning, but she might have alerts set up for when people post something about Amy or *Born Killer*. He types #BornKiller into the search bar and doesn't have to scroll for long before he spots a post that momentarily quickens his heart.

A user calling themselves BornKiller4Real has posted a picture of Jessie, standing alone in woodland, wearing the red Wrecking Ball World Tour T-shirt he bought her when they went to see Springsteen for her twenty-first birthday. She's been caught in profile, her head turned to one side, brow furrowed, as if she's just heard a sound somewhere off in the woods and has turned her head in its direction. The post was uploaded at 8.30 p.m. yesterday evening.

What the hell was Jessie doing in the woods – presumably Cooper's Wood – at that time, he thinks, then something clicks in the back of his mind and his heart quickly calms.

Regardless of when the photo was posted, it couldn't have been taken yesterday. Jessie lost the T-shirt she's wearing in it years ago. He knows this because it was her favourite, and she was so upset when she lost it that he offered to buy her a replacement, but she said it wouldn't be the same. The photo must be an old one, taken while she was making *Born Killer*. Some fan must have got hold of it and posted it online. Some of them go crazy for behind-the-scenes photos. Besides, it wasn't a photo that Elaine was so worked up about.

He scrolls further down the feed and another post from BornKiller4Real appears, a video rather than a photo. On the screen is a freeze frame of Connor, sitting on a brown sofa, in a dingy-looking living room.

Martin looks up and eyes Connor, who's still sitting at the table, the flickering candlelight giving him a moody, almost devilish aspect. Didn't he say to himself, in the car, that if Jessie was in some sort of trouble, there's a good chance Connor would be behind it?

'What?' Connor says.

'Nothing,' says Martin, then he turns the volume up on his phone and presses play and the image of Connor comes to life, takes a drag of his roll-up cigarette, then sits back with a sigh and says, *You ever think about what we did?*

# 57

## Jessie – 6.05 a.m.

When Fiona next speaks, she no longer sounds robotic. She no longer sounds like Fiona at all.

'Didn't I tell you, if you want to see your family again, you have to be ready to tell the truth,' she says. 'If you'd have done that sooner, this whole thing could have been over by now.'

Chloe?

No. It can't be her. It just can't be.

Being down here, in the cold and the dark and the wet, has sent me mad. That's what this must be. Right now, Fiona – the real Fiona, who *is* an emergency call handler, of course – is still on the other end of the line, calling my name, over and over, trying desperately to pull me back to reality. But my damaged mind has retreated. It has sent me to some alternate, upside-down universe, deep in my subconscious. Or perhaps I've already slipped under the water and my oxygen-starved brain is misfiring, inventing random scenarios that couldn't possibly be real.

That must be what's happened, because that makes a damn sight more sense than Fiona being Chloe. Anything makes more sense than that, doesn't it?

'Chloe . . . ? Is that you?'

She sighs. 'I was worried you'd worked it out ages ago.'

'But your voice—'

'Oh, that part was easy,' she says, gleefully. 'I used an app, on my computer. I've been using one for ages when I game online. If you don't, you get all creepy men saying stuff to you. But if you change your voice, to like, an older woman, or a man, they mostly leave you alone.'

I know computers are capable of all sorts of things, that people can put a celebrity's face and voice on top of another actor's and make them say anything they want them to. But this is different. Surely Chloe couldn't have changed her voice over a phone call?

'That's not possible,' I say.

'Of course it's possible,' says Chloe, with a laugh. 'There are a few apps that'll do it. I used one called Clownfish, because it's free. You can change the pitch, sound like a man, a woman, or even an alien, if you want. It's not perfect, and maybe if you weren't so messed up you'd have realised sooner. But it did the job.'

My God, it's really her. All this time, she's been on the other end of the line, pretending that help was on the way.

'But . . . but why?' I stammer. 'Why would you do this to me? My leg . . . you made me . . .' She has tortured me, there's no other word for it. She could have called for help, but instead she has kept me down here. She made me pull a root out of my thigh . . .

'Because I wanted you to suffer, that's why,' she spits back. 'And because you're a liar. You lied about *everything* and I've given you all these chances to come clean and you still haven't done it.'

'I don't know what you mean,' I cry. 'I don't know what you want me to say!'

'I want you to tell the truth, about Connor. About what he did.'

'But he's innocent. He didn't *do* anything. You know this, Chloe!' God, what am I doing, arguing with her? I need to end the call right now, use whatever battery I have left to phone someone who can actually help me.

She's still talking. '. . . you lied for him,' she says. 'You covered for him, again and again, and I've been trying to help you to come clean, to tell the truth. But you're, like, so stubborn sometimes.'

I fumble with the phone to end the call, but the touchscreen is unable to register the press of my wet fingers.

'Jessie? What are you doing?' Chloe says. 'Jessie? Don't hang up on me. Don't you *dare* hang up on me.'

'Shut up! Shut up, shut up!' I shout.

'I'm the only one who can save you . . .'

# 58

## Martin – 6.10 a.m.

The footage looks like it could be a clip from *Born Killer*, but doesn't look like something Jessie would shoot. The quality is poor, and the camera work shaky. Plus, Martin has watched both seasons of *Born Killer* more than once, and has no recollection of this scene being in any of the episodes.

Jessie's voice comes from off camera: *We were just kids, Con. We didn't know what we were doing. If we could go back and change things . . .*

Unseen footage? A fragment rescued from the cutting room floor?

*I still feel guilty, though*, says Connor. *About the accident. It's our fault. It all started with us*. Which is bad enough, but then he goes and caps it off with: *If we hadn't done what we did, she'd still be alive.*

The clip stutters, then starts again from the beginning, *You ever think about what we did?*

Martin presses stop, scrolls down to check the number of views. It's in the tens of thousands, and the number is climbing before his eyes. It's going viral. He scrolls down a little further, just enough to reveal the first of many comments: *See!!! Always knew he did it, and that she was in on it.*

No wonder Elaine was upset. Anyone who sees the video could be forgiven for thinking the worst: that Connor is guilty, and that Jessie covered for him. And while Martin couldn't care less what people think about Connor, at best this little snippet from the cutting-room floor could ruin Jessie's career. At worst, it could do a hell of a lot more damage than that.

Martin turns to Connor, who is staring at the phone, slack-jawed.

'What is this?' he says, incredulous. 'That's me. That's my house. How . . . ?'

'I don't know,' Martin replies. 'Someone calling themselves BornKiller4Real posted it. Could be anybody. Maybe Jessie was hacked and somebody stole the footage off her computer?'

'Shit.' Connor holds his head in his hands, then stands and paces a quick half-circle around the kitchen.

'I don't understand,' says Frank. 'This is real?' He looks at Connor, his eyes narrowing with suspicion. 'You said those things?'

Connor stops moving. 'Yeah, but . . .' He rubs a hand over his face. 'It's not . . . we weren't . . .' He turns to Martin, a pleading look in his eyes.

Martin is loath to come to Connor's rescue, would gladly leave him floundering if this was just about him, but it isn't. It's about Jessie too. It's about all of them.

'He's right,' he tells Frank. 'It looks bad, but they're not talking about Amy and the well. They're talking about something else. Something that happened when we were kids.'

'Yeah,' Connor jumps in. 'That's right. It was just . . . a misunderstanding.'

Not the word Martin would use, but he supposes it'll do.

'The night Amy went missing, there was an argument, between the four of us,' Martin explains to Frank. 'Amy got upset and stormed off. If she hadn't, she'd have still been with us, and never have been pushed into the well. She'd have been safe. That's what he means, when he says it's their fault, isn't it, Connor?'

Connor nods. 'Exactly.'

'Hmm,' says Frank, sounding unconvinced. 'I suppose . . . these things happen. Kids fight, fall out over silly things.'

'That's what it was,' says Connor. 'Just a silly argument.'

'But you realise what people are going to think when they see this?' Franks continues. 'Doesn't matter what the truth is. They'll make up their own minds, jump to conclusions.'

They will. And the repercussions could be disastrous.

'Look, it'll be OK,' Martin says. 'Maybe Jessie can put out some sort of statement once she's back. She can explain that it's taken out of context, that it isn't what it sounds like.' With luck, she can come up with a credible explanation and shut this thing down before it gets out of hand.

Frank points at the phone. 'Who on earth would want to do this? Who'd put such a thing on the internet, knowing the trouble it might cause?'

Poor, innocent Frank, thinks Martin. He probably has no idea what some people can be like online, treating stirring up trouble like it's their full-time job.

'That's exactly why they've posted it,' he explains. 'Some people are obsessed with *Born Killer*, and not in a good way.'

'Well, can't we get them to take it down?'

'Even if we could, I'm afraid it's too late for that. It's already gone viral. And the chances of us finding out who did this . . .' Martin shakes his head. 'It could be someone halfway across the world, for all we know.'

Connor slams a fist down on the kitchen worktop.

'No,' he says. 'I know *exactly* who did this.'

'You do?' says Frank.

'Yeah, and they're not halfway across the world, they're right here, in Westhaven. It's the same person who's been messing with me. Sending me hate mail, death threats. Leaving dead animals on my doorstep.'

This is the first Martin has heard of this, though he's not entirely surprised. The occasional piece of hate mail is probably par for the course for someone convicted of murdering a child.

'But that's different,' he says. 'Jessie's had trouble in the past, mean comments and threats online, a few nasty letters to her agent. But she's never been sent any dead animals through the post.'

Frank clears his throat. 'Ah . . . that might not be entirely accurate,' he says.

They turn to look at him.

'Frank?'

'A few days ago, I found a box, outside. I think a fox must have got into it. There were feathers, everywhere. The remains of a little bird. I threw it out right away, didn't want to upset the girls.'

'There was note with it, wasn't there?' Connor says.

Frank nods. 'I thought it was just kids, messing around,' he says, sheepishly. 'I didn't think it was anything serious.'

Not serious? Someone leaving dead animals on your doorstep and making death threats? This sounds pretty serious to Martin, and all of sudden, the fact that Jessie has been out of touch all night, that his only contact with her has been a short phone call during which he could barely hear a word she said, no longer feels like the result of stormy weather and bad phone reception. That feeling in his bones, that something is seriously wrong, is back and stronger than ever.

He turns to Connor. 'These death threats, what did they say?'

'Well, they weren't wishing me a happy birthday, Martin,' says Connor. 'What do you think they said?' Then he heads out of the room, with Frank calling after him.

'Where are you going?'

'I'm going to go and see the person who's behind all this,' Connor calls back.

'Don't do anything stupid now,' Frank says. 'Let's call the police, let them deal with it.'

'He *is* the police,' Connor shouts from the hallway, then they hear the sound of the front door opening and the wind whipping down the hall.

Frank looks to Martin, his face a question mark, but Martin has already made up his mind. If there's even a chance somebody has done something to Jessie, hurt her, or worse, he has to go too.

'Keep an eye on Freya,' he calls to Frank over his shoulder, and he heads after Connor, out into the storm.

# 59

## Jessie – 6.15 a.m.

Seven per cent battery remaining. Not a lot, but it should be enough. I hold the phone above the waterline, dial three nines in a row and hit the call button, pray to God that it goes through. The weather is no better, and the signal no doubt still terrible. Will it make any difference that I'm calling 999? Probably not. No signal is no signal, whoever you're calling.

*Please connect, please connect . . .*

One ring, then a male voice answers: 'Hello, what's your emergency?'

Unlike when I first spoke to Fiona – or Chloe – I don't feel any great sense of relief. It's too late for that. All I can do now is explain where I am and hope they can get to me in time.

'I'm trapped, in Dutton's Well, in Cooper's Wood,' I tell the operator. 'I was speaking to someone who said they were one of you but . . . You need to get people here, right now. I'm going to drown. I don't have long left—'

'You've fallen into a well? Have I got that right?'

'Someone pushed me . . .' No time to explain. 'It doesn't matter. There's water down here, and it's getting higher. I don't have much time left. You have to help me.'

The clatter of a keyboard in the background. 'OK, please try to remain calm. Help is being arranged for you. Can you tell me your name, please?'

'Jessie.'

'And how old are you, Jessie?'

'Thirty-one,' I tell him, as if it matters.

Further questions follow. He asks how long I have been down

here, about my injuries, how cold I am, if I have been drinking, and as I give my answers, I can feel time moving, slipping away from me. Seconds turn into minutes and the rain pours and the water continues to rise. It's up to my shoulders now, the chill of it lapping at the base of my throat, the chill of it seeping into my body.

Chloe's right, I realise. It's too late.

I don't know exactly how long I have left before the water is too high or the cold too bad for me to go on, but I know it isn't long. Even if I could move my legs to help me tread water, I feel so weak I don't think I'd have the strength to do it for more than a few minutes. And while much of what Chloe told me over the phone while she was pretending to be Fiona was a fiction, the storm up above is very real. All of the fake reasons she gave for why help hadn't arrived – the fallen trees, the blocked roads, the flooding – are real reasons why it's going to take them time to get to me. Time that I don't have.

'You have to hurry,' I tell the operator. 'I don't have long.'

'OK,' he says. 'Try to remain calm. Help is on its way to you right now. Is there anything you can do to keep your head above the water? Can you try to climb?'

'No,' I tell him. Been there, tried that.

They know where I am, and they know time is running out. There's nothing more to gain from staying on the line with him. I think of Chloe, how she dropped the phone down to me, then was somehow able to call as Fiona just moments later. She must be close by. If she is, maybe what she said just before I hung up on her is true. Maybe she really is the only one who can save me now.

'I've got to go,' I tell the operator. 'But please hurry.' And I hang up.

# 60

## Martin – 6.25 a.m.

Connor gives Martin a vague set of instructions. 'Up the hill, turn left. Keep going for a couple of miles,' he says. 'I'll tell you when to turn after that.'

'You know where he lives?'

Connor nods. 'His parents' old farm, up in Larkhall.' When Martin tilts his head, Connor adds, with a shrug, 'He keeps an eye on me, I keep an eye on him.'

Great, thinks Martin. So, John Dalton's been making death threats to Connor, and Connor's been spying on Dalton. There's no way on earth this isn't going to turn into a total shit show.

The smart thing to do would be to turn the car around, go back to Frank's, call the police and let them handle it. But while the idea that Dalton might have done something to Jessie feels terrifying and unreal, it doesn't sound so far-fetched. Somebody sent her that dead bird, and released that video footage. Somebody is trying to ruin her. And who has more of a motive than John Dalton?

'We're just going to talk to him, right?' Martin says, over the sound of the rain drumming on the car's roof.

'Sure,' Connor says, staring grimly at the road ahead. 'Just talk.'

Being alone with Connor makes Martin feel queasy. Angry too, in a way he hasn't been in a long time. No matter, he thinks. They don't have to be friends, don't even have to talk to each other. They just need to find Jessie. But soon enough, even the small mercy of silence is taken away from him.

Connor clears his throat. 'The way I was with you, back when we were kids . . .' he says. 'It wasn't cool, wasn't right.' He clears his throat. 'If I could go back, do things differently, I would. Just so you know.'

Is he trying to apologise? Is that what that was supposed to be?

Of course, thinks Martin. These days, Connor likes to present himself as a gentle giant, who wants nothing more than to be left in peace to care for his ailing grandmother. Well, he can fool some people, but he can't fool Martin.

'Let's just focus on finding Jessie,' Martin says.

Connor shoots him a stony-faced look. 'Fair enough,' he says. 'Right at the next turn.'

How typical of him, to think that he can make things right with a half-arsed apology. That's the problem with people like Connor Starling. They only care about the consequences of their actions once it's too late, once the damage has been done. And make no mistake, Connor has done plenty of damage. The man's a liability. He was a rotten kid, and Martin would put money on him being a rotten adult too.

'Why did you do it?' Martin asks, his anger suddenly boiling over. 'That day you pushed me over and ripped up my library book. Why?'

Connor considers it for a moment. 'Dunno,' he says. 'Maybe I was jealous of you.'

What a ridiculous idea. At thirteen years old, Connor was nearly six feet tall. He was popular, he could run, he could fight. He was the school bad-boy – just about every girl had a crush on him. And while those things might not have got him very far in life, back when they were kids, they counted for something.

Martin lets out a laugh. 'Sure you were,' he says.

'I was,' Connor says. 'You were smart, you came from a nice part of town, lived in a nice house, with nice parents. You had nice clothes. You had everything, I had nothing.'

It's true that Martin did live in a nice part of Westhaven, in a nice house, and his parents did their best to look after him. But how could Connor have possibly known any of that at first sight?

'Impressive,' Martin says. 'You knew all that about me from the moment you saw me, sitting on that bench, reading my book and minding my own business?'

Connor nods. 'Kind of.' He interrupts himself, points. 'Next left.' Then goes on. 'I could tell what kind of kid you were by the new

Nikes on your feet, the way your clothes were all neat and ironed. All that stuff? It adds up, says something about you.'

'Your powers of deduction are truly astounding,' Martin says.

Connor turns to him. 'Don't tell me it wasn't the same for you. That you didn't think I was going to be trouble the moment you laid eyes on me, because of the way I looked, the way I dressed. You wouldn't even look at me, never mind talk to me.'

'Because the first thing you did was insult me. And you *were* trouble, weren't you? In case you've forgotten, you were the one who stole my book and pushed me over.'

'Yeah, sorry about that,' Connor says. 'I was having a bad time at home, and when I saw someone like you, I wanted them to have a bad time too.'

'That's why you did it? You wanted to ruin my day just to make yourself feel better?'

'Maybe,' says Connor. 'Look, I was a bad kid, OK? I didn't think before I opened my mouth, or before I lashed out. I was angry, all the time. I know I hurt people, and I know I can't take any of that back no matter how much I wish I could. I don't expect forgiveness. Sometimes . . .' He tips back his head, as if he can peer through the roof of the car at the stormy sky above. 'Sometimes I think you'd have all been better off if you hadn't met me.'

Is he fishing for sympathy? Well if he is, he's come to the wrong place.

'Hate to say it,' says Martin. 'But I think you might be right about that.'

The truth is, it feels good, after all this time, to put into words what he's never been able to share with Jessie: it was Connor's fault, all of it. When he came into their lives he turned everything upside down. He wasn't just a bad influence, he was reckless, dangerous. If not for him, everything would have been fine and – Martin is certain of this – Amy would still be alive today.

'Take the next left, then pull over,' Connor says.

Martin slows down as they approach a gap in the hedgerows that line the road on either side. The car's headlights illuminate the muddy ground as Martin turns in, shine their way up a dirt track, at the end of which is a run-down cottage surrounded by several outbuildings in various stages of disrepair. An old Land Rover is parked up, its tyres sinking into the earth, and the rusted carcasses of various pieces of farm equipment lurk in the shadows.

Martin parks up, and they sit, observing the house through the rain-spattered windscreen. It looks dark, unlived in.

'He moved here after his divorce,' Connor says. 'He lives alone.' Then he gets out of the car, closes the door behind him with a soft clunk. Martin follows suit, stepping out in the rain, his feet immediately sinking up to the ankles in a thick slurry of mud and manure.

Connor moves silently towards the front door of the cottage, and Martin follows. Once there, they step under a small porch, out of the rain, and Connor hammers on the door with his fist.

'We're just going to talk to him, right?' says Martin. 'Find out if he knows anything?'

'Right,' says Connor, but from the way he's rolling his shoulders and shifting his weight from foot to foot, like a boxer in his corner waiting for the bell, it looks like talking is the last thing on his mind.

# 61

Jessie – 6.30 a.m.

'. . . told you,' Chloe says, when she answers my call. 'It's too late now. Nobody else can save you. The . . . way you'll get out of there, is if you do as I say.'

She sounds different. Not just from how she sounded as Fiona, when she was using an app to disguise her voice, but from the Chloe I thought I knew. The Chloe who would flick the hair out of her eyes in a way that reminded me of my best friend. The Chloe who chased Freya around the garden and ended up rolling around the lawn, laughing so hard that there were tears in her eyes.

Was it all an act? Part of some big plan to lure me here so she could force me to talk?

I don't believe that. I don't accept that the curious, kind young girl I met wasn't the real her. Something must have turned her against me. Or someone.

'Is it Oscar?' I say. 'Is he making you do this? Because if he is, and if you're trying to protect him—'

'You don't know the first thing about him,' she says. 'You keep acting like he's some terrible person and he's not. He's . . . boyfriend, and he's the only one who cares about me.'

'That's not true,' I say. 'I care about you. And I met your dad yesterday. He cares about you too, very much.'

She lets out a snort of derision. 'If you'd really met my dad, you'd know he doesn't give a shit about me . . . trying to get rid of me for years. At least Oscar wants me around, at least he's there for me. At least . . . loves me.'

She's running hot with emotion, with hurt and anger. I think of her dad yesterday, keen to connect with his daughter, to have his little girl back, but bemused by the unruly teen she has turned into. No wonder Chloe found comfort with Oscar and his family. And maybe that suited Oscar just fine. Maybe Oscar liked having someone younger around who he could control and manipulate. I wonder if she's reciting his words now, and picture him, whispering in her ear: *I'm the only one who's there for you, the only one who loves you . . .*

'If you're protecting him, then you're going to get in trouble too. If he killed Evan—'

'He didn't kill him!' she shouts. 'He's not a murderer. What happened was an accident.'

There it is. The answer I've been looking for.

Is it madness, to feel the thrill of uncovering the truth, while I'm stuck down here with so little time left? Probably. But I can't help wanting to know more, wanting to know how Evan's story ended.

'What happened, Chloe? Were you there? Did you see him do it?'

'It was an accident, that's all.' She's being propelled by her anger now, so eager to prove her boyfriend isn't to blame that the details come tumbling out of her. 'Oscar told me *exactly* what happened. He was just messing around, teasing him, like he always did. Like we all did.'

Like they *all* did? Chloe included? I wonder about that story she told me, about Evan asking her to the dance, about them becoming 'sort of' friends. Was any of it true?

'It was Evan who started it,' she says. 'Oscar was just trying to defend himself. He didn't mean to hurt Evan. He only hit him, like, two times, at most. Then Evan fell down and hit his head on something and wouldn't get back up. But that's not Oscar's fault, is it? Oscar didn't make him hit his head; you can't blame him for that.'

Bill said whoever killed Evan gave him a real working over, beat him black and blue. Oscar hit Evan a lot more than twice. Isn't the more likely scenario that, when Evan stood up to his much bigger, stronger bully, Oscar decided to teach him a lesson? That he hit him, knocked him down, then kept on hitting him? And when he was finished, when he saw the damage he'd done, instead of getting the help that could have saved Evan's life, he walked away, left him there on the forest floor to bleed to death.

And then what?

'He asked you to cover for him, didn't he?' Demanded, perhaps? Grabbed her hard by the wrist and told her exactly what to say when she came knocking at my door?

'He's my boyfriend,' Chloe says, as if that's reason enough for all the lies that followed. 'He shouldn't have to go to prison, just because of an accident.'

'OK,' I say. 'But even if it happened just the way Oscar says it did, you should still tell the truth, you still have to do the right thing. Just think of Evan's family.'

'Oh, that's rich,' she says. 'Coming from you.'

There's real venom in her voice, and while I can understand her wanting to protect Oscar, I don't know where all this anger towards me has come from. Has he got in her head, convinced her that I'm not only his enemy, but hers too?

'Chloe, listen to me,' I say. 'This isn't you, I know it isn't. You're a good kid, and if I've hurt you, or upset you in any way, then I'm sorry, truly I am. If you help me out of here, we can work all of this out. Nobody knows it was you who put me down here, and nobody has to. If you help me out, I won't tell anyone, I swear.'

Silence on the other end of the line.

'Please, Chloe. If you won't do it for me, then do it for Freya. You like Freya, don't you? I know she likes you. She even drew a picture of the two of you, playing in the garden.'

Still nothing.

'Freya needs me. She's only a little girl. She doesn't deserve to lose her mum like this.'

On the other end of the line, Chloe erupts, 'Neither did I!'

'Of course you didn't—'

Her words are muffled through her tears. 'I didn't deserve to have my mum taken away either, but that's what happened. And you lied . . . covered it up, to save Connor.'

I don't understand. It's as if she has conflated two things – her mother's death, and Amy's murder. And then something clicks in the back of my mind, and everything falls into place: why she did this to me, who she really is. All of it.

# 62

## Martin – 6.33 a.m.

The second Dalton opens the door in his underwear, with a confused *what-time-do-you-call-this* look on his face, Connor charges forward. Dalton tries to push the door shut but Connor slams his shoulder into it twice in quick succession. The first blow rattles Dalton, but he manages to not only stay on his feet, but stand firm. The second blow hits harder, sending him stumbling back down the hall as the door swings wide and slams into the wall. Dalton collides with the newel post at the foot of the stairs, and the impact throws him off balance as it knocks the wind out of him. He goes down hard, lands on his side.

Martin watches all of this happen in disbelief. He knew Connor was on edge, that he was spoiling for a fight, but he hadn't expected things to escalate so quickly.

'Connor, stop!' he shouts, but Connor isn't listening. As Dalton scrambles up onto all fours, Connor bears down on him, plants a muddy boot on his hip and shoves, sending him sprawling.

'Where is she?' Connor shouts. 'What have you done with her?'

'What are you talking about?' Dalton shouts. 'Get out of my house!' He shuffles backwards, trying to put some space between himself and his attacker.

Martin doubts he'll be able to overpower Connor, but if he can slow him down, distract him maybe . . .

He moves up behind Connor and taps him on the shoulder. 'All right,' he says, in his most commanding voice. 'I've got it from here.' Then he puts himself between the two men, one hand held out in front of Connor's chest to hold him at bay.

Connor looks at him as if he's lost his mind.

'Mr Dalton?' Martin says. 'I'm sorry about all this, but I'm Jessie Hamill's husband, and she's gone missing. We're trying to find her.'

'I don't care who you are,' Dalton snarls, as he clambers to his feet.

'We need to know if you've seen her, if you've heard from her. If you know anything—'

'Of course he knows something,' Connor shouts, his very limited patience having worn thin. He points at Dalton. 'You're the one who's been sending us death threats. You're the one who put that video online.'

Dalton's face creases in confusion. 'What video? Death threats? I don't know what you're talking about,' he says. Now Martin thinks about it, while he can believe Dalton might have sent a death threat or two in his time, he's not so convinced he'd have the knowhow to hack into Jessie's computer to retrieve old *Born Killer* footage. What is he, in his late fifties? Of course, it's possible he's a computer whizz, and that somewhere in this old run-down farmhouse, there's a whole bank of computers devoted to cracking the online passwords of people he thinks have wronged him. But Martin doubts it.

Connor, on the other hand . . .

'Oh, come on,' Connor says, his hand flailing in frustration. 'Just admit it.'

'Connor, please,' Martin says, then, 'Mr Dalton, if you could please help us. When did you last see Jessie?'

'Yesterday afternoon,' Dalton says, without taking his eyes off Connor. 'I saw her in town.'

'He's lying,' Connor snarls.

'She was with a little girl and her dad. They were eating ice cream.'

Martin looks over at Connor, who shrugs. Neither of them have any idea whether Dalton's telling the truth or not, and Connor doesn't seem to care much either way.

He takes a step forward. 'If you've hurt her . . .'

'You're insane,' Dalton fires back. 'And you're a child murderer. You should still be locked up.'

Connor explodes. 'You ruined everything for me, you took away thirteen years of my life.'

'Oh, and you think it's been easy for me? Losing my job, my family?'

'Because you *lied*.'

'How many times do I have to say it: I did *not* plant that bag.'

'Oh, it just magically appeared there, huh? Nobody else could see it but you.' As Connor rants, Martin watches Dalton's eyes flick to his left, like he's searching for something. 'Isn't that convenient? You always had it in for me. You were just looking for an excuse . . .'

It happens in a matter of seconds. Dalton drops to one knee, as if he's struggling to catch his breath, then his hand dips out of sight, under the stairs, and there's the sound of a zip being unfastened. When he straightens, he's holding something in his hand – a small black tube. A torch? Does Dalton really think he can hold Connor at bay with a torch? Then Dalton whips his arm back, then down, and the tube extends with a satisfying click. It's a telescopic baton, the kind that the police use.

He points it first at Martin, then at Connor. 'You'd better get out of here, both of you, before I do something I'll regret.'

Martin backs away towards the still open door. 'All right, Mr Dalton,' he says. 'We're just trying to find Jessie, that's all.'

Connor doesn't move. He stays exactly where he is, his feet planted firmly on the hallway floor, a strange expression on his face that Martin can't place.

Dalton whacks the baton into his open palm, then takes a step forward. 'I'm warning you.'

Martin tugs at Connor's forearm. 'Connor? Come on, let's go.' Connor shrugs him off without a word. It's almost like he wants Dalton to attack him.

Maybe that's it, thinks Martin. He wants Dalton to hit him, so he has an excuse to hit him back. He's probably dreamt about this moment a thousand times, dreamt of getting payback for the thirteen years he lost. And Dalton? Maybe he wants it too. Not only does he blame Connor for all his misfortunes, but as far as he's concerned, the man standing in front of him is a child killer.

They're both just as bad, and just as dangerous, as each other, thinks Martin. Putting himself between two people like that will only end badly for him.

'Connor, please,' he tries one last time. 'This isn't going to help us find Jessie.'

But it's as if Connor can't hear him. Or maybe he just doesn't want to.

Someone's going to get seriously hurt here, maybe even killed, Martin thinks. And there isn't a thing he can do about it.

Then a voice calls out from the doorway. 'Drop it, Dalton. And, Connor? Step back, right now, or I'll arrest the both of you.'

# 63

## Jessie – 6.35 a.m.

'How much battery do you have left?' asks Chloe.

I take the phone away from my ear, and the surface of the water, now lapping around my neck, is briefly illuminated as I check the reading at the top right of the screen.

'Five per cent,' I tell her.

'Should be enough,' she says. 'Now, I'm going to ask you some questions, and you'd better answer me.'

I know the truth she wants to hear. I think I even know the moment she became suspicious, when her mission to divert attention away from her boyfriend turned into something else. It was when she saw the video of Connor, and he mentioned the accident.

The next day, when I told her about me and Connor kissing, I told the truth. The night Mum and Dad sat me down and broke the news of Mum's cancer, I really did go looking for Amy and end up at Connor's. He really did comfort me, look after me, and we really did kiss. You could maybe call that an accident, at a stretch. It was, after all, a mistake. Neither of us meant for it to happen and we regretted it immediately.

But that wasn't the accident Connor was talking about in the video.

'Chloe, please. I'll tell you everything, I swear. Just *help* me.'

My teeth chatter, my body shakes and shivers. I can't last much longer down here, I know I can't. If the water doesn't kill me, the cold will.

'Just answer my questions,' Chloe says. 'And then we'll see.'

'You can't be serious!' I'm dying down here, and she wants to interview me?

'The twelfth of February, 2007, between 7 and 11 p.m. Who were you with?'

'Don't do this,' I plead.

This can't be happening. I can't spend my final moments like this. 'Who were you with?'

Help is on the way, but the chances of it getting here in time are growing slimmer by the second. But if Chloe is close by, and if I do as she asks, perhaps she could still save me.

I don't have a choice. I have to give Chloe her interview.

The twelfth of February 2007 is almost sixteen years ago, but the events of that evening are seared into my mind. I know exactly who I was with that night.

'Amy and Martin,' I tell her.

'And what were you doing?'

'Watching a film, at Amy's house.' I take a shuddering breath as the memory comes back to me, our quiet evening disturbed by a knock at the door. 'Connor arrived, said he wanted us to go with him, that he had something to show us. We walked up the hill, up to the estate where he lived, round the back of the houses. There was a car. He said it was his grandad's.'

'What kind of car?'

'I don't remember,' I cry.

'Try harder.'

Although the car often features in my dreams, I'm always inside it, hurtling down dark county lanes at speed. I never see it from the outside.

'It was small. Black, maybe dark blue. That's all I remember, I swear.'

'Then what happened?'

'Connor . . . he had the keys, said we should go for a drive, just up the alleyway a few times. Martin and Amy said he was crazy, that we'd get into trouble.'

'And you?'

'I thought it would be fun. Exciting.'

Even though she couldn't possibly have known about the kiss, Amy had been acting weird with me for days. Perhaps because of the secret we shared, I found myself feeling more aligned with Connor, rather than my best friend, or my sensible boyfriend. I knew Connor driving without a licence was wrong, but it was his grandad's car. It wasn't like he was stealing it and we were only going to go a short way.

'Martin tried to talk us out of it, but I told him to . . .' A shiver shakes through me. 'I told him to stop being such a wimp. I got into the passenger seat, he got in the back. Amy didn't want to be left there on her own, so she got in next to him, then Connor took off. He drove up the alleyway, like he said he would, but when he got to the end, he didn't turn around and come back. He kept going, drove through town.'

I remember Martin and Amy in the back seat, shouting at Connor, telling him to turn back, to slow down, to stop and let them out, but he wouldn't. He kept looking over at me and grinning, like he was doing this for me. And maybe he was.

'He drove us to the edge of town, at the top of the valley, then pulled over. Said he wanted to show us the view, how nice it was up there. All the stars, the little lights in the town. It was . . . peaceful. At least it would have been if Martin and Amy weren't so mad. They kept saying we were going to be in big trouble, that we were going to go to prison. Martin kept imagining he could hear sirens, saying the police were probably already looking for us. Amy started crying and that did it. Connor said he was sorry and, after a bit, we drove back, along the Lansdown Road.'

It's the part I replay in my dreams, driving under the shadow of the trees, with only the car's headlights to keep the night at bay. And the faster we went, the better I felt. It was as if I were leaving everything behind, all the bad things that were happening to me – Mum's illness, what happened with Connor, Amy being annoyed at me.

'Then, out of nowhere, I saw . . . a person, in the middle of the road.'

The headlights lit her up from behind, painted her bright white. She didn't see us coming, barely had time to turn her head. I remember the screech of tyres, my body slamming against the side door as the car lurched to the left, then a horrible thud followed by the silence of disbelief. The car stopped and we sat there, looking at each other, terrified. Then the screaming started.

'You hit her,' Chloe says.

'I tried to go back, I swear I did. I got out of the car and started running, but Connor grabbed me, stopped me. That's when he told me the car wasn't his grandad's, that he'd stolen it. He said we had to go. We were all so scared and in shock, we just did what we were told. He dropped us off at the edge of town, told us to walk back to Amy's, sneak in and pretend we'd never left, and that's exactly what we did.'

The sound of Chloe sobbing comes over the line. 'That was the accident,' she says. 'Not some stupid kiss.'

'Yes,' I gasp, as the cold water closes around my throat.

'"If we hadn't done what we did, she'd still be alive," Connor said. He didn't mean Amy, he meant my mum, didn't he? You lied to me . . . you lied about the car he stole.'

She's right. I lied; we all did.

We agreed to say that we were at Amy's, all night. Even Connor. The police came for him eventually. Someone had seen him behind the wheel, recognised him, but he swore he was with us. They wouldn't have believed him if it was just his word, but maybe because Amy, Martin and I were three polite, well-brought-up kids, from the nice part of town, they believed us.

'Chloe, please . . .'

'That's why you made Born Killer, isn't it? It had to be you, because somebody else . . . uncover the truth, but you could make sure it stayed buried. You didn't care about finding Amy's killer—'

'No! That's not true—'

'—you just wanted to make sure your secret stayed hidden. But I saw through you.' She's frantic now, the words pouring out of her between sobs. 'The first time I watched Born Killer, I knew . . . wasn't right. I even told my dad, but he wouldn't listen. He said I was being silly, that he'd moved on and there was no . . . digging up the past. He said a thirteen-year-old kid was hardly likely to know better than the police. My own *dad* wouldn't believe me. So I tried telling other people, but there's, like, a million theories online about Connor and Amy and . . .' She dissolves into tears, her breaths coming in quick, hitching gasps.

'Chloe, listen to me, please. It was a terrible accident, and I'm so, so sorry it happened, really I am, but this isn't going to fix anything—'

'It was just a hunch, at first. I needed proof, I just didn't . . . how to get it. And then you came back to town and . . .'

She planned it all, right from the start, I realise. Wormed her way into my life so she could get the evidence she needed.

She goes on. 'Then I saw the way you lied when I found the video, and knew I'd have to find a way to stop you controlling the story, because that's what you do, isn't it? It's what you've always done. Well not anymore. I'm the one telling the story now, and the whole world . . . know what you did. Everyone is going to know that Connor killed my mum, and that you covered for him.'

'It wasn't like that,' I cry.

'Tell the truth!'

'I swear to God.'

It's the truth, and it's the reason I fought so hard to free Connor, and to find Amy's killer. Because it's all connected. It all comes back to that terrible night.

'We didn't lie to protect Connor,' I tell Chloe. 'Because on the way back, he wasn't the one driving.'

# 64

## Martin – 6.42 a.m.

Martin has only met Bill once before, at the first public screening of episode one of *Born Killer*. He'd seemed pleasant enough, and he'd certainly looked pleased for Jessie, though she'd been unable to persuade him to take part in the Q&A session held at the end.

At the after-party, Bill had waited patiently in line for his moment to speak to Jessie, then had given her a brief hug, kissed her on both cheeks, then excused himself in time to catch the last train back to Westhaven. He had struck Martin as a quiet, serious sort of man, his small frame and portly figure somewhat at odds with the tough, no-nonsense detective Jessie had made him out to be. But as Bill steps through the doorway of Dalton's house, the rain streaming from his overcoat and lightning flickering in the sky behind him, Martin gets it.

Bill carries with him a natural sense of authority, and seems to command the respect of both Connor and Dalton, who have frozen in place with guilty expressions on their faces, like misbehaving schoolchildren caught in the act by their headmaster. Dalton lowers the baton, Connor unclenches his fists, and before long, Bill has them sitting at opposite ends of Dalton's kitchen table.

He glares at each of them in turn, points his finger. 'I don't want to hear a word out of either of you. Got it?' Martin half expects either Connor or Dalton to object and for the whole thing to start up again, but Connor mumbles an OK and Dalton nods, and they both fold their arms over their chests, sulky expressions on their faces.

Bill turns to Martin. 'Now, do you want to tell me what's going on here? Frank called, said all hell was about to break loose.'

So that's why he turned up out of the blue. Thank God for Frank.

'It's Jessie,' Martin explains. 'She's gone missing.'

He explains about Jessie leaving Frank's before the storm last night, about her not coming home and not answering her phone. 'She's been out of contact all night. It's not like her, to leave Freya like that.'

'I see,' says Bill. 'And nobody has heard from her since yesterday?'

'Right,' says Martin, before catching himself. 'I mean, no, that's not quite true. I spoke to her, sort of. She called when I was driving over, but the signal was so bad I couldn't hear a thing, then it cut off.'

'And there's been nothing since?'

Martin shakes his head. 'Nope. And Frank says he found a dead bird, outside the house the other day, along with a threatening note. A death threat. The same thing's been happening to Connor. And then there is this.'

Martin takes out his phone and opens Twitter, which is still on the BornKiller4Real account. He hands it over to Bill, who takes it, then moves it back and forth in front of his face before reaching inside his coat and pulling out a pair of reading glasses. He turns to Connor. 'That right, son? You've been getting death threats?' Connor nods. 'And you think John here is responsible?'

Connor rolls his eyes. 'Who else would it be?'

'Christ almighty,' says Dalton, through gritted teeth. 'I've told you already, I don't know anything about no death threats. In case you've forgotten, my nephew was killed last week. If you think I've got time to be writing letters and shoving dead animals through people's letterboxes, then you've lost the plot.'

Connor smirks. 'Well, it wouldn't surprise me.'

'Oh yeah?' Dalton gets to his feet and Connor does the same, and there's a brief shouting match before Bill drowns them both out.

'If you two want to knock lumps out of each other, you'll have plenty of opportunity once we've found Jessie. Now for God's sake, sit down. You're behaving like children.'

They do as they're told, albeit begrudgingly, while Bill puts on his glasses and picks up the phone. 'Martin, talk to me,' he says. 'What am I looking at here?'

'There's a video and a picture,' Martin explains, 'both posted in the last hour, by someone calling themselves BornKiller4Real. The video is of some . . . unreleased footage. Something Jessie would never have put out there herself.'

'You think someone's trying to intimidate her?'

'I think they're trying to hurt her, ruin her career, cause trouble. But whoever it is, they could be posting from anywhere.'

'Hmm.' Bill rubs a hand over his face. 'Maybe forensics could track them down,' he says.

Martin watches Bill scroll down to the photo of Jessie up in woodland, then he looks up at Martin, ashen faced. 'This look like Cooper's Wood to you? I mean, I know trees look pretty much the same everywhere, but . . .'

'Yeah,' says Martin. 'I thought so too.'

'And this was taken yesterday evening? If she was up there when the storm hit, she could have got stranded . . .'

Martin shakes his head. 'It was *posted* yesterday, but that doesn't mean it was taken yesterday. It's an old photo. It must have been taken when she was up here making *Born Killer*. See the T-shirt she's wearing? She lost it, years ago.'

'You're sure about that?'

Martin nods, then Dalton's voice comes from over his shoulder. He's leaning over, looking at the phone's screen. 'I think you'll find she was wearing that yesterday, when I saw her in town,' he says.

Martin turns to him. 'She can't have been . . .'

'Let me see,' says Connor, and Bill angles the phone in his direction. 'Yeah,' he says, once he's looked. 'I think he might be right.'

'Oh, I'm right,' says Dalton. 'I know what I saw.'

Bill hands back the phone. 'I'm going to call this in. Maybe she twisted an ankle, got stuck out there, or maybe . . .' He bites his lip, looks concerned.

'Maybe what?' says Martin.

'I don't know,' says Bill. 'But if this was taken last night, we know one thing. She wasn't out there on her own.'

It takes Martin a moment to process Bill's words. He looks at the photo again, half expecting to see a sinister figure hidden among the trees, before it hits him, and his heart sinks. Jessie wasn't alone, because Jessie didn't take the photo. And now that mildly startled expression on her face takes on new meaning. What if it wasn't an animal that scared her, but a person? Perhaps the same person who killed Evan Cullen?

Martin heads for the door, hears chairs clatter behind him as the other men get to their feet. Dalton snatches his keys off the kitchen counter.

'Come on, I'll drive,' he announces. 'You won't get more than five minutes down the trail in that car of yours.'

If Connor has objections about sharing a car with Dalton, he keeps them to himself. The only thing that matters now is finding Jessie.

Moments later, Martin and Connor are squeezed into the back of Dalton's Land Rover as it rattles down narrow country lanes, Bill following behind in his police car. They charge through the storm, through deep puddles and around tight bends, the rain a constant drumroll on the car's metal roof. When they arrive at the turn for the picnic area that marks the start of the trail into Cooper's Wood, Dalton takes a sharp right and turns in.

As the Old Mill Tearooms come into view, Martin notices two things. First, that Jessie's car is in the car park, taking up two spaces instead of one. It looks like it was parked in a hurry. The second thing he notices is that there are lights on in the Old Mill Tearooms.

# 65

Jessie – 6.44 a.m.

Connor said he'd teach me how to drive, and I remember thinking that sounded like fun, but I don't think that's why I got behind the wheel. I think the real reason was because I knew Amy was pulling away from me. There was no way she could have known about the kiss – I hadn't said anything, and knew Connor wouldn't have either – but she could tell something was wrong. We were best friends, like sisters.

I hated myself for what I'd done to Amy, but my feelings were muddled. The guilt and self-loathing transformed into something else, into a red-hot anger at the world, for making Mum ill, and for making me do something so stupid that I risked losing my best friend. Somehow, I even found a way to blame Amy. If she'd been there when I needed her, I told myself, then I wouldn't have ended up alone with Connor, and I wouldn't have kissed him.

So, while Amy cried and repeatedly asked to be taken home, and Martin fretted and whined about us all being sent to prison, I switched seats with Connor. He told me which pedals did what, and after stalling a few times, I sort of got the hang of it.

I liked how just a gentle touch on the pedal would make us go faster, how the smallest turn of the wheel would make the huge metal box we were all sitting in point in a different direction. Most of all, I liked the feeling of being in control, for once.

I drove faster and faster, racing down the dark, narrow roads at the top of town. The others – even Connor – told me to slow down, but I didn't see why I should. It was late, the roads were clear. There was nobody around for miles.

And then suddenly there was. A young woman materialised in the middle of the road like some awful magic trick.

I froze, too scared to do anything because I suddenly couldn't remember which pedal did what. Connor tried to help, reaching over to snatch the wheel, but it was too late. The car swerved, but not enough. There was an awful sound, a deep, hollow crunch, and then the woman was gone, and Connor was climbing over me to stop the car.

'You're lying,' says Chloe. 'You're still trying to protect him.'

'No,' I say. 'It was Connor who protected me. When we saw the news the next day, and I understood what I'd done, I was going to turn myself in. Amy was terrified, kept saying she didn't want to lose me. Martin said it was all Connor's fault, that he should take the fall. After all, he was the one who'd stolen the car, and he never should have let me behind the wheel. Connor insisted we do nothing. He said there was no use ruining anyone's life over an accident. Besides, he'd already got rid of the car. They wouldn't be able to trace it back to us.'

'What did he do with it?'

'He told us he'd put it somewhere nobody would ever find it.'

'And why didn't you turn yourself in?'

I've thought about this so many times, wondered what stopped me from doing the right thing. The truth is, I wasn't just worried for myself, I was worried for Mum too. She was so ill, I thought that if she found out what I'd done, it might kill her. So I told myself I'd wait until she got through her next round of chemo, until she was feeling stronger, then I'd do it. Go to the police, tell them the truth. But, in the end, that didn't happen.

'I was too scared,' I tell Chloe. 'Scared of what might happen to me, and to my mum. And I know that's no excuse, but it's the truth. And then, a few months later, everything changed.'

'When Amy found out about Connor.'

'Yes. She was mad at him, but she was *really* mad at me. She said she was going to turn me in, tell everyone what I'd done. I don't know if she said it because she was angry, or if she really meant it.'

'So you . . . killed her, to stop her from telling the truth?'

'God no! I swear. I didn't *want* her to go to the police, but at the same time . . . a part of me was relieved she was going to do the right thing because I was too scared to. When she left us that night, it really was the last time I saw her. I don't know why she went into the woods, or who she was with. I wish to God I did.'

'Then . . . have been Connor. He did it to save you, and to save himself.'

'No! He loved her. He would never have hurt her.'

I hear Chloe sniff on the other side of the line, swallow back tears. 'I've recorded everything,' she tells me. 'Every word. And now I'm going to share it online and everyone's going to . . . what you did, and who you really are.'

Perhaps I deserve that much, for taking Chloe's mum away from her when she was just a baby, for cheating on Amy, for the many lies I've told. But I don't deserve to die down here in the dark.

'Do what you have to,' I tell Chloe. 'But please, don't leave me down here. Don't let Freya grow up without a mum too. None of this is her fault. She shouldn't have to lose me because of something terrible I did when I was a stupid kid. Chloe, please . . .'

Nothing.

'Chloe?'

She isn't there. The line has gone dead. I look at the screen and a white rectangle flashes a few times before the phone dims to black and turns itself off.

I'm out of battery. And I'm out of time.

# 66

## Martin – 6.55 a.m.

As Martin steps out of the car and into the pouring rain, he immediately feels that tight fist of worry in his stomach start to unclench. That warm, yellow glow, visible behind the tearooms' closed curtains, is a beacon. It signifies that everything is going be OK after all. Jessie's inside, and probably has been all night, which means she's had access to food, water and shelter. She's safe and she's well, just like he thought she said over the phone.

Car trouble, he tells himself. That'll be what happened here. Jessie's old Fiat has been on its last legs – or wheels – for months now. They've been talking about getting her a replacement for ages, because all sorts of things can go wrong with old cars, and often do at the most inconvenient of times. Jessie returned from her walk in the woods to find the car's battery was flat, and with the storm incoming, and no phone signal, felt her only option was to take shelter inside the tearooms. Obviously, they'd have already been closed for the night by then, so she'd have had to have broken in by forcing a door, or smashing a window. But better that, and pay for the damage later, than spending the night out in the cold and rain.

Martin jogs over to the front door of the tearooms through the rain, and is immediately soaked through to the skin, but he's getting used to that by now. He hammers on the door with his fist.

'Jess? It's me. You in there? Jessie?'

Bill's cruiser pulls into the car park, as Martin knocks again.

He stands back, listens for a response while Connor and Dalton, keeping a wary distance from each other, come up behind him, Dalton immediately pressing his face up to one of the windows, trying to peer through a paper-thin gap between the curtains.

'Maybe they just left the lights on?' says Connor, but then Dalton hollers over the sound of the wind.

'Think I see movement in there.'

Martin knocks for a third time, beats on the door with the flat of his fist, hard enough for it to hurt. The storm is loud, but if Jessie's in there, she must be able to hear him. So why the hell isn't she answering?

'Anything?' Bill calls out as he joins them. Martin notices that Bill is carrying a large metal torch, not that they'll need it inside the café, seeing as the lights are on, but it looks heavy, like it could do some damage.

When Martin shakes his head, Bill turns to Dalton.

'What do you reckon?' he says. 'Think we've got cause to believe somebody's in there, that maybe they're hurt?'

'Reckon so,' says Dalton.

'Connor? You care to do the honours?' Bill says, and Connor can't seem to resist a half-smile to himself. It's probably been a long time since he's broken into somewhere, thinks Martin. And perhaps he broke into this very building once when he was younger, because he certainly doesn't need to think about how he's going to gain access for long.

'There's a door, this way,' he says.

They follow him down the side of the building, to a small, fenced-off yard, where the rain drums on the lids of a pair of large metal bins and cigarette butts pirouette in a water-logged ashtray. Connor stoops down, picks up a half-brick lying on the ground and approaches the door, ready to smash the lock, but he doesn't need to use it. When he tests the handle, it swings open with a squeal. Somebody *is* here.

Bill leads the way inside, followed by Martin, then Connor, with Dalton bringing up the rear. They move down a short corridor, past a small kitchen, customer toilets and a cleaner's cupboard, and into the main seating area, where mismatched chairs gather around circular tables with condiments arranged on the checked plastic tablecloths.

'Hello?' Bill calls out. Nothing. 'Nobody here,' he says.

'There was.' Connor points to a table in the far corner. It's covered in empty crisp packets, chocolate wrappers and soft-drinks cans. He goes over, bends down and lifts something up off the floor. 'Sleeping bag,' he says, before dropping it.

Would Jessie have had a sleeping bag with her when she came to the woods? Martin doesn't think so.

'Whoever was here, maybe we scared them off,' says Dalton.

He could be right. Maybe whoever was hiding in here made a run for it out the back as soon as they heard him banging on the door. But then where the hell is Jessie?

'All right,' says Bill. 'Let's head up the trail, keep our eyes peeled.'

They all nod and start to head back the way they came, but part-way down the corridor, Bill holds up a hand. 'Wait,' he whispers. He has come to a stop outside the cleaner's cupboard.

'You hear something?' he says.

Martin shakes his head. It's hard to hear anything over the sound of the wind outside and the rain battering against the windows, but Dalton nods, steps by Connor and joins Bill by the cupboard door.

'Jessie, that you?' Bill shouts.

It can't be, thinks Martin. If it was, she'd have come out when she heard his voice. Bill seems to think so too, because he knocks on the door with the back of his torch.

'Police,' he announces. 'I'm going to need you to come out of there.' When there's no response, he tries a different approach. 'Listen here, I don't have time for playing games, so either you come out, or I'm going to drag you out. Do you hear me? It's your choice.'

Still nothing.

Bill looks over to Dalton, and there's an exchange of expressions between them; their years of experience as police officers doing the talking for them. Dalton moves to cover the other side of the door and nods. He's ready.

Bill reaches for the door's handle and begins a silent countdown: *One, two* . . . But before he reaches three, the door bursts open.

What follows happens so quickly, it catches all of them by surprise. Not one, but two people come barrelling out of the cupboard. Bill is knocked over by the force of the door swinging wide, while Dalton catches an elbow to the face. He rears back as a man in a dark hoodie exits the cupboard at a full run. He dives right, heading for the tearooms' back door, calling out a single word as he does.

'Run!'

Bill and Dalton, both dazed, can only turn and watch him go. Neither of them even sees the second, smaller intruder, slink out of the cupboard, clutching something to their chest. But Martin sees, and he moves with a speed he didn't know he had in him. He snatches out a hand, manages to grab a fistful of the second person's hoodie and yanks them backwards so hard that their feet leave the ground. He pulls the figure to him, wraps his arms around their body and holds them tight.

'Get *off* me,' a voice shouts, and as they wriggle and squirm, their hood peels back and Martin sees that it's a young girl. In shock, he almost *does* let go, but then he hears raised voices and looks up to see that he's not the only one who managed to snare an intruder.

Connor has the other man restrained, an arm twisted behind their back. He marches them down the corridor, back into the light.

They're just kids. Teenagers. The girl can't be more than fifteen, and while the boy might be tall and broad shouldered, he can't be much more than a few years older.

Bill is back on his feet. 'Bring 'em in here,' he shouts, and while Dalton blocks the corridor, Martin and Connor both release their captives into the seating area.

The two kids back themselves into a corner, the girl clutching what Martin can now see is a laptop to her body.

Bill switches on his torch, the beam powerful and bright, even in the light of the tearooms, and shines it at each of the kids in turn. Only then does Martin notice that the girl looks sort of like Amy. She's dressed like her too, in ripped jeans, band T-shirt and hoodie.

'Now, what the hell are you two doing in here?' Bill says.

'Nothing,' says the boy, lifting an arm to shield his eyes. 'We were camping out, but the storm came, so . . . we broke in. Then we heard you banging. How were we to know you were police?'

'Camping, eh? Jesus,' Bill shakes his head. 'You know a boy was killed in those woods last week? Beaten to death, he was.'

The boy says nothing, while the girl sniffs and looks down at her feet.

They know all right, thinks Martin. That's probably why they were camping out in the first place. *Born Killer* has made Cooper's Wood into a tourist destination for a certain kind of twisted fan. Is it any wonder that a second murder might bring more weirdos to the woods?

'Sit down, both of you,' Bill orders, and the kids shuffle over to one of the tables, pull up chairs and sit, shooting nervous glances at each other.

'Hold on,' Dalton says to the girl. 'I know you. You were with Jessie, at Evan's vigil. You were taking photos.'

The girl's eyes flick over to Dalton, then she looks down at the table, says nothing.

'Is that right?' says Martin. 'Are you Chloe, the girl Jessie's been working with?'

There's no response, though she holds the laptop she's carrying tighter to her chest.

Martin slides into the chair opposite her. 'Jessie's missing,' he explains. 'If you know anything about where she might be . . .' A thought occurs to him, and he leans in closer. 'Were you in the woods with her last night?'

'Hey, leave her alone, man,' the boy says. He tries to stand, but Dalton, who has moved behind him, reaches down and grabs the boy's shoulder, pushes him back down into his seat.

'Easy there,' he says.

Martin continues. 'My wife is missing,' he says. 'Do you understand? It's dangerous out there. We have to find her. If you know anything...'

The girl looks back at him, defiance in her eyes. Still, she says nothing.

'I'd better call this in,' says Bill. He pats his pockets. 'Shit. Left my radio in the car. John? Connor? Keep them here. I'll be back in a minute.'

As Bill heads outside, Martin studies the girl. Why does she seem so angry? he wonders. And why the attitude? If she doesn't know anything, all she has to do is say.

'Look, if you know where Jessie is, you have to tell us,' he says. 'If she's been hurt, or if she's in some sort of trouble, we need to know, before it's too late.' And finally there's a reaction from her, though not the one he was hoping for.

The corner of her mouth turns up in a smirk. 'It's already too late,' she says.

What the hell does that mean? He reaches over the table, grabs her by her slim shoulders, shakes her. 'Where is she? You know where she is, right?'

'Get *off* her, man,' the boy tries to stand again, but Dalton holds him firm.

The girl only shakes her head, the look in her eyes one of complete and utter contempt, of deep burning hatred. Martin wonders how anybody could hate somebody they've never even met before so much. And in that moment he's certain that she's done something to Jessie, he can feel it in his bones.

'What have you done?' he says.

She tips her head on one side. 'What have *I* done?' she replies.

The back door of the tearooms opens with a clatter and Bill's quick footsteps echo down the corridor before he reappears, breathless and panicked.

'Martin, we've found her,' he says. 'We know where she is.'

# 67

## Martin – 7.05 a.m.

The Land Rover's headlights push back the darkness, illuminating the trail as they rumble onwards through the torrential rain. Thank God for Dalton, Martin thinks. There's not a chance in hell he'd have got the Prius up here.

Connor shouts to him over the din of the rain. 'Can't you go any faster?'

'I'm trying,' Martin shouts back, as he wrestles with the wheel and the two of them are thrown around in their seats.

Just hang on, Jessie, he thinks. A few more minutes and we'll be there.

Then Connor lets out a shout and points straight ahead. Martin slams on the breaks.

A tree is lying across the trail, blocking their way. While Martin tries to work out if they can drive around it, or if he can use the Land Rover to push the tree out of the way – no and no, he concludes – Connor jumps out, runs through the rain to the fallen tree and lowers himself down, braces his back against its trunk, plants his feet in the mud and starts to push with everything he's got. There is a little movement, the tree's trunk shifting in the mud, but then Connor's feet slip out from under him and he goes down. He gets back up, wipes the rain out of his eyes and tries again, this time pushing with his shoulder. Again, there is a little movement before his feet lose their grip. This time he goes down hard, gets a face full of mud.

This is going to take forever, Martin thinks.

He grabs the torch from the back of the car and gets out, then shouts and waves to attract Connor's attention. When Connor looks, Martin signals that he's going on foot. Connor nods, and he sets off down the trail, running as fast as he can.

The ground is sodden underfoot. In places, his feet sink deep into the mud and he has to work to free them before he can go any further, but he keeps going, even after his shoes are sucked right off his feet. He runs, as hard as he has ever run, until his heart pounds so hard in his chest that it hurts.

Will he be able to find the path that leads to the well? It's been fifteen years since he was last here. But when he reaches the place where instinct tells him it should be, it takes him only a few seconds to locate the point at which the trail branches off. He runs down the path, slipping and sliding in the mud, branches scraping at his face and arms, then he ducks down under the tunnel of trees and comes out into the clearing. He sees the well and races over to it, shouting Jessie's name.

He shines the torch down into the darkness, the light gliding over the wet stone, then he leans over and peers into the well and sees the torchlight, reflecting back at him off the gently churning water. There's nothing down there.

They got it wrong, he thinks. Oh, thank God, they got it wrong.

Then a flash of white breaks the surface. It's only there for a second, but that's long enough for Martin to recognise the shape of a hand, of pale fingers desperately grasping, like they're trying to grab a fistful of air.

She's down there. She's really down there.

He moves around the well's perimeter, calling her name over and over, 'Jessie! *Jessie!*'

But there's not a hint of movement in the waters below.

He looks over his shoulder, desperate, distraught. Help is coming – he can hear sirens in the distance – but by the time they get here, it will be too late, he realises. And he steps up onto the rim of the well, and jumps.

# 68

## Jessie – 7.10 a.m.

I draw in a final breath and hold it as the water washes over my mouth and nose. A moment later there's a rushing sound as it fills my ears.

I think of Freya, my sweet, perfect little girl, hold a picture of her in my mind, as I close my eyes and the water covers my face. How blessed I was to have her. I will miss her so, *so* much. Thank God she'll still have Martin, my sweet, kind, brilliant husband.

My lungs spasm, and the desperate need for oxygen takes over. A final, convulsive breath forces my mouth open, and the dirty water rushes in. I want to keep fighting. For Freya, and Martin. For Dad too, but I've nothing left to give. My body is a dead weight, my thoughts are turning into liquid.

I fight to take one last breath, twisting and turning beneath the water, but suddenly I'm lost. My feet can't find the bottom. I no longer know which way is up and which way is down, which is madness, because I'm in a well just four feet across, submerged in less than six feet of water, but it's as if I'm drowning in the depths of a vast ocean. No matter which way I turn, there is only darkness.

A feeling of immense pressure inside me in my chest and in my head. It builds, expands until it fills me up, until it's all there is, and I know that this is the end. I'm finished.

My life does not flash before my eyes. There's no blinding white light, no tunnel with the people I've lost at its end, beckoning me to join them. But in my final moments, I am relieved beyond measure to find that there is . . . *something* – a flicker of a feeling, a warm sensation, remembered from long ago. A connection I have missed so much.

Amy is with me. My best friend.

I can *feel* her, can hear her voice in my head, the way I used to when we'd talk to each other using only our eyes.

*Don't give up*, she tells me. *You have to keep fighting . . .*

I open my eyes, and through the murky water see a haze of shimmering light. The opening to the well, far above me.

*That's it . . . You can do it, Jess . . .*

I will not let the water take me. I will not die in this well. I will not—

I reach for the light, my hand breaks through the water's surface . . .

An explosion.

Water erupts around me, as if the storm up above has found its way down into the well and has me in its teeth. I'm shaken back and forth like a rat in a dog's mouth. Something clamps around my upper arm and hauls me upwards. I feel cold air on my face. I'm out of the water, or at least a part of me is.

Someone is shaking me, shouting, *Breathe, breathe!* over and over.

Rescue has come after all, I realise. If only they'd got here sooner.

The light begins to fade, my consciousness ebbing away, and the last thing I hear before the darkness floods in is a man's voice, an urgent, desperate cry – *I've got her! Help me! Help!* – and although I know it's the end, I take some small comfort from the fact that, whoever my rescuer is, he sounds a little like my husband.

# BORN KILLER –
# SHOOTING SCRIPT

## S03 – E01: FOLIE À DEUX

**STUART MITCHELL (Chloe's Father)**: 'That woman killed my wife, it's as simple as that. She ran her over, left our little baby girl without a mum, then made her fortune telling lies about it. She only came clean because she was forced to, and she gets a grand total of six months in prison – *six months*. While my little girl gets locked away for four years, when she didn't kill anybody. You tell me – where's the justice in that?'

**INTERVIEWER**: 'But if Jessica Hamill hadn't been rescued by her husband . . .'

**STUART MITCHELL**: 'So they say. But they say lots of things, don't they? That Chloe planned this whole thing, that she sent hate mail and dead animals to people, that she pretended to be someone else, that she practically tortured this woman . . .'

**INTERVIEWER**: 'So . . . you're saying she didn't do these things?'

**STUART MITCHELL**: 'Look, I'm not claiming that Chloe is perfect, but I know my daughter – I know the real her. And I know, in my heart, that she wouldn't have done half the stuff they accuse her of. Or, if she *did* do those things, she was doing them because of him. Because he made her.'

**INTERVIEWER:** 'Oscar, you mean?'

**STUART MITCHELL**: 'Exactly. I never liked him, could tell he was trouble from the start. The first time I met him, I just knew something wasn't quite right with him. I could see it in his eyes.'

# 69

*One year later*

## Martin

Sitting on the picnic bench, outside the Old Mill Tearooms, Martin watches his daughter fidget in the seat across from him, notices the way her eyes are drawn to that dark tunnel of trees at the start of the trail that leads into Cooper's Wood. She gets this way sometimes, when Jessie is out of sight for too long. Restless, fearful. Worried that Jessie might not come back. Nine months is a hell of a long time for a six-year-old to be without their mum.

He waves a hand to attract her attention. 'Hey, sweetheart, you OK?'

She turns to him and nods, then asks, for the second time, 'Why can't I go with Mummy?'

'We've talked about this,' he says. 'Because Mummy has something important she needs to do, and she wants to be by herself while she does it. But I promise you that she's OK, and that she'll be back very soon.'

'But *why* does she want to be on her own?' Freya pouts.

'Because.'

'But *why* because?'

'What are you, four years old?'

'No.' She laughs, then rolls her eyes as if he is being very silly. 'I'm six now, Daddy.'

'Ah yes, that's right. So that means you're old enough to understand that Mummy wants a bit of peace and quiet while she says goodbye to somebody.'

Freya looks puzzled. 'How can Mummy say goodbye to somebody if she's on her own?'

Good question, thinks Martin. He tries to think of a way to explain, to help her understand.

'Sometimes, when somebody says goodbye, they're just saying it for themselves, to make them feel better about the other person having gone away. So it doesn't matter if the other person isn't there to hear them. Does that make sense?'

Freya frowns. 'Sort of.'

'I'll tell you what, when Mummy gets back, maybe she'll explain it to you, if you ask her nicely. Anyway, we're OK here, aren't we? Do you want another drink? Or do you want to take your dad on at football? I'll give you a three-goal head start. What do you reckon?'

She'd usually scoff at the suggestion of him going easy on her, but today she only shrugs. She's unhappy and unsettled, and who could blame her.

The last year has been hard on all of them. For Jessie, of course, because she had to leave Freya and him behind. A surprisingly swift trial resulted in a custodial sentence for the accidental death of Julie Mitchell, mother of Chloe Mitchell – nine months, three of which were deemed to have been served while on remand.

For Martin, those nine months were long and lonely, but for Freya, they must have felt like an eternity. Even if, as far as she was concerned, Mummy was simply away on a very important work trip. How long that particular piece of misdirection will hold up, Martin isn't sure. That anxious look Freya gets in her eyes when Jessie leaves the room, even for a moment, makes him worry that she already suspects something. He's tried his best to shield her, but it's probably only a matter of time before one of her schoolmates lets something slip, or she stumbles upon an article in a paper, or online. God knows, the story was everywhere for a while: footage of Chloe and Oscar being bundled into police vans with blankets over their heads; countless column inches poring over every gruesome detail of Jessie's time in the well; think pieces weighing Jessie's nine-month sentence against the four years Chloe received for kidnap and assisting an offender, and the life sentence, with a minimum of sixteen years served, Oscar was given for Evan's murder. And with the forthcoming release of season three of *Born Killer* – made without Jessie's approval or involvement, of course – it looks like the story won't be going away anytime soon.

If only Freya knew what today means, he thinks. If she understood that it is a momentous day: the day when her mum not only says goodbye to her childhood friend Amy, but also to *Born Killer*, for good. Soon, they'll be heading back to London, having put all this behind them.

Things will be different now. Jessie needs to work out what she wants to do with her life, seeing as she's done making crime documentaries. But she'll get there – she is brilliant, after all. The most important thing is that she'll be home, for good. And while there's always the chance that others might want to tell Amy's story, nobody is going to put their heart and soul into it the way Jessie did, which also means Martin isn't going anywhere.

It was a tense few months when Jessie first told him she was going to make a documentary about Amy's murder. He thought he was in real trouble at first, that it would only be a matter of time before she uncovered the truth. He even contemplated running away, flying to some far-flung country to start a new life. But as much as he was terrified of getting found out, he couldn't face the idea of leaving Jessie behind.

Fortunately, as the investigation progressed, he realised that Jessie wasn't in the least bit suspicious of him, and never would be. She thought of him as a gentle person, who would never hurt another soul, if he could possibly help it. She just didn't look at him *that* way, didn't think him capable of such cruelty.

When he thinks back to *that* night, he barely remembers the argument about the kiss, though he remembers the aftermath: Jessie and Amy both in tears; making Jessie give him back the ring he'd bought her for Valentine's Day; Amy threatening to go to the police to tell them about the accident before storming off. And he remembers later that night, when Amy called up to his bedroom window.

She didn't say she wanted to talk, didn't say much at all at first, but he thought it made sense, the two of them being together. The two wounded parties, both hurt and betrayed. More than anyone, they knew how the other was feeling.

They ambled through the town, across the valley, all the way up to Cooper's Wood.

It was still light when they walked along the trail and Amy took him down the secret little path to the well.

'Connor used to bring me here,' she told him, peering off into the trees wistfully, as if her relationship had ended not several hours ago, but years earlier. She took a seat on a fallen tree, put her head in her hands, and wept. 'She was supposed to be my best friend,' she wailed when she surfaced for air.

He sat down next to her and put his arm around her shaking shoulders and that seemed to make her feel better for a while. But after she'd dried her tears, she looked up at him with an angry look in her eye and said the oddest thing.

'Maybe they *should* be together. They suit each other, don't you think? They're both crazy. So maybe that means . . . me and you?'

She'd never shown any interest in him before. In fact, she'd often seemed to find him irritating, as if he were an interloper, getting in the way of her and Jessie's friendship. Nevertheless, she leaned in and pressed her mouth against his, and her tongue was suddenly between his teeth. As she kissed him, she ran a hand over his chest and a shiver ran through him. It was then that she found the ring, plucked it from his shirt breast pocket and slipped it on her finger.

'See?' she said, her eyes red and sad. 'Doesn't it look better on me?'

He shook his head. He didn't want this, any of it. Even if Jessie had cheated on him, it felt deeply wrong to be kissing Amy, as if they were setting off down a path they could never return from.

'Can you give it back please?' he said.

Amy laughed. 'I'm just messing. I wasn't being serious.'

'I know,' he said. 'Just . . . I don't like you that way.'

She nodded. 'Good,' she said, a mean look in her eyes. 'Because I don't like you either.' Which wasn't quite what he'd said to her. She went on, 'Why would I ever want to be with you, anyway? I mean, look at you. You're a loser. Everyone thinks so, even Jessie.'

'That's not true,' he said.

'Oh, it is. She told me. She only went out with you because she felt sorry for you.'

That stung, because he suspected there was some truth to it. He felt the prick of tears at the back of his throat. He wanted to go home.

'Just give me the ring,' he said, putting out his hand.

Amy puts her hands behind her back. 'No way. It's mine now,' she said. 'I'm keeping it.'

He got to his feet, tried to wrestle the ring from her, but she skipped away from him, then danced in circles, laughing. She was supposed to be his friend, but she was acting like one of the kids who used to bully him. But at least with Amy he had the physical advantage. He went for the ring again, feigning right, and when she ducked left and tried to spin away from him, he grabbed her around the middle. She fought to break free of him, twisted and turned her body, then pushed against him with both hands. When he let go, she toppled backwards, ending up sprawled on top of the rusted iron grate that covered the old well.

She sat up, unhurt but a little stunned, then looked down at her dress. There was a smear of orange across the hem, where it had rubbed against the rusted grate. 'Look what you did!' she cried. 'You ruined my dress!'

'And you took my ring!' Martin shouted back.

'God, you are *such* a loser,' she said, then she went quiet for a moment before bursting into tears again. 'I hate her,' she sobbed. 'I hate her so much.'

Martin thought about going over and comforting her, but she was being so horrible to him it felt wise to keep his distance. Still, it was starting to get dark. He was hardly going to leave her to walk home alone through the woods.

'I think I'm going to go now,' he told her. 'Do you want to walk with me?'

'Yeah. Sorry.' She sniffed, then pushed the hair out of her eyes. 'I didn't mean those things. I'm just so . . . I dunno.'

'I know,' Martin said, as he watched her shuffle forward on her bottom so she could hop down off the well. But before she had the chance to climb down, there came a horrible metallic squeal from beneath her, like the pained cry of an injured animal.

Amy froze, lifted her head and looked at him, her eyes wide with fear.

'Martin—' she said, his name turning into a high-pitched scream as the section of the grate she was sitting on collapsed inwards, as if it were on a hinge. Amy's feet shot up in the air as her body tipped backwards. Martin rushed forward, managing to reach her just in time to snatch a handful of her dress in his fist and stop her from falling further.

'Pull me up! Pull me up!' she screamed.

With his other hand he got a firm hold of her leg, ready to pull her to safety.

Then he hesitated.

Did Jessie really think he was a loser? he wondered. Is that why she'd cheated on him with Connor? And when she and Amy exchanged those looks with each other then burst out laughing, were they laughing at him? Maybe they were. He thought back to the moment he'd demanded Jessie return the ring he'd bought for her. He'd hoped she would refuse, that she'd insist on keeping it, on fighting for their relationship. Instead, she'd wrenched it off her finger and all but thrown it at him before chasing after Amy. She might have been upset about him breaking up with her, but what really mattered to her, as always, was her best friend.

'What are you waiting for?' shouted Amy. 'Help me. Pull. Me. Up!'

He had a firm enough grip, and Amy wasn't heavy. He could have pulled her to safety without too much effort. But as she shouted at him, cursed him, called him names, he found that he didn't want to help her. He was tired of being second best.

'Martin, come on!' she shouted, and at that moment, he let go of her leg and relaxed his grip on her dress. The fabric slipped through his fingers, and he felt something click into place inside his chest, like he'd just found the key to a door he'd been trying to unlock for a very long time.

'What are you—' he heard Amy start to say, but her words were drowned out by another one of those metallic squeals as the rest of the grate gave way beneath her, and she slipped out of view.

Martin gets another soft drink from the tearooms for Freya, and a packet of crisps for good measure. Once she's finished eating, they kick a football around on the grass for a while, until Freya gets breathless. She comes to a stop, puts her hand to her chest and calls over to him.

'Daddy, I need my breather.'

He goes to her, crouches down to her level, gives her a big hug then pulls back and looks in her the eye.

'It's right here,' he tells her, patting the bulge in his hip pocket. 'But before I give it to you, I want you to take a few deep breaths – look at me – take a few breaths, let's slow things down. In through the nose, out through the mouth. Do it with me.'

He shows her how, and she copies him, pulling in air through her nose so that her chest inflates, then pushing the air out between her pursed lips.

'Remember, you're the one in control here, not your asthma,' he tells her.

She keeps going, taking slow, controlled breaths, until finally she looks at him and smiles. 'I think it worked!' she says.

'You're sure? You can have your inhaler if you need it. The important thing is that you tried.'

She shakes her head. 'I don't need it now.'

'All right!' Martin high-fives her. 'Good girl. Now, go and play, but take it easy, OK?'

'OK, Daddy,' she says, and she runs back to her football.

He knows it won't work every time. He can't cure her, but maybe he can help her not to be so reliant on her medication. Besides, she'll hopefully grow out of her asthma entirely as she gets older, then he won't have to listen to the awful crackle and wheeze of her constricted breathing when she's having an attack, a sound that never fails to take him right back to the moment Amy fell into the well.

His first thought, after she slipped into the darkness, was: I've killed her. And with that, he almost turned and ran. But then he heard a frightened moan that froze him in his tracks.

He inched forward, braved a look over the rim of the well, and there she was, tangled up in what was left of the metal grate that had collapsed under her weight. He could see blood smeared across her forehead, and her arm was twisted at an odd angle, like it had an extra elbow. The rest of her was submerged in a pool of filthy-looking water. Seeing her like that made him feel sick to his stomach.

She called up to him in a broken whisper. 'Martin? Are you . . . there? Help . . . me.'

She did *not* sound good. He pulled back, out of sight, pretended not have heard her.

'Martin?'

Her breaths were coming in short, sharp, wheezing gasps, like she was an old man of ninety.

'My inhaler . . . It's in . . . my bag . . . Need it.'

He looked over to the fallen tree where they had been sitting just moments earlier, and saw Amy's bag lying on the ground. He went over and picked it up, checked inside it. Beneath her purse and her phone, and a bunch of other girl stuff, he could see her blue asthma inhaler, the one he'd seen her use dozens of times when she got breathless during sports, or if they'd walked a long way.

He took the inhaler out of her bag, weighed it in his hand.

He could drop it down to her, then go and get help. He'd have to explain that there'd been an accident, but that would be OK. Accidents happen all the time, and it wasn't like he'd actually pushed her in. Although . . . she was awfully mad at him, and at Jessie. What if she told the police he'd pushed her? And what if she told them about the woman Jessie hit while she was driving? They'd lock Jessie up, take her away from him forever.

A brilliant and terrible idea came to him, how he could make sure he didn't get in trouble, and how he could make sure Amy would never tell anyone about the car accident. Not only that, but if he was smart about it, perhaps he could get Connor out of their lives for good too.

But he couldn't just leave her here, could he?

'Martin?' Amy wheezed, her breaths growing shallower by the second. 'Are you . . . still . . . there?'

He put Amy's inhaler back in her bag, slung the bag over his shoulder, then put his hands over his ears and turned and walked away. He only removed his hands once he'd reached the main trail, by which time her cries were so thin, with so little breath behind them, he could hardly hear them at all.

The next morning, when Jessie called and told him Amy was missing, it was like their fight had never happened. She asked him to come over, said she was sorry for everything and that she needed him – what a wonderful thing *that* was to hear. So, he went to her, comforted her, and they joined in the search for Amy. Before long, Connor appeared, of course, but that didn't worry Martin. He had a plan for how to deal with his old bully. All he needed to do was to plant Amy's bag in Connor's bedroom, and he was pretty sure that, given Connor's reputation, the rest would take care of itself.

# 70

## Jessie

The clearing looks different today. Birds sing in the trees and sunlight breaks through the woodland canopy in mote-filled rays, dappling the forest floor in patches. It is quiet, and peaceful. Soul-nourishing, the way that nature can be on warm, bright days, when it feels like you've rediscovered a gift from God you forgot he gave you.

After what happened to me last year, and after some local campaigning, Westhaven Council finally got their act together. Rather than trying to pretend the well didn't exist, and hoping Cooper's Wood would swallow it up once and for all, they decided the better – not to mention, safer – option would be to create a proper path leading up to the well and turn it into a memorial.

Now, there's no need to push your way through the trees, arms held aloft to protect your face from sharp branches. You simply diverge off the main trail when you reach the signpost and walk down the winding path lined with wood-chippings, until you arrive at the fenced-off clearing. There is no litter, there are no empty beer cans lying on the ground, or ancient pages from dirty magazines. There's a small wooden bench for sitting on, and a rubbish bin that is emptied on a regular basis. The well no longer sits back, half hidden in the brush. Now it stands proud of the trees, and not only has it been filled with concrete, but a large planter has been placed on top, full of beautiful wildflowers.

As I draw near, I see something on the well's rim – a row of tiny plastic figurines. Some are rather crudely painted, while others are highly detailed. There's a dwarf, an elf, some sort of wizard, a barbarian, and so on. They must have been put here by Peter Rand and Evan's friends from the games club. I wonder, is that why Evan visited the library on the evening before he was killed? Not to find Connor, as I'd assumed, but to find his friends? I grow tearful at the thought. Evan had such a short, unhappy life, and he met such a horrible end at the hands of his bully, Oscar. But he was not without friends, despite what Chloe told me.

Below the figures, a plaque on the well's side reads: *This space is dedicated to the memories of Amy Barnes (1992–2007) and Evan Cullen (2008–2023).*

I crouch down, run my hand over the letters, the brass ice-cold against my skin.

I tried to say goodbye to Amy here once before, but didn't get the chance to finish. And maybe that's a good thing, because while I don't remember much about the moment I almost drowned, I remember that Amy was with me. She came to me when I needed her most. If not for her, I wouldn't have made the final, desperate attempt to reach the surface. Martin wouldn't have seen my hand, and wouldn't have jumped in to save me. It's thanks to Amy that I'm alive today.

Not that I think her spirit, or any other part of her, is down there now. But this is where she last lived and breathed, and it's where I last felt her presence. It feels right to do it here.

I sit on the bench and take out the little box Elaine left with Dad before she moved away. I was surprised she bothered after she found out about the lies I'd told. Dad suspects John Dalton played a part in softening her hard feelings towards me. Against the odds, Dalton has emerged as a voice of reason in all this, and played a central role in the campaign to turn the well into a memorial for his nephew and Amy.

Inside the box are photographs, flyers for concerts that we went to, little notes that we wrote to each other, a few items of jewellery, an old The Smileaways CD. Little pieces of Amy that Elaine saved for me.

I settle on a photograph of me and Amy at the seaside with the flashing lights of an arcade behind us. Objectively, it is a bad photo. It's out of focus, the horizon is off kilter, and the two windswept subjects aren't even looking at the camera. They're looking at each other, smiling as the wind whips their hair in front of their faces. But Amy and I look like we're having a blast. We always did love the seaside.

It's my favourite of the photos Elaine left for me, which I think means it has to be the one. While I don't know the rules for this sort of ceremony, I'm guessing I can't just choose any old picture. It has to feel like a sacrifice. It has to mean something.

I take out the lighter, flick the wheel and touch the flame to the corner of the photograph. A moment, then the corner blackens and curls, and the picture blisters and deforms. I drop the burning photo to the ground before it singes my fingers, and extinguish the remains with my foot, then pick up what's left and carry it over to the bin. Returning to the bench, I put the lid back on the box, then take one last, lingering look around the clearing.

*I'm going now, Amy, and I don't think I'm ever coming back here again. I'm sorry I couldn't finish your story, but I tried my best, I swear I did. I miss you. I love you. Goodbye.*

As I walk back along the trail, towards my husband and my little girl, I feel faintly silly, as if I've accomplished nothing. But perhaps burning the photograph isn't about how I feel today, but how I'll feel tomorrow, and the next day, and the day after that. Today will act like a marker in my memory, like one of the lines on Freya's bedroom doorframe that records how tall she is at a particular moment in time. It will remind me that I came here and that I said goodbye to Amy, and to the well.

Fifteen minutes later, the trail begins to widen, and the view opens up. Beyond the tearooms, framed by the trees, Westhaven shimmers in the distance, as broken as it is beautiful.

The open wound left behind by *Born Killer* is worse than ever now. Interest in the town I grew up in, and the child-murders that happened here, is at an all-time high, thanks to BlinkView – and thanks to me, of course. I was the one who started this story, driven not only by the hope of getting justice for Amy and Connor, but by the need to control the narrative, to ensure that Amy's parents didn't bring some other filmmaker to town who might expose the awful truth about what happened to Chloe's mother.

If half the town hated me before, now it seems as if I'm despised by everyone here, except for Dad and Connor. I know I brought that on myself, and that no matter how many times I apologise for the damage I've done, it will never be enough.

Secrets are heavy things to live with. Sometimes, so is the truth.

Up ahead, I spy Martin and Freya, playing football on the grass in front of tearooms, and I come to a stop, step off the path and move behind a tree so I can watch them without being seen. I listen to their shouts and laughter, and marvel at how lucky I am, how blessed. I came so close to losing them both because of the lies I told and the secrets I kept.

Well, there will be no more lies, no more secrets.

I watch Freya kick the ball to Martin then turn to look in my direction. She scans the trees, searching for me. Poor thing. I can hardly leave the room to use the bathroom without her worrying I'm going to disappear again.

*Don't worry, love*, I think. *I'm right here. I'm not going anywhere.*

I move to step out from behind the tree and that's when I stumble, and drop Amy's box of things. It slips from my grasp, hits the floor and pops open, the contents spilling out over the woodland floor.

I crouch down, gather up each photo, flyer, handwritten note – each and every memory – until there is only one left. The ring. It's a cheap thing, a silver band with a small red stone set in it. Elaine told Dad that Amy was wearing it when they pulled her out of the well. I haven't looked at it closely until now, couldn't quite bear the thought of handling something Amy was wearing when she took her last breath, but now I pick it up and slip it onto the end of my finger, then put the lid back on the box and tuck it under my arm.

I straighten, step out from the shadow of the tree, and take a few steps, looking at Amy's ring as I walk, the way the sunlight glints off the stone . . .

I come to a stop. Elaine must have made a mistake. This ring didn't belong to Amy.

It's the one Martin bought me for Valentine's Day the year Amy died, the one he demanded I return to him when he found out that I'd kissed Connor.

When we got back together, I asked him if I could have it back, but he told me he'd lost it. He promised to buy me a replacement, but

I told him not to, because I didn't deserve it. Why should he have to buy me a new ring after what I'd done to him? Instead, I bought him one, a silver signet ring that he still wears to this day – although he has had to have it altered a few times.

If Martin lost the ring, how could it possibly have ended up on Amy's finger when they pulled her out of the well? It doesn't make sense. The only way Amy could have been in possession of the ring on the night she died, is if Martin gave it to her. But he can't have. He went straight home after the argument, and stayed there until I called him the following morning to tell him that Amy was missing. The last time he saw Amy was the last time *any* of us saw Amy, wasn't it? At least that's what he told me, and told the police.

Please don't tell me he lied?

I look up in time to see that I've been spotted. Martin and Freya are looking in my direction with huge grins on their faces. Freya tugs at Martin's sleeve and asks him something and he rolls his eyes in an exaggerated fashion, then nods, *Go on then* . . . She sets off in a run towards me while Martin shrugs behind her and smiles.

Please God no. Not Martin. Not *my* Martin?

Ever since I saved him from drowning, I've always thought of him as . . . not weak, exactly, but *soft*. A kind, gentle soul, with goodness in his heart. It's what first attracted me to him, and what I've always loved about him most. It's what makes him such a supportive partner, and a brilliant dad to Freya. But is that why, in all the years I've searched for Amy's killer, it never once occurred to me to look at the man I share my life, and my bed, with? The man I have a daughter with?

A year ago, he drove halfway across the country in the dead of night because he was worried Freya might have an asthma attack. Then he ran through a storm to find me and, despite the fact he is half-terrified of water, jumped into a well to save my life. He is a brilliant father and a wonderful husband, and I wouldn't be here today if it weren't for him. And yet . . .

It sounds impossible, but have I been blind to the real him all along? He's always been there for me, ever since we were kids. He's always put me first, above everything, and everybody else. Always wanted me for himself . . .

My God, if he did it . . . When I think of all the pain he might have caused; to Amy, of course, but also to Connor, to Elaine and Rob, to this town and these people. To me.

'Mummy!' Freya calls out as she races to meet me. I drop down to one knee as she launches herself into my arms. 'You were gone for ages!' she says.

'I know, sweetheart, but I'm back now.' I hug and kiss her, then take her by the hand, and we walk away from the woods, back to Martin.

'Everything OK?' he says, when we get close, and I nod while I search his face for some sign that he's not the man I've known for all these years, that behind those kind eyes of his lie wickedness and cruelty. But all I see is my husband.

He leans in and kisses my cheek. 'Well done,' he says, into my ear. 'You did it. It's over now. It's really over.'

'Yeah,' I say.

'You can move on. No more *Born Killer*. Not now, not ever, right?' He smiles.

'Right,' I say, my throat suddenly so dry that it hurts.

Martin picks up the football and tucks it under his arm. 'Who wants to go home?' he says, and Freya lets out a cheer. When I don't respond, he looks over to me. 'You OK, hon? You look tired. Tell you what, when we get back, I'll run you a bath, bring you a nice glass of wine. After that, we can curl up on the sofa, watch some BlinkView if you like?'

'Sounds heavenly,' I say, in a daze.

As we start the long drive back to London, and Westhaven shrinks to nothing in the rear-view mirror, I think of Amy, and all the years I spent trying to give her the ending she deserves. And I look at the ring on my finger and shoot Martin a tight smile while I wonder: what ending does he deserve? Perhaps he's wrong about *Born Killer*. Perhaps it isn't over. Perhaps I can finish Amy's story after all.

# Acknowledgements

My thanks to the team at Embla Books, especially to my editor Jane Snelgrove, who worked very hard to make sense of this strange story of a woman trapped in a well during a storm, and the troubled person who put her there. Also to my agent Stephanie Glencross, for her continued support and for helping me work through how to get Jessie out of the horrible situation I put her in.

Thank you to my writing friends, Josh Winning, Tom Newman, Jake Webb, Patrick Wray and Andrea Robinson, for their encouragement and for being there when I need them, and to my non-writing friends, Mark Critchell, Fred Dutton, and the much-missed Mark Mitchell, for the same.

Thank you to my mentor, Alexandra (A.K.) Benedict, a wonderful writer and a brilliant teacher, and to my mum and dad, who continue to be the most supportive parents a person could wish for.

Finally, thank you to my wife Bailey, for putting up with me, and to Rufus, who continues to be the greatest dog in the world.

# About the Author

P S Cunliffe was born and grew up in Newton-le-Willows, Merseyside. A musician, artist and writer, he holds degrees in Fine Art and Creative Writing. He has spent the last twenty years working in digital marketing for some of the world's biggest websites and brands, and now lives in North London. For more information, please see his website at paulcunliffe.com.

# About Embla Books

Embla Books is a digital-first publisher of standout commercial adult fiction. Passionate about storytelling, the team at Embla publish books that will make you 'laugh, love, look over your shoulder and lose sleep'. Launched by Bonnier Books UK in 2021, the imprint is named after the first woman from the creation myth in Norse mythology, who was carved by the gods from a tree trunk found on the seashore – an image of the kind of creative work and crafting that writers do, and a symbol of how stories shape our lives.

Find out about some of our other books and stay in touch:

X, Facebook, Instagram: @emblabooks
Newsletter: https://bit.ly/emblanewsletter

Milton Keynes UK
Ingram Content Group UK Ltd.
UKHW011833090124
435754UK00001B/8